PATIENCE STOUT was born in Hillingdon a
and Colston's Girls' School in Bristol. On co
Patience's family moved to Raasay in the
discovered that helping out on the family far
the Scottish mainland was not ideal for a seventeen year-old, she
joined the army. Patience married four years later into an army family and
raised two daughters.

When the girls were away at boarding school, Patience trained to be
a nurse, stepping into midwifery and health visiting.

Always interested in the Orient, Patience travelled to India, China
and the Middle East. Retiring to Cyprus, she enjoyed studying Indian
history and the East India Company. Combining her experience of the
Hebrides with her love of India and the 'John Company', she wrote this
historical novel.

Ropes of Sand

Patience Stout

SilverWood

Published in 2019 by SilverWood Books

SilverWood Books Ltd
14 Small Street, Bristol, BS1 1DE, United Kingdom
www.silverwoodbooks.co.uk

ISBN 978-1-78132-840-8 (paperback)
ISBN 978-1-78132-861-3 (ebook)

British Library Cataloguing in Publication Data
A CIP catalogue record for this book is available from the British Library

Page design and typesetting by SilverWood Books
Printed on responsibly sourced paper

Thank you to Emma Corbett for all her care and diligence in bringing *Ropes of Sand* to life.

Handed down through the mists of ages comes a legend which tells us that the islands that make up the Hebrides were an afterthought – a casual casting from heaven of precious stones left over from the Creation.

In fine weather this legend is easy to believe for, set in a sapphire sea beneath an azure sky, the bleak and barren islands possess a divine beauty. But more often than not fierce winds shriek across the islands from the west: vicious, merciless winds that batter the land and its people. On such days it is easier to believe that it was the Devil himself who fashioned the Hebrides to tempt souls into the jaws of Hell. The islanders were torn between the Devil and the Almighty. Neighbour spied on neighbour and tittle-tattled to the minister whose job it was to exact retribution for wrongdoing on behalf of God.

Generations of islanders and ministers have come and gone, but the sins have remained the same, and will remain so throughout eternity as human nature is ever the same.

FINLAY

CHAPTER 1

All that could be seen of wee Jimmy were the backs of his legs and patches of his backside glowing pinkly through his tattered *breeks*. The rest of him was bent at right angles, his upper body resting on a deep stone sill with his head thrust through a tiny unglazed window. He was on lookout duty, and if he saw the lay elders or, worse still, the minister himself, it was his responsibility to warn those huddled round the fire. Outside the black house the first gale of approaching winter caught the island in its gnashing jaws. Wee Jimmy was protected from the worst of the rain by a turf heather roof, but when the wind came in vicious gusts it was blown, sharp as needles, straight into his face. His ears and nose grew colder, but inside the black house, where a fire burned, his backside was as warm as if he had been on the sharp end of a *skelping*.

The black house consisted of two rooms, the smaller of which was the winter quarters for a cow and heifer calf. In the larger room peat smouldered and sparked in the central fireplace. With the window stuffed full of wee Jimmy and the hole in the thatch above the hearth full of debris, there was nowhere for the heat to go but round and round the rooms. Peat smoke mingled with the steamy breath from the cattle and the acrid smell of dung.

Five people sat by the fire, freed from their week's toil at the kelp, for the laird, and hoping for the weather to ease by morning for the one day they had to work their own patch of ground. But foremost in their minds was the rumour that had swept across the island with the wind.

'Ach, but *hougmangandie*,' said one. 'And a son of the *manse*, too.'

'I wish I'd been there to see the minister's face.'

'My, but its furious he must be with Finlay, *chust*.'

A bottle was passed round, and the slurp of giggle water being poured into cups alerted a sixth who lay dying on an iron bedstead pushed against the back wall. The curtain, there to screen him from view, was yanked to one side.

'Where's mine?' asked a querulous voice. 'I'm no' dead yet that I *canna* still enjoy a wee dram.'

His old *wifey* hobbled across the room. 'Dinna fret,' she scolded. 'Here's yours.' She poured some down his throat and he coughed and spluttered.

'Ach. You'll kill me,' he gasped when he came up for air. He wiped his wet chin with his fingers, and then sucked them clean of whisky.

'Aye, so I will,' agreed his wife. 'But no' tonight.' She padded back to her place beside the fire. 'Yon Finlay's a fool,' she said. 'Always has been. But Sadie now. I never thought she'd get caught. It'll be the *Kirk Session* for sure.' The others nodded in agreement.

'About time too. The way she chases after the men. Still, she's a daftie to mess wi' a son of the manse. The minister will no' like it.'

'Oh, we'd all like it with Sadie.' The men laughed.

'*Haud yer wheesht!*'

There was a sudden clatter as wee Jimmy squirmed backwards and fell off the crate he had been standing on. 'Quick. It's the minister, hisself,' he whispered.

In a flurry of activity, cups were drained of whisky and refilled with tea, and the old wifey hid the incriminating bottle beneath the dying man's bedcovers. By the time the door of the black house opened, and the minister stepped inside with a squall of wind and rain, all was a picture of innocence. Five people sat beside the fire nursing cups of tea, the dying man lay with his hands crossed on his chest, eyes open, and wee Jimmy had joined the cattle at the far end.

'Is it yourself, Reverend?' said Ishbel. 'Will you take tea?'

The minister peered through the swirling smoke. His eyes darted back and forth for signs of sin and his nose twitched with the smell of the whisky.

'Thank you, no, Mistress Macdonald. I just called by to see the old man. I'll not be stopping. Mayhap I'll say a wee prayer.'

He crossed the room and bent over the dying man. His nostrils flared with the alcoholic fumes emanating from the damp nightshirt. 'How are you, Angus?' His tone was indifferent and betrayed his lack of interest in the old man's welfare. 'Still here I see. Mayhap the good Lord doesn't want you, smelling of the whisky the way you do.'

The minister began to pray, and the wee prayer went on and on. The five people beside the fire stood in respect for the Almighty. Then, before the minister came to an end of praying, the dying man stretched out his arm and brandished the whisky bottle. He flung the bedcovers back and tried to swing his legs to the ground.

'What are you doing, man?' gasped the minister. 'Are you in that much of a hurry to get to your grave?' He snatched the bottle away. 'And you can't be taking this where you're going.'

'I need a piddle,' said the dying man. His legs could not support his weight and he fell to the floor.

The minister took a hasty step backwards. His nose wrinkled and his mouth pursed in distaste. He turned to the people beside the fire and saw that they were red in the face with suppressed laughter.

'He needs attention,' said the minister. 'Seeing as how he's not dying just yet.' And he left without another word.

'My, but he's an old he-bugger, chust,' whined the dying man after his needs had been attended to and he was tucked into bed again.

'Aye, so he is,' echoed the others.

The Reverend Lachlan Nicolson, uncrowned king of the Hebridean Isle of Toronsay, trudged homeward with his collar up and his head down against the gale. He was aware that he was hated, but that did not bother him. All he required of his parishioners was their unquestioning obedience to God's will. Woe betide anyone accused of drunkenness, wife-beating, theft or violation of the Sabbath. He would have them up before the Kirk Session as quick as a wink. But as his feet squelched across the boggy ground, it was not hatred that Lachlan could feel snapping at his heels; it was scorn and derision. He grew hot and cold with the thought of those ragged *scallags* in their black house laughing at him behind his back. And all because of Finlay, whom he had failed to beat into submission in spite of seventeen years of trying. They would all have heard about Finlay by now. He pushed his thoughts of Sadie MacLeod into dark corners of his mind and tried to focus on how to maintain control over his parishioners when he had, so clearly, failed to keep his own house in order. By God, he swore as he reached the manse, that boy will be the death of me.

*

11

Four months had passed since Finlay had taken the first step that would lead him to stand before the Kirk Session. That day in early June was the first truly warm day of the year. May had been generous with its sunshine, but the winter's chill had lingered on. This first day of summer came with a sudden rise in temperature, which brought folk out and put smiles on their faces. Sunshine sparkled on a deep blue sea and the *machair* on Toronsay bloomed as flowers of every hue covered the grasslands – poppies, red and white clover, blue harebells and speedwell, yellow pansies and wild orchids of many colours. The plaintive cry of lapwings vied with the raucous screech of gulls, and the air was filled with the beating of wings and the salty tang of the sea.

Murdo and Finlay chased each other along the water's edge. Their shoes dangled from their fingers and their feet sent sprays of white sand in their wake. Oyster-catchers scattered at their approach, and in the still warmth of the afternoon the ceaseless noise of the sea was hushed.

'Wait for me,' called Murdo.

Finlay dropped onto the soft sand where a matted fringe of marram grass marked the edge of the shore. A few moments later Murdo flopped down beside Finlay.

'I couldn't keep up with you,' he panted. 'My feet kept sinking into the sand.'

'That's because you don't have the benefit of ducks' feet,' chuckled Finlay, wriggling his own webbed toes.

Murdo threw a pebble into the sea and watched the ever-increasing circle of ripples on the surface before turning to his brother. 'What are you going to do with your life, Finlay? You can't stay here for ever.'

Finlay uttered a mirthless laugh. 'Oh, yes I can. Father won't let me go. I did ask him for a testificat a while back so that I could join a Highland Regiment. He refused, of course. He needs me here as his whipping boy. Anyway, I need to be here for Ma.'

'Ma has Elspeth and me. We can keep an eye out for her.'

'Elspeth's married now, and you'll be off to the university soon. I have to stay.' Finlay threw a pebble into the sea. He cast sidelong look at Murdo. 'If you've any sense at all, you won't come back after the university. I know I wouldn't in your place.'

'You'd join a regiment?'

Finlay shook his head. 'I'd go to Uncle Donald in Glasgow and ask to work my passage to America. There's so much world out there, Murdo, and all we know of it is what we've seen on maps in the schoolhouse. Why not use your testificat to escape Father's plans for you? You could do so much more – be so much more – than a minister of religion. I can't believe it's what you really want to do. Is it?'

'I've not given it much thought. It's what he expects of me.'

'Yes, but it's your life, and you have to live it, not him. If you follow in his footsteps you'll end up just like him. I couldn't bear to see you turn into Father. Anyway, you have a choice, and my advice to you is to think carefully about your future. Most of us are held here by the bully in the pulpit, but he's going to set you free because he thinks you'll come back. You should grab that freedom with both hands before it's too late.'

Murdo took a deep breath filled with the smell of seaweed. The sea lapped gently against strands of kelp, stirring them before retreating. Oystercatchers paddled at the water's edge, dipping their beaks in search of food. The sun dipped below Temptation Hill. Whispers of pink tinged the gathering clouds and a light breeze stirred the marram grass. The sudden drop in temperature alerted Finlay to the passing time. He jumped up and brushed sand from his breeches.

'Come on,' he said. 'We'd better hurry back or we'll be late for tea.'

Murdo trotted homewards a few strides behind his brother. He was troubled by Finlay's words, and yet they struck a chord deep within him, forcing him to face what he had refused to acknowledge. Finlay was right; he did not want to become a minister like his Father. He wanted a life at sea. When he sat in the kirk on the Sabbath his gaze was always drawn to the view of the sea through the window and he longed to be at the fishing. And he would be the first to admit that when he was at the fishing his thoughts never strayed to the kirk. He was fourteen years old and there was no need for decisions to be made yet, but that time was fast approaching, and tempting like the devil.

Halfway home, and still out of sight of the village, three young women sauntered towards them with their arms linked. As they approached Finlay noticed with lascivious interest that the one in the centre was Sadie MacLeod. She was flanked by two of her cousins. Sadie's only claims to beauty were her abundance of red hair and her magnificent body. She was a sharp-featured woman in her mid-twenties who had the misfortune to have one eye fixed at its outer corner, which gave her a shifty look. But she was willing, or so Finlay had heard.

Sadie swerved so that the young women would be brought face to face with the Nicolson brothers although she only had eyes for Finlay. His eyes were as blue as a summer sky, his white skin flushed from an afternoon spent in the sun. Sadie narrowed her eyes. Finlay Nicolson was no longer a boy. This past winter had seen him shed his childhood and it was a young man who stood before her – fresh, innocent and ripe for the picking. The years of repression he must have endured beneath the weight of his father's pious presence could easily be made to erupt into a sexual frenzy, and Sadie thought that it might be fun to try out the son of the manse.

Finlay scarcely glanced at the faces of the women. His eyes were drawn inexorably from one buxom bosom to the next. Murdo looked from Finlay to Sadie and his heart sank. She was clearly intent on mischief. Sheena and Ailsa giggled as Sadie moved her body, emphasising each and every curve. Finlay reddened to the tips of his ears as she ran her eyes up and down the full length of his body. Her lips parted revealing white, even teeth and the tip of her tongue.

'Like what you see?' she taunted, shaking her shoulders so that her ample breasts swung against her loose-fitting homespun dress.

'Ach. Away home wi' ye,' said Finlay with a smile. ''Tis almost the Sabbath. You'll get yourself in trouble if you're out late.'

'Are ye asking?' leered Sadie.

Before Finlay could answer, she darted forward and pressed her mouth against the side of his face. 'Meet me by the far cairn as soon as it's dark,' she whispered. Then she ran a hot tongue back and forth across his ear.

All three women roared with laughter, and then they kicked up their heels and ran off, without a backward glance. Murdo and Finlay stared after them.

'Jezebel,' muttered Murdo. 'Come away home, Finlay. Take no notice of Sadie MacLeod.'

The brothers hurried towards the village. With dusk falling the islanders were busy at their evening chores. There was always more to do on a Saturday evening than on other days of the week because preparations had to be made for the Sabbath when no work at all was permitted. Hens waited hungrily in doorways whilst folk tended their potato patches. Tough drudges of wives cleaned hearths and re-laid fires with peat from stacks at the end of their black houses. Then they prepared the evening meal, and the next day's, too. It would be dark before they were done, but they would rest on the morrow.

Murdo and Finlay called greetings as they passed, but there was no time to stop and talk. Work must be finished, and the Nicolson brothers must present themselves for tea on time. As they came in sight of the manse they could see their father standing at the open door with a Bible in his hands. They hurried up the path and followed him indoors. Lachlan went straight to the dining room, but Murdo and Finlay made their way to the scullery first to dowse their hands and faces with cold spring water taken from pail by the back door.

Lachlan kept the manse austere as a snowdrift, but he enjoyed his food and was generous with its provision. There was a haunch of venison, mutton broth with bread, lightly boiled eggs, mealy tatties in their skins, broiled haddock and oatmeal cakes. To drink was tea, coffee and sweet milk from one of their own cows. There was no alcohol. Lachlan did not even keep a drop of whisky or brandy hidden away for medicinal purposes. The drinking of alcohol was a sin, and any islander caught in possession of the local whisky, distilled illicitly from the grains of barley and oats, was brought before the Kirk Session and punished.

When Murdo and Finlay entered the dining room, Elspeth and her husband Torquil, the local schoolmaster, were already seated. The boys sat facing them and they waited in silence for their mother. Finlay winked across the table and Torquil hissed his disapproval. Torquil was of one mind with Lachlan: Saturday evenings were a serious preparation for the Sabbath; there was no place for frivolity.

Moira drifted into the room like a wraith and took her position at the far end of the table opposite Lachlan. Finlay smiled at her and the others nodded a greeting, but she seemed not to notice them. Her face was blank, the faraway look in her eyes betraying her indifference to her surroundings.

Morag, their domestic, brought all the food to the table at once and the family helped themselves. The meal was eaten in silence and, apart from Murdo and Torquil, they shrank beneath the overwhelming menace of the man at the head of the table. Heads were bent, shoulders hunched, each trying to escape notice or censure. Lachlan's gaze passed from one to another. He had a nose for wrongdoing and could sniff it out from the darkest corner. He did not miss Finlay's preoccupation with whatever everlasting sight he had reconstructed from his meeting with Sadie that evening. Moira did not deign to notice, taking no part in the proceedings. Her face was impassive, but it was of her firstborn that she always thought when they joined together for family prayers after their meal. Angus had run away from home following the worst beating Lachlan afflicted on any of his children. No trace of him could be found on the island, and with one dinghy reported missing, it was assumed that he had drowned in the treacherous waters of the Minch. It was inconceivable that a twelve-year-old could have reached the mainland in such a boat. Not knowing for certain what had become of her boy, Moira was tormented with hope, however forlorn that hope had become over the years. And that spark of hope flickered into flame at unexpected moments so that she knew no peace.

Murdo found it difficult to concentrate that evening. Finlay had put temptation in his way. Thoughts of a life at sea seduced his mind, distracting him from the words that had always brought him comfort, and whilst Lachlan threatened them with the deep, dark, bottomless pit that awaited all sinners, Murdo began to question his father's plans for him.

Finlay thought of Sadie MacLeod.

She was the subject of much speculation and gossip, and Finlay knew that his father had tried in the past to drag her before the Kirk Session. But he lacked hard evidence against her and she would either have to be caught in the act or reported by someone. And what man would do that when it would mean that he, too, would incur the wrath of the Kirk. Accusations by suspicious, outraged wives were not enough by themselves.

Behind Old Fergie's barn, those who were indiscreet inflamed village lads with their talk of the liberties Sadie permitted. Finlay's heart pounded as he anticipated what might await him later in the evening. His face reddened and his breathing quickened as he thought of what was hidden beneath Sadie MacLeod's skirts. He became so engrossed in his fantasy that he missed the 'Amen' at the conclusion of the prayer before becoming aware of his father's face, contorted with anger as he glared at him.

Finlay dragged himself back from his imagination, and as father began to read a chapter from the Bible, Finlay wondered how much truth there was in the village talk. Lachlan never spoke of his past, but it was common knowledge that he had joined a ship belonging to the East India Company when he was a boy. The yarns spun by the old folk on winter nights about Lachlan's adventures were figments of fertile imaginations, but he was not the only man who had been to sea. Some of those added lurid tales of their own – stories about young Chinese girls on flower boats and Indian beauties dripping with pearls and gold. Fantasy blended with fact and now, years later, most of the islanders stated their firm belief that their minister was spending the latter part of his life atoning for his early years. Finlay wanted to scream 'bloody hypocrite' at his father, but as his back was still raw from the previous day's beating he was in no hurry to invite another so soon.

After prayers were over, the family moved into the sitting room with its sofas and soft chairs. Morag lit candles and placed them on side tables, and then set about clearing the dishes and re-laying the table for the next day.

Lachlan leaned back in his chair, stretched his legs out in front of him and patted his stomach. 'It's been a grand day,' he said. 'The good Lord has surely shone on us in His mercy.'

'Aye,' agreed Torquil. 'And it's set fair for tomorrow as well.'

'Indeed. I doubt Calum Dhu will live to see it though. I looked in on him this afternoon. He's on his last legs now. My, but he's been a long time in the dying.'

'And him only sixty,' exclaimed Torquil. 'That's no age to be dying, for sure.'

'Aye, well. That's the demon drink for you,' said Lachlan, his face full of pious disdain. 'Serves the man right. No good ever comes of the whisky. Now the Devil to claim his own. I'll be called out tonight anyway. His folks will need a wee prayer.'

Finlay's heart sank. He sat by the window watching the sun drown in the sea to the west and trying to judge how long it would take him to reach the old cairn in the dark. He did not turn round when his father spoke, but his face fell as he realised that he stood no chance of slipping out to meet Sadie MacLeod if his father sat up late. He could not begin to imagine her fury should he fail to meet her at the appointed time and knew that she would not give him a second chance.

Moira and Elspeth sat together on one of the sofas. Elspeth picked some sewing out of the workbasket on the floor. She threaded wool into a large-eyed needle and attacked a hole in the heel of one of Murdo's socks. On each of her visits to her childhood home, Elspeth left with a pile of mending from the basket. Moira had become so detached from life's particulars that she did not notice how the pile of darning and mending spilled over the workbasket, nor did she have any appreciation of how the pile disappeared at the end of each week. Elspeth darned, patched and mended seams and hems, and Murdo and Finlay remained respectably clothed.

Mindful of Finlay's comment earlier in the day, Murdo took a good look at his mother and was shocked to see how much she had aged. He took her for granted because she was always there, and he had not noticed her metamorphosis from vibrant woman to frightened wife. Murdo had only a vague memory of older brother Angus and, apart from Elspeth and Finlay, his other siblings had all died within days of being born. Now, as he looked at his mother, Murdo saw the lines on her face deepen as she drew her lips into a thin line, and he wondered if she was remembering. She never spoke of the lost ones, but suddenly the tragedy of her life showed on her face, and Murdo was embarrassed and shocked.

There was a sudden, urgent knocking at the front door and a few moments later Morag ushered in Calum Dhu's son. He removed his hat and touched his forelock.

'Can you come, Minister?' he said. 'It's time.'

Lachlan heaved himself out of his chair. 'I don't know how long I'll be,' he called over his shoulder. 'Don't wait up.'

'Calum Dhu will be missed,' said Elspeth after they heard the door slam behind Lachlan. 'He's the best shoemaker we've got.'

'Not since he took to the bottle,' argued Torquil.

'Even so,' replied Elspeth. 'His son doesn't do such a good repair.'

'Well, he's too young to die, right enough,' intervened Murdo before a row developed between his sister and her husband. 'He might have lived if we had a wee hospital on the island.'

Elspeth shuddered. 'Those places are charnel houses. We don't need one on Toronsay. I'd sooner be dead than go in one.'

'If you were dead already they wouldn't have you,' said Torquil.

The islanders were rarely ill unless a traveller to Toronsay brought sickness with him, apart from the scourge of tuberculosis when they were all likely to be ill at the same time. There was no doctor on the island, just a village woman to help with the laying out of the deceased and to attend birthing. People fell ill and either they recovered or they died.

Moira stood up. 'Death is not something to be joked about,' she admonished. 'You may think it amusing when it involves someone else, but it comes to us all sooner or later.' Her eyes swept around the room. 'I'll away to my bed,' she said. 'Goodnight.'

Torquil stood up. 'We'd better be off,' he said. 'Come, Elspeth. We must be home before Sabbath.'

'Why?' sneered Elspeth as she rose to her feet. 'In case we turn into evil spirits?'

Torquil sucked at his teeth. 'May you be forgiven your ungodliness,' he hissed. 'What's wrong with you, woman?'

Elspeth followed Torquil into the hall. At the door she turned and raised her eyebrows at Finlay. He grinned back at her.

'You are risking your souls,' said Murdo self-righteously.

Finlay laughed again. 'Ach, but you don't know whether to really believe in superstitious nonsense any more, do you? I can see it in your face.'

Murdo looked away. He wanted to believe it. He had believed in it all his life, but now that Finlay was tempting him again he wavered. He wanted it to be true, but now he was not sure. He picked up the last candle.

'I'm going to bed,' he said. 'Are you coming?'

'I'll be up in a minute,' said Finlay.

Murdo undressed quickly and climbed into the bed he shared with his brother. He pulled the blanket to his chin and stared at ceiling. The flickering candlelight set shadows on the walls. When Finlay entered the room, he crossed to the window and peered through the glass.

'Come to bed,' murmured Murdo.

'In a minute. Snuff out the candle and go to sleep.'

Murdo spat on his fingers and pinched the flame. With no light in the room the window was no longer like a black mirror. Finlay's reflection was gone and now Murdo could see his silhouette against the darkening turquoise of the sky. There was no moon and it was not yet dark enough for stars to appear. At this time of the year darkness was but a short interval between dusk and dawn.

As soon as Finlay believed Murdo to be asleep, he bent down to

19

remove his shoes. He tiptoed to the door, carrying his shoes, and opened it an inch. The click of the latch alerted Murdo, who was awake instantly. Finlay slipped from the room. Murdo jumped out of bed and pulled on his breeches. He tugged his shirt over his head as he followed his brother from the manse.

Finlay was forced to move slowly because of the lack of moonlight and the need to be silent. If anyone saw or heard him prowling about at this hour on a Saturday night his father would know of it before morning. He skirted round the single storey dwelling, slinking along in the shadows of dry stonewalls. All the black houses were in darkness. No one would wish to waste a precious candle, if indeed there was a candle to waste. Folk went to bed when night fell and rose again when it was light.

He was about to dart across the open ground beside Old Fergie's barn when he froze to the spot. A door was open and Finlay could hear Peggy and Alasdair Macdonald shouting at one another, Alasdair being chased by his wife. They ran round in circles, flapping their arms.

'I canna catch him,' shouted Alasdair.

'Ach, you're *nae mair* use than a kettle wi' nae *spoot*,' shrieked Peggy, who retained her Clydeside accent in spite of having spent fifty years on Toronsay. 'You get yon rooster *oot frae* they hens.'

'I canna.' Alasdair's voice was drowned by a sudden squawking. Feathers flew into the air. 'Buggeration,' he swore. 'I almost had him.'

Peggy Macdonald raised her eyes to heaven. She rolled up her sleeves and entered the fray with pointed elbows. 'Oot o' my way.' She strutted after the rooster, clapping her hands.

'Ach, leave him be,' sighed Alasdair. 'What harm can he do?'

'Ye *ken* fine what harm, Ali Mac,' shouted Peggy. 'And he'll nae be doin' it on the Sabbath.'

Peggy flapped her skirts and steered the bird towards her husband. Eventually, between the two of them, they managed to catch it and Alasdair imprisoned it in a wooden crate, where it would remain until Monday morning. Satisfied at last that the Sabbath would not be violated by their randy rooster, Peggy and Alasdair retreated into their black house, slamming the door behind them. The silence set Finlay's ears ringing.

As soon as he judged it safe to move, Finlay ran across the open ground and headed for the island loch before turning back towards the shore. Murdo spotted him as he passed Ruari's croft before losing sight of him again in the dark mass of Temptation Hill. In the last flicker of daylight Murdo gingerly crossed the slimy steppingstones in the peaty water of a burn. After the heavy rains of the previous days, water surged rapidly between the mossy banks on either side. He struggled to remain upright as he only had one hand free to use as a counterbalance. The fingers of his left hand were clamped to his nose against the stench of the tumble of rocks that formed the dwelling of Mad Bella. Then, as he flitted across her potato patch, Mad Bella emerged wreathed in clouds of peat smoke. She called to Murdo and the hairs on the back of his neck stood on end.

'Leave him be, young Murdo,' she croaked. 'Leave him be and come away in for a *strupach*.' Murdo hesitated. 'Come away in,' she insisted, and Murdo did not dare to argue or disobey.

All the children on Toronsay knew for certain that Mad Bella was a witch. It was only as they grew up without knowing of anyone who had been turned into a toad or who had been made to disappear, that they came to accept with reluctance that Mad Bella did not, after all, possess supernatural powers. Then their childish fear of her turned indignant, disappointment tinged with contempt. Murdo's feelings towards Mad Bella hovered between fear and indignation, but fear had the upper hand as he entered her home.

It stank. Mad Bella shared her dilapidated black house with her hens and her milch cow. The cow was out to grass for the summer, but there were hens everywhere – on the home-made table, the rickety chairs, and on the pile of sacking in the corner that served as Mad Bella's bed. Sooty peat smoke blackened the interiors of all the dwellings, but the blackness of Mad Bella's house was liberally spattered with countless years of hen's droppings. Defeated by the smoke and the hens, she had long ago abandoned any pretence of house cleaning.

She had always lived alone. She had never married, and her idiosyncratic ways, together with her reputation for being fey, ensured that the islanders kept her at arm's length. Unless they had need of her that is, for Mad Bella was known to brew up roots and cast the bones, so that a slow but steady trickle of women beat a clandestine path to her door if they had sinned with a man and needed help, or if they wished to have their fortunes told – when they would marry, or when they would bear a son. Lachlan maintained that Mad Bella had the mark of the Devil on her. He would preach against her ungodly ways, and these sermons were listened to with more interest than the congregation could usually muster, but Mad Bella paid him no more heed than she would a fleabite.

'Sit ye down, sit ye down,' she said to Murdo, pushing hens off one of the chairs.

A battered kettle balanced on stacks of burning peat in the room, tottering dangerously as it boiled, and sending spouts of steam curling upwards with the smoke. Very little of it found its way through the small opening in the thatch above, and it wasn't long before Murdo's eyes began to stream with the sting of smoke. Mad Bella set a pan of milk on the fire and whilst it warmed she dusted the insides of two chipped mugs with her dirty fingers. When the milk was hot and frothy, she filled the mugs and handed one to Murdo. The table wobbled and some of the milk was spilled. Mad Bella grunted as she bent down and stuffed a bit of crumpled rag under one of the legs to hold it steady. The table was roughly made from bits and pieces of driftwood. It was held together with twine and rusty nails, but it served its purpose.

Mad Bella handed Murdo an oatcake before settling herself on the chair opposite him. 'Now,' she said. 'Just what do you think you're doing out at this hour of a Saturday night? As if I didn't know already.'

Murdo had never been so close to the old woman. He stared at her with interest. A few black hairs sprouted from her chin, but it was her eyes that held Murdo's gaze: black as berries, they seemed to bore into his soul.

'I only wanted to know where Finlay was going.'

'Ach.' Mad Bella shook her head and wagged a finger. 'Yon Finlay's a fool, young Murdo, and he'll no' be needing you this night.'

She pushed up her sleeves and tucked her bulky skirts around her bony legs. A lifetime of carrying heavy loads like a beast of burden had left her bent almost double. Her hair was a matted patchwork of grey and white, but her black eyes were bright and intelligent, and she still had her wits about her. 'Seventy past' is how the islanders would give her age, but she was nearer ninety.

Murdo's eyes travelled around the hovel Mad Bella called home. He raised his mug of milk. He put his lips inside the mug to avoid the rim coming into contact with his mouth and slurped noisily. His eyes came to rest on the bones. Mad Bella saw his interest. She crossed the room to fetch the bones and scattered them on the table in front of Murdo.

'Do you want to know your future, young Murdo?' she cooed, fluttering her dirty fingers over the bones. 'I can tell you what sort of life is in front of you. As a minister, or something else maybe?'

Murdo gulped. A tiny part of him did want to know what his future held, but he was his father's son and his father had taught him well.

'Fortune-telling is the Devil's work,' he said primly. 'My father says that you are a black angel from hell.'

Mad Bella threw her head back and laughed, but her laughter stopped abruptly and she thrust her face close to Murdo. 'And he would know, wouldn't he chust? Him being something close to the Devil himself. The Kirk might have called him, but he's going to the other place.' She pointed to the ground. 'Hellfire awaits your father.'

Murdo shivered, and Mad Bella wiped a dewdrop from the end of her nose with the back of her hand.

'The Kirk doesn't call you, young Murdo,' she said. 'Your father is pushing you where you don't belong.'

She grabbed a handful of bones – ribs, shoulder blades and leg bones of mice and other small animals – and pushed them to one side of the table, leaving just one sickly white skull. Peat smoke swirled around them and the acrid smell of hens' droppings together with the smell of Mad Bella's unwashed body and clothes made breathing difficult. Murdo was mesmerised as Mad Bella nudged the skull with a scrawny forefinger. She closed her eyes and began to sway from side to side.

Murdo covered his ears with his hands. 'Stop it!' he yelled, frightened almost witless. 'I don't want to know.' He jumped up and knocked the table over, which brought Mad Bella out of her trance.

'What did I say?' she asked.

'Nothing.' Murdo began to weep.

'Aye, well,' sighed Mad Bella. 'I saw a lot more than nothing. I saw the sea and I saw fire. Such a fire it was.' She shuddered. 'Religion will keep you in chains all the days of your life if you let it.' She leant forward and grasped Murdo's hands in her own. 'Dinna fret, laddie. You'll get your heart's desire, but for the very life of me I canna see why.'

She bent down to pick up scattered bones. Murdo could not bring himself to touch them. He backed towards the door.

'What about Finlay?'

'What about him?' said Mad Bella. 'I dinna need the bones to tell me his future. Yesteryear Finlay was all teeths and feets, and today he's all breeks. Leave him be, young Murdo. He'll be making more than enough trouble for himself without your help. You wait and see. Now, away home wi' ye afore your father knows you're not in your bed.'

Finlay's destination lay well beyond the village. The old cairn stood in the shadow of the remnants of a castle, the one-true seat of a clan chieftain. The reason for the cairn having been built was a mystery. Some said that the stones had been piled one on top of another in memory of a boatload of fishermen lost at sea. The more romantically inclined favoured the idea that it had been built by a woman whose sweetheart had died, and that each stone marked a year of tears shed in remembrance of lost love. But whatever the truth, the stones had been piled high so long ago that the cairn was now partially covered by wind-blown sand, and spindles of grass sprouted through the lower levels.

Finlay moved stealthily in the dark. It was a relief to reach the old cairn and glimpse Sadie's red hair. A part of him had not really believed that she would be there waiting for him. As soon as she saw him, Sadie grabbed Finlay's hand and pulled him over the ridge on which the cairn was built.

'Keep your head down,' she whispered. 'Did anyone see you?'

Finlay shook his head. 'I don't think so. I came by the home farm so no one would guess I was coming here even if I was seen.'

Over the years the prevailing winds had carved a cave-like hollow on the far side of the ridge. Sadie pulled Finlay inside it. There was no room to stand up, and Finlay lay trembling beside Sadie, breathing in the heathery smell of her hair and concentrating on the sensation of her large, soft breasts against his chest. Now that his fantasies were about to become reality, Finlay was suddenly overcome with shyness. In spite of all the brave talk he had heard behind Old Fergie's barn, he did not know what to do, and he was terrified that Sadie would laugh at his ignorance. But when her scorching tongue darted about his ears and her fingers crept inside his breeches, he abandoned himself into her capable hands.

They met each Saturday throughout the summer, driven solely by lust. And each Sabbath that followed, Finlay's contempt for his father grew as he faced him in the pulpit. Heaven was not some abstract place to be hoped for after death. Heaven was here on earth with a woman beneath you, drawing you into herself until you drowned in the throbbing glory of sexual fulfilment. But what could that vindictive old man know of real passion? Sex belonged to the young, and Finlay found it impossible to imagine his father as ever having been a young man.

One evening at the end of September, when Finlay began to strip off his clothes as soon as reached the old cairn, Sadie burst into tears. Finlay hesitated. The wind outside the hollow was rising, whipping the sea to foam, and the pounding of the waves on the shore found their echo in Finlay's heart. Although the night was warm he felt icily cold, and even before Sadie spoke he knew what she would say.

'I'm going to have a bairn,' she wailed. 'Oh, my God. A bairn. What am I going to do? My father will kill me.' She chewed her knuckles and tears poured down her cheeks.

Finlay stared at her in horror. He had a sick feeling at the pit of his stomach.

'How?'

Sadie's woeful expression turned to anger in an instant. 'Don't "how" me, Finlay Nicolson,' she snapped. 'You ken fine how. You've done it enough times.'

'How do I know it's mine? Who's been with half the village lads? Could be anyone's bairn.'

'Of course it's yours,' yelled Sadie.

Finlay felt a surge of panic. 'Well, I don't believe you.'

With a scream Sadie launched herself at him, clawing with her nails and pulling his hair. Finlay ran from her, tugging at his breeches as he fled. He yelped with pain as a stone Sadie flung at him caught him on the back his head. He kept running, and Sadie sank to her knees in misery.

Finlay did not go straight home. He needed time to think, and when he had put some distance between himself and Sadie, he put his shoes down and waded into the sea to rinse the blood from his hair. The sting of the salty water on his split scalp made him wince and brought tears to his eyes. When the bleeding had stopped, he crouched shivering against a lichen-covered boulder and agonised over what he was going to say to his parents.

His instinct was to run, but there was no way of leaving the island now until the fishing boats put out on Monday morning. He was going to have to tell his parents, and then sit in the kirk for the morning service, bludgeoned by the enormity of what he had done. Young and frightened of the consequences, Finlay gave no thought to Sadie's predicament. He thought only of how he might extricate himself from the situation. Anyhow, he thought in his ignorance, she could be wrong. Iona Macdonald down at Clachan was always claiming to be pregnant but never went on to have a bairn. He sat until the first streaks of morning lit the eastern sky before creeping back to the manse; he had decided to say nothing at all unless Sadie made trouble for him.

Sadie, all alone in the dark after Finlay's desertion, felt fear for the first time in her life. She did not know what to do and could think of no one to whom she could turn except for Mad Bella, and she was terrified of that old witch. Still, she had to pass Mad Bella's on her way home and as she approached she saw the old crone sitting on her doorstep smoking a clay pipe. Light from the peat fire behind her cast flickering shadows on the back wall and put Mad Bella into silhouette against the flames. Hunched over her pipe Mad Bella looked like a crooked hobgoblin, and Sadie shrank back with dread. She knew that she was too far from the light for Mad Bella to see her, but the old witch knew she was there all the same. She beckoned to Sadie.

'I've been expecting you,' she croaked.

Sadie began to shake from head to feet. She turned to run, but Mad Bella called after her. 'Come away in before anyone sees you. I'll no' bite.'

Sadie had no choice. She crossed the unkempt garden and followed Mad Bella indoors. Mad Bella waved hens off the chairs and indicated to Sadie that she was to sit down. Sadie perched on the edge of her seat. Mad Bella's piercing black eyes held to Sadie's one good one, red rimmed from crying.

After some minutes of silence Mad Bella looked Sadie up and down and pursed her lips. 'How many monthlies have you missed?' she asked.

Sadie gasped at the bluntness of the question, but she answered without hesitation. 'Four, I think.'

'Four, you think. Do you no' ken how many?'

Sadie shook her head. 'It's at least three,' she said. 'But it could be four.'

Mad Bella tutted and sighed. 'You should have come sooner. If it's more than two I canna promise what you want. It's dangerous anyway, the more so the further you are. Do you ken what you're asking?'

Sadie nodded. 'I canna have a bairn.'

'How come you've never been caught before?' asked Mad Bella. 'I can't imagine Finlay's more of a man than any other on Toronsay.'

Sadie looked at her feet. 'I've never done it with anyone else,' she mumbled.

Mad Bella stared at Sadie in surprise. It was hard to believe that Sadie had remained a virgin in spite of all the talk about her, and yet Mad Bella had no sense that Sadie was lying as she spoke. Sadie sat slumped in her chair, shoulders drooping, and with despair on her face. Gone was the cocky, blatantly sensual young woman all the men fell for, and in her place was a frightened girl just like others who had called on Mad Bella for help.

'Does Finlay agree with what you want to do?'

Sadie shook her head. 'He says it's not his.'

Mad Bella snorted. 'Just like a man,' she said. 'They leave the woman to pay the price for their fun.' She leant forward and grasped Sadie's hands. 'Are you sure you won't face up to it and tell your parents? It's the safest way for you.'

'I canna,' whispered Sadie. 'My father will kill me.'

'My medicine might kill you,' said Mad Bella flatly, releasing Sadie's hands.

Sadie blinked away fresh tears. 'Please help me, Mistress Bella,' she pleaded.

Mad Bella looked at her through narrowed eyes. 'Oh, "Mistress Bella" is it, now that you need my help? I remember you when you were a wee bairn,' she said. 'You used to torment me and destroy my crops. You thought it didn't matter because I was just a crazy *cailleach* who counted for nothing. "Mistress Bella" indeed, when it's Mad Bella behind my back.'

'I'm sorry,' sobbed Sadie. 'Children can be cruel and we were all frightened of you because of your spells.'

Mad Bella cackled. Her laughter peppered the inside of the black house and bounced off the walls. 'People are always frightened of things they dinna understand. But I'm no' a witch, Sadie MacLeod, and I don't cast spells. My second sight is a gift from the Almighty, and my knowledge of herbs plants is the result of years of trial and error. And fear doesn't keep folk away from my door when they need help they canna get anywhere else.'

27

Sadie snivelled into her fists. Mad Bella crossed to a shelf by the unglazed window. On the shelf was a row of bottles and several boxes containing Mad Bella's precious collection of potions, powders and leaves. She reached for one of the boxes and removed the lid, shaking a spoonful of leaves into a dirty mug. Then she poured hot water from the singing kettle onto the leaves and stirred them with a bent twig. She brought the mug to the table and sat it before Sadie. Sadie stared into the steaming, swirling brew.

'What will happen after I've drunk it?'

'Hard to tell,' answered Mad Bella. 'You will get a dreadful headache, and don't eat anything before tomorrow afternoon or you'll be very sick. Other than that I don't know because you've come too late. If the medicine works you will have stomach cramps and you'll bleed heavily. You could even bleed to death. If you're as far gone as you think, you'll have a labour and produce a tiny bairn that you'll have to bury. It won't live. If it's too late for the medicine to work you will still be very ill, and you'll still be pregnant. But I'm warning you, Sadie. You could easily die and I'll deny you were ever here. Do you understand me?'

Sadie nodded dumbly. She did not want to die. She wanted the baby to die. Finlay, too, because he had betrayed her. It was unfair that she should have to face the shame and humiliation of an unwanted pregnancy whilst he could walk away unscathed. She hated Finlay Nicolson and she hated this bairn. She picked up the mug, eyed its contents warily and took a small sip. It tasted vile, and she spat it out.

'Drink it quickly if you're going to drink it at all,' said Mad Bella. 'There's no sense in letting the taste linger on your tongue.'

Sadie tossed the rest of the mixture down her throat. She put the mug down on the table and shuddered. 'Thank you, Mistress Bella,' she said.

Mad Bella nodded. 'Now away home wi' ye. Go to bed and stay there until it's over one way or the other. I can do no more for you. Except pray, perhaps. And Finlay's father would say that prayers to the Devil are nought but curses.'

Sadie rose from her chair. Mad Bella took her arm and led her outside. 'I hope it works for you. But I doubt it will.'

CHAPTER 2

When Sadie looked down at her naked body she cursed the unwanted thing growing inside her that would make her fat and ugly. Mad Bella's medication had proved useless. Already blue veins had appeared on the milky white skin of Sadie's large breasts, breasts that Toronsay's men folk loved to fondle and bury their faces in. She shuddered with disgust. No man would lust after her anymore, and yet her entire existence was focussed on clandestine encounters with men. She had always been scornful of the wives whose husbands panted after her, and she enjoyed the embarrassed longing in men's eyes, especially in the kirk where their false piety made her want to laugh out loud. Now she would have to face the smug satisfaction on the faces of those same wives. And she would have to face the wrath of the Kirk. Nothing remained secret on Toronsay forever, and there was no hiding from the Minister and his creatures. It was a miracle that she had not been discovered before now, but Sadie had no intention of burning in Hell alone. She would drag Finlay Nicolson down with her every inch of the way into the flames.

After a month had passed since Finlay fled from Sadie at the old cairn he thought he was safe. It was not until the beginning of November that Sadie's secret became common knowledge. Walking through the village one evening with the wind against her, moulding her homespun dress to her body, there was no mistaking the shape of pregnancy, and her mother knew of it before Sadie reached home. Eager tongues wagged, thrilled to be the bearers of salacious gossip, whilst wives who were suspicious of their husbands felt panic rise in their breasts. If Sadie MacLeod was finally pregnant, whose man was the father of the bairn she carried? Please God, not mine, went the prayer in one black house after another.

Chrissie Macdonald had no husband to worry about. He had been in the ground these past ten years, having had the decency to die before Sadie

MacLeod was old enough to interest him. Chrissie was jealous of Sadie, as only one woman can be of another. A skinny woman herself, she was no match for Sadie's voluptuous charms, and although she would have liked another husband she was all too aware that no man would pay heed to her when he had Sadie to play with. With her eyes glittering in triumph, Chrissie was thrilled to be the one who would tell the MacLeods about their wayward daughter. She hurried along the stony path that led to the MacLeods' front door.

'Hello,' she called. 'Are ye in?'

Mrs MacLeod came to the door. 'Is it yourself, Chrissie? *Ciamar a tha thu*? I'll make tea.'

Chrissie followed Sadie's mother indoors. A vast pan of water on the fire emitted eerie squeals as the cockles being boiled opened and spat out grains of sand. Oatmeal was ready on the side and, once shelled, the cockles would be rolled in the oatmeal and fried for supper. Mrs MacLeod poured tea and picked up her knitting.

'What brings you here, then?' She asked when they were settled at the table.

Chrissie shifted in her seat. Mrs MacLeod's hospitality put her at a disadvantage and she was just a little ashamed.

'I just wanted to say how sorry I was about Sadie's trouble.'

'Our Sadie? What trouble would that be, chust?'

Chrissie's sharp eyes raked over the older woman's face. Her bewilderment showed that she had no idea that her daughter was in any trouble.

'I don't understand,' said Mrs MacLeod, she put her knitting on the table beside her and took the pan of cockles off the fire. 'What trouble are you talking about?'

Chrissie stood up, embarrassed now and wishing she had not been so ready to tell tales. The MacLeods were nice people, it was only their daughter who was a disgrace.

'Aye, well,' she muttered. 'I'm sorry if I've spoken out of turn. I thought you must know already.' She hurried away leaving Mrs MacLeod standing in the doorway staring after her.

'What did that dried up *cailleach* want?' asked Mr MacLeod as his wife sat down again at the kitchen table.

Mrs MacLeod looked puzzled. 'She said she was sorry to hear about our Sadie. I don't know what she's talking about.'

Even so, there was a nagging doubt in her mind as she thought back over recent weeks. She stared unseeingly into the fire as the pieces of the puzzle fell into place. In the hour between Chrissie's visit and Sadie's arrival home Mrs MacLeod aged ten years.

As soon as Sadie crossed the threshold she knew that her secret was out. Her mother's face was pinched and her brows were pulled so close together that there seemed to be no gap between them. Sadie put the milk pail she carried in a corner and draped a cloth over the top. Her mother watched her every move.

'You might as well tell us, girl,' she said flatly. 'We're bound to know sooner or later. Chrissie Macdonald has already been here to tell us you have a problem.'

Sadie sank to the floor. She crossed her arms and rocked slowly back and forth. Tears sprang from her eyes and dripped onto her sleeves. Her mother looked at her sharply. Sadie was not given to weeping. Mrs MacLeod guessed the reason and trembled with the shock and the shame of it.

'You're with child, aren't you?' She said quietly.

Mr MacLeod jumped to his feet and bellowed like an angry bull. 'She canna be!'

He rounded on Sadie and struck her across the face. Sadie cowered before him. Her parents stared helplessly at each other. It was the worst thing that could have happened to them – Sadie, their daughter, with child but without a husband. Sadie, the ugly one that no man would ever want to wed, who was their insurance against being left to fend for themselves in old age. Now this – a man's plaything with no ring on her finger.

'Is it true?' he yelled at her. Sadie hugged her knees without answering.

'Ach,' spat Mr MacLeod. 'Who's the father? Mayhap we can get him to wed you. Who is it?'

Sadie shook her head. 'I canna tell you,' she whimpered. Sadie continued to rock back and forth. It was clear that she was not going to tell them what they wanted to know. But Sadie was merely biding her time. She had already planned it. It was already decided what she was going to say, and to whom she would say it.

'It's true, then,' groaned Mr MacLeod. 'A married man no less. Get up. You're coming with me to the manse right now.'

'We can't go to the manse at this hour,' gasped Mrs MacLeod. 'We'll have to wait until tomorrow.'

'No,' said Mr MacLeod. He grabbed Sadie's wrist and yanked her to her feet. 'We're going now.'

With Mrs MacLeod still protesting that the Minister should not be disturbed until the next day, the three of them set out along the path. Faces peered from black houses and villagers ceased toiling their patches of soil to witness their progress through the village. Rumour, the staple fare of small communities, had spread like wildfire and Sadie's pregnancy was already causing rows between husbands and wives. Small bets were placed on likely suspects, and the names of some of these gave rise to coarse laughter as the sexual prowess of the elderly, the infirm or the mentally deficient was discussed amongst the men.

The manse was quiet as the grave. Lachlan sat at his table, a sheet of paper in front of him and his open Bible at his right hand. He was making notes for a sermon. His theme was Popery, the rites and rituals of Roman Catholicism being close to devil worship in his estimation. It was Catriona McQuigg, married to the Irishman, who had prompted a return to this well-worn theme. She had recently opened a 'dame' school in her house which was attracting attention. Several girls had been withdrawn from the parish school to attend this new independent enterprise and Lachlan was incensed by its popularity. His quill scratched at a furious pace and his indignation rose with every word he wrote. So when Morag ushered the MacLeods into his presence he was already an angry man. He glared at the intruders.

'We must speak with you,' apologised Mr MacLeod. 'The matter couldn't wait. Our daughter has transgressed, and we need guidance.'

Lachlan looked at the red-haired young woman who stood between her parents. One glance was all he needed to divine her transgression – *hougmagandie*. He felt a surge of triumph. Sadie MacLeod brought before him at last. He had waited a long time for this, and now he savoured the moment. Now she was in his power. He waved Morag away.

'Sit down,' he said to the MacLeods.

They perched stiffly on the edge of their seats. Lachlan's eyes bored into Sadie's face, willing her to look at him. He felt no pity or mercy for her. Whoever the man was who shared her sin, he would be caught and punished; but it was always the woman's fault when a man fell from grace, so hers was the greater transgression.

The setting sun cast Lachlan's shadow onto the wall. He was a man spare of frame with stooped shoulders. His skull-like head rested on a scrawny neck with a prominent Adam's apple and on the wall his shadow resembled a black vulture. The silence in the room was broken by Sadie's father.

'She's with child,' he blurted out. 'And her unwed.'

Lachlan drew in his breath sharply. This was worse than he expected. Fornication was one thing, bringing a bastard into the world quite another. It was inevitable, he supposed, given the young woman's promiscuity. The only surprise was that it had not happened sooner. Sadie MacLeod flaunted her body before every man on Toronsay. It was a pity about that squinting eye, but she could be forgiven her face with a body like hers. It was difficult for any garment to conceal. Lachlan flushed as he thought of the hours he had spent on his knees in penitence for the lust he felt for Sadie MacLeod and her scornful rejection of him ten years earlier.

Lost in his thoughts, Lachlan was caught unawares as Sadie suddenly looked straight at him with her one good eye. Her lip curled with contempt, and Lachlan knew that she, too, was remembering the scene between them when she was little more than a child: he with his breeches round his ankles and she doubled up with laughter at the sight of his flaccid penis. Divine intervention had rendered him impotent at the very moment that Sadie's magnificent body was revealed to him in all its glory. God had had mercy on him and he had not sinned.

'Have you nothing to say, Minister?' Mr MacLeod's voice brought Lachlan back to reality, and he hardened his heart against Sadie MacLeod.

'Is it true? Who is the father?'

Sadie glared at Lachlan. She thought him a sanctimonious prig, and no better than the rest of them for all his preaching. A vision of his nakedness swam before her eyes. He may have fathered eight children, but it was a pathetically small, wrinkled specimen of manhood he had hoped to charm her with; and she only thirteen years old at the time.

'Tis your own son,' she said with triumph. 'Finlay is the father.'

There was a moment of stunned silence before Mrs MacLeod became hysterical. Mr MacLeod caught Sadie a vicious blow on the side of the

33

head, making her scream, then he punched her in the face. Blood dripped down her chin from a split lip.

Lachlan turned pale. He banged his fist on the table. The inkpot rattled and blobs of black ink spattered onto the paper.

'Liar! Jezebel! How dare you drag my son's name into this?'

'Because it's true,' sneered Sadie. 'Finlay is the father of the bastard.'

Lachlan sank against the back of his chair. In spite of himself, he believed her. His hot temper transformed into a cold fury. That such behaviour should have been discovered in his parish at all was damnable, but that this depravity had been indulged in by his own son, a son of the manse, was a bitter pill to swallow. He rose from his chair, crossed the room, opened the door and bellowed Finlay's name into the hall.

When he heard his father shout his name a second time Finlay came with Murdo at his heels. They reached the top of the stairs and Murdo peered over the banister. The hall was empty. Finlay hunched his shoulders and went downstairs. Murdo stopped halfway, and then he sat and stared through the banister rails through the open dining room door and hoped that his presence would not be noticed. He wondered what dreadful thing his brother had done to have been summoned to the dining room instead of being taken outside for a whipping.

When Finlay reached the door, his father spoke in a soft voice, which unnerved Finlay more than his ranting ever did. There was something ominously controlled about Lachlan's voice, and Finlay found himself wishing for the belt rather than whatever his father was planning to do to him.

'Come here, laddie,' said Lachlan. 'You have some explaining to do and we're waiting to hear what you have to say for yourself.'

When Finlay failed to respond, Lachlan fought to quell the loathing he felt for his son. Wherever there was trouble, there was Finlay right in the thick of it, and with some plausible excuse as to why it was not really his fault. Well, this time Finlay would answer for his sins without Lachlan raising so much a finger towards him.

'Well?' said Lachlan. 'We're waiting.'

Finlay remained silent. What could he say? It was obvious that Sadie had denounced him; what more did they expect?

Moira drifted into the room and sat by the window. Her face was pale, and she did not need to be told the reason for the MacLeods being there. Finlay felt a pang of remorse at being the cause of yet more sorrow being heaped upon his mother's shoulders. He clenched his jaw and wondered how a blissful summer should have come to such a bitter end.

'Is it a coward you are?' sneered Lachlan. 'Or are you being wilfully perverse?'

Finlay dithered. Before he had a chance to answer, Mr MacLeod's temper snapped. He brought his fist down on the table.

'What have you done to my daughter?' he thundered.

Finlay's eyes came to rest on Mr MacLeod's face. 'No more nor no less than she has done to me.'

'And just what do you intend to do about it?' asked Lachlan, when he recovered from Finlay's insolence.

Finlay stood helplessly before his father. Do? What did they expect him to do?

'Is it a gentleman you are, Finlay Nicolson?' asked Mrs MacLeod. 'You must marry Sadie and make an honest woman of her, chust.'

Finlay was appalled. Good God, he thought, I cannot possibly marry Sadie MacLeod. 'I'll not marry her,' he said.

Sadie began to weep, and her parents gasped at Finlay's reply. 'I'll not marry her, and that's final,' he repeated.

There was a moment of tense silence before Moira spoke in quiet but determined defence of her son.

'Hard as it may seem on Sadie, Finlay is right,' she said. 'He is too young to marry, and there is no reason why it should be him rather than any of the other lads in the village. Sadie's behaviour has always been the subject of much gossip as you must know.'

'That's not true,' cried Sadie.

'How dare you insult my daughter?' roared Mr MacLeod. 'And what about the bairn? Whose name will it bear? Who will support it?' He slammed his fist down on the table again. 'Is our Sadie to be the mother of a bastard child whilst your son shirks his responsibilities? Answer me that.'

'She is certain that Finlay is the father of her child, is she?' asked Moira.

'How can you doubt it?' sobbed Mrs MacLeod. 'Sadie was always a good girl. She's never given us a moment's worry. 'Tis your son who's depraved. He led her astray.'

Lachlan stared at the MacLeods in disbelief. He wondered how it was possible that they were unaware that their daughter was a whore. Moira spoke again.

'Sadie is twenty-four,' she said. 'That makes her seven years older than Finlay and quite old enough to know what she was doing when she took a boy to her bed.'

Lachlan stood up wearily. 'We're going round in circles. There's no point in discussing it further. The matter will be referred to the Kirk Session. Both Sadie and Finlay will be summoned to appear before the Session to account for their wickedness.' His voice brooked no argument and the MacLeods hung their heads. 'Now it's best that you return home. I bid you goodnight.'

After Sadie and her parents left the manse, Lachlan and Finlay glared at each other in silence for several minutes. Then Lachlan crossed the room and opened the door of a handsome cabinet. He withdrew a heavy book and brought it to the table.

Finlay had no difficulty in recognising the book. It was the Book of Discipline, Lachlan's means of maintaining order within the household. In it he faithfully recorded each transgression and punishment against the sinner's name. Lachlan leafed through the pages until he came to the last entry. He took up his quill, dipped it in the ink, and Finlay and Moira watched as he wrote in his spidery hand. The scratch of the quill was the only sound in the room. When he finished writing Lachlan blotted the ink and then pushed the Book of Discipline towards Finlay.

'Read what I have written.'

Finlay was accustomed to seeing his name appear against his many wrongdoings, but this was his first truly serious offence. He stared at the words.

'Read it aloud.'

Finlay's voice shook as he read what his father had written. He felt the stirrings of shame.

'Name: Finlay Nicolson. Transgression: Fornication. Punishment: To be determined by the Kirk Session.'

'Now get out of my sight,' hissed Lachlan.

CHAPTER 3

Across the island folk whispered together in doorways, along beaten tracks between the black houses and the sea, and over their giggle water in the evenings. Time and again wee Jimmy was stuffed into the window as more people crammed into the black house. Forbidden whisky loosened tongues and fuelled fanciful conversations.

'Yon Finlay'll no' be the only one. You mark my words.'

'Aye, I could name several in the village, chust.'

'And all the men in Clachan,' said the dying man in the bed against the rear wall.

'What? Are you no' dead yet? And there was I thinking it was a skellington in the bed.'

'Shut your mouth and bring me a wee dram.'

'He's taking a long time to die, right enough. Or is he shamming just to get the world and his wife to wait on him hand and foot?'

'I heard that,' said the dying man. 'Nothing wrong wi' my ears even if the rest of me's nigh at the last gasp.'

The dying man's mouth was stopped with whisky and he fell into a deep sleep almost immediately. The conversation returned to fornication.

'It's wild orgies they've been having. I heard that Finlay wore horns on his head like the Devil hisself and that Sadie gave herself to one after another.'

'Lucky buggers then, that's all I can say. How many of you got that far?'

Whisky was tipped down throats and chairs creaked as the men shifted their weight. Truth was, none of them had but none cared to admit it. They squinted at each other in the firelight, but the subject was quietly dropped.

In the manse the atmosphere could have been cut with a knife. No one spoke. Moira kept to her room. Finlay roamed the moors from dawn to dark. In an effort at reconciliation, Murdo approached his father.

'It wasn't Finlay's fault,' he pleaded. 'Sadie MacLeod is a wanton. You said so yourself many a time. Finlay wouldn't have sinned if she hadn't made him do it.'

Lachlan frowned at Murdo. 'If you are to become a minister you must understand that a community can only be saved if each person within that community lives a good and godly life. To have one sinner amongst us places all our souls in danger of damnation. Finlay did not have to do what he did. He chose to do it and he knew what he was doing. And as long as there are weak-willed and lecherous men amongst us who are prepared to indulge in depravity, there will be wicked women ready and willing to snatch them from the rightful path. Fornication is evil, and there is never an excuse for it. Now an innocent child will suffer the stigma for life of having been born a bastard. Don't waste your pity on Finlay. He is not worth it, nor does he deserve it.'

Murdo left his father, and Lachlan stared through the window at a steely grey sea.

He could not have relented even if he had wished to. He was obliged to punish wrongdoers and he relished the power he wielded over his parishioners. But there was more to it: he wanted to make Finlay suffer for succeeding where he himself had failed. He was jealous of his son.

After the initial delight and amusement felt by the islanders that a son of the manse should have been caught out, the realisation that Finlay's sin jeopardised all their souls began to sink in. The disapproval of the islanders closed around the Nicolsons like a steel trap. Tentacles of fear reached beyond the family in the manse. Torquil McBeth, schoolmaster and Lachlan's son-in-law, was not the only man on Toronsay to dread what Sadie might reveal when she was under interrogation.

On the evening before the Kirk Session was to be held, Torquil sat and gazed moodily into the fire. His black hair hung untidily about his shoulders and the bald spot on the crown of his head was clearly visible. He tied his hair back on schooldays to disguise his baldness so that the children did not make fun of him. There were few balding men on Toronsay, most being blessed with thick black hair to complement their blue eyes. At some angles Torquil was a handsome man, but as he stared into his peat fire that evening Elspeth caught his resemblance to the Nicolsons' cow.

Elspeth sat at her spinning wheel and cast furtive glances at her husband. She lacked the good looks of her brothers and was a plain young woman with mousy hair. When Torquil had first shown an interest in her she had been flattered, and she agreed to be his wife in spite of having no love for him; he had a position, a certain social standing and a steady income so that her future would be secure. They had been married for four years, and if Elspeth could not say that she was blissfully happy, she was far from being miserable.

Their evenings were usually filled with amiable chatter, but this evening Torquil was silent. Elspeth assumed that his gloom and unease were due to the fact that, as clerk to the Kirk Session, he would be one of those required to pass judgement on her brother. In spite of it being common gossip that most of the island's menfolk had dallied with Sadie MacLeod, it did not occur to Elspeth that Torquil might also have been involved with her in the past. Unaware of her husband's fear for the next day, Elspeth set about wheedling and cajoling him to be merciful.

'He's just a boy, Torquie,' she pleaded. 'I know Finlay is wild and stupid, but he's not a wicked person. If Sadie MacLeod decided to get her claws into him he couldn't have stood a chance. Don't be too hard on him.'

Torquil shifted uneasily in his chair. In truth there was nothing he could do to help Finlay. He was just the clerk. There were others more powerful than he who were bound to demand their pound of flesh.

'It won't be my decision,' he said. 'Your brother is a fool, and he only has himself to blame for the predicament he's in. He knew what he was doing, and he knew that it was a sin.'

'His only crime is having been caught,' snapped Elspeth. 'Everyone knows that Sadie MacLeod is nothing but a trollop. There are plenty of others guilty of the same thing. They've just got away with it so far.'

Torquil flushed. 'Finlay's crime was hougmagandie,' he said. 'Getting caught was his misfortune, not his crime. I'll do what I can, but if Finlay admits his guilt, which he's bound to do sooner or later, he will deserve whatever punishment is meted out to him.'

'But...'

'Haud yer wheesht, woman,' sighed Torquil. 'The subject is closed. The Lord will guide us during the Session.'

Elspeth glared across the room at her husband. She knew that it was useless to argue further. Torquil would only lose his temper, and then he might be less well disposed towards Finlay in the morning. With her lips compressed into a thin, tight line she returned to her spinning. In her anger she began to turn the wheel faster and faster until Torquil, driven mad by the whirring noise, rose to his feet and stamped out of the room.

Torquil dreaded the forthcoming session. So far, in common with the other lay elders, his responsibilities had been confined to administrative matters, such as the poor fund and the curriculum of the parish school. Those few civil crimes with which he had been concerned related to violations of the Sabbath, domestic violence and drunkenness. This would be his first experience of hearing an offence as serious as hougmagandie.

Had the guilty woman been anyone other than Sadie MacLeod, Torquil would have been less squeamish. He was terrified that Sadie would name him as one of those who had benefited from her promiscuous charms. Marriage had not erased the memory of his encounters with Sadie from his mind. Elspeth was a passive woman in bed, although Torquil would have been none the wiser if he had not been with Sadie. But now, whenever he saw Sadie or heard her name mentioned, he relived the feel of hands and hot tongue all over his body, biting, teasing inflaming him beyond measure. He wished Elspeth was more like her. He would never forget Sadie's passion even though she had always denied him full consummation. Now he wondered if that was the secret of her hold over men – there was always the hope of the final act pulsating between them without the promise ever being fulfilled. Finlay Nicolson was a lucky bugger, chust.

During the night the wind increased. By morning Toronsay was gripped in the teeth of a gale. Ferocious winds blew rain in horizontal sheets and churned the pewter-coloured sea, sending drifts of spume into the air. Folk stayed indoors for fear of being blown off their feet. Those who would have some excuse to loiter in the vicinity of the kirk to witness what they could of the proceedings had to content themselves with peering through cracks in the dry-stone walls of their black houses.

Lachlan, Finlay and Murdo ate their oatmeal *brose* in silence and Morag crept about on tiptoe carrying plates to and from the kitchen. When the men of the family had all been served, Morag took a tray upstairs to Moira. Moira had lapsed into melancholy, withdrawing from society altogether. She fretted about Finlay's appearance before the Kirk Session in the certain knowledge of the humbling his free spirit would undergo. Finlay might be a rapscallion, but he had a special place in Moira's heart and she feared more for him now than she had during the many beatings he had suffered at his father's hands.

Elspeth arrived before they had finished breakfast. She drew up a chair beside Murdo and would wait with him while the Session took place so that he did not brood by himself. She was loyal and protective of her family, never having managed to transfer that loyalty to Torquil. Part of her own censure of Sadie MacLeod was due to the envy of the ease with which Sadie, with no husband, had become pregnant so casually, when she herself, with a husband, was disappointed month after month. Her life was dull and uninspiring, and Elspeth remained more daughter than wife, more Nicolson than McBeth.

After breakfast Lachlan and Finlay donned their cloaks and left the manse. They clung to one another in the fierce wind as matter of necessity, each of them loathing the physical contact with one another. Murdo and Elspeth watched until they were out of sight. Upstairs, unseen and despairing, Moira leaned against a window with her eyes glued to the back of Finlay's head.

Murdo stayed at the window downstairs. He wiped condensation away with his sleeve. Raindrops chased each other down the panes of glass, but he stared past them into the deserted bleakness outside. Realisation of what being a minister really meant began to sink in. It was not confined to posturing in the kirk with canny sermons and conducting baptisms, marriages and funerals. There was this other, darker side that Murdo had known little about. 'Judge not, that ye be not judged', the Bible said, and yet that was exactly what his father was about to do. And not without a hint of enjoyment either, thought Murdo, who had seen the gleam in his father's eyes. Murdo lowered his forehead onto his folded arms to hide the tears in his eyes. He was sick at heart as he waited for Finlay and his father to return to the manse, and in the depths of his soul he rejected his father's plans for him.

Toronsay was a small island and possessed few men of substance to serve as lay elders, so the Kirk Session that was to sit in judgement over Finlay and Sadie consisted of the most pious members of the community. They had been elected to their positions for life and were responsible for supporting Lachlan in his supervision of strict moral discipline.

Finlay and Sadie knew these men, but now their familiar faces were closed, their eyes hostile, and they were like strangers. They sat on tall-backed oaken pews, devout and godly men, conscious of their own saintliness. Torquil dipped a quill into a bottle of ink and held it poised in readiness over a pile of papers. Of these men, only one could say with all honesty that he had never lusted after Sadie MacLeod.

Old Donald Gillies was in his late seventies. As a younger man he had been the precentor in the kirk until his voice began to fail and another man took his place. For more than twenty years his rich baritone voice had filled the kirk on each Sabbath day as he led the congregation in the chanting of psalms. He was a thin weed of a man with a humourless face and enormous ears. Some said that Old Donald could hear a whisper from one end of the island to the other with those ears and a following wind.

It was Old Donald who led the questioning. Finlay and Sadie stood before the men who would act as judge and jury. There was no one to speak in their defence, and they were completely at the mercy of the Kirk Session. It was cold inside the vast building and their voices echoed in the emptiness. The walls were grey in the drab light that seeped through the windows, and the men were dressed in dark clothes. It was like a funeral without the wry humour that attended those occasions.

Finlay's eyes darted about the kirk seeking escape, but there was no escape. The door was not locked and he was free to leave, only there was nowhere for him to go. His father could cast him out of the parish, but he was tied to the island because of his mother.

He glanced at Sadie. She stood with her head held high and glared at the lay elders with contempt. Sadie could not deny the charge against her since her pregnancy and unmarried state proclaimed her guilt; but Finlay continued to protest his innocence. It was a futile gesture. All men confessed eventually under intense interrogation.

Old Donald turned a sour face to Sadie. 'Where is the alleged guilt supposed to have taken place?'

As far as Sadie was concerned, the fact that she now stood before the Kirk Session was due entirely to men's unbridled lust. Without men she would not have been brought face to face with those po-faced sanctimonious pigs. She bristled with anger at the unfairness of her situation.

'What do you mean "alleged"?' she said in a clear voice. 'It happened. Look at me. Do you think I got like this on my own?' She put a hand on her swollen belly. 'You men are all the same. You think you can do what you like because you're not the ones to take trouble home with you.' She glared at Old Donald. 'You must have wept into your pisspot that your spies let you down this time.'

Old Donald bridled with indignation at Sadie's insolence. 'You'll keep a civil tongue in your head when you speak to us, Sadie MacLeod. Answer the question. Where did you meet?'

Sadie shrugged. 'At the old cairn.'

'And did the guilt occur on just one occasion or did it happen more than once?'

Sadie glanced sideways at Finlay. He stared straight ahead. His eyes were bright, his teeth clenched, his cheeks two livid patches. She was pleased to see that he looked scared to death.

'Which of you would only want to be with me the once?' She sneered. 'Of course it was more than once. We met every Saturday through summer past, and he'd better not say different or you can add telling lies to his list of crimes.'

There was silence as all eyes turned to Finlay. Lachlan snarled at his son. 'Is this true? Have you been violating the Sabbath all these months as well as lying with this whore?'

Finlay stared at the wall behind his father's head.

'Huh!' said Sadie. 'He's too much of a coward to admit it, chust. Would any of you admit it?' She stared hard at each accusing face in turn. She saw them flush, saw the fear in their eyes, and she laughed.

Torquil kept his eyes down and scribbled furiously. He expected Sadie to denounce him at any moment. The others fidgeted with their sleeves. Only Old Donald dared to look her in the eye before turning his attention to Finlay.

'Are you prepared to confess now and save us all a lot of heartache?'

'No,' said Finlay. 'She may have been with someone, but she can't prove that it was me. It could have been anyone.'

Sadie leapt at him and raked her nails down his face. 'You're a liar, Finlay Nicolson. You know it was you, and I know it was you. I've never done it with anyone else.'

There was a sudden deathly hush. Lachlan and the other lay elders had the grace to blush. Except for Old Donald, who had not been involved with Sadie, they each knew that she was speaking the truth. Sadie had allowed them total freedom with her body except for full intercourse. In spite of all the talk about her, nobody had boasted of having had her, although none had admitted to having failed in their attempts. If she was now accusing Finlay of being the father of her bairn, then he probably was.

Unaware of the agonised thoughts of the other lay elders, Old Donald pursed his lips and narrowed his eyes. He had no sympathy with either Finlay or Sadie. They were an affront to all decent people, and now his own salvation was in jeopardy because of them. It was time to play his trump card and bring these proceedings to a conclusion.

'We have a witness,' he said into the cold, stale air of the kirk.

He spoke slowly, enunciating each word with smug satisfaction. The stilted words dropped like hailstones on glass, shattering Sadie's defiance. Finlay's mouth went dry, his pulse pounded in his ears and beads of perspiration formed along his hairline. Involuntarily they turned to each other in shock and disbelief.

Old Donald leant towards Torquil and whispered, 'Bring her in if she's here.'

Mad Bella hovered in the porch, cold and wet. It had been a dangerous walk from the edge of the moor and she had twice been blown over. She had been of a mind to ignore the summons to attend the Kirk Session, but she was no fool. Nor was she so certain of resting at peace after her death that she was prepared to snap her fingers at the Kirk and all it stood for. She believed that death was final, and folk made their own heaven or hell here on earth. But, if she were mistaken, she would have to stand before her Maker and to account for herself, so it was safer to hedge her bets and pay lip service to Lachlan and his creatures. Even so she was in no mood to be humoured, and when Torquil took hold of her to lead her into the kirk, she snatched her arm from his grip.

'I *dinna* need your help,' she told him.

Torquil stepped back and withdrew his hand as quickly as if he had been stung. Mad Bella stepped inside and shuffled past the rows of carved benches and pews, tapping her stick on the stone floor. She brought with her an air of decay and a smell of ordure made worse because her clothes were wet.

Sadie began to tremble. She glared at Finlay who replied with a slight shrug of his shoulders. Sadie had told no one of her visit to Mad Bella and the old woman's medicine, but now she expected Mad Bella to reveal the secret shame of what she had tried to do. But just as Sadie never spoke of her assignations, so Mad Bella kept her own counsel over the unfortunate women who sought her help. She would tell no lies to the Kirk Session for fear of her own salvation, but she would sooner die than betray a confidence.

'Now, Mistress Bella,' began Old Donald. 'We want you to tell us what you saw on Saturday evenings during summer past.'

Mad Bella's piercing black eyes darted back and forth, and her lips twitched. 'I'm no afeared o' you, Donald Gillies,' she growled. 'I ken when you were a wee bairn in wet breeks, chust.'

She stood defiantly before him, and the other lay elders bent their heads to hide their smiles. Lachlan pulled a white handkerchief from his pocket and held it against his nose.

'I'm not afraid of you either, you crazy *cailleach*,' replied Old Donald smoothly. 'In spite of your wee bones and your evil eye. You'll stand before God sooner than I shall. You told the Minister that you saw Finlay out at night. Is that correct, or do you want to withdraw your statement?'

Mad Bella chewed her lower lip. She looked at Finlay and shrugged.

'Mistress Bella,' said Lachlan, fighting his irritation. 'Please repeat what you told me earlier – that you saw Finlay going to the far cairn to meet Sadie MacLeod.'

'I never said that,' retorted Mad Bella. 'Dinna put words into my mouth. How would I ken where he was going or who he'd be meeting?'

'Ah,' said Norman MacLeod, spotting the flaw in her statement. 'So you did see Finlay out on Saturday nights then?'

Mad Bella was trapped. She waved her skinny arms in the air. 'Aye, so I did,' she shouted. 'So I did. I saw him, chust. That's all. I saw him by the burn, and that's all you can make me say.'

'It's enough,' said Lachlan. 'Thank you for your testimony, Mistress Bella. You can go now.'

'I'm going anyway,' she snapped. 'I'm saying nothing more.'

'You don't need to.' Old Donald smiled with malice. 'You've told us what we wanted to hear.'

Mad Bella cast her eyes over each of the lay elders until they came to rest on Lachlan. 'Ach,' she said. 'I wonder who is the real sinner here, chust.'

She stamped out of the kirk. Lachlan rose from his seat and went to open a window in spite of the gale blowing outside. They all took a few welcome breaths of fresh air, but the smell of Mad Bella had seeped into every corner.

'Now will you admit to the guilt?' Lachlan said to his son when he resumed his seat. 'You've no choice really.'

Finlay hung his head. 'No.'

Old Donald licked his lips. 'Very well,' he said, turning to Sadie. 'As Finlay refuses to admit to being with you, and therefore denies being the father of the child you bear, you must tell us the details of what took place between you. Then we'll decide whether or not he is guilty.'

He leant forward, eager to learn the intimate details of the illicit couplings. Finlay blushed to the roots of his hair, and only Lachlan felt he could not bear to hear what Sadie would say.

'Have the decency to spare her,' he snarled at Finlay. 'You know she is telling the truth. How can you stand there and continue to deny it?'

Finlay quailed. He had thought that by remaining silent the lay elders would give him the benefit of the doubt. But the lechery he saw in the old men's eyes as they waited, slack-mouthed, for Sadie to reveal what had passed between them filled him with disgust. He spoke to relieve them both of the humiliation.

'I admit the charge of hougmagandie,' he said sullenly.

'At last,' breathed Lachlan. 'Finally we have some stirring of a guilty conscience.'

'I do not admit to being the father of the bairn,' added Finlay.

The lay elders held a brief consultation. Their verdict was never in doubt. Old Donald spoke for them all.

'We find you both guilty on your own admission of having committed hougmagandie. Also, we find that you, Finlay Nicolson, are the father of the child. You will both appear before the congregation of the kirk for a minimum of four Sabbaths. If we feel that you are not truly penitent in that time we will increase the number of your appearances. Finlay, you will support the child for ten years. That is all. You may go.'

CHAPTER 4

Life continued its daily progress as Finlay and Sadie awaited the first public penance. Buoyed by anticipation of the spectacle to come, the villagers set about their chores with lighter hearts. Cows were milked and the excess was set in pans for the skimming cream made into butter; more peat was cut and added to stacks at the end of each black house; crofters scratched at stubborn patches of ground; herrings and mackerel were salted and hung from rafters above fires; and the wind and rain provided a grey tapestry of gloom.

Sadie was confined to the space beside her bed. Neither of her parents would speak to her. Her shame was their shame; her humiliation, their humiliation. And when it came, her penance would be theirs too. Sadie watched her mother put thick, sour milk left from the skimming of cream into saucepans on the fire. When it was ready crowdie floated to the top and Mrs MacLeod poured the whey. She put some of the fresh crowdie to one side for use over the next day or so, and then added salt to what remained. Then she lined the press with muslin and ladled in the crowdie to mature into cheese for the winter. When she finished she poured some of the whey into a beaker and gave it to Sadie to drink; it was as sharp as the look on Mrs MacLeod face. And all the while she banged each utensil against pots and pans as if the noise would relieve her temper.

Finlay played no part in the preparations for winter. Each day he rose at first light. Morag dished him up a bowl of porridge, which he ate without tasting its rich creaminess, and then he left the manse, not to return until nightfall. Only Murdo knew where Finlay went, but if Finlay was aware that his young brother followed him at a discreet distance, he gave no sign of it.

Most days Finlay climbed Temptation Hill and sat on its crest where he could see the whole of Toronsay spread before him. The upward thrust of Temptation Hill divided Toronsay into two unequal halves. The narrower, eastern side was largely uninhabited with just a few scattered bothies visited only by fishermen when it was the season to fish. Here, the inhospitable bracken-covered land dropped steeply to a narrow strip of shingle and deep water. It was on the wider, western side of the island that folk lived, crammed into black houses and scratching a living from the land and the kelp. The moorland between east and west was peppered with derelict dwellings, abandoned when islanders were forcibly moved to make way for the sheep. There were no trees on the island and the landscape was bleak, so that the profusion of colour provided by the machair each spring was the Lord's annual miracle.

During these lonely, desolate days Finlay sat in the fading heather and stared over a land of a thousand memories. Sometimes he watched the beyond-the-pale Irishman as he fished inshore, but most of the time he stared straight ahead seeing nothing. He berated himself for his stupidity and cowardice, and he hated Sadie. Most of all he hated the Kirk. He tried to will himself into an acceptance of the power of religious belief: the belief that to have one sinner amongst them jeopardised salvation for the entire congregation; the belief that either they were all saved or they were all damned. But he could not. He tried to see that his Father acted only out of a fervent desire to ensure their rightful places in heaven. But he could not. He saw only that his Father was a tyrant whose harsh rule over his flock must surely stem from a desperate need to atone for sins of his own. It was this hatred that burned within Finlay that saved him from the melancholy.

On the day before the penance the wind shrieked across the island, battering gulls off course and buffeting a golden eagle which hovered in the sky above the two brothers. From a distance came the thunder of waves breaking on the shingle far below. The clouds were so low that there was no visible margin between sky and sea, and only the white crests of angry waves marked one from the other. Murdo sat in a pile of bracken and felt moisture from the sodden earth seep through his breeches until his buttocks were icy cold.

The Sabbath dawned grey and wet, but the wind had dropped. They arrived early at the kirk and Murdo went straight to his usual seat on the front bench on the right-hand side. There was a small group of villagers already sitting talking amongst themselves as members of the congregation arrived in clumps of half a dozen or more, all in their best black suits.

The kirk would need to fill with bodies for there to be sufficient warmth to make it a comfortable place to be for an hour and a half. Folk arrived with more enthusiasm than was usual. The MacLeods from the next village were there, jaws chomping on goodness knows what, looking like a herd of cows chewing the cud. And the McBeths were there with their brood of ten children, one a year and each resembling a startled white rabbit with red-rimmed blue eyes. Even those whose frailty or infirmity furnished them with an excuse to stay at home on the Sabbath managed to trek to the kirk that morning. Feet shuffled and stamped to keep the blood moving and tubercular coughs punctuated whispered conversations. The benches filled quickly and the atmosphere was tense with a show of piety.

Elspeth slid along the bench towards Murdo squeezed his hand. She looked round at the assembled congregation, but none would catch her eye. It was clear that they considered all the Nicolsons to be tainted by Finlay's sin, and that they wanted to avoid the contagion. Elspeth sniffed her contempt for their assumed righteousness. There was scarcely a man present who had not enjoyed Sadie MacLeod's favours, and she had overheard wives screaming very unchristian words at their husbands during rows over the trollop.

Quietness settled over the assembled islanders as Lachlan entered the kirk. His steps were heavy, as though he carried the weight of God and all his angels on his shoulders. He reached the front and turned to face his congregation. They were his flock, but they were not his people. He was an outsider, not born to island ways, and although he had lived on Toronsay for many years, and in spite of his marriage to an islander, he knew that he would only ever be recognised as an inhabitant of Toronsay, never as one of them. He had always believed that being an outsider endowed him with a certain mystique, but there were times when he had wished he might bridge the gulf between them, and now, for the first time, he wished that he had stirred himself to learn more of the barbaric language.

He frowned and drew his lips into a thin, unsmiling line. The islanders stared back at him with inscrutable black eyes, and he avoided looking directly at their faces. But he missed nothing. Rain spattered against the windows and moisture seeped from sodden clothing to drip in muddy pools between the rows of worshippers. The air was filled with the smell of dampness and the manure that clung to Alistair

MacDonald's old boots. Lachlan had lost count of the number of times he had told Ali Mac to remove those boots before he entered the House of God.

It seemed the kirk had never been so full, many of the men obliged to stand. But there remained one empty seat, glaringly obvious to all, and Lachlan's face reddened with anger when he saw it. He would take his wife to task when he returned home after the service. Moira could not be permitted to go her own way. The Sabbath had its purpose and she could not hold herself apart from it.

Lachlan held his hand up for silence, although no one was talking. Then he took a deep breath and began.

'Let us pray.'

It takes time for a congregation of three hundred to get to their feet, and the noise of so much movement echoed to the rafters. Lachlan waited patiently until there was silence once more.

'The soul that sinneth, it shall die. May the good Lord look down on us in our repentance as we pray for His forgiveness.'

The starting prayer went on and on. Murdo had the impression that his father was deliberately spinning it out to delay the proceedings, but even Lachlan could not go on indefinitely. Finally the congregation sank onto the benches, relieved to take the weight off their feet. Then Andy MacDonald, the precentor, mounted the few steps into the lower of the two carved oak pulpits and raised his voice to lead the congregation in the psalm.

'Oh Lord God, to whom vengeance belongeth; Oh God, to whom vengeance belongeth, show thy self.' His untrained tenor voice held them in thrall.

As he repeated each line in turn the congregation joined in the chant. They sang with feeling; some good voices, some out of tune, but all sang from the depths of their souls. Their lives were hard, the land and weather harsh and relentless, but still they praised their Lord on each Sabbath day with a depth of emotion that could soften the heart of the most hardened unbeliever.

When the psalm came to an end and Andy MacDonald had returned to his seat, Lachlan climbed into the upper pulpit. He rested his hands on the edge and stared at the faces raised to his. They were all alert and expectant; there was no one there that Lachlan could shame into wakefulness with his acid tongue. No one slept in the kirk that morning. He could feel the shifting of power as his congregation began to withdraw its support for his ministry. He ruled Toronsay with their tacit consent, and that consent was based on fear, but now that fear had turned to ridicule and contempt, and Lachlan's little empire was beginning to crumble. They understood that if Lachlan was unable to keep his own house in order, what help was there for the rest of them? With a heavy heart Lachlan addressed his flock.

'We are all of us divided into two groups: those of us who will achieve salvation, and those sinners who face damnation for all eternity. We have two such sinners here today who will appear before us in penitence and humility. Finlay Nicolson and Sadie MacLeod have dishonoured God and this congregation by committing the sin of hougmagandie.' He raised a finger and pointed towards the door. 'Bring them forth.'

Torquil led Finlay and Sadie into the kirk. Folk looked over their shoulders and craned their necks to catch a glimpse of them. They were clad in sackcloth and stumbled as they made their way to the front of the kirk. Lachlan left the pulpit. With slow and deliberate step he brought forward the short-legged cutty stool – the stool of repentance. He placed it in the centre in front of the congregation. Finlay's face was ashen, and Sadie wept silently, her earlier defiance having left her. It was the ultimate humiliation, as standing on the cutty stool made him clearly visible to everyone present, in a position of ridicule and censure. It had the desired effect in that it broke Finlay's spirit. He wept like a bairn, exactly as his father intended that he should.

Murdo watched the proceedings with mounting horror. He glanced sideways at those seated nearest to him, expecting to see some measure of sympathy on their faces towards the two transgressors. Instead, he was shocked to see no trace of compassion. They sat smug-faced and complacent in the certain knowledge of their own purity and sinlessness. With the unblinking disapproval of all directed towards them, Finlay and Sadie had to remain where they were throughout Lachlan's interminable sermon, the second psalm and the final prayer. As soon as the benediction was over Murdo fled the kirk.

Moira had struggled downstairs with Morag's help, anxious to be there for Finlay the moment he arrived. She sat wrapped in a blanket beside a feeble fire, and Lachlan pounced on her as soon as he entered the room.

'You were not in your place this morning,' he snapped. 'It is bad enough to have a son shamed in public without his sin being compounded by your disobedience. There were others present this morning who are considerably more frail than you. Explain yourself?'

Moira turned dull eyes towards her husband, summoning one last spark of revolt against all he stood for.

'I had no desire to witness you and your religion humiliate Finlay.'

'But it was your duty to be there,' said Lachlan. 'The Lord expects you to attend the kirk on the Sabbath day.'

'No, it is you who expects me to be there,' argued Moira. 'The Lord only requires that I remember the Sabbath and keep it holy.'

Lachlan was scandalized. He stopped his pacing and stared open-mouthed at his wife. 'This is blasphemy,' he roared. 'Am I to bring you before the Kirk Session next? What has come over you, woman?'

Moira shrank into the blanket around her shoulders. When she spoke her voice was filled with sadness and she chose her words with care. 'I have spent the last days since the Kirk Session thinking long and hard about your God and His mysterious ways. I am sorry to say that I want nothing more to do with Him. I have no wish to worship or believe in a God who is so unjust; a God who killed three of my bairns almost before their lives took hold. Whatever did they do to so offend God that he should have seen fit to rob them of their lives?'

Lachlan turned purple with anger, and a blood vessel pulsed rapidly in his temple. 'How dare you question God's purpose? You will rot in the deep, dark, bottomless pit for what you have just said. And instead of thinking what the bairns did that they died so young, you should think about what sins you committed that the good Lord punished you by their loss. You will go to hell, my dear.'

'I don't care,' retorted Moira. 'The sooner the better as far as I'm concerned. It can't be any worse than life here with you.'

Murdo gasped with horror. He could not bear to hear any more. Everything had happened so quickly that his brain reeled. All he could think of was Finlay's warning that he would turn into their Father if he became a minister. He raced upstairs and stuffed some fresh clothes into a bundle, and then, heedless of the fact that it was the Sabbath, he ran from the manse. He did not stop to draw breath until he reached the eastern side of the island with its swirling below. He was there. The Irishman sat in his dinghy fishing for saithe amongst the rocks. He looked up as Murdo appeared over the brow and rested on his oars.

Murdo had known Paddy McQuigg would be there because he was always at the fishing regardless of the day of the week. The lapsed Roman Catholic scorned the island's religion and paid Lachlan no heed. Had he ever attended the kirk when Lachlan preached against heresy and popery, he would not have been able to prevent himself from laughing out loud, so it was prudent of him to give the village a wide berth on the Sabbath. Even so, he knew of the Kirk Session and its verdict, and guessed what had taken place in the name of God that morning. A plague on all religions, he muttered under his breath.

It was Paddy's wife who had opened the dame school which had so incensed Lachlan. Catriona had been surprised and encouraged by the support it received from the villagers. Although Catriona was island-born she was frowned on by kith and kin – which included the majority of the villagers due to intermarriage – for having what the islanders regarded as an irregular marriage. Catriona and Paddy had been married in a register office on the mainland, and in the eyes of the pious on Toronsay this was no marriage at all. But the acceptance of her little school marked a change in their attitude.

Murdo stared down at the man in the dinghy. Here was his salvation, his means of leaving the island right now instead of waiting for the fishing boats in the morning. He hesitated for a brief moment as thoughts of the worry he would cause his family brought tears to his eyes, but then he plunged headlong down the cliff, scrambling through dense bracken, slithering and sliding down the rock face and sending loose stones clattering to the narrow beach below.

CHAPTER 5

It was almost dusk before Murdo was deemed to be truly missing. A soft, fresh mantle of mist had settled over Toronsay and with a louring sky bringing an early nightfall there was little daylight left in which to mount an extensive search. Lachlan went about the village collecting able-bodied men to scour the island for his boy. They turned out in force and set off in all directions. Those who would head for the northern most tip of the island carried lanterns. They would stay out all night, resting in ruined bothies during the darkest hours. Others searched closer to home, side by side in long rows, beating at the bracken with their *cromags* and poking into every nook and cranny. No one had seen Murdo slip out of the manse, and although Paddy McQuigg's boat was not anchored in its usual place, it was pure speculation that he had spirited Murdo away. The Irishman was often at the fishing on the Sabbath day.

Lachlan did not join in the search as he had the evening service to conduct. The Lord's work must be done and prayers must be said for Murdo's safe return. His congregation was composed almost entirely of women. No more than half a dozen men, ancient, decrepit or mentally deficient, sat on the benches. All the rest were out on the moors. Hard, stony faces that had been directed towards Finlay and Sadie that morning now fixed themselves on their Minister.

There was surprise amongst the islanders that it should have been Lachlan's shadow who had made a run for it rather than Finlay who, it was agreed, had endured more cruelty at his Father's hands than any child should have to bear. And they had a sneaking admiration for the golden boy who had found the courage to break free from Lachlan's tyranny. None had any sympathy for Lachlan himself. If it were not for the wrath of God and the deep, dark bottomless pit that awaited them if they rebelled, they too would turn their backs on Lachlan and all he represented.

After the service the congregation emerged out of candlelight into darkness. This time of year, when the days were short and the nights long, seemed to emphasise the fact that God, with his Church, was the light of the world. Outside the lamp-lit kirk the devil waited, and inside the manse Moira waited for news of her son.

Two hours after setting foot on the moors, a small group collected at the foot of Temptation Hill, amongst them Ali Mac and his wife Peggy. Cold and exhausted they had little strength left to continue the search. Ali Mac produced a bottle from beneath his dripping cloak and after taking a large swig of whisky – for the warmth, you understand – he passed it round the others. Peggy produced some oatcakes and those were also shared. They huddled in the lea of Fergie's barn.

'He canna be here or we'd have found him,' said Ali Mac. Rain drizzled down his face and leaked between his collar and his neck. 'We canna search any more till morning. It's not safe on the moors without a light.' It was so dark that there was not even the silhouette of a bush to be seen.

'Aye, and we'll catch pneumony, chust.'

'The best we can hope is that the Irishman has him.'

Others voiced their agreement. 'Better him than Mad Bella. She'd eat him for supper, like as not.'

'Dinna be *sae* daft,' said Peggy. 'Gimme that bottle afore ye drink any mair and lose your brains altogether.'

'Mayhap he's away with the fairy folk.'

'Well, we canna do any more tonight. He'd have come back home if he'd been hungry, so someone must be sheltering him.'

'Or he could have fallen and be lying somewhere with a broken leg. Or he could have been sucked into a bog.'

'Jonah,' said Ali Mac. 'Anyroad, we'd better head home now.'

'Aye, but who'll tell the Minister we haven't found the boy?'

All eyes turned to Iain McBeth. An inoffensive little man, bedraggled by the rain, he opened his eyes wide. 'Ah no,' he protested. 'I'm no' going. I'm concerned for the boy, right enough, but I dinna owe that ol' he-bugger anything after what he did to me. I did nae even have a drink.'

The others laughed. 'All right, all right,' said Iain, brandishing the whisky bottle. 'I was *going* to have one, right enough. I admit to that. I was holding the glass, chust. But I hadn't had so much as a wee *drap* afore he caught me.'

'I expect old Donald Gillies heard you pour it,' said Farquor MacLeod. 'He's got ears like bats' wings, chust. I swear they swivel on his head like eyes on stalks.'

There was general laughter before the gravity of the situation calmed them down once more. It was no laughing matter, and against his will it was Iain McBeth, the disgraced precentor hauled before the Kirk Session for the drinking of whisky, who went to break the news to the Nicolsons.

Silver and brass gleamed in the candlelight and the mahogany side table glowed deep red in the light from the log fire in the hearth. The room with its curtains drawn against the night was warm and cosy; the three people sitting waiting for news were cold and anxious. Lachlan glowered from his armchair, unable to understand the disaster the Almighty had inflicted on him. He had committed no sin and therefore did not deserve a punishment such as this.

Moira remained where she had sat all day, huddled in a blanket, her face devoid of expression. Locked inside herself she had raged and wept, prayed and cursed until she was spent of all emotion. She accepted Murdo's loss as God's retribution for her rejection of Him, but that did not make it easier to bear.

Finlay had drawn up a chair beside his mother. He sat close to her with an arm draped around her shoulders. From time to time he glanced at the man opposite who should have been comforting Moira but was too wrapped up in his own torment to spare any consideration for anyone else's heartache. Finlay did not share his parents' anxiety. He guessed that Murdo had persuaded Paddy McQuigg to help him leave Toronsay. He fought to keep the triumph and satisfaction from his face as he pictured his young brother sailing on the high seas, and if he suffered momentary concerns it was only because the Minch was an unpredictable stretch of sea, and Murdo could meet a watery end off the shores of the island before his new life began. He did not pray for Murdo's safe return: he prayed for his freedom.

When Morag opened the door for Iain McBeth to enter the room Lachlan sprang from his armchair. Moira's eyes held a momentary gleam of hope, which died as soon as she saw the messenger's face.

'Well? What news, man? Have you found him?' said Lachlan.

Iain McBeth twirled the brim of his hat round and round in his hands, moisture dripping from his cloak.

'I'm so sorry, Mistress Moira,' he said with a catch in his voice. 'We've done all we can tonight. We'll start again at first light.'

Lachlan turned on the poor man, his helplessness making him angry. 'How can I trust you? How do I know for sure that you've looked in all the derelict bothies?' He raved. 'I've only your word for it, and if any of you have the drink in you…'

Iain McBeth flushed. 'Aye, we did chust. Each and every one of them. All the barns and outhouses too. We canna find him. We'll try again tomorrow. I'm sorry.' He turned to leave but paused at the door. 'Mind, none of us has looked in the kirk. He could have sneaked in there after the Service.'

Lachlan's head jerked up. The kirk. Of course, why had he not thought of that? It was the obvious place for Murdo to be. He pushed past Iain McBeth and strode from the manse, his heart pounding with hope. But the kirk was empty. Murdo was not there. Lachlan raced up and down the aisles, peering between and beneath the rows of benches and pews. He climbed the steps into each of the pulpits. He looked everywhere, but the kirk was empty. Lachlan sank to his knees with grief.

'My son, my beautiful son,' he wept. 'Why have you deserted me?' His shoulders heaved and the sound of his cries filled the cavernous building.

When his grief burnt itself out Lachlan cast around for someone to blame for his loss. And he blamed the only other presence there with him in the kirk. It was God's fault. The fanaticism with which Lachlan had worshipped God became a bitter and venomous reproach. In his twisted, mentally disturbed state Lachlan saw Murdo as his sacrifice to God, and yet God had not saved his son. He had saved Abraham's son Isaac. Now Lachlan would punish God for his abandonment of him.

Outside in the night the wind whistled through cracks and crevasses and moaned across the moors. On the high ground came the first snow flurry of winter. Folk huddled together in their beds, cows breathed warmth into black houses, hens clustered in coops. Moira and Finlay sat up all night. Lachlan did not return home.

The following morning Finlay found his father in the kirk. Lachlan had hanged himself with his leather belt. On its side beneath his feet lay the cutty stool – the stool of repentance.

CHAPTER 6

On a warm day in June 1826, Oxford Street teemed with life. Horse-drawn omnibuses and hansom cabs hustled up and down, sending pedestrians sprinting out of the way with fear for their lives. Half a dozen Ethiopian serenaders gave a pleasing rendering of 'Old Mr Coon'. Further down the street a blind musician scraped a tune on a fiddle, his affliction earning him more than his performance.

Dozens of elegant ladies converged on Dickens and Smith. The store had taken delivery of a new consignment of silks from China and shawls from Kashmir. In the window was a display of gloves and hosiery, and large paper boxes from which spilled all manner of materials. Every inch of the window space was used, with lengths of printed cottons, lace-edged handkerchiefs and worked collars all set out to their best effect with the intention of luring customers inside.

The haberdashery store was packed with people. Although they were not welcome, a few poorly dressed women mingled with the wealthy. They had come to dream and admire, but if they strayed too close to an assistant they were swiftly escorted to the door. There was no room and no patience today for anyone who could not afford to buy.

The Garthwaites's lacquered carriage halted outside the store and the footman jumped down to assist Lady Cecilia and her two daughters to alight. They swept through the door and Lady Cecilia wrinkled her nose in distaste at the less than edifying sight of a scramble of ladies vying with one another to snatch the choicest of fabrics. She strode forward, looking neither to her left nor right, with Miriam and Alice trailing behind her. Other ladies drew aside to make a path for them, and an assistant immediately brought a chair for Lady Cecilia to sit on at the counter. The Garthwaite family were well known in high society. They possessed the two most prized assets – noble birth on Lady Cecilia's side and great wealth on her husband's. It was Lady Cecilia's good breeding that ensured their place in society rather than their wealth, but both bring power and, with it, the envy of those who lack one or the other, or both. Lady Cecilia never spared a thought for such a vulgar thing as money, but she was protective of her position and conscious of the privileges it brought.

The assistant laid bolts of every hue on the counter before Lady Cecilia. She fingered some of them, assessing their quality. She and her daughters were to have new gowns made for the ball the Garthwaites were to host in Miriam's honour. Miriam was newly returned from Belgium where she had spent a year at a finishing school. The ball was planned as a means of launching her into society and parading her before prospective suitors. She was eighteen years old, and a brilliant marriage for her was foremost in the minds of her parents.

Alice, two years younger than Miriam, stood at her mother's elbow. She was a short, plump girl, entirely lacking the grace and elegance of her mother and sister. She was overwhelmed by the sumptuous array of silks on the counter. This would be her first ball, although she had already been warned that she would only be allowed to stay until the supper break, at which point she would be sent home to bed. Her heart seethed with resentment, and now she could have burst into tears. She knew that no matter how much she pleaded she would not be permitted to choose for herself. Nevertheless, she gave it a try.

'Please can I have the purple, Mama?' She asked with a whine.

'Of course not, child,' came the swift reply. 'Don't be absurd. Your gown will be white.'

Alice stamped her foot in vexation. 'It's not fair,' she sulked. 'You always make me wear white. I'm sick of white.'

Several elegant heads topped with extravagant millinery turned in the Garthwaites' direction.

'All girls of your age wear white,' said Lady Cecilia, through clenched teeth. 'Besides, purple is so funereal.' Alice scowled. 'Put your face straight at once, child,' scolded Lady Cecilia. 'If you wish to behave like an infant you'll be treated like one. We'll leave you behind in your old nursery.'

Lady Cecilia looked down her nose at her dumpy younger daughter and sighed. Finding a husband for her when the time came would be no easy task. 'You will wear white,' she said. 'But you may choose ribbons in whatever colours take your fancy.'

Alice stomped off to another part of the shop where the ribbons and lace were wound round large cards shaped like bobbins.

Miriam selected a bolt of ivory silk from the counter. The assistant brought a mirror, and Miriam held a length of the material against her, turning this way and that to assess the effect of the ivory against her skin.

'That suits you very well,' approved Lady Cecilia. 'You may have it.'

'Thank you, Mama,' said Miriam with a sweet smile that masked her feelings of triumph. 'What will you wear?'

Lady Cecilia sighed. Even at her age she was still a beautiful woman. When she was young she had been the belle of every ball, but when she saw how vibrantly young Miriam had looked a moment ago as she held the ivory silk against her, Lady Cecilia had felt the first icy tentacles of age creep towards her. She feared growing old.

'What about the green?' suggested Alice, who had returned to her mother's side having selected purple for her ribbons as the only way to include that colour in her gown.

Lady Cecilia frowned. How could she have produced a daughter so utterly lacking in taste? She cast her eyes around the store.

'No, not the green,' she said. She pointed at a bolt of silk on another counter. The assistant fetched it immediately and unrolled a length for her appraisal.

'Oh, Mama,' breathed Miriam. 'It's perfect.'

The silk was a rich blood red, a colour that shrieked to be worn by a lady of elegance and self-confidence. Lady Cecilia would look magnificent, and she knew it. Her spirits rose suddenly: she was not past it after all. She could not compete with Miriam's youth, but she would outshine her in every other way. What more could she possibly want?

With their purchases complete Lady Cecilia arranged for them to be delivered, and then she led her daughters from the store. No sooner had she placed one foot on the step of the carriage than she stopped in surprise.

'Good heavens,' she exclaimed. 'There's your Uncle Stuart. We haven't seen him for an age.' She waved to attract his attention.

Stuart Ross Esquire was not alone, and Miriam was less interested in her godfather than she was in his companion. He had thrown his head back and was laughing at something Uncle Stuart had said. Miriam was captivated by him. His laugh was infectious and brought a smile to the corners of her own mouth. She had an unaccountable, overwhelming desire to laugh with him, and to go on laughing with him for the rest of her life. Without knowing the least thing about him, not even his name, Miriam Garthwaite fell in love.

The two gentlemen crossed the road, dodging deftly between the carriages and cabs that travelled up and down Oxford Street. Stuart Ross raised his hat in greeting.

'What a pleasant surprise,' he said as he bowed over Lady Cecilia's hand. 'My wife only commented the other day on how long it has been since we last saw you.' He turned to Miriam. 'How elegant you have become, my dear. Your time in Belgium was well spent, I see.'

He acknowledged Alice with a perfunctory nod, but quickly realised that Lady Cecilia was staring at his companion.

'Forgive me,' he said. 'I am forgetting my manners. Allow me to present my protégé, Captain Murdo Nicolson.'

Murdo cut a fine figure in his uniform of a sea captain with the East India Company. He wore his blue coat, with its light gold embroidery and shiny yellow buttons, and his buff waistcoat and breeches with immense pride, his ambition in life achieved. Seventeen years had passed since he fled the Isle of Toronsay and he had grown to be tall, his handsome face tanned by a thousand tropical suns.

He removed his hat in a sweeping gesture and bent to kiss each of the Garthwaite hands in turn. Murdo's first impression of Miriam was one of surprise for she looked foreign, and he was intrigued that a lady as fair as Lady Cecilia should have borne such a daughter, especially when also compared with the younger girl.

'How do you do?' said Murdo, and Miriam blushed with pleasure as his blue eyes smiled into her dark brown ones.

Miriam Garthwaite was not what was considered a beauty, but her appearance was sufficiently striking to cause heads to turn. She was slender and of average height, but her thick black hair and olive skin were startling beneath an English sky. For her unusual colouring she owed a debt of gratitude to her paternal grandfather, who had returned from one of his sea voyages complete with a foreign bride. Her name was Zeinab, which was as exotic as her dusky beauty, and did nothing to appease the Garthwaite family; they were appalled at the addition of a foreigner to their country estates.

Murdo had to drag his eyes away from Miriam when Lady Cecilia spoke to him. She had been looking speculatively at the sea captain and thought that a light-hearted dalliance with him might be amusing.

'You must come to the ball we are hosting in my daughter's honour,' she gushed. 'I absolutely insist.'

'In that case, how can I refuse?' said Murdo. He smiled at Lady Cecilia, but his smile did not reach his eyes. He was well rehearsed in the ways of women and recognised the unspoken invitation in her eyes; he had no intention of being drawn into her web.

Lady Cecilia turned to Stuart Ross. 'You must bring Captain Nicolson with you,' she said. 'Oh, and Mrs Nicolson too, of course,' she added hurriedly.

'Thank you, Lady Cecilia,' said Murdo. 'But I am not married.'

Miriam's heart lurched. She had quite thought that he must have a wife, and the news that he did not sent a wave of relief through her. She blushed when the sea captain smiled at her, certain that he could read her thoughts, and by the time they reached home Miriam Garthwaite was totally smitten. She rushed straight to her room, threw herself on her bed, and endeavoured to recall every glance and expression Captain Murdo Nicolson had directed towards her during their brief encounter. Alice, meanwhile, went to find her father to complain about the white gown her mother insisted she had to wear to the ball.

It is difficult to imagine two sisters as unalike as Miriam and Alice: the one dark, poised and accomplished, and the other fair, graceless and vacuous. Miriam appeared to have inherited little or nothing from their mother's side of the family, taking after her father and grandmother, whereas Alice, with her blond hair and blue eyes, possessed none of the characteristics of her father's side of the family. Grandfather Julian Garthwaite's acquisition of a foreign bride had for years alienated his family, dismayed that foreign blood would now pollute future generations of Garthwaites, but Zeinab's beauty and generosity of spirit had slowly won them over and over time she earned their grudging acceptance. Julian had been dead now for many years, but Zeinab, stone deaf, was still alive, and she spent her declining years toasting her toes on the fender in front of the fire in her son's home in the winter or sitting with an Afghan blanket over her knees in her favourite corner of the rose garden in the summer.

Julian and Zeinab produced two sons, neither of whom inherited their mother's colouring other than the dark brown velvet of her eyes.

Jeremy, the younger son who had to make his own way in the world, was commissioned into an infantry regiment and was killed in a skirmish overseas, but Ali, the first-born, was very much the man-about-town. He was tall and handsome, his fair hair strikingly at odds with his dark eyes, but his face wore a constant sulky expression. He hated his mother and was ashamed of her foreignness; nor could he forgive her for compounding that insult by endowing him with a foreign name. He could, and did, pretend that Ali was a shortened version of Alexander, and his friends saw no reason to question that; but he knew, he knew that his name was Ali, and the presence of his alien mother in his house was a perpetual thorn in his side, a daily reminder of his 'touch of the tar brush'.

Ali inherited the Garthwaite fortune at the age of twenty-eight and within a year had married the aristocratic Lady Cecilia Wallace. He never understood why she had consented to be his wife when she must have known that any children they were blessed with would be of mixed blood. He was so ashamed of this taint in himself that he could not bring himself to believe her when she professed to love him, preferring to believe instead that she had married him for his money. However, over the years Lady Cecilia's love for her husband died, and their marriage became an empty shell. She grew tired of Ali's constant denigration of his mother for her presumed humble origins and his readiness to take umbrage at any inference of a slight he perceived against his parentage. Nowadays Ali Garthwaite stood on the sidelines and watched cynically as Lady Cecilia flirted outrageously with all and sundry, caring very little just as long as there was no scandal, whilst he sought solace with a French dancer he had established in a flat in the West End.

When she was born Miriam's appearance had been a shock to Ali Garthwaite. For years he distanced himself from her as she reminded him too much of his despised mother, so when Lady Cecilia had suggested that Miriam be sent to a finishing school in Belgium he had been keen to agree as he saw it as a means of removing the girl from his presence altogether. When Miriam returned home, a comely and accomplished young woman, Ali Garthwaite realised that with his wealth and his wife's connections she could make a brilliant marriage, even allowing for her colouring. The more he thought about it, the higher his expectations became of finding a husband of considerable standing for her. After all, he thought with distaste, there were men whose fancy turned towards a dusky beauty. The ball was to be the first step in the fulfilment of Ali Garthwaite's ambition for Miriam.

In the evening following the excursion to Dickens and Smith, Lady Cecilia recounted each detail to her bored husband.

'Miriam will look especially lovely in the ivory silk,' she said after dinner. 'It's exactly right for her colouring, and I'm quite certain that she will attract a good deal of attention. I would not be in the least surprised if she received several offers of marriage during the course of the summer.'

The mention of Miriam's colouring was a mistake, and Ali Garthwaite scowled. 'Well, don't go putting any silly ideas into her head,' he said. 'She had better not harbour any notion of marrying where she pleases. I intend her to make a brilliant match. An earl perhaps, or even a duke.'

Lady Cecilia glanced sharply at her husband. Although it was perfectly usual for marriages to be arranged in the upper echelons of society, she had always regarded such cold-blooded transactions as legalised rape if the bride was not a willing partner. She considered herself fortunate to have succeeded in manoeuvring her own father into permitting her to marry a man of her own choosing, and she was concerned for her older daughter.

'Miriam is not a piece of meat to be hawked before potential buyers,' she said.

Ali Garthwaite raised his eyebrows in surprise. 'Isn't she? I was under the distinct impression that that is exactly what marriage is about for women. They are paraded before prospective bridegrooms, and then they are sold off to the highest bidder.'

Lady Cecilia was shocked by his attitude. She watched in silence as her husband crossed to the sepulchral white marble fireplace where he stood and stared moodily into the empty grate.

'This is our daughter we are talking about,' she said. 'I hope you will allow her some say in the matter. I trust that you do not intend to force her to marry someone of your choosing that she finds odious.'

Ali Garthwaite laughed shortly. 'She will do as she is told,' he said. 'And she'll not find a duke odious, I'll be bound.'

Ali Garthwaite's main concern that his daughters marry well had more to do with the future of the family fortune than for any regard for their welfare. He had no son – the lack of which was entirely the fault of his wife – so it was of paramount importance that Miriam and Alice should marry into money. Only then could he be reasonably certain that his fortune would not be squandered in the future by some impecunious son-in-law. Of course, should there be a grandson then the Garthwaite estates would go directly to him, but first his daughters must marry, and Miriam was now of an age to do so.

CHAPTER 7

It should have been obvious to anyone who looked at her that Miriam was in love. She radiated happiness, walked as though on air, picked at her food and had a permanently distracted manner; but there are none so blind as those who will not see. Ali Garthwaite and Lady Cecilia did not see, and Miriam's hopes and dreams were allowed to run riot because neither of her parents exerted any restraining influence over her.

On the evening of the ball, as she sat in front of the dressing table mirror, whilst Bessie the maid brushed her long hair until it shone like silk, Miriam could scarcely sit still for excitement. In less than an hour's time she would see him again – Captain Murdo Nicolson of the East India Company, the man who had stolen her heart with a glance. Her pulse pounded in her ears and she had butterflies in her stomach.

At Lady Cecilia's suggestion Bessie wound Miriam's hair into a chignon before fastening a string of pearls around her throat. The overall effect was dazzling. Miriam looked like an exotic flower: a magnolia or a creamy frangipani blossom. Alice was consumed with envy. She hated her own white dress and the purple ribbons she had unwisely chosen, and now she fretted that she would be a wallflower all night. But it was love that imparted a special beauty to Miriam that evening, and the rapid beating of her heart when she met the sea captain for the second time that added colour to her cheeks.

Lady Cecilia looked sensational. Her fading fair hair was swept unfashionably high, the better to display her rubies. She had pinched her cheeks and bitten her lips to flood them with colour, and her eyes, the colour of wild bluebells, sparkled as she flirted with Captain Nicolson. Inside her head she was still only twenty years old and she expected to conquer him just as she had conquered countless others before him, but although Murdo played his part as an attentive guest he showed no interest in Lady Cecilia as a physically desirable woman, and she was piqued when he left her side to join the throng gathered around her older daughter. It was a bitter pill to swallow: to be upstaged and forced to face her advancing years when she was still so full of the hopes and desires life's experiences had failed to completely quell. She could have wept in despair, and she realised suddenly that the red silk had been a mistake after all. She felt like a cheap harlot. Desperately trying to maintain her dignity, Lady Cecilia's voice rose ever higher, and her laugh was brittle. Her smile was fixed almost to a grimace and her eyes were glazed, but she knew that she had lost, for every gentleman in the room, and not a few of the ladies, had turned their attention to Miriam.

Murdo bowed before her. He was conscious of the honour bestowed on him in having been invited to the ball. His wealth alone would not have secured him a place in such society, and he was grateful for his association with Stuart Ross, who belonged here by reason of birth.

'I trust there are still some unclaimed dances on your card, Miss Garthwaite, or am I too late?' he asked.

Miriam felt her cheeks flame. 'No, you are not too late,' she breathed, and handed him her dance card with its tiny pencil attached by a silken cord.

Murdo signed his name against three dances, which was daring in so new an acquaintance and was bound to cause comment. Miriam could have swooned with delight, but someone else quickly claimed her dance card.

Rupert Fitzroy, the Earl of Averton, knew that he was staring at the Garthwaite girl. He scarcely recognised the elegant young woman she had become from the ordinary girl he had known for most of his life. He could not take his eyes from her, and there is nothing like the attraction of one gentleman to a young lady for bringing that lady's desirability to the notice of others. Fitzroy mentally dismissed the unimportant sea captain as he felt desire stir within him. He wondered how it was possible that he had not noticed before that Miriam Garthwaite was beautiful.

Lady Constance Ainsley watched her escort with mounting concern. She was a plain young woman, well aware that her face was too thin and angular to even be considered attractive, but she was, nevertheless, a lady. Miss Miriam Garthwaite was a nobody in spite of her mother's title and her father's fortune. Fitzroy's ill-concealed interest in her was shameful, and Lady Constance was irritated and embarrassed by it. She considered her marriage to the Earl of Averton to be a virtual certainty, as did her parents, even though he had made no offer as yet. He was her regular escort, and in an unguarded moment she had rashly intimated to friends that they were as good as betrothed. It was galling to see him so obviously interested in someone else, and Lady Constance's sudden feelings of insecurity made her spiteful.

'I cannot think what the Garthwaite girl thinks she looks like with her hair like that,' she said haughtily, shaking her own mouse-brown locks and hoping to regain Fitzroy's attention.

The Earl frowned in reply. Lady Constance bit her lower lip and tapped her closed fan in the palm of her hand. Unable, or unwilling, to admit defeat she became more disparaging.

'Actually, I don't really know why we accepted this invitation,' she said. 'The Garthwaites are not our social equals after all. Isn't there a coloured ancestor lurking in the background somewhere? That would certainly account for Miss Garthwaite's swarthy complexion.'

Too late, Lady Constance realised that she had overstepped the mark. The words had been uttered and the Earl, whose face was suffused with anger, was clearly not prepared to forgive them. He rose on his long, aristocratic legs, bowed politely to Lady Constance and her parents, and without a backward glance he crossed the floor to claim a dance with the lowly Miriam Garthwaite.

'What a pleasure it is to see you in town again,' said Fitzroy. 'You have been away a long time.'

'I have been in Belgium this past year,' replied Miriam.

'Ah, I see,' said Fitzroy. 'I thought that you must have decided to bury yourself in your family's estates in darkest Derbyshire.'

'That's hardly likely. It's much more lively here.'

The music began again, and Fitzroy proffered his arm. 'Our dance, I believe.'

He led Miriam to the dance floor where they took their places for the cotillion. Miriam found it difficult to concentrate. All she could think about was Captain Nicolson, and her eyes followed him as he circulated amongst the guests. Each time their gaze met she was overwhelmed by the rush of feelings he aroused in her. Her distraction only served to inflame the Earl further, and when the dance came to an end he asked permission to accompany her for the refreshments during the interval. Miriam forced herself to pay attention to him. There was something in the way he looked at her that made her ill at ease.

'Surely you have a partner for this evening?' she said. 'Are you not Lady Constance's escort?'

Fitzroy bowed his head in assent. 'I accompanied the Ainsleys, that is true,' he said. 'But I am my own man, Miss Garthwaite, and I choose to be with you now.'

Miriam hesitated. She had made no prior arrangement to pass the interval with anyone in particular although she knew with whom she wished to be. As if in answer to her unspoken prayer for deliverance from the Earl of Averton, the sea captain appeared at her side.

'Excuse me,' he said to Fitzroy. 'I have come to claim my partner for supper.'

Murdo offered his arm to Miriam and Fitzroy stood aside to let them pass, but he followed at a discreet distance, unwilling to let Miriam out of his sight. The evening passed in a whirl of cotillions and quadrilles, but Miriam only came alive when she danced with Murdo, and the final dance of the evening, a waltz, was his. The waltz was still frowned upon by many as being unseemly, and as she twirled round the floor in the arms of the sea captain the feel of his body against hers transported Miriam to previously undreamt-of heights of pleasure that would have shocked her mother and infuriated her father had they taken notice of their daughter and her unsuitable partner.

The Earl of Averton's interest in Miriam had not passed unnoticed. Sir Jerome and Lady Gertrude Ainsley felt that he had publicly humiliated them, and Lady Constance was mortified to have been deserted by her escort for Miriam Garthwaite of all people. But in contrast to the Ainsleys' blighted hopes, the Garthwaites were jubilant over the obvious interest Rupert Fitzroy showed towards their daughter. Ali Garthwaite was cock-a-hoop: if Fitzroy married Miriam, she would have a title and the whole family would rise in society. He was so blinded by his hopes that he failed to notice Miriam's regard for Captain Nicolson and paid no heed to their dancing together. Even if he had seen the way they looked at each other he would have dismissed any attachment out of hand, as the sea captain was far too insignificant to be considered as a suitor for his daughter.

*

Alice did not mince her words. A few days after the ball, as they travelled home from a luncheon at which Fitzroy refused to leave Miriam's side, she took her sister to task.

'You are a fool, Miriam,' she said. 'I'd have the Earl like a shot if he asked me. I'd take anyone with a title, no matter what he was like. I can't imagine what more you could possibly want. He is an earl, he's young, he's rich and he's handsome. I don't understand you.'

'There is more to life than a title,' said Miriam.

'Well, you surely can't prefer that sea captain,' said Alice. 'He is an old man. Anyway, I'm certain that Fitzroy plans to make you an offer and you will have to accept it. Father will not allow you to refuse him.'

Miriam pulled a face. She did not need her younger sister to tell her of Fitzroy's intentions. She already lived in dread of the day when he would approach her father. Fitzroy was everything Alice said he was, but even if she had never set eyes on the sea captain she would not have considered marrying the Earl of Averton, because of the unfathomable darkness in his brooding eyes. In fact, he frightened her, but now that she had fallen in love with Captain Nicolson she would rather die than marry the Earl or anyone else.

When an invitation arrived for Miriam to spend a few weeks with her godparents it could not have been more welcome, for it would free her from the unwanted attentions of Fitzroy and provide her with opportunities of seeing the object of her adoration. Even more agreeable was the fact that the invitation had not been extended to include Alice, so she would not be able to report to their parents on Miriam's behaviour. She oversaw the packing of her trunk with a lightness of heart, full of hopes for the future, and she dismissed Fitzroy from her mind.

CHAPTER 8

When Murdo fled the Isle of Toronsay and made his way to Glasgow, he had no difficulty finding his uncle, who was well known in the tobacco trade. Donald Nicolson was a man of a different stamp from his brother. While Lachlan had studied for the ministry and then taken a post in the islands, Donald remained in Glasgow following his own university career. He met and married the younger daughter of one of Glasgow's tobacco barons. He was absorbed into the family firm and rapidly exhibited a flair for the business, so that by the time of his fifth wedding anniversary he had already been made a junior partner. Frightened of the sea, he was solely concerned with the Port Glasgow end of the business. The Kerr, Ross and Nicolson Company controlled a significant amount of the tobacco trade between Scotland and Chesapeake in America, and Donald Nicolson became a rich man.

He was delighted to help Murdo forge a life for himself away from Toronsay and the Church and offered him a position on one of the tobacco ships sailing to America, but Murdo had other ideas. As the fishing boat on which he had sailed from Oban approached Greenock he had his first sight of an East Indiaman, and now his heart was set on becoming the captain of one of those majestic vessels – the Lords of the Seas. When he told his uncle of his dream, Donald Nicolson wrote to his brother-in-law, Stuart Ross, and packed Murdo off to London. But he did more than this: in an exceptionally generous gesture he provided Murdo with a capital sum of five hundred pounds, which was a necessity if the boy was to become a midshipman.

'I'll pay you back one day,' Murdo promised, but his uncle dismissed the offer.

'I'll not hear of it,' he said. 'It pleases me to be able to help you. In any case, there are no pockets in a shroud, so I might as well put some of my money to good use whilst I am still alive to see the benefit.'

After several years at sea with the East India Company, Stuart Ross Esquire had become a 'Ship's Husband' and now managed three ships for the Company. Before he was prepared to obtain a position for Murdo as a midshipman on board one of his ships, Stuart Ross enrolled him at the Oriental Institute to acquire a working knowledge of Hindustani and Persian, and he also arranged a period of instruction in navigation for him. Only when Stuart Ross was completely satisfied with Murdo's progress did he announce that he would sail as a midshipman on board the Dundonald, on which Murdo would make his first voyage to India.

Under the patronage of Donald Nicolson and Stuart Ross, Murdo advanced and prospered, and now he was the captain of the Brochel Castle, of which his benefactors were part owners.

At the Garthwaites' summer ball Murdo had been amused and flattered that Miriam Garthwaite took such an instant liking to him, but with the difference in their ages, and with his mind occupied with his forthcoming voyage in November, he had thought no more about her. However, now that Miriam was staying with her relatives, and Murdo called at the Ross establishment on most days, they were much in each other's company. Together with Aunt Dora they visited museums, art galleries and the opera, and they walked in London's beautiful parks.

Miriam was too young and innocent to hide her feelings and Murdo became quite taken with her, but the idea of marriage did not enter his mind although it was foremost in hers. Miriam was dispirited when her visit came to an end without the dashing sea captain having given any indication that she meant as much to him as he did to her. She returned home with her head filled with romantic and fanciful notions, her idea of Murdo unreal and idealised.

Matters came to a head at the end of September. Ali Garthwaite strutted about the drawing room, puffed with pride. The Earl of Averton had made an offer for Miriam, and he had given Fitzroy permission to approach his daughter. Ali Garthwaite sent for Miriam to apprise her of the Earl's intentions, certain that she would be overwhelmed by the honour being bestowed upon her. He was taken completely by surprise when Miriam, far from being pleased, was positively furious.

'How could you have given him permission to propose to me without speaking to me first?' she stormed. 'I don't want to marry the Earl of Averton, and I shall refuse his offer.'

Her father met her anger with his own. 'Confound it. You will do as you are told, my girl,' he shouted. The self-satisfied smugness had been wiped from his face to be replaced by mottled fury. 'The Earl is a magnificent catch. Most girls would not hesitate to marry him. Think about it – you would be a countess. What possible objection can you have to such a match?'

Miriam's face was stubborn, her cheeks flushed. 'I agree with you that Fitzroy is an eligible man, but not for me. I will not marry him, and I shall refuse to be alone with him, which will save us both the embarrassment of my rejection of him.'

'You will not refuse,' shouted Ali Garthwaite. 'What is the world coming to that you can stand there and openly defy me? You have been put in a position where the entire family has the opportunity of reaping some benefit. If you are a countess, Alice will be able to make a brilliant marriage when her time comes.'

'I do not intend to marry the Earl of Averton just so that Alice might marry a title.' Miriam's eyes blazed.

Ali Garthwaite paced up and down, coming to a halt by the bay window. His pale, yellow hair glinted in a shaft of sunlight.

'You will accept Fitzroy, or else,' he said after a short silence. His voice was ominously quiet.

'Or else what?'

'I'll cut you off without a shilling, that's what.' Miriam blanched. 'Hah!' Ali Garthwaite was triumphant. 'I thought that might make you see things differently. You women are all the same. Money, money, money – what would you do without it? You would baulk at marrying a pauper, wouldn't you?'

'Not if I loved him,' said Miriam in a final show of defiance.

Her father gave a scornful laugh. 'Love?' he sneered. 'What has that got to do with anything? Love comes after marriage for women, and outside of marriage for most men. You can forget about love. I have given Fitzroy permission to speak to you after our dinner party next week, and you will accept his offer. Now get out of my sight.' He waved Miriam from the room.

Miriam did not know what to do. She had no financial independence and was under the absolute control of her father. In her despair she took her troubles to the one person who never failed to give comfort.

Zeinab sat in a cane chair with a knitted shawl around her shoulders and an Afghan blanket over her knees. She was still a beautiful woman even though her hair was now snowy white, and she dozed in the gentle warmth of the autumn afternoon. Miriam placed her hand on her grandmother's arm and Zeinab opened her eyes. She raised her arms and Miriam knelt beside her with her head in her grandmother's lap. While Miriam wept, Zeinab stroked her hair and waited for the storm to pass.

In spite of her deafness Zeinab was not unaware of events occurring within the family. She had never learned to read or write so it was not possible to communicate with her in writing, but over the years she had taught herself some rudimentary lip-reading so that, although unable to follow whole sentences, she managed to grasp the general drift of conversations. Locked into her silent world she had become adept at reading facial expressions and interpreting gestures. Zeinab had watched the Earl of Averton's brooding gaze as he sat opposite her when he visited, but she had also seen the look on Miriam's face on the evening of the ball when her eyes followed Captain Nicolson as he moved about the room. She did not need to be told what distressed her granddaughter.

Deafness had not robbed Zeinab of the power of speech. Her words were sometimes slurred and indistinct, but the family understood her and now her words soothed Miriam.

'You must follow your heart, my dear, for that is where happiness lies. Love may not last for ever, but to have loved truly and been loved in return is the greatest gift we mortals can give to one another.'

Miriam looked up so that Zeinab could watch her mouth. 'I love Captain Nicolson, Grandmama, but Father says that I must marry the Earl of Averton. I don't know what to do.'

'Does my son know you love the captain?'

The light of hope dawned for Miriam. 'No, he doesn't,' she said. 'Of course, he doesn't know. I haven't told him.'

'Then perhaps you should,' said Zeinab. 'Marriage to a man you love may be strewn with stones, but marriage to a man against one's inclination is a nightmare doomed to failure. A true marriage is more than just a financial settlement, whatever your father may think.'

Miriam kissed Zeinab's cheek. 'Thank you, Grandmama,' she whispered.

She ran straight to her father's study, but she was not given the opportunity to explain to him as Ali Garthwaite refused to either see or speak to her until she had accepted the Earl's proposal of marriage. Miriam was frantic, and in her panic she did something no lady would have dreamt of doing – she wrote to Captain Nicolson.

No sooner had she sent the letter than she wished she could have it back: not because she had written anything she wished to retract, but because she was worried that Captain Nicolson would think her unforgivably shameless. Her face burned with embarrassment as she recalled the words of love she had written. Her heart pounded with fear, but also with excitement for having done something so outrageous. With the letter sent there was nothing further she could do, so Miriam waited on tenterhooks for a reply; but none came that day or the next, and she could only hope and pray that he would be at the place where she had suggested that they meet.

Murdo did not call on the Ross household for three days, and Miriam's letter lay on the silver salver on the hall table awaiting his visit. When he arrived, Murdo took the letter into the library. He rang the bell and asked the maid to bring tea, then settled himself in one of Uncle Stuart's leather chairs, stretched his legs out in front of him, and slit open the envelope. He read the letter several times before folding it carefully and placing it in his breast pocket. He sipped his hot tea, and his face creased into a deep frown as he wondered what to do for the best.

He had arrived with a spring in his step, his thoughts full of the sea and his forthcoming voyage. Miriam's letter brought him down to earth with a jolt. He was a little annoyed to be faced with such a dilemma when he had other pressing matters to attend to, and yet he recognised that Miriam must have been in considerable distress to write to him at all. It was not something that a lady would do.

Murdo pitied women their lot in life. They were forever subject to one man or another and permitted no freedom. Those who were treated kindly were fortunate, but often they were miserable or ill-used. An image of Fitzroy sprang into his mind. There was something about him that betrayed a potential for violence, and Murdo doubted whether the Earl would use the power he would wield over his wife with much mercy should she give him cause for displeasure. He would wish to spare Miriam that as he would hate to see her crushed into a replica of his mother.

There was only one certain way of saving Miriam from such a fate and that was for Murdo to marry her himself. She had made it perfectly clear in her letter that she would welcome such a proposal, but she was too young to really know what she was suggesting. She would not have given a thought to how different their lives had been and how little they had in common. She had been raised in a world of luxury, and although Murdo was in a position to enable her to continue a similar mode of living, his own boyhood as a son of the manse on a windswept island had left him indifferent to the trappings of wealth. He had amassed a small fortune not because he was a miser, but because he led a frugal life from choice. He doubted whether Miriam would enjoy such simplicity. There was also the fact to take into consideration that he spent much of his time on board ship. There were captains who permitted their wives to sail with them, but Murdo had never been in favour of such an arrangement. A captain's wife could make or break a happy ship and making the wrong choice of bride was a recipe for disaster. He supposed that he could leave the sea on marriage, but he was far from certain that he was ready to do so yet.

There were so many valid reasons not to marry Miriam and only one he could think of in favour of it: the fact that he had no desire to lead a celibate life. Murdo lost his virginity on a flower boat in Whampoa on his second voyage, his first and only voyage to the Far East. The dainty Chinese girl he saw perched on a red cushion seemed little more than a child at first glance, but she unveiled a perfectly formed woman's body from her robe. This child-woman introduced Murdo to shameless lust and sexuality, and in spite of the many married women who had invited him to share their beds over the ensuing years, he had sought in vain to recapture the exquisite pain of that first throbbing encounter with the Chinese girl. He had never lain with a virgin, and perhaps Miriam's lean and untried body would bring him what he was looking for. With his eyes closed, and his tea growing cold beside him, Murdo thought about making love to the delightful Miriam Garthwaite.

They met at Gunter's Tea Shop in Berkeley Square, a short distance from the Garthwaites' London residence and the only place where a young lady could meet a gentleman without a chaperon. Murdo was there first and leaned against the railings watching snatched meetings between couples until Miriam's carriage arrived. He raised his hat in greeting.

'Good afternoon, Miss Garthwaite.'

'Good afternoon, Captain Nicolson.' Miriam's face was pale, and she wound a handkerchief round and round her fingers. 'You must think ill of me.'

Murdo climbed into the carriage beside Miriam and signalled to a waiter to bring sorbets.

'Has your father changed his mind since you wrote to me?'

Miriam shook her head and tears sparkled in her eyes. 'He won't even see me. I don't know what to do. It was Grandmama who suggested that I tell my father how I feel, but he refuses to let me speak to him. I am so ashamed of having written to you, but you were the only person I could think of who might be able to help me.'

The waiter dodged between the carriages to bring the ices, and Murdo and Miriam ate them in silence.

'When I did not hear from you I didn't know what to think,' said Miriam. 'You must have been cross with me, for you have given me no cause to write what I did. And quite shocked that I should be so unladylike.'

Murdo could not hide a smile. 'I am not easily shocked, Miss Garthwaite, and to receive words of undying love from one so young and beautiful as you are can only flatter an old man's ego.'

'Now you are laughing at me.'

'Not really,' said Murdo. 'I didn't reply to your letter as I only received it last evening, and I realise that you would not have written as you did unless you were desperate. Do you still feel the same now or has the cold light of day made you see things differently?'

'I still feel the same,' said Miriam in a small voice. Her head was bent but she could feel Murdo's eyes on her. 'I can't – won't – marry the Earl of Averton whatever the outcome of our meeting here today.'

'But why? Your worlds are similar. You know the same people, share the same friends, and he has a title. I can see why your father approves such a match.'

A tear splashed onto Miriam's hand and she let it trickle onto her skirt. 'I am a little frightened of him. His smile never reaches his eyes. And I love you.'

'You would marry me without knowing the first thing about me?' asked Murdo.

'I know that I love you. Isn't that enough?'

Murdo shook his head. 'Not really, my dear. Marriage isn't just about love, and if that's all we have you could come to hate me in the end.'

'I could never hate you,' said Miriam. 'And marriage isn't just about money either. That's all my father thinks about, but Grandmama says there is more to marriage than money. When you laugh it makes me want to laugh with you. When I see a shadow of concern cross your brow it weighs heavily on my heart too. I have lived and breathed for you from the moment I first saw you outside Dickens and Smith's.' She began to tremble with embarrassment. 'Forgive me, Captain Nicolson, I have no right to talk to you like this.'

Murdo watched her weep silently into her sodden handkerchief and his heart softened. He took her hand and raised it to his lips.

'Well then,' he said. 'Would you take an old sailor for your husband since you refuse the dashing young Earl of Averton?'

Miriam raised her tear-stained face and her eyes searched his. 'I don't ask for your love, Captain Nicolson, but could you learn to care for me in time?'

'My dear Miss Garthwaite,' he replied. 'If I did not care for you already I would not be here with you right now.'

'Then I accept your offer of marriage gladly,' said Miriam.

Murdo threw his head back and laughed. 'How very demure and ladylike you have become all of a sudden now that you have got what you wanted.'

Miriam flinched. 'I will be a good wife to you, I promise,' she whispered.

'I am glad to hear it,' said Murdo. 'But first I have to face your father, and I am not at all confident that he will consent to our marriage.'

Murdo was full of foreboding on the evening of the Garthwaites' dinner party. As his carriage rattled up the drive gusts of wind whipped fallen leaves into the air. Soon it would rain, which only added to Murdo's sense of gloom. Miriam had selected this particular evening because there would be too many guests present for there to be an unseemly row should her father raise any objections to Murdo's suit. In spite of Miriam's belief that her father would agree to the match, Murdo was far from certain that Ali Garthwaite would embrace him as a suitable husband for his daughter when weighed against the lure of a title.

Miriam dressed with especial care, certain that her engagement to Captain Nicolson would be announced after dinner. Her high-waisted gown was of white diaphanous georgette with a froth of lace around the neckline and spilling over her shoulders. Her heavy black hair hung to her waist, brushed to perfection by her maid Bessie. Once Miriam was dressed, she peered through the window to watch for Murdo's arrival and was in time to see him climb down from his carriage. She saw him speak briefly to his driver before he strode to the stone steps which led to the entrance. Miriam ran from her room and flew down the stairs to meet him, but by the time she reached the lower floor Murdo was already being ushered into the library. She pressed her ear to the door, eager and excited, but as she eavesdropped on the interview between Murdo and her father, Miriam thought that she would die of shame.

Ali Garthwaite was in an expansive mood and received Murdo with more civility than would have been the case had he not been looking forward to the dinner party with such anticipation.

'What can I do for you?' he asked. 'Captain Nicolson, isn't it?'

Murdo gritted his teeth. 'It would be foolish to beat about the bush, sir,' he said. 'I have come to seek your permission to ask for Miss Garthwaite's hand in marriage.'

There was a brief, astonished silence before Ali Garthwaite roared with laughter. Murdo flushed with anger and embarrassment. Feeling more like an awkward schoolboy than a fully-fledged sea captain, he made the mistake of attributing Garthwaite's mirth to a mistaken understanding of his means.

'I am possessed of reasonable wealth, sir,' he explained. 'Your daughter will want for nothing as I am well able to maintain her in the manner to which she is accustomed. You must be aware of the potential for making fortunes when in the employ of the Honourable Company.'

But Miriam's father continued to laugh and Murdo floundered.

'You don't see it, do you?' spluttered Ali Garthwaite. 'It is not a question of money, Captain Nicolson, rather a matter of breeding. I have no intention of marrying either of my daughters to a man who earns his living.'

'You misunderstand me, sir,' said Murdo. 'I have the command of my ship, but I sail because I choose to not because I must. I should leave the sea on the occasion of my marriage. Neither I nor my heirs need ever earn his living.'

Ali Garthwaite stood up and wiped the tears of laughter from his eyes. 'Go away, Captain Nicolson,' he sneered. 'The state of your personal circumstances is of no consequence to me. My daughter's engagement to Rupert Fitzroy, the Earl of Averton, is to be announced this evening. I will overlook your impudence and will forget that you have spoken to me on this matter. I suggest that you do likewise.'

Murdo turned on his heel and strode from the library. He retrieved his hat and left the brightly lit mansion, which already teemed with guests and was full of noisy chatter.

The instant she heard her father laugh at Murdo, Miriam fled upstairs to her room. She had no fixed plan in her head, but she called for Bessie to fetch her cloak. The cloak was brought, and Bessie draped it around Miriam's shoulders. Then Miriam raced back downstairs, pulling the hood over her head to conceal her face as she ran. She squeezed between a few startled guests, slipped through the front door, skipped lightly down the stone steps and crossed to Murdo's carriage, to where she suspected he would soon be returning. The driver looked down at her but did not speak. The horses jostled against each other, and their harnesses jingled as she climbed into the empty carriage. Once inside, she curled into a ball in the corner and covered herself completely with her black cloak. She had only intended to speak to Murdo, to apologise to him for her father's rudeness, but as he approached the carriage Murdo called to the driver to drive on, and he was still mounting the steps as the carriage moved off down the street. He was too deeply immersed in his own dark thoughts to notice the black lump against the far side of the carriage until Miriam uncovered her face and peered out from beneath her cloak. He was appalled.

'What on earth do you think you are doing?' he gasped.

Miriam was not prepared for his look of shock and disapproval. 'Please don't be angry with me,' she said. 'I can't bear it.'

Murdo sighed. What a child she was! 'I'm not angry with you, my dear,' he said. 'If I appear angry it is because of your father, not you, but I am very concerned. Even if I took you straight back home there would be a scandal. Have you any idea of the damage you have done to your reputation? God, what a mess.'

Miriam began to cry. Murdo sat with a face like thunder, and all the while the carriage bore them further away from the Garthwaite residence.

Eventually Murdo handed Miriam a handkerchief since she appeared not to have one of her own.

'Here, dry your eyes. If we are going to elope you might as well look happy about it.'

'Elope?' gasped Miriam. 'Is that what we are going to do?'

'An elopement is more honourable than the alternative reason for you stowing away in my carriage in the dark. What was in your mind?'

'I just wanted to apologise for the way my father treated you. You see, I eavesdropped outside the door of the library. When I heard him laugh at you I was mortified; you have no idea how ashamed I felt – of him, not of myself. So I slipped in here to catch a private word with you and to say sorry; but then the carriage drove off before you saw me and before I had a chance to explain. I hadn't expected this to happen,' she paused for breath. 'Where are we going?'

'To Uncle Stuart and Aunt Dora. They will know what to do, but don't expect them to be pleased. What we are doing is unforgivable, but at least we can put it right, in a manner of speaking.'

They continued the journey in silence. Miriam was frightened to speak in case she made matters worse, and Murdo was worried sick at the damage done to her reputation. Also, he felt trapped. It was one thing to be gallant and offer to marry Miriam, quite another to be forced into a corner like this. He was plagued with misgivings, but there was no way back now. Their course was set, and there was nothing he could do but play his part to the bitter end. Why had he allowed himself to be seduced by thoughts of Miriam's nubile body? What a fool he had been.

Stuart and Dora Ross were every bit as cross as Murdo expected them to be, and he flinched beneath their anger.

'What were you thinking of? Have you completely lost your senses?' stormed Stuart Ross.

Miriam was upset and ashamed. Nothing was turning out as she had anticipated. When Murdo announced that they were eloping she had thought that he would be as excited as she was, but he just seemed distracted and worried. Confusion reduced her to tears, but she knew that it was her own recklessness that had brought them to this.

'I'm sorry, Uncle Stuart,' she wept. 'It's all my fault, and none of this was planned. Captain Nicolson had no idea that I was going to hide in his carriage, and I had only meant to talk to him. Anyway, I am glad that

I have run away from home. I couldn't do what my father insisted I do.'

'My dear girl,' said Stuart Ross. 'You haven't just run away from home. That could have been overlooked and quietly dealt with. The fact is that you have eloped, and the scandal of it will blight your entire family.' A sudden thought occurred to him and he turned to Murdo. 'You haven't already...?'

'No,' said Murdo quickly, anticipating the question and wishing to spare Miriam's blushes. And God knows, he thought, intimacy was the last thing on his mind at that moment.

'Well, that's a blessing at any rate,' said Stuart Ross. 'At least her honour is intact even if her reputation is in shreds. Well, what's done is done and can't be undone. One thing is certain, though, and that is that Miriam's father is bound to come here as soon as he realises that she is missing.'

'No,' gasped Miriam. 'He'll force me to return home with him. I would sooner die.'

Dora Ross spoke up. 'I take it that you two plan to marry?' Murdo nodded. 'Then the best thing would be for you to go to your ship, Murdo, so that you are not here when Mr Garthwaite arrives. That way we might be able to persuade him to allow Miriam to spend a few days with us on the grounds that she needs time to think things through. He need not know that it was you who brought her here although he may well guess the truth.'

'Thank you, Aunt Dora,' said Murdo with relief. 'I will attend to the matter of a special licence and arrange for the marriage to take place as soon as possible.'

Aunt Dora nodded. She was as shocked as her husband over this elopement, but a wedding was always certain to soften her heart. She loved Miriam and Murdo and approved the match, though not the manner of its making.

'You had best go now, quickly,' she said to Murdo. 'Mr Garthwaite could arrive at any moment.'

Murdo grabbed his cap. 'Thank you both for your help. I will get a message to you about the arrangements and I'll see you next in church.'

Miriam's head jerked up. 'Do you mean to say that I will not see you again before our wedding?' she gasped.

'It's best for you both,' said Stuart Ross. 'We need to salvage as much of your reputation as we can, and separating you is the best way to do it. It may help to mollify your father if he knows that you are not together.'

Miriam's eyes filled with tears again. She went to the door to watch Murdo leave and her heart sank when he did not turn to look back at her. She had sudden qualms about what he really felt for her and what their future held.

CHAPTER 9

Lady Cecilia Garthwaite, vexed and agitated, ran to her husband. 'Miriam has disappeared,' she cried.

'Don't be absurd. She can't have disappeared. Where would she have gone?'

'I don't know. Alice and I have looked all over the house and we can't find her anywhere. No one seems to have seen her.'

Ali Garthwaite frowned. 'Send someone to search the gardens. She can't have gone far away, and our guests have begun to arrive for dinner. I expect the Earl of Averton at any moment.'

'I've already done that,' said Lady Cecilia. 'It has started to rain so she is hardly likely to be outside. What are we going to do?'

Ali Garthwaite paced up and down. 'Confound the girl. That's what comes of sending girls abroad to complete their education. I knew it would lead to no good. Damned foreigners. They've stuffed her head full of nonsense. What am I going to say to the Earl? What can she be thinking of to disappear on the evening of her betrothal?'

All of a sudden he knew. It came to him in a flash, and fear clutched at him as the truth dawned.

'She's run off with that bloody sea captain,' he spluttered.

Lady Cecilia's face drained of colour and she sat down hurriedly. 'Run off? Eloped?' She screamed with the horror of it.

'We'll soon get to the bottom of it,' said her husband. 'Alice will know where they have gone and what their intentions are.'

'Alice? No, you're mistaken. Alice had no more idea than I about Miriam's disappearance. If Alice had known anything she would have come and told us. You know what a sneak she is.'

Ali Garthwaite rang for Miriam's maid. When she slunk into the room, Bessie smoothed the front of her bib-fronted apron and stood in front of the master with her eyes cast down. She did not like the master and was afraid that he had sent for her to dismiss her for some imagined error.

'When did you last see your mistress?'

'Well, sir,' said Bessie with a curtsey. 'I helped her dress for dinner and I brushed her hair.' She paused.

'Yes, yes,' said Ali Garthwaite. 'Get on with it.'

'Well, sir,' continued Bessie. 'Miss Garthwaite came downstairs, and then she came back for her cloak.'

Bessie fell silent. She was a stout girl with red cheeks and hands, and she had not been in the family's employ for more than a few months. She did not want to get her nice young mistress into trouble.

'And? What then?' Ali Garthwaite was exasperated with the dull-witted maid.

'Please, sir. I don't know, sir. I didn't see her after.'

'Did you see her go out?' asked Lady Cecilia.

'No, madam, I did not. It had started to rain so I didn't think she would be going out.'

'Did she take anything with her when she left her room?'

'No, madam.'

'Very well, you may go, Bessie. Thank you.'

As soon as the maid had gone Lady Cecilia turned to her husband with relief. 'There! She can't have gone far if she took nothing with her,' she said. 'She can't have run away – eloped – as you suggest. She would have planned for that and taken a valise with her. She would have needed more than the clothes she had on her back.'

'I'll warrant that that is exactly what she has done though,' said Ali Garthwaite.

'Well, if you are right, the captain will be easy to find. Stuart Ross will know the name of his ship. You must leave immediately, my dear, and bring her back home. I'll tell our guests that there has been a sudden family illness and you have been called away. I'm sure they will understand.'

Ali Garthwaite scowled. 'What about the Earl? What am I going to say to him? He will suspect something if Miriam is not here.'

Lady Cecilia dabbed at her eyes. 'I can't believe it of her,' she sobbed. 'She's ruined. The Earl won't have her now, and Alice will never be able to marry into decent society after this.'

Alice. Ali Garthwaite had forgotten about Alice. Miriam had

destroyed everything. After a minute of chewing at his bottom lip until he drew blood, Ali Garthwaite came to a decision, and when he spoke his voice was bitter.

'Miriam and the damned captain can go to hell,' he said. 'I have no intention of going after them, and there is to be no further contact between her and either you or Alice. I will not have her name mentioned in my house ever again. Is that understood?'

'But she is our daughter,' gasped Lady Cecilia.

'Not any more,' growled Ali Garthwaite. 'She has violated the honour of our entire family – and for a mere sailor too. It is unworthy of her. As far as the Garthwaite family is concerned, as of this evening, Miriam is dead.'

The day of the wedding dawned bright, but cold. In the short time available to them Dora Ross had managed to rustle up a limited trousseau for the bride, who had fled her home without so much as a change of linen. Miriam was to be married in the white gown she had worn on that day although the gauzy material was wholly unsuitable for the crisp autumn weather. Miriam was radiant. Stuart and Dora Ross looked tense and faintly disapproving, but their supportive presence lent an air of decency to the occasion. This was no way for a marriage to take place – in secret, as if there were something of which to be greatly ashamed, but it was infinitely preferable to there being no marriage at all.

John Birch, Murdo's first mate on board the *Brochel Castle,* stood as groomsman with Dora Ross's sister the only other person present to witness Murdo and Miriam take their vows. Cold emanated from the stone walls of the church, and even the vicar in his robes shivered and rubbed his hands together for warmth. Their voices echoed thinly in the vast cavern of a building, and Murdo hated the furtive atmosphere around the ceremony during which he and Miriam solemnly pledged their lives to one another.

Afterwards the small wedding party returned to the Ross's house for refreshments before the newlyweds left for a brief honeymoon in Brighton. Murdo dropped his bombshell on the journey there.

'My ship sails for India in three weeks,' he said. There was no way to say it kindly to soften the blow, and he dreaded Miriam's reaction.

Miriam felt the bottom fall out of her world. All her hopes and dreams seemed turned to ashes, and she realised just how little she really knew of the man she had married.

'India? In three weeks? You didn't tell me.'

'You didn't exactly give me the chance,' said Murdo with a smile. 'Your letter and our unplanned elopement happened at such an unseemly pace that I have hardly drawn breath since I left your father's study.'

'I am so sorry for the trouble I've caused,' sighed Miriam. 'While I was at Uncle Stuart's I had time to reflect on what I've done, and I realise that you must feel as if I've tricked you into marriage when that was not my intention at all. Are you very cross with me?'

'No, I am not cross with you,' said Murdo. I was at first, but not now.'

'What must I do while you sail for India? I don't want to go back home even though my father cannot now force me to marry the Earl of Averton. Should we ask Aunt Dora and Uncle Stuart if I can stay with them?'

Murdo looked at his bride with surprise. He had not expected her calm acceptance of the fact that he was to leave her so soon. Tears or recriminations would have been easier to understand though harder to bear.

'You don't seem to mind my going away,' he said.

'Of course I mind,' she replied. 'I mind very much. How could I not? But I married a sailor, and I know that a sailor's wife will always take second place to his ship. I will manage. I just hope that Aunt Dora will let me stay with them.'

'It wouldn't be a very good idea,' said Murdo. 'Their lives would be adversely affected if you stayed with them, and that would not be fair. You don't seem to fully realise the repercussions our elopement will have. You won't be received in polite society any more, and they would be snubbed by association.'

Miriam frowned. 'I had not thought of that; but surely everything will be all right now that we are married?'

'I doubt it,' said Murdo. 'We have sinned, you and I. We have become untouchables. The best thing would be for you to sail to India with me. Society cannot reach us on the high seas, and by the time we return things may have changed. Memories are short.'

Miriam was silent as she digested Murdo's words. It was several minutes before she fully realised what he had said. She turned to him with shining eyes.

'Sail with you?' she gasped. 'Oh, Murdo, I would love that. But I have heard you say that you disapprove of captains taking their wives on board with them.'

'That's true,' Murdo nodded. 'So you will have a huge responsibility for proving me wrong; but I warn you, my dear, the *Brochel Castle* is my ship. I command her, and all who sail in her.'

'I understand,' said Miriam. 'I won't disappoint you, and I have just vowed to obey you.'

'Then see that you do,' he said, not unkindly.

As she lay in bed on her wedding night waiting for Murdo to join her, Miriam was nervous and excited. She thought of the goings-on of the marital bed as Janine Piganeau, with whom she had shared a room at the ladies' college in Belgium, had divulged to her. The subject was never discussed at home, and Lady Cecilia implied to her daughters that the details were too abhorrent even to be whispered. Janine Piganeau's lurid descriptions had intrigued Miriam rather than frightened her, so that although she was an innocent bride, she was not an entirely ignorant one. When Murdo climbed into bed beside her and took her in his arms she trembled.

'Snuff the candle,' she whispered.

'Certainly not,' he replied.

When she awoke on the first day of her life as Mrs Nicolson, Miriam watched her new husband through half-closed eyes. Murdo had risen from the bed and sat by the window gazing out to sea. He looked dishevelled, and Miriam smiled to herself as she thought of the night of loving they had shared. She was so happy that it did not occur to her that Murdo could be anything other than happy too, but Murdo's thoughts were a tumble of contradictions. Something was lacking: that something that he was forever seeking. It was not that Miriam did not please him because after her initial shyness she had proved to be as passionate as he was himself, and for this he was truly grateful; so why did he feel less than satisfied? Was he yearning for something which simply did not exist? But he had felt it with the Chinese child-woman; surely it was not too much to hope to find it again?

He sighed heavily and returned to bed where Miriam's delight in him and their lovemaking at least made him pleased that she would be accompanying him on his long voyage to India. In any event, he had committed himself now and would have to make the best of it. He pulled the covers over their heads and drew Miriam towards him.

CHAPTER 10

Miriam thought – hoped – that she was going to die. She lay in her cot in the captain's cabin with waves of nausea engulfing her with every movement of the ship. At first, she had felt so ill she feared she would die. Now, four days into the voyage, she looked forward to death as a welcome relief from her torment. Taffy Evans, Murdo's steward, forced her to sip weak tea and nibble on a dry biscuit every two hours. The very thought of food made her retch, so she pretended to be asleep each time she heard the steward tap on the door before he entered, but he was not deceived.

'Please, Mrs Nicolson,' he implored. 'Even a small amount will settle your stomach for a while and make you feel a little better.'

Miriam was too ashamed of her weakness to complain, and she was forced to admit to herself that the crumbs of biscuit did help. The cabin stank of her perspiration and her sickness, and she was mortified to be such a failure. Her cot, which was suspended from the ceiling, swayed gently each time she moved so she lay completely still for long periods. The cot resembled a wooden coffin minus its lid, and she wondered vaguely if this was a deliberate design, and that its lid came separately, ready to be nailed into place so that she and the cot could be tipped over the ship's rail when death finally claimed her.

Murdo was kind. Miriam had thought that he would be angry, but he had shrugged.

'You'll be over it soon,' he said. 'I used to be almost as bad.'

'You? I don't believe it.'

Murdo dabbed at her forehead with a damp flannel. 'It's true, and I'm told that Admiral Nelson also used to suffer from mal-de-mer, so you are in good company.'

A whole week passed before Miriam, still weak and unsteady on her feet, was able to climb out of her cot and sit in a chair, but by the end of the second week she had gained her sea legs. It was good to go on deck and feel the salt spray on her face, and she pottered about in the vegetable garden Murdo cultivated on the poop deck.

Her favourite time was the hour before dusk when, looking upwards, the ship's masts appeared to touch the sky, and looking down from the deck over the side of the ship, the deepening blackness that is the sea at night seemed so far away. In that hour before the darkness of the night enveloped them the ship's band played haunting folk tunes, lullabies and songs of love. Here and there a member of the crew would sing softly or hum the melody in a sonorous bass. Lanterns were lit; seamen, their chores over for the day, gathered on the forecastle to relax and smoke; passengers strolled on deck before turning in for the night, and the sun slipped lower in the sky until it sank into the waters at the horizon.

So often, when one has looked forward to something with eager anticipation, the reality does not meet one's expectations. This was so for Miriam. She was disappointed with India. It was exciting at first: the exotic sights and smells; the boom of cannon each time a ship arrived or departed; the forest of masts of hundreds of ships anchored off Calcutta; and the grace and charm of the palatial bungalow provided for her and Murdo, but the novelty and glamour quickly faded in the overwhelming brightness and heat.

Their names were included in the list of guests for receptions at Government House and they were swallowed into a hectic social round, but it was this that Miriam most disliked: the way in which the British conducted themselves without making any allowances for the foreignness of India. She found the ritual of calling tedious, the evening drives in carriages and buggies unimaginative, and the manner in which everyone dressed – top hats, tails, busks and parasols – faintly ridiculous. She would have much preferred to have been able to mingle more with the local population and travel to see something of the country.

They were four months in harbour, four months during which Miriam became more and more miserable. It did not help that the weather was oppressive and sapped her strength. She had to force herself to show an interest in Murdo's affairs, but he saw through her pretence, and the fact that she never complained began to irritate him. He almost wished that she would reproach him for bringing her to India because then they could have had a row, which might have cleared the air. As it was Murdo began to return home later in the evenings, leaving Miriam to retire for the night alone.

It was a relief for them both when the time came to board ship for the voyage home. Although she had dreaded the return of the seasickness that had plagued her on the outward voyage, Miriam now almost welcomed it because it meant that she had left the hated country behind. Her abiding pleasurable memory of India was the perfume of camphor candles and sandalwood, everything else she was happy to forget.

In order to occupy the long hours at sea Miriam had purchased some lengths of Indian cotton and embroidery silks, and she whiled away the time on deck making a set of bed curtains for Murdo's cot; but part way home she was seized once again with bouts of sickness. It was the ship's surgeon who suspected that the captain's wife was pregnant, and he approached Murdo with his suspicions.

Murdo was aghast. 'Are you certain?' he asked.

'Well, I haven't examined her,' replied the surgeon. 'But the pattern of your wife's sickness suggests that she is with child.'

Murdo cursed. With a fair wind behind them they should reach home before the child was born, but voyages were unpredictable and, if the winds failed, Miriam faced being brought to bed on board ship, and that could herald death or disaster for both her and the child. He blamed himself for not having taken more care, but in truth he had not considered the possibility of pregnancy, which was foolish of him considering Miriam's youth and the frequency of their lovemaking.

Miriam, sensitive to Murdo's concern without realising his fears for her, became steadily more withdrawn. She had been delighted to learn that she was bearing a child, but she misinterpreted Murdo's furrowed brow as meaning that he was angry with her. Rather than confront her fears she put a distance between them. Murdo fretted day and night over each change in the wind's direction, but they reached England safely and in time. Murdo took Miriam straight to Stuart and Dora Ross where they were welcomed with open arms. Aunt Dora fussed over Miriam, insisting that she lie on the sofa with her feet up, but Miriam found it difficult to comply because after the long voyage her brain tricked her into thinking that the sofa and the floor beneath it were moving as if she were still on-board ship. That evening Miriam wrote a letter to her parents requesting that she be allowed to come home for her confinement. Only a day or so later she was shocked and distressed to receive a letter from her father's lawyer forbidding her return and insisting that she made no further attempt to contact her family. Miriam ignored this and wrote immediately to Alice for an explanation, taking the precaution of asking Aunt Dora to address the envelope rather than trying to disguise her own handwriting.

When it arrived, Alice took the letter to her room to read it, totally unsuspecting of its contents. Alice had always been jealous of her older sister, and to her envy was added the fury and smouldering resentment caused by the blighting of her marriage prospects when Miriam eloped with Captain Nicolson; but now she had news of her own to boast about, so without her parents' knowledge she replied to Miriam's letter. She wrote to congratulate her on the forthcoming birth of her firstborn, but then, in unmistakable spite, she wrote that there was no hope that their parents might relent and agree to see Miriam because, as far as they were concerned, she was dead.

Alice's letter contained two other items of news. Firstly, that Zeinab, their grandmother, had died shortly after being told of Miriam's disgrace, the implication being that her death was Miriam's fault. Secondly, she wrote that she was about to be married to Sir Edward Wickham; and she expressly wrote, for it was underlined three times, that she was to become Lady Alice.

The shock and grief cause by Alice's letter thrust Miriam into labour. Once again it was Aunt Dora who rushed around coping with the crisis. She sent the maids bustling back and forth. Up the stairs they trudged carrying jugs and bowls of steaming hot water, only to trail back down again later with the water cold and unused.

Miriam's labour was long and difficult. As the hours passed she could no longer prevent herself from moaning out loud as each wave of pain gripped her. When she began to scream, Murdo, who had been waiting white-faced and tight-lipped in the study, could stand it no longer. He bounded up the stairs two at a time and burst into the hot, stuffy bedroom.

'Out! Get out!' screeched Aunt Dora. 'This is no place for a gentleman.' She rushed towards him, flapping a towel in his face.

But Murdo had seen worse sights at sea. To Aunt Dora's horror he crossed the room and knelt beside Miriam. Wild-eyed, she grabbed his hand so fiercely that he winced. Her teeth chattered with fear.

'I'm going to die, Murdo,' she whimpered.

Another spasm of pain convulsed her, and when it passed she turned to Murdo once more.

'I don't mean to be so pathetic, Murdo, but it hurts so. Something doesn't feel right and I'm so frightened,' she whimpered. 'I don't want to die.' Her eyes closed briefly, but then another scream brought Murdo to his feet.

'You are not going to die, my dear,' he soothed. 'Aunt Dora is here, and I am going to fetch the doctor for you. This has gone on long enough.'

The doctor's face was grave when he sought Murdo after he had examined Miriam, and Murdo feared the worst.

'The baby is lying in the wrong position,' the doctor explained. 'I will do what I can and, if it is God's will, they will both survive, but it will go hard with your wife.'

Murdo sank into a chair. When he reached the door, the doctor turned back to face Murdo.

'If you have any faith, I suggest that you pray for them. And also for me.' He closed the door softly behind him.

Faith! Murdo gave a mirthless laugh as he poured himself a large glass of Stuart Ross's best brandy. Faith in what? Faith in whom? He had abandoned his faith on the day that Finlay was humiliated in God's name on the Isle of Toronsay. There was no one there to pray to. If there really were a merciful God somewhere, why did He permit such suffering on earth? No, he had no faith, not any more; but a superstitious fear of being wrong made him offer a brief prayer for the lives of his wife and child – just in case there was Someone there after all.

A wail! Murdo's morose introspection was interrupted by a baby's cry. He leapt to his feet and wrenched open the door. For a moment the only sound he could hear was that of footsteps overhead, but then it came again – the unmistakable, affronted, indignant cry of a newborn baby. Murdo's heart lurched. His child was alive. Thank God, he said to himself automatically.

The doctor was not long in coming downstairs. 'Congratulations, Captain Nicolson, you have a fine, healthy daughter.'

'And my wife?' asked Murdo. 'What of my wife?'

'She'll do,' said the doctor. 'She is asleep now, exhausted and weak, but she is young, and she will recover.'

Tears filled Murdo's eyes. He shook the doctor's hand. 'Thank you,' he said simply. 'Thank you.'

After Miriam had had a rest, Aunt Dora summoned Murdo. 'You can stay for a few minutes, but Miriam must not get excited, and the baby needs to sleep.'

Murdo crossed the room and stood looking down at his wife. Black smudges coloured the delicate skin beneath her dark eyes. She was pale, but her expression was one of triumph as she pulled the shawl from the baby's face so that Murdo could see his daughter. He bent over and put his finger into the tiny hand, and it was instantly held fast. He smiled with pleasure. The baby opened her smoky blue eyes and stared at him. Her face was red and crumpled, and a mass of black hair poked from beneath a frilly cap. Murdo was lost for words.

'Isn't she beautiful?' whispered Miriam. 'She is going to be as dark as my grandmother, I think. What shall we call her?'

'Alexandra,' said Murdo without hesitation.

Miriam frowned. Tiredness and emotion sent tears flowing down her cheeks.

'I'm sorry if you do not care for the name,' said Murdo gently. 'But it was my mother's middle name.'

'It's not that,' said Miriam. 'It's just that Alexandra will be shortened to Ali, and that's my father's name. I don't think that I can bear that.'

'Nor I,' said Murdo, thinking of his last interview with Ali Garthwaite. 'It's easily remedied though. We will call her Lexy.'

Miriam nodded and closed her eyes. Murdo took the baby from the crook of her arm and laid her in her cradle before tiptoeing from the room.

CHAPTER 11

Miriam had known from the beginning that Murdo would not be able to honour his pledge to leave his life at sea. He could not hide from her that he found life in London irksome. She watched his eyes glaze over when they were in chattering company and knew that the siren song of the sea still held him fast. On their long voyage to India, in the first flush of their married life together, Murdo had told Miriam a little of his early years in the Hebrides; sufficient for her to understand that he was not brought up to the superficiality of their life in London; sufficient for her to know that sooner or later she would lose him. For Murdo the sea would always come first. She understood, but it saddened Miriam to realise that he would also leave his daughter without a qualm.

Lexy was just past her second birthday and already showing signs of the beauty she would become. She was darker than Miriam, inheriting all her physical attributes from Zeinab, but she had her father's direct gaze and stoicism. She was a delightful child and, were it not for Lexy, Miriam knew she would not be able to bear the parting from Murdo that she knew would come, so she devoted herself to her daughter as a means of protecting herself from despair and desolation.

When a note arrived from Stuart Ross for Murdo, he left immediately for the Jerusalem Coffee House. He stepped from a cold and foggy November day into the steamy room, which was crammed with people and steeped in the smells of wine, coffee and tobacco smoke. The instant Murdo entered this familiar world his spirits soared. He had been away too long; this was where he belonged. Here ships' husbands and owners, merchants and insurance brokers met to discuss trade and policies. Stuart Ross caught sight of Murdo and beckoned him to join him in a dark corner of the coffee house. Two mugs of coffee steamed on the table in front of him.

'What news?' asked Murdo, whose crossing of the room had been constantly interrupted by the surprised greetings of the peoples of the sea welcoming him back to the fold.

Uncle Stuart's face was long and solemn. 'Not good, I'm afraid. McKendrick is sick unto death. He'll not be able to sail next week.'

'I'm sorry to hear that,' said Murdo. 'Who is taking command?'

Uncle Stuart scratched his chin. 'It rather depends on you. I asked you here to offer you the *Brochel Castle* again. It's very short notice, I know, but it would be short notice for anyone since the ship is due to sail on Wednesday. I don't know how you will feel about it now that you have a family, but I thought I would give you first refusal.'

Murdo took a deep breath. He felt as if he had suddenly shed years, so heavily had the last two lain on him. He did not hesitate to accept the offer.

'I need it,' he said. 'Only another captain would understand.'

'I do.' Stuart Ross nodded. 'How are Miriam and Lexy?'

'Both well,' said Murdo. 'It's not that I want to leave them, but I belong on the sea. I don't think I will ever be able to settle on land. How did you do it?'

'Didn't have a choice, dear boy. Dicky heart,' replied Stuart Ross, lightly tapping his chest. 'How will Miriam take the news that you are to sail again?'

Murdo smiled faintly. 'You know, I really do believe that she has seen it coming. You know what she's like. She never complains about anything, but I don't want to take the baby on such a voyage, and Miriam won't be lonely with a child to care for.'

'We will watch over them for you.'

'I know you will,' said Murdo. 'That makes leaving less of a worry for me. It makes me savage that the Garthwaites still refuse to see them.'

There was a disturbance as a large gentleman pushed his way through the crowd towards them.

'Ah! I hoped I would find you here,' he said. 'I'm afraid that I have some terrible news.'

Murdo looked sharply at his lawyer. Ernest Frobisher took a sheaf of papers from his case and settled himself beside Murdo and Stuart Ross.

'I'm glad you are both here. Have either of you heard from Glasgow of late?'

Murdo and Stuart Ross shook their heads. 'No. Why?'

Ernest Frobisher frowned. 'There is no easy way to tell you this, but I'm afraid that Donald Nicolson has passed away.'

Murdo gasped, scarcely able to take in the lawyer's words. The news of his uncle's death distressed him far more than that of his father's would have done. Donald Nicolson had been more than a father to him. He had also been his benefactor, financing him through his early years with the East India Company until he had risen to the rank of first mate, from which time he had been able to support himself on his own salary together with monies raised from private trade. The news left him numb with shock.

'How did it happen?' asked Stuart Ross. 'And how long ago?'

'It would appear that he passed away peacefully in his sleep a couple of weeks ago,' replied Ernest Frobisher. 'I rushed here as soon as I heard.'

'Have you any news of my sister?' asked Stuart Ross.

'According to Mr Nicolson's lawyer she and your nieces have been well provided for, but I should imagine that they are much shocked by the suddenness of it.'

Stuart Ross stood up. 'I must make arrangements to travel to Glasgow immediately.' He turned to Murdo. 'This puts a different perspective on next week's sailing. You might wish to reconsider.'

Murdo looked glum. 'I have given you my word. I shall still sail. The voyage will give me time to adjust to our loss. Give my love to Aunt Mary and tell her that I will write before I leave.'

Stuart Ross strode from the Jerusalem Coffee House leaving Murdo and the lawyer in an island of sadness amidst the uproar of shipping business being conducted around them.

'I'm sorry,' said the lawyer.

'Thank you for coming to tell us personally.'

'Did your uncle ever discuss his business affairs with you?'

Murdo's head jerked up in surprise. 'No. Why would he?'

'Then you are not aware that Mr Nicolson named you his sole beneficiary after provision for your aunt and cousins?'

Murdo sucked in his breath. 'Surely not? I think there must be a mistake. My father and older brother would have a claim before me.'

Ernest Frobisher shook his head. 'It is you that he has named. Nobody else. I think he was very proud of you and what you have achieved.'

He handed Murdo a copy of his uncle's last will and testament in which Murdo read that the family home and contents, plus a sum of money, were to be held in trust for his aunt and cousins, but that the remainder of the estate, comprising stocks, shares, his share in the tobacco company and a bank account containing fifty thousand pounds, was to come to him unreservedly. Altogether it was a vast sum, and Murdo's head reeled.

'I would suggest that you travel to Glasgow with Mr Ross,' said the lawyer. 'You have much to attend to.'

Murdo shook his head. 'I sail for India on Wednesday. I am committed to that, and as yet my wife doesn't even know about it. It's too difficult to make other arrangements for the voyage at such short notice. I'll go to Glasgow when I return.'

'But that could be two years from now,' protested the lawyer.

'Even so,' said Murdo. 'I must leave the details to you and Uncle Donald's lawyer until then.'

'But you have no need to sail now. You need never work again.'

Murdo smiled grimly. 'If you were my banker you would know that I haven't had to work for years. And as my father used to say, Mr Frobisher, the Devil soon finds work for idle hands to do.'

The lawyer nodded. Murdo drummed his fingers on the table in front of him.

'I would rather my wife was not informed of the contents of the will,' he said. 'I will tell her in my own time when I have made some decisions.'

The two men shook hands and parted company. Murdo left Cowper's Court and walked down to the Thames, shaking his head at coachmen touting for business. He ordered a tankard of ale at an inn and sat gazing unseeingly through a grimy window at the busy river. Hundreds of craft – barges with brown sails, lighters, ships and boats of every size and description – jostled for space on the river as they drifted up and down stream, but Murdo barely noticed them. He sat by himself with a lump in his throat as he said a silent farewell to his Uncle Donald.

When he had finished his drink Murdo left the inn and hailed a cab to take him home. Miriam knew that something was wrong as soon as he entered the drawing room. She rang for the nursemaid to take Lexy and sent for a tray of tea. One of the things Murdo appreciated about his wife was that she rarely asked questions. She was not one to pry and was the most uninquisitive woman he had ever known. Never had he appreciated this quality in her so much as now, as she sat quietly and waited for him to speak.

The maid brought the tea with a plate of hot-buttered scones. Murdo was not hungry, but was glad of the tea, almost draining his cup before he spoke. There were two things he wanted to tell her, and he did not know which of them to say first.

'Uncle Donald has passed away,' he said eventually.

'Oh, my dear, I am so sorry. I know how much he meant to you.' Miriam's face was full of concern. 'I expect you will want to go to Glasgow. I'll call the maid to pack your things.'

She moved towards the bell, but Murdo held up his hand to stop her. 'I'm not going,' he said. 'Uncle Stuart is going immediately.'

'How sad for your Aunt Mary,' said Miriam. She had never met any of Murdo's relatives, but she knew of the Nicolsons in Glasgow for Murdo often spoke of them, and there were regular letters.

'It has been a terrible shock,' said Murdo. 'I have no idea whether or not he had been ill. It seems he passed away in his sleep. I think it must have been quite sudden as I'm sure Aunt Mary would have written of it had he been ill.' He made no mention of his inheritance. 'There's something else I have to tell you. The reason I cannot go to Glasgow is because Uncle Stuart offered me the *Brochel Castle*, and I had only just accepted when Ernest Frobisher arrived with the news about Uncle Donald. I sail for Calcutta on Wednesday. I know it is short notice, but the captain who was to take command is seriously ill and so I was the first person that Uncle Stuart thought of to take his place. I sail without you, but you must not think of this as meaning that I don't care for you or Lexy. I love you both very much.'

Miriam went and knelt at his feet. She laid her head in his lap to hide her tears, and her voice was muffled against his knees.

'It's all right, Murdo dear,' she said softly. 'I have had you with me far longer than I expected to. I have always known that you would not be able to keep your pledge to leave the sea. But it's all right. I do understand. The time has come for me to give you back to your ship.'

ANJANA

CHAPTER 12

Murdo stood at the deck rail and peered into the white mist which engulfed the ship, truncating the bowsprit and main masts. The mist was dense, the air hot and humid. They had been becalmed for five days; boredom and lethargy stalked the decks, and in the silence that surrounded them all sounds were magnified so that the passengers felt constrained to talk in whispers. The *Brochel Castle* was motionless, and her sails hung undisturbed, like pieces of stage scenery. All around her rose the stench of the ship's waste, released into the sea, but held fast against her by the still waters. Murdo had ordered the lowering of boats several times so that the ship could be towed into cleaner waters, but until the weather changed they could only smoulder in the lap of the gods. They had been blown off course during a storm and had lost contact with their convoy of East Indiamen. Now they were alone on the high seas; marooned in sinister isolation.

Murdo chafed at the delay. With most of the poultry and many of the other animals already butchered and eaten, he was concerned about the remaining store of food. They were several weeks behind schedule and he had no idea when they would have the opportunity to take on more supplies. With the lemon juice running short he feared scurvy amongst his crew, and there was already an outbreak of fever amongst the Company's Marine. It was hard to shake off a creeping conviction that they had been cursed.

On the sixth day there were two deaths – one, a marine, the other, a passenger. In the late afternoon Murdo assembled the ship's crew and passengers for the funeral service. Fear and sorrow added to the prevailing air of dreariness. The white mist and unnerving stillness played on superstitions, and even Murdo was not immune from a sense of malevolence in their situation.

'Deliver us from evil,' he muttered under his breath.

The ship's bell was struck, and a party of marines marched forward carrying the bodies of the deceased, the dead marine draped with the union flag. Murdo conducted the service in sepulchral undertones, and each person present was deeply affected by the ghostly atmosphere.

'I am the resurrection and the life, saith the Lord: he that believeth in me, though he were dead, yet shall he live: and whosoever liveth and believeth in me shall never die,' chanted Murdo. He felt icy fingers of superstitious fear creep up his spine. Who was he to conduct this holy service when he had turned his back on God?

The Company's Marine fired a volley. There was a roll on a drum, and the planks on which the bodies rested were raised to the rail.

'We therefore commit their bodies to the deep.'

The bodies slid, one from beneath the flag, the other from its covering of canvas, and after a brief, tense pause there came the splash as the bodies sank to their watery grave. People breathed more freely. Then there was silence once more; total silence in the white mist.

'Dismiss the men, Mr Birch.'

Crew and passengers turned to leave. Moments later Murdo sensed an infinitesimal lightening of the air, a ghost's breath, before the shy flutter of a sail caught his eye. A slight movement of the deck beneath his feet, the creak of a rope, and he knew it was over. Wind at last! Orders were given, sails hoisted, and crewmen rushed to their posts, scattering the passengers right and left.

Murdo shivered. He had the sudden, unaccountable conviction that the two bodies he had just committed to the deep had been an unintentional sacrifice, and now that they had appeased the gods of the seas, they were free to continue on their way. The powerful impression of a malevolent spirit somewhere in the ocean around them, a malignant and sinister water demon that thirsted for the souls of men, filled Murdo with terror. It was a bad omen and boded ill for the entire voyage.

It was March before the *Brochel Castle* arrived in Calcutta and rejoined the fleet, which was anchored close to Fort William. It was the time of the northeast monsoons, which made their passage up the Hooghly River against the wind and treacherous tides, but the weather at this time was at its most agreeable. A single cannon fired a salute to acknowledge their arrival, and soon pandemonium broke out as relieved relatives shouted from the quayside. Excitement animated the weary travellers, loosening their tongues as they shouted back and waved coloured handkerchiefs to attract attention.

Numerous small boats quickly surrounded them. 'How much? How much?' Dark skinned natives held up two or three fingers and shouted 'rupees' in reply. Then came a loud clamour of bargaining as the price of being ferried ashore was haggled down to a few annas. Porters jostled each other on the quay, manoeuvring themselves into the best positions for the opportunity of carrying luggage to the waiting *gharries* for a few annas more.

Murdo gazed at the scene, content and at peace with the world. He had brought his ship safely to port, and now he was free to indulge his love of India. As the sun set, casting a peach-coloured glow, sudden intense flashes of gold were reflected from shiny surfaces touched by the light. The *ghats* leading down to the river filled with faithful Hindus come to perform their evening *puja*. An elderly woman, waist deep in the water with her wet sari stuck to her wizened frame, scooped water into her hands and raised it to the setting sun. As she did so, river water trickled through her fingers and caught the light like broken strings of glass beads. Before his unnerving experience following the committal at sea Murdo would have been scornful of her offering to the sun, but not now. Now he smiled grimly to himself as he realised how appalled his father would be to know just how tenuous his faith had become.

After the cramped conditions on board, Murdo revelled in the luxury of the spacious bungalow obtained for him by his banian – his Indian general steward – and he wasted no time in ridding himself of the journey's filth. No sooner had he inspected the bungalow and taken tea, then he clapped his hands.

'*Koi-hai?*' A servant appeared and Murdo ordered hot water for a bath. While he waited he wandered out onto the veranda which overlooked the Hooghly and watched the comings and goings on the river. Cannon boomed at frequent intervals, and it seemed that the vast number of ships left no room for manoeuvre. Murdo knew the dangers and recognised the skills of other captains as they inched their ships into position.

The bathroom was at the rear of the bungalow. A servant stripped Murdo of his sweat-stained, evil-smelling uniform and took it away. Murdo lowered himself into the water and sighed with pleasure. The servant returned with more hot water in a brass jug, a small bowl and a folded towel. He knelt beside Murdo and shampooed his greasy hair. Murdo wallowed in the bath until the water cooled, then he soaped his body and stood up in the bath so that the servant could pour clean water over him to rinse off the lather. He stepped from the bath with water streaming from his body and was immediately cocooned in a fluffy white towel. Then he sat in a chair whilst months of golden growth were meticulously shaved from his face. By the time his toilet was complete, his belongings had been unpacked and neatly put away by someone as yet unseen.

Over the course of the next few days, Murdo attended to his private trade, the means by which he augmented his £120 annual salary from the Company. Already on the outward voyage he had netted a considerable sum from fares charged to his passengers, but now he set about purchasing chests of the finest tea, tubs of camphor and crates of oranges, all of which would be auctioned in London by the East India Company for his personal enrichment. Most of this business was conducted through his banian, but on his previous voyages to India Murdo had purchased goods which he had not declared. Being small and easily concealed about his person, his enterprises had brought him significant financial gain, and although he was now a rich man, even without his recent vast inheritance, he decided to risk a further venture into the illegal business of smuggling.

Diamonds. A man might sell his soul for less.

Years earlier, when he had first entered the establishment of Vijay Chatterjee (the very best diamond merchant in the whole of India, he would have you know), Murdo had known little about these precious gems other than that they fetched high prices in London; but he quickly learned that a diamond which is immersed in water will be dry when it is removed. and that a diamond can only be scratched by another diamond. They were small details, but crucial for protecting himself from being duped into purchasing fake gems. Now Murdo wended his way along the bustling alleys of the bazaar, where shops were busy with merchants selling spices, sticky sweetmeats in silver paper, silks, trinkets and wedding finery. He passed them all with barely a glance until he came to the one he sought.

'Welcome back, Captain,' said Vijay Chatterjee. 'I trust you had a pleasant voyage.'

He clapped his hands and the *char-wallah* brought tea, and then merchant and client sat down to do business together. The precious stones came from the mines at Golconda, which at that time was the sole source of the world's diamonds. Vijay Chatterjee spread a square of black silk on the counter and tipped some uncut diamonds onto it. He leaned back in his chair, sipped his tea, and watched the sea captain through hooded eyes. The last time Captain Nicolson had visited the shop he had driven a hard bargain, but he had still paid more than the merchant would have accepted for the gems he bought and was likely to do so again. Vijay Chatterjee was not fooled by Murdo's show of carefully examining the diamonds, but he had put a selection of gems of varying value in front of him from which Murdo could choose those he guessed would bring him a good price in England. They were not his most precious diamonds – those he reserved for nawabs and maharajas – but nor were they by any means worthless. The captain would make a profit whichever of the gems he bought.

When Murdo was satisfied with his selection, he and Vijay Chatterjee made an entertaining game of haggling over the price, and when this business was successfully completed Murdo commissioned a double row of pearls to be made for Miriam.

'It is always a pleasure to do business with you, Captain Nicolson,' said Vijay Chatterjee as he accompanied Murdo to the street outside his shop. 'Before you go, I wonder if you would accept an invitation to a *nautch* at my house next week in honour of my son's fifth birthday? You are welcome to bring a friend with you.'

Murdo was flattered. Such entertainments were far less common these days than they had once been, and the days of Europeans and Indians mixing freely together were fast disappearing. He was delighted to be granted the opportunity of a glimpse into the past.

'Thank you very much,' he said. 'That is most kind of you. I am honoured to accept your invitation. If it is acceptable to you I should like to bring my first mate with me.'

'Of course.'

Arrangements were made, directions given, and Murdo returned to his bungalow from where he sent a message to John Birch regarding the nautch. During the days leading up to the party, Murdo's anticipation increased with every passing hour. He did not know what to expect, other than dancing girls, but his imagination ran riot. He hoped for the exotic and the erotic; and he would not be disappointed.

CHAPTER 13

'Come along, Anjana. Get yourself off that cushion and come and give me a hand. Am I to do all the organising myself?' Malati Chatterjee frowned at her younger sister. She really was the giddy limit sometimes.

Anjana pouted. 'It's your house, Malati, and it's your party tonight. Why do you need my help? You seem to be managing perfectly well on your own. The servants haven't had a moment's peace since you got out of bed this morning.' She gave an elaborate yawn.

Malati sighed. It was true that the nautch party was being held partly in her honour. She had suggested to Vijay that the birthday of their eldest son be marked with a nautch, and he had readily agreed. She had not bothered to remind him that her birthday fell on the same day as their son's because, as a mere woman, her birthday would normally pass without comment; but she loved the idea of celebrating it with a nautch and could now do so using her son's as an excuse. She did not actually require Anjana's assistance, but her sister's lethargy irked her. Anjana's melancholy was understandable and Malati frequently berated herself for her lack of charity towards her, but Anjana would try the very patience of the saints the Europeans worshipped.

Malati left Anjana to her solitude and went to inspect the grounds. It was dusk, and the gardens were illuminated by hundreds of lamps. The flickering light sparked flashes of brilliance in the cascading waters of the fountain. Now that the paths had been watered to settle the day's dust, all the windows were thrown wide open, and Malati sighed with pleasure. On this, her fifth inspection, she found nothing to criticise in the preparations. She clapped her hands in excitement – her twentieth birthday was going to be wonderful.

Unusually, Malati and Anjana were not expected to seclude themselves completely from the outside world, as was the situation for many women. They were married to two men who were related to each other – an uncle and his nephew – both of whom were proud of their wives and saw no need to hide them away. The two sisters were the youngest children of a family of five daughters and two sons, whose parents, having lost their livelihood in a disastrous flood, had despaired of being able to provide dowries for them. When they were still just children, Malati had feared that she would never be married. No merchant of her own caste would want her without a dowry, and she would never entertain the idea of marriage to a man of a lower caste.

'We'll be nobodies if we don't have husbands,' she had grumbled to Anjana at the wedding of an older brother.

Anjana had pulled a face. 'Women are nobodies whether they are married or not. At least if we don't have a husband we won't have a mother-in-law to beat us. Anyway, I don't care if I never get married.'

'How can you say that?' countered Malati. 'I want a husband and I want lots of babies. How can you not want babies?'

Anjana had shrugged in reply. There were two years between them in age, and both girls were beautiful. Malati was taller and plumper than her sister; Anjana was dainty and graceful.

One day Anjana caught the eye of Ramohun Chatterjee. The wealthy diamond merchant approached her parents, but although they were delighted that he desired their daughter, they were dismayed at their inability to provide a dowry. Embarrassed, they explained why they must decline the marriage proposal, but Ramohun Chatterjee desired Anjana's young body more than he required a dowry, as he was already a rich man. Anjana's parents accepted the diamond merchant's renewed proposal with alacrity, and suddenly Anjana found herself betrothed to the old man.

During the negotiations for the marriage, Ramohun Chatterjee had been accompanied by his nephew, who fell in love with Malati at first sight. Vijay Chatterjee made a similar offer to that of his uncle's – that he would marry Malati with only a token dowry for the sake of appearances. Malati was thrilled with her handsome young husband, making Anjana's situation all the harder to bear, for the young twelve-year old was understandably appalled by the elderly man she was being forced to marry.

Anjana left her home to live with her new husband's family where she would remain until she bore a son. Ramohun promised her that when she had fulfilled this expectation he would move her to an establishment of her own. Anjana was bitterly unhappy. Old Mrs Chatterjee was a martinet who made her life a misery. She was in her sixties, a vast age, and her life, cushioned by her son, was more comfortable than she, as a widow, could reasonably expect. Her good fortune did not serve to make her any less spiteful, and she missed no opportunity to pinch and punch Anjana in the privacy of the *zenana* where Ramohun could not see, or to complain to Ramohun about her irritating passivity.

Anjana's aloof detachment acted as a goad to Ramohun. As she became used to her new husband's sexual requirements, and ceased to show her disgust and revulsion, he tried to rouse her to some degree of passion; but it was a forlorn hope. because Anjana lapsed into a self-induced trance whenever he summoned her to his bed. Had he not been so desperate for a son Ramohun might have abandoned her and sought solace with a mistress, but he needed a son. His first wife had given him three daughters, all of them now significantly older than Anjana. He had to have a son to take over his business, and it was of paramount importance that he had a son to light his funeral pyre when his time came. The intermittent pain he felt in his chest warned him that time was running short, so he sent for Anjana most nights and tried to ignore her remoteness.

In the zenana, Anjana refrained from becoming embroiled in the intrigues and scandal-mongering inevitable in a house of women. She appeared to live in a world of her own and her impassivity provoked old Mrs Chatterjee into a never-ending stream of abuse, which only served to drive Anjana further into retreat. In her desire to protect herself Anjana became adept at self-hypnosis, effectively switching herself off from her stressful surroundings. She infuriated everyone around her apart from Malati, and Anjana only came alive when she was with her sister.

When she finally became pregnant both Ramohun and Anjana were overjoyed: Ramohun because he expected her to produce the son he craved, and Anjana because she would have someone to love. But old Mrs Chatterjee was incensed by the self-satisfied expression on Anjana's face. She dared Anjana to produce a daughter for her son.

'He'll cast you out then, and no bones about it,' she said vindictively. 'And good riddance too.'

Anjana took no notice of her mother-in-law and spent most of her time with her sister. Malati was expecting her second child. She had borne Vijay a son nine months after their marriage, and Anjana loved to play with her nephew Rakesh. She seized every opportunity to escape her own home and her hostile mother-in-law.

The baby was a boy. Ramohun showered Anjana with gifts of gold, rubies and diamonds. There was nothing he would not do for her, and no end to his pride in having fathered a son at the grand old age of forty-six. Anjana could do no wrong in his eyes. Anything she desired was hers for the asking, and what she most wanted was to live somewhere – anywhere – away from old Mrs Chatterjee.

'The good-for-nothing is not caring for your son properly,' she sneaked to Ramohun. 'She leaves him crying for hours on end. You've got your son now so get rid of her. She's a weird one and you would be better off without her.'

But Ramohun's delight was such that his mother's lies and complaints fell on deaf ears. On the day she moved out of the Chatterjee family home, Anjana sought old Mrs Chatterjee to give vent to her feelings in a rare display of animation, confident in her position now that she was the mother of a son.

'When the time comes for Pran to marry,' she said to the old lady. I shall never submit his bride to the treatment you have meted out to me.'

Stung, old Mrs Chatterjee replied, 'I have not treated you any differently from the way I was treated when I joined my husband in his family home.'

'Then that only makes it worse,' said Anjana. 'Unless you enjoyed being treated so cruelly, you should not have inflicted the same pain and humiliation on me.'

'It is custom.' The old lady shrugged. 'It is not a question of what one enjoys.'

'That doesn't make it right,' said Anjana.

Away from Ramohun's mother Anjana devoted herself to her baby and was tolerably happy. The joy she felt at having produced a son was the first deep emotion she had ever experienced, and she began to blossom. Malati gave birth to a second son and Anjana and Pran were frequent visitors to her home.

Disaster came swiftly, like a thief in the night. In the heat and humidity towards the end of the monsoon season, Calcutta unleashed a miasma of pestilence. Pran succumbed to a fever and died before he reached his first birthday. Shocked and stricken, Anjana retreated into a trance. She stared at Ramohun as if he were a stranger. The only person she responded to was her sister, so it was at Malati's home that Anjana stayed until the worst of the shock and grief had passed.

Three years and two more sons later, Malati invited Anjana and Ramohun to join the birthday celebrations, but when the day of the nautch came Ramohun felt unwell and decided to stay at home. He had been tired of late and now he lacked the motivation to do more than sit in a chair and stare into space.

'You go, Anjana,' Ramohun said. 'There's no need for you to miss the party because of me. It will do you good to have some fun.'

'Are you in pain?' asked Anjana. 'Would you like me to send for a doctor?'

Ramohun shook his head. 'No, I'm not in any pain and I don't want a doctor. They are all quacks and charlatans, and they make you even sicker than you were before with all their disgusting pills and potions. I'm all right. I just feel tired. I'll be better after a few days of rest. Vijay will look after the business. He does most of the work now anyway. You go and enjoy yourself.'

Malati was more concerned for Ramohun than her sister was. Ramohun was growing old and the death of his baby son had aged him, robbing him of the vitality that fathering a son had given him. Malati was worried for Anjana's future because Ramohun did not look as though he would live to be as old as his mother.

'What's wrong with him?' she asked.

'He says he is tired. He is not in pain and refuses to see a doctor. He looks a little puffy and he is breathless sometimes. I'm sure it's nothing terrible. Anyway, it suits me very well that he prefers to stay at home.'

Malati held her tongue, but she thought that if Anjana took a close look at herself some day she might see where much of the blame lay for her own misery. Instantly Malati felt contrite. Who was she to criticise? She had four healthy and growing sons whereas poor Anjana had lost her firstborn and there had been no more babies. She doubted if she could have borne such tragedy any better than Anjana and resolved once again to try to be more charitable towards her sister.

CHAPTER 14

The night was hot and sultry. As Murdo dressed for the evening's entertainment he reflected that in England it was probably cool and wet. Spring flowers would be shooting in the borders of his garden, and Miriam and Lexy would still be enjoying hot crumpets cooked on a toasting fork over a roaring fire. He thought of the cool and the wet and his wife, but he did not hanker after them. He did not miss them, and he felt a pang of shame when he realised how seldom he had thought of his wife and daughter over the past months. How was it possible to have all but forgotten them? He knew that he had lusted after Miriam rather than loved her, although a measure of love had come with the satisfying of that lust and the birth of his daughter. He had heard that the Indians believed that women were born without souls and were intended purely for the sexual pleasure of men; could it be that he was of the same mind? Was there no meeting of minds and hearts between him and Miriam? No, he admitted to himself, there was not.

Murdo's face was solemn as he and John Birch were driven to the Chatterjees' *haveli*, but his mood lightened as they were shown into a room of sumptuous size and elegance. The shutters and windows along one side of the room were opened wide onto the terrace and formal water garden beyond where lamplight flickered in lanterns which were suspended from the branches of trees, pools of yellow in the blackness. The other three walls were decorated with painted panels of birds and flowers, and across one end wall, jutting from above, was a gallery screened with latticed sandalwood. Cushions and bolsters were scattered all around the room on the richly carpeted floor for the comfort of the guests later in the evening.

There was a sprinkling of other Europeans amongst the predomi-nantly Indian guests, but Murdo was quick to notice that there were no ladies present. He knew that it was unlikely that Indian ladies of quality would have been permitted to appear in mixed company, but that did not explain the absence of memsahibs.

'I wonder if no invitations were extended to European ladies?' Murdo mused to John Birch.

'It's more likely that our memsahibs would have refused any invitation to attend a nautch. Things are very different these days. Most of us, the ladies especially, have become far too prejudiced to mingle in Indian company,' replied the first mate. 'The fools don't know what they're missing. This promises to be a wonderful evening, and I, for one, am really looking forward to it.'

Murdo nodded. 'My wife would have harboured no qualms about coming to a nautch. She found India very boring just being with our own people all the time. She could hardly wait to leave here, but I think she would have liked it better if she had had opportunities like this. I must take care to remember the proceedings from start to finish so that I can regale her with the details when we get home.'

They were interrupted with the request that everyone move to the terrace, and Murdo and John Birch joined the others outside. The air was filled with the smell of burning incense and the sweet heady perfume of night flowers. Sparkling fireflies danced in swarms beneath the trees and stars shone brightly in the sky above.

First there came the jugglers, then snake charmers, sword swallowers, contortionists and fire-eaters, all of whom held their audience in thrall. When they moved indoors again, Murdo declined the offer of a hookah pipe, but John Birch settled himself on a bolster to enjoy a smoke.

Hidden behind the ornately carved screen of the gallery Anjana and Malati spied on the assembled party. They had watched the outdoor entertainments from an upper window and five-year-old Rakesh was naturally over-excited, clamouring to be allowed to go downstairs. Malati was also impatient to join the rest of the celebrations, but it was time for Rakesh to go to bed. She called for the *ayah* to take the tired, cross little boy away and then turned to her sister.

'Come on, Anjana. Let's go down.'

Anjana shook her head. 'You go, Malati,' she said. 'I shall stay and watch from here.'

Malati stamped her foot in vexation. 'Honestly, Anjana. Here we are, both of us fortunate to have husbands who don't insist that we hide ourselves away, and you treat the privilege lightly. Most women would give almost anything to enjoy our freedoms. Don't you realise how lucky we are?'

But Anjana was not listening. Peering from the shadows of the gallery she viewed the lamp-lit room below as if it were a scene from a stage play, and her attention was caught by a tall, golden-haired sea captain. She gazed at him with interest and made no reply to Malati's nagging.

'Well, suit yourself,' said Malati. 'You can stay here and be miserable all on your own. I'm going to go and enjoy my birthday party.' She swept from the gallery and went downstairs to join her guests.

Murdo was astonished to see her cross the room to stand beside her husband, conscious of the honour bestowed on the assembled company by her presence. She brought with her the scent of musk and fragrant oils. He inclined his head towards John Birch.

'I have seen many lovely Indian women, but Mrs Chatterjee is a rose amongst thorns,' he whispered.

John Birch nodded his agreement. 'We must hope that the dancing girls are at least half as beautiful,' he replied with a lascivious grin.

They did not have long to wait. Three musicians entered carrying a *tabla, dholak* and harmonium, and the singers followed them. Murdo lounged back against his bolster and relaxed as he listened to the strangely hypnotic music. He closed his eyes in pleasure and a hint of a smile lifted the corners of his mouth.

Anjana watched him from her hiding place. The apertures in the screen provided ample opportunity for her to observe the proceedings without being seen. She had not been in close proximity to Europeans before, but she had seen them parading along the Strand and had always thought them pale and pasty in appearance; but Murdo's tanned face against his golden hair appealed to her, and as she drank in and memorised every detail of this fine-looking sea captain, she fell in love. Although Anjana had been married for several years she had never known desire, but now passion coursed through every fibre of her being. She yearned for this foreigner with an intensity that almost caused her pain, and her empty, unfulfilled existence was suddenly flooded with tense excitement. She trembled with unfamiliar emotions.

Murdo opened his eyes, conscious of being watched. He glanced around the room, but everyone was staring at the singers. Nobody appeared to be paying him any attention, but the feeling persisted, and he felt ill at ease. He turned back to the evening's entertainment. The singers had finished now, and the dancers took their place. There were six nautch girls and three men, and Murdo tried to put his unease aside so that he could concentrate on the part of the evening he had most looked forward to. The dancers were dark skinned; much darker than Malati's pale mahogany complexion, and all six were beautiful. They wore gaily-coloured dresses, each with a border of silver or gold, and beneath their petticoats peeped full satin trousers that almost covered anklets of bells above dainty bare feet. They were all heavily bedecked with jewellery – bangles, necklaces, rings on their fingers and toes and in their ears, and the nautch girls covered their heads with highly embroidered *dupattas*.

As the evening wore on the music became fast and furious, and the dancing increasingly uninhibited. The breathtaking display of eroticism and agility held the audience spellbound. Murdo's senses were fully aroused. Dark women had always attracted him, and the beauty of these sultry exotic dancers inflamed him and fired his imagination with desire.

Refreshments were served after the dancing. The Indian guests were led away to eat in a separate room from the Europeans, but Vijay and Malati mingled politely with all their guests. None of the Europeans was introduced to Mrs Chatterjee. Murdo studied her with interest, surprised that the diamond merchant permitted his wife such latitude, and as he looked at her he saw her eyes open with surprise and disbelief. He turned to see what had caused her to look so, but he sensed the newcomer's presence almost before he saw her.

Anjana had waited until the nautch was almost ended before acting on the overwhelming compulsion she felt to join the company. She hurried down the stairs leading from the gallery to the marble-floored hallway below, and then she glided into the room where everyone was gathered in preparation for the firework display which would bring the evening to an end. She crossed the floor, acutely aware of Murdo's gaze and yet studiously avoiding him.

Murdo was dazzled by her. If he had likened Malati to a rose amongst thorns, then this young woman's beauty would make even the most wondrous orchid pale to insignificance beside her. She was simply exquisite. Her almond-shaped eyes dominated an oval face with its finely chiselled nose and full lips. She was petite, but her body was voluptuous beneath graceful folds of yards of fine gauzy fabric, and her thick black hair fell over her shoulders like a cape.

Murdo was conscious that he was staring and forced himself to look away, but his eyes kept returning to that lovely face. It was a face that must surely have set the heart of every gentleman present pounding, and it intoxicated Murdo with the contradictory desires of lust and a wish to protect its owner from harm.

It was inevitable that their eyes would meet, and when finally they did each of them gasped with the intensity of feeling that flashed between them across the crowded room. Time stood still for them both. They were not introduced and did not speak to one another. When the firework display came to an end and it was time to leave, Murdo did not know her name and had no idea who she might be, but he wanted her more than he had ever wanted anyone or anything. He wanted her more than life itself.

Anjana returned home a few days after the nautch. Murdo might know nothing about her, but she knew exactly who he was. Careful, sly questioning about the guests had led Vijay to disclose the names and positions of all the Europeans who had attended the celebrations. Anjana had been careful to show no particular interest in any of the details, but the names of Captain Nicolson and his ship, the *Brochel Castle,* were imprinted on her mind like a tattoo, never to be erased. It was a small matter to send a servant to discover where he lived.

Ramohun's health had deteriorated whilst she was away. She found him sitting in a wicker chair staring through an open window into the garden. The shutters were open so that sunlight filtering through the latticed window cast patterns on the wall behind his head. The *mali* was busy in the garden, and the clip clip clip of his pruning shears penetrated the room from outside together with a babble of female voices. Anjana watched Ramohun for a moment. He was slumped to one side, his chin resting on his hand, and his breathing was laboured. She crossed to his side and knelt beside him.

'Did you enjoy yourself?' he asked.

'Yes, thank you,' she replied. 'I had not expected to, but Malati planned it all so well, and the fireworks and entertainments really were spectacular.'

'I'm glad,' sighed Ramohun. He struggled to sit in a more upright position. 'As you can see, things don't go well for me.'

'You do look ill,' said Anjana. 'Would you like to see a doctor now?'

Ramohun shook his head. 'There's nothing anyone can do for me,' he said. He did not turn to look at his young wife as he spoke. 'Anjana, I think I am dying.'

Anjana had never been interested in Ramohun's welfare, and she had not spared him so much as a passing thought whilst she had been with her sister, even though she had known that he was unwell, but now she stiffened at his words. She focussed her attention on this old man she scarcely knew in spite of their married years together, and for the first time she took note of his flushed cheeks and the bluish tinge of his lips and fingernails. She wished that she could feel something for him, because he had been good to her, but he left her empty inside.

She sighed heavily and Ramohun turned to her. He was not frightened of dying, but he had many regrets, so many unfulfilled wishes and intentions. Sadness and concern for Anjana were etched on his face in heavy lines. Life for a childless widow in India was cruel, and she was still so young. He must write to Vijay and ask him to take care of Anjana for him when he was gone.

The gaiety of the laughing women in the garden began to grate on his nerves. It irritated him to think that they would live on regardless after he was reduced to ashes. Anjana noticed his distress and called for the shutters to be closed. When it was quiet Ramohun dozed a little. Anjana stayed beside him for a while before rising to go to her own quarters. Her movement woke him.

'I want you to do something for me,' he said. Anjana bowed her head in submission. 'I want you to go to the temple and pray for me.'

Anjana's head jerked up in surprise. They rarely attended the temple, and Ramohun's request was as unusual as it was unexpected.

'The temple? Why there? I can pray for you here.'

Ramohun felt a surge of pity for Anjana, and also for himself. He had failed in his duty to please his wife, and notwithstanding the difference in age between them, he had tried to please her. At least, he had tried in the beginning. There was something about Anjana that discouraged intimacy, and he had long ago abandoned any attempt to understand her. Worst of all, he would die without a son. What sin had he committed that the gods should have denied him that for which all men yearned? He sighed again. 'Karma,' he whispered. 'Please do this one thing for me, Anjana.' She nodded her assent, disturbed by the doomed look in his eyes.

The early evening air was filled with the perfume of jasmine and frangipani. In the garden a shadowy figure poured water onto the dust around the house to settle it before the windows could be opened to allow fresh air inside. Anjana was happier when she was away from her home, but this evening she was troubled. For the first time she faced the fact that Ramohun was unlikely to live for much longer, and it dawned on her that her approaching widowhood gave her a certain freedom – not the freedom of having no husband because she was well aware of the pitiful life of widows; but the freedom to do whatever she wished to do until such time as widowhood was thrust upon her. The realisation that she only had a short time for herself focussed her mind on what she could do with that time, be it weeks or only a matter of days.

When she reached the Temple of Kali she stepped out of her sandals and raised a hand to ring the temple bell that would alert the goddess Kali to her presence. Small oil lamps lit the interior of the temple and their spooky light emphasised the eerie atmosphere. Other worshippers performing their individual acts of devotion came and went. Anjana moved into the inner sanctum and joined the throng circling the idol, and then she laid her offerings of money and marigolds before Kali. She squatted in front of the goddess in silent prayer for Ramohun. She prayed that he would have a long life, although this prayer was offered without any desire on her part that it might be answered. She prayed that he would be spared pain, and she hoped in her heart that this prayer would be heard, for the only person on whom she wished any harm to befall was old Mrs Chatterjee. Finally, she offered a fervent prayer for herself.

'Oh Mother, you took away my only son. Now I ask for something in return. Only give me the Englishman with the golden hair and I shall ask for nothing more. If you grant me this one desire I shall submit to your will, and anything else you ask of me shall be freely given.'

CHAPTER 15

Murdo was restless. He could not rid his mind of the beautiful woman he had seen at the nautch. It was well that his duties both on board and ashore were light and required little of his personal time and attention because his thoughts were filled with the scent of musk, the sensuous drape of silk against a graceful body, and a pair of shy almond eyes rimmed with kohl.

The evening was young, but already the doors and shutters which had been closed against the sun all day were thrown open to allow the wind, which always came at this time of day, to blow through all the rooms of the bungalow. Murdo wandered into the garden and the strong wind ruffled his hair, sweeping it back from his face and cooling his brow. The hibiscus, jasmine, rose and oleander bushes provided a riot of colour and filled the air with perfume, but it was not the scent of the musk he so craved, and he was not at peace.

It was the time of day for civilians and the military to parade themselves in their finery; a time to take the air before attending various social entertainments, and Murdo had an hour to fill before he was to dine with Colonel Radcliffe and his lady. He called for his *syce* to bring his stallion and rode without enthusiasm down the Strand, the long broad road that ran by the side of the Hooghly River, close to the hundreds of ships moored midstream. The ghats leading down to the river were busy: some with the Hindu faithful come to perform the rituals of their evening puja, and others with porters carrying merchandise on and off the ships. Murdo joined the Europeans who conducted their own evening ritual on horseback or in buggies and carriages, meeting and greeting friends and acquaintances in a flurry of silk, whalebone and parasols, top hats and tails, and colourful uniforms. He rode past imposing porticoed mansions set in immaculate gardens along the Strand towards Fort William, and he nodded politely to right and left at people to whom he neither knew nor cared whether he had been introduced.

Afterwards, he could not have said what it was that prompted him to turn his horse away from the muddy brown waters of the Hooghly and ride past the racecourse into Kalighat Road. It was not what he would have called a sudden impulse that made him change direction. It was more as if he were being drawn by an invisible thread. It was an irresistible force, and he made no effort to fight it.

He arrived at a temple that was surrounded by worshippers. All humanity was represented there – cripples, beggars, women in colourful saris, men in *dhotis* with their mouths stained with *betel* juice, and sellers of marigolds and paan and sweetmeats. The hubbub was immense and entangled. Murdo was both fascinated and repelled, but he felt an unaccountable urge to go inside the temple. He dismounted and tossed the reins to a boy with the promise of a few annas if he would look after the horse, and then he strode towards the entrance.

'Sahib! Sahib!' The urgent cry came from a skinny old man whose teeth and gums were stained red. He pointed at Murdo's boots and indicated by sign language that he must remove them if he intended to enter the temple. Murdo removed his boots, and the old man set them side by side amongst worn and dusty sandals left in his care. When they reached the top of the steps, worshippers rang the temple bell before going inside. Murdo did as they did.

Black-faced, her tongue hanging grotesquely from her mouth, the goddess Kali is not for the faint-hearted European, and Murdo reeled from the shock of such hideousness. Kali is possessed of four arms. In one hand she holds the head of a demon, in another a sword, and her remaining pair of hands is raised to bless her followers. Dead heads hang from her earrings, skulls form her necklace, and a girdle of human hands encompasses her body. Beneath her feet lies the body of her husband, and her three eyes represent past, present and future. This, then, is the goddess Kali, creator and destroyer, who grants peace to all who worship her.

Murdo was the more repelled to see the object of his desire in an attitude of silent prayer before the idol, but the ugliness of the one only served to enhance the beauty of the other. Anjana's eyes were glazed and unseeing, her face screened from the light, and Murdo waited, scarcely daring to breathe lest he should startle her.

She knew that he was there. She had known the instant he set foot inside the temple that Kali had heard her prayer. Her heart drummed against her ribs as she came out of her trance. After a moment she turned round and smiled at him, knowing full well that she was taking the first step on a dangerous path that would lead to her doom. With that one tentative smile she knew that she had sealed her fate.

Murdo was breathless with pleasure as he returned her smile. Anjana rose to her feet in one graceful movement. She raised clasped hands to her forehead and turned to leave the temple. As she glided past Murdo her musky perfume wafted around her. Murdo followed her outside. She folded herself into her palanquin and he gazed after her as she was borne away. They had not spoken, nor had they arranged to meet again, but each knew that when they did so the path they had chosen would – could – only lead to paradise, heartache and damnation. In a daze of rapture Murdo donned his boots, paid the old man who had guarded them and the boy who had held his horse, mounted and rode away. He was almost back at his bungalow before he remembered his dinner engagement and turned his horse again.

There were twenty seated for dinner. As always there were more gentlemen present than ladies, and Murdo found himself sandwiched between an infantry captain and a magistrate, both of whom had plenty to say and saved Murdo from having to add much to the conversation, but every so often he had to wrench his thoughts away from the woman he desired to answer a direct question.

'I can't think how you men can bear to spend so much of your lives in a wooden coffin on the high seas,' said the captain. 'How do you manage it?'

'The air is fresh,' murmured Murdo in reply.

'True enough,' joined in the magistrate. 'The air here is full of pestilence. It's no wonder that few of us last long. Why so many gentlemen want the memsahibs to come here I can't imagine. They'll either die off in no time or go to seed like Mrs Atkins down there next to Colonel Radcliffe, or they'll go mad. Mrs Atkins can't be more than twenty-five and looks more like fifty. Better they all stay in Blighty. Then we can amuse ourselves with the local beauties to our hearts' content, what?' He belched, winked and nudged Murdo in the ribs. 'Have you lifted the veil yet?'

Murdo felt his face redden, but the captain and the magistrate did not notice. They began a discourse across Murdo on the joys of the local women and their skills in the arts of love.

'Well, Captain Nicolson,' said the magistrate to Murdo when the captain paused to draw breath. 'Whatever they say about the Kama Sutra, it ain't possible, dear boy. Believe me, I've tried it. Only the gods. Only the gods – more's the pity, what?'

Murdo left the dinner party at the earliest opportunity. He sat up half the night in contemplation, but not once did his thoughts turn to the wife and child who waited patiently in London for his return. He thought only of the beautiful Indian woman who had cast a spell over him. He dismissed any concerns for the differences in their customs and beliefs. They did not matter to him nor, he believed, did they matter to her, and, in any case, he had already renounced his religion. He was vaguely aware that she would lose caste if they embarked on an affair, but he was ignorant of the implications of that loss. All the men he knew who had had affairs with local women had been with followers of Islam as it was more difficult to meet Hindus, so he had not heard the matter of caste mentioned except in passing. However, even if he had known that discovery would condemn Anjana to a wretched existence on the very edges of society, friendless and penniless, he would still not have fully understood and, not understanding, he would not have stepped back from the brink to protect her from such a fate. He loved and wanted her, and that was all that mattered to him.

Anjana returned home from the Temple of Kali with her mind full of schemes designed to bring about another meeting with the sea captain. She gave no thought to the risk to her own position even though she knew that he would have to leave her and return to England where she assumed he must have a family waiting for him. She cared nothing for such things. She knew only that she loved him, and that a few days spent alone with him would help her to face the rest of her life. She had every intention of grasping a few hours of happiness before the death she saw looming ever closer.

Anjana and Ramohun sat together in their lamp-lit garden listening to the tinkling of the fountain and the plop of the goldfish in the water. Anjana's serene expression was in marked contrast to her habitual mournfulness and it did not pass unnoticed by Ramohun. He thought that Anjana must have received some personal comfort from her visit to the temple and so he encouraged her to go there again.

'Would you pray for me at the temple every day?' he asked. 'It brought me peace knowing that you had offered prayers for me there today.'

Anjana shrugged. 'If that is what you wish me to do then of course I will do as you ask.'

Ramohun frowned in irritation. He had offered Anjana an olive branch and she had spurned it. Damn the woman. He had tried his best. What was wrong with him? What was it about him that she maintained such an air of total indifference towards him? He hungered for some display of feeling from her – hatred if she could not love, even pity or sympathy now that he was dying. Anything would be preferable to her utter lack of emotion. Was he some sort of monster? Or was she?

He was suddenly angered by her presence. 'Go,' he said, waving a dismissive hand at her. 'Go back to your sister and stay there.'

Anjana turned to him. Ramohun looked ill and she could almost feel sorry for him this evening. 'If you really are dying, I should stay here with you,' she said.

Her unexpected concern surprised Ramohun, but it was too late now. He had lived too long in isolation from Anjana.

'I cannot stand to look at you any more,' he sighed. 'And I don't want you here when I die. I shall send for my mother to be with me. Just go away and leave me alone.' He turned his back on Anjana and she withdrew.

If Anjana had harboured any misgivings as to the course she was about to take, she did so no longer. Ramohun had unwittingly provided her with the perfect solution: he would think that she was with Malati whilst her sister would believe her to be at home with him; and all the while she would be in paradise with Captain Murdo Nicolson. The arrangement was perfect. It was meant to be. It was karma. She went to her quarters and changed into the white muslin of the common people, and then she slipped out of her home.

Murdo had known that she would come to him. When the bearer ushered Anjana into his presence, Murdo rose to greet her. He scarcely recognised her in the simple clothes and yet she was even more beautiful than he remembered. Her luminous black hair hung in a thick plait down her back and she wore the red bindi mark on her forehead. The bearer withdrew, silently closing the door behind him so that they were left alone. It was Anjana who spoke first.

'For us there is no past and no future, only the present,' she said in a low voice. 'We must live for the now because it is all we have.'

Murdo did not know how to answer this woman who offered herself to him, and whom he desired with every fibre of his being. She stepped towards him, close but not touching. He could smell her perfume; feel the warmth of her body and her breath against his face as she gazed up at him. They stood for some time, not moving, just gazing deeply into each other's eyes, and their desire smouldered into blazing passion until they trembled beneath their self-imposed restraint. Murdo could stand the intensity no longer. He held out his arms to her and Anjana stepped into the heat of his embrace. They drowned in each other's sensuality.

In the dewy early morning light Anjana's face was still flushed with excitement. Murdo had unleashed a capacity in her for shameless eroticism and all her pent-up feelings of frustration were set free; and Murdo knew that he had found that unknown something that had been missing from his life. The strange, irresistible attraction he felt for Anjana stirred the whole of Murdo's being to its very depths, and the chilling numbness left his heart. But in falling so deeply in love they both knew that they had crossed an invisible divide and could never go back. They had given themselves totally and unreservedly for all time.

A chink of sunlight through the shutters fell across Anjana's body and Murdo traced its straight line with his finger. She opened her eyes and smiled lazily into his, and once again they were lost to all but themselves; locked in their precious world of love.

For almost three months Murdo and Anjana lived only for each other. They lost all sense of time as lazy days of delight dissolved into nights of burning passion. There was no other world outside the bungalow, only this place and this moment in time for evermore.

CHAPTER 16

Malati was in the garden playing with her sons when the bearer came onto the veranda with a letter. He stood silently in the shadows and waited for her to notice him. Rakesh and Arun chased after one of the peacocks, which managed to strut two steps ahead of them in regal iridescent blue and turquoise whilst Rashid, having newly found his feet, tottered and tripped several yards behind. The baby slept on Malati's lap and did not wake when she shook with laughter at the antics of her boys. When Malati caught sight of the bearer, she waved him to her side. She took the letter from the tray, and the bearer salaamed and withdrew.

The letter was addressed to Anjana. Malati stared at it in surprise, not understanding why it should have been sent to her house. She signalled to the ayah to watch over the children and took the letter inside to her husband. Vijay looked up from his business correspondence and shook his head in bewilderment at the letter.

'Why would anyone write to your sister at this address?'

'I don't know,' replied Malati.

'She isn't here, is she?'

'No, she went home a few days after the nautch. That was weeks ago. It's not like her to stay away from me like this.'

Vijay scratched his head. 'That's very odd.' He summoned the bearer. 'Where did this letter come from? Who brought it here?'

'A servant from your uncle's house came with it a few minutes ago.'

Vijay frowned. 'You may go,' he said. The bearer glided silently away.

'Anjana can't be at home then,' said Malati. 'But where can she be? The letter might be important.'

'Well, my uncle obviously thinks that she is here. I know that your sister is a strange woman, but I would not have expected her to leave home. Where would she have gone?'

123

Malati shrugged her shoulders helplessly. 'I can't imagine,' she said. 'It's not like Anjana. She would come here if she were troubled. Perhaps something has happened to her. Maybe we should call the police.'

The truth hit her with a sickening blow and she was suddenly afraid. There was only one place Anjana would have gone willingly. Malati's hands flew to her face and she paled with the shock of it. Vijay looked at her with suspicion.

'You know, don't you?' he said. 'Where is she?'

'I don't know for certain,' whispered Malati. 'But I can guess where she is. You will be appalled.'

'Why? Where has she gone?'

'I think she might be with that sea captain. The one who came to the birthday nautch.'

Vijay cast his mind back. 'I don't remember.'

'The one with the golden hair,' said Malati.

'Captain Nicolson?' Vijay's jaw dropped in disbelief. 'She wouldn't. She couldn't. I thought he was a gentleman.' His mouth set in a grim line. 'I shall kill them both,' he growled.

Malati laid a restraining hand on his arm. 'I could be wrong, Vijay, but if I am right Anjana has gone to him because he is the only person in the world who can make her happy.'

Vijay shook her off. He was scandalized and needed a few minutes for the full horror of it to sink in. He slit open the letter, read it and passed it to Malati.

'We must send her a message immediately, but if your sister is with the Englishman I will not have her in this house again. She has made herself an outcast.'

'But Anjana is dear to me,' protested Malati. 'Whatever she has done I could not bear it if we were parted forever. Please don't cast her out, Vijay. If you know where the captain is staying send a message there to tell her about her husband, but let's not decide her future right now.'

'Future? What future? If she had remained true to my uncle then I would have welcomed her into our family, but not now. Now she will be a widow like any other, unwanted and an affront to society.'

'You are too cruel,' cried Malati. 'What sort of a life has she had? Married to an old man when she was still a child. If she is with the captain, then I am glad for her. I'm glad that she has been able to find a measure of love at last.'

Vijay strode from the room leaving Malati in tears. She collapsed into a cushion and buried her face in its softness.

'Anjana, Anjana, what have you done?' she wept.

Anjana did not need to open the letter to know what it contained because she had long expected it. It must have been Malati who had guessed where to find her, and she knew that it must have cost her sister dear to reveal her secret. But it didn't matter any more. It was over. The dream had ended, and the nightmare was about to begin. She went to Murdo with tears glistening in her eyes.

'My husband is dead,' she said quietly. 'I must go home.'

Murdo pulled her towards him and held her close. He kissed away her tears, not realising that they were shed for him.

'Shall I come with you?' he whispered into her hair.

'You must not.' Anjana held her hands to Murdo's face and gazed deeply into his eyes. 'Whatever happens, you must believe me when I tell you that I love you more than life itself,' she said. 'I will always love you.'

Murdo stroked her hair. He smiled gently. 'I love you too, my dearest one, more than words can say. A day or two apart may seem a lifetime, but it is only a matter of hours. Go and do what you have to do. I will wait here for you to return to me.'

A cold shiver of fear ran down his spine. 'You will come back to me, won't you? If you don't, I shall search for you to the ends of the earth for I cannot live without you.'

Anjana held him tightly against her, imprinting the feel of him on her body to give her the strength she knew that she would need. Then she was gone. She took nothing with her, and she left as suddenly and as silently as she had arrived. Murdo tried to quell the rising sense of foreboding he felt within his heart. He sat alone, wrapped in emptiness, and waited for Anjana to return to him, counting each second as it passed.

That first night without her was hot and humid, and without a wind it was too warm for sleep. Murdo's thoughts were concentrated on Anjana, and he could not rid himself of the conviction that she was in torment because of her husband's death even though she had told him of her unhappy marriage. Without her presence beside him, the heat, the boom of the cannon and the jagged sound of pariah dogs fighting somewhere in the distance disturbed the peace and tranquillity Murdo had come to take for granted. She will come back to me, he told himself. And yet there was a dreadful, nagging suspicion that she would not.

Anjana left Murdo with the certain knowledge that she would never return. She could only hope that one day his love for her would help him to understand: to understand that she had no choice; to understand that her ways were not his ways. If she had not been so sure of his absolute love for her she would not have been able to follow the path she had chosen, the consequence of which she feared might cause him to lose his mind or turn his love to hatred. But she was sure of his love and his love gave her strength, and one day, one day in the bleak and lonely future, Murdo would understand because of that love.

No sooner had Anjana stepped across the threshold of her home than old Mrs Chatterjee flew at her, tearing at her hair and her clothes, and clawing at Anjana's face.

'Where have you been, you worthless good-for-nothing?' she screeched. 'What have you been up to while your husband lay dying?'

Anjana ignored the old lady. Malati, who had been sitting and waiting with Ramohun's mother for Anjana to return, rose from her seat.

'I must talk with you,' she said. 'Alone.'

Anjana led the way to her quarters. Malati faced her sister, distressed and anxious, but Anjana had already retreated into her own inner world.

'I guessed where you would be,' said Malati. 'I don't know what to say to you. Vijay is so angry. He won't let you come and live with us. You are to be an outcast. Oh, Anjana, whatever made you do it?' She collapsed onto the bed and wept bitterly.

Anjana's face softened. She sat beside Malati and took her hand, 'I'm sorry to have caused so much trouble,' she said. 'But you must not concern yourself about me. I won't be an outcast.'

Malati sat bolt upright, her tear-stained face stricken with horror. 'Surely you're not going back to him?'

Anjana shook her head. Her face was sad and she spoke in a whisper. 'I don't expect you to understand, dear Malati, but in the past few weeks I have lived a whole lifetime of happiness such as even you could not comprehend. I have given and received more love than anyone has a right to expect in this cruel world. My only fear is that he may not be able to

126

understand why I am going to do what I must. And my only regret is that I shall end our baby's life with my own. I doubt if he would ever accept that, so you must not tell him when you carry out my last wishes.'

Malati stared at her sister with horror as it dawned on her what Anjana intended to do. 'You can't, Anjana,' she gasped. 'It is too awful. For pity's sake, don't do it.'

Anjana smiled, which chilled Malati to the core. 'I can do it, and I must,' said Anjana. 'I am doing it to set him free. I have to let him return to his own life or he may come to hate me in years to come. If I had not foreseen this ending for me I would not have gone to him, even though my heart would always have been his. I began this with my eyes open, and I shall not shirk from its ending.'

She moved towards a carved cabinet beside the window. She opened one of its doors and removed a sandalwood casket.

'This is what I want you to do for me when it's all over,' she said. 'Captain Nicolson has a young daughter and I want you to give him this for her. It is my gift to his daughter, so he must take it. Tell him that it is for Lexy.'

Malati trembled as she took the casket, marvelling that her sister could remain so calm in the face of the terrible death she had planned for herself. 'I promise I will do as you wish,' she said.

CHAPTER 17

In the heat of the east funerals must follow swiftly after death, so as the blood red sun went down only hours after Ramohun left this world for the next, his funeral procession moved towards the cremation ghats on the banks of the River Hooghly. His body, covered with a red shroud, was carried on the bed on which he had died. Friends and relatives joining the procession added more shrouds, some of which would be burned with Ramohun, others given to the poor. Near the end of the column someone banged on a drum, which helped Anjana ease herself into a state of detachment from her surroundings. No one in the streets paused to look at the sad procession – death was all too commonplace to arouse even the mildest curiosity.

Before they left the house, Malati offered Anjana a small bottle. 'Drink this poppy juice, Anjana,' she urged. 'It will help you.'

But Anjana refused the opiate. She had no need of its narcotic spell.

The pile of sandalwood was large, for Ramohun had been a rich man. His closest relatives lifted his body from the bed and immersed it in the river through which the holy waters of the Ganges flow. After purification Ramohun's body was placed on the funeral pyre. The moment had come. Anjana turned to Malati and clasped her hands.

'Farewell, my dearest sister,' she murmured. 'Don't mourn for too long, and please take my gift to Captain Nicolson. I am relying on you.'

Malati's eyes filled with tears. She nodded silently, unable to speak for sorrow, and she watched aghast as Anjana climbed onto the pyre. Until this moment Malati had not really believed that Anjana would go through with what she had planned. There was a collective intake of breath as the mourners realised what they were about to witness.

Dressed in simple white muslin Anjana sat beside her husband's body, but she did not touch him. She took a deep breath and stared straight in front of her. She was not afraid to die this way. Death meant nothing to her, and she had known that she would become *sati* the moment Ramohun had told her that he was dying.

As he was Ramohun's closest male relative, Vijay took a brand of wood and set it alight. He walked right round the funeral pyre before touching the lighted brand to it. The sandalwood spat and spluttered into flames. Anjana prayed silently to the goddess Kali.

'I thank thee, Oh Mother, for granting my desire. I take all blame upon myself for what we have done.'

A light breeze fanned the flames. The material draped around Anjana's body flared, but she did not flinch. When the fire engulfed her, her final thoughts were of Murdo.

'I am with you, my beloved. Always and always I shall be with you.'

Malati watched her sister's self-immolation with mounting horror. She wanted to scream at her to stop doing this dreadful thing but mingled with her revulsion was a sense of pride and admiration. In tune with the pulsing atmosphere around her, Malati paid tribute to Anjana's courage and the calm manner in which she faced her death. But there was pity, too, for the unborn child.

Malati, Vijay and old Mrs Chatterjee remained at the cremation site for the three hours it took for Ramohun and Anjana to burn. Old Mrs Chatterjee was distraught.

'I misjudged her,' she cried. 'I never believed that she loved my son. I was wrong to treat her so badly, because she must have loved him dearly to have burned with him.'

When it was over Vijay scattered the ashes in the river. Malati stood by the ghat and tore at her hair. And drums beat a tattoo for Anjana. In her lifetime she had been as nothing, but by becoming sati Anjana's name would live for evermore in glory and honour.

'Sahib.' The bearer shook Murdo from his reverie. He had slept in a cane chair on the veranda, drifting in and out of sleep because of the heat.

'What is it?'

'A Mr and Mrs Chatterjee wish to speak with you.'

Murdo was fully awake in an instant. His heart lurched, and he was filled with dread. The diamond merchant would have come alone if he had wished to see him on a matter of business, but if his wife were with him it could only mean one thing – they had come to speak to him about Anjana, and he could feel himself shrink from what they might say; but they had sought him out and he could not refuse to see them.

'Show them in.'

They were ushered into the sitting room where Murdo joined them. He went through the polite formalities of seating them in comfortable chairs and offering tea, which they declined. Vijay Chatterjee balanced something bulky and wrapped in brocade on his knee. His wife sat with her eyes cast down demurely and with her hands resting in her lap. From the haunting sadness on their faces Murdo knew that they had only bad news to tell him. He shrivelled in his chair, ageing ten years in as many seconds, and he had to fight the tide of despair that threatened to engulf him.

From beneath her lowered lids Malati scrutinised the face of the man her sister had loved so deeply. It had taken all her powers of persuasion for Vijay to agree to her accompanying him on this visit, but after much pleading and argument he accepted that she should be the one to tell Captain Nicolson what he had to know. She sat for several minutes wondering how best to tell him; wondering how well he had really known Anjana and what she had told him of herself; and she agonised over how much of their culture he understood, for that would be crucial to how he would bear the news. All the sentences she had rehearsed so carefully in her mind seemed now to be inappropriate and she struggled with what she had to say, but it was Murdo who spoke first, and he made it easier for her.

'Anjana is dead, isn't she?' His voice was flat, his eyes bleak.

Malati nodded in reply. 'I am very sorry.'

'I feared so,' said Murdo. 'What happened to her?'

Malati paused only long enough to take a deep breath. 'What I am going to tell you is going to cause you much pain,' she said. 'My sister was certain that you would understand and that you would forgive her, but I doubt if you will and that concerns me greatly. I doubt if any European is capable of truly understanding Hindu customs.'

Murdo frowned. Something about what Mrs Chatterjee was saying did not sound right. What was all this about understanding and forgiveness?

'What is it that you are trying to tell me, Mrs Chatterjee?' he asked.

'Did you know that my sister was married?'

Murdo nodded. 'Of course. She left yesterday because her husband had just died. I don't see what that has got to do with it. What has happened to Anjana? Has there been an accident?'

Malati ignored the question. 'Her husband died of heart problems. His health had been failing for some time and his death was not unexpected. Life for a widow in India is cruel, Captain Nicolson. Unwanted and never allowed to remarry, Anjana would have had to exist on the very edges of society. She made herself an outcast when she became involved with you, and I'm afraid we could not have taken her into our home as we would otherwise have done. Anjana knew what she was doing, and she took the only course open to her. Her end was honourable.'

Murdo's heart pounded with horror. 'Are you trying to tell me that Anjana took her own life? That her death was not an accident?'

'She became sati, Captain Nicolson.'

The words reverberated around the room. Murdo sprang from his seat and reeled across the floor, scattering furniture and breaking ornaments as he went.

'*Sati?*' He was appalled. '*Sati*! Oh, my God. My God. She burned herself alive?'

Malati gazed at him with pity. Anjana was wrong: this man could never understand or accept what she had done. Murdo's head throbbed and he felt physically sick. How could he ever bear it? To lose Anjana was worse than to have lost his own life, but to lose her in such a manner!

'It's barbaric,' he shouted, desperately trying to quell the bile rising in his throat. He stared at the Chatterjees but only saw how unreadable the expression was in their foreign eyes. The full beauty, the mystery and the violence of India exploded in his mind.

'Christ!' he said bitterly. 'What a country. What kind of people are you?'

'It is our custom,' said Malati quietly.

Murdo sat down again and his face was sullen. 'Well, I know that she did not sacrifice herself for her husband,' he said. 'I also know that she would not have sacrificed herself for our sin. The sin was not so very great, after all. So why did she do it? She must have known that I would not have forsaken her.'

'It was a sacrifice for life, Captain Nicolson – your life. She died to set you free. She knew that you must return soon to your country and your duty to your family, and she fully accepted her fate. She knew that she had to do what she did or she and the child…' Malati gasped and clamped her hand to her mouth, horrified that she had inadvertently divulged Anjana's secret.

Murdo's face was ashen and he shook violently. 'Child? You mean that Anjana was carrying my baby? God forgive me. What have I done?'

He lowered his head and buried his face in his hands. He was overcome with sorrow, and a deep sense of shame pervaded his soul. Shame was quickly replaced with loathing: loathing for the act of sati that had robbed him of the woman he loved, and loathing for the crime Anjana had committed in killing their child.

Malati spoke again. 'I hope that you will be able to forgive my sister in time, Captain Nicolson,' she said. 'Be proud of her because what she did took great courage.'

Murdo glared at Malati and she recoiled from the hatred in his eyes. 'Proud?' he snarled. 'I can feel no pride. I can feel only shame and disgust. Please do not misunderstand me, because I shall never forget Anjana. She has my heart and my love until the day I die, but you are right in thinking that I will not be able to understand or forgive what she has done.'

He stood up and bowed to the Chatterjees. 'Thank you for coming in person to tell me about Anjana. I am very sorry for the hurt I have caused your family.'

Vijay and Malati rose to take their leave. 'There is one final thing,' said Malati. She took the package from her husband. 'Anjana asked me to give you this.'

Murdo shook his head. 'Take it away. I need no reminder of her.'

'It is not yours to refuse, Captain Nicolson. It is a bequest from my sister to your daughter, Lexy. Please do not insult Anjana's memory by spurning her gift.'

Murdo shrugged and Malati placed the package on a table. 'As you wish.'

The moment the front door closed behind them Murdo groped his way to his room, blinded by tears. With an animal cry of pain, he threw himself down on his bed to begin the agonising journey that leads from shock to acceptance. He was fortunate that it was only days before he sailed from Calcutta, homeward bound, never to return. The duty of command would help him through the early days of his torture.

When the *Brochel Castle* began its journey down the River Hooghly, a solitary seabird flew to the top of the tallest mast and stayed there until they reached the sea. Then, with a plaintive cry, it spread its wings and soared into the blue above. It flew back in the direction they had come, and it took Murdo's lost and lonely soul with it.

Anjana had not set him free. She had bound him to her for evermore.

CHAPTER 18

The Isle of Toronsay shuddered in the teeth of a gale. With no trees to hinder its momentum the wind shrieked across the land, driving the rain in horizontal torrents before it and sweeping away everything in its path that was not fastened to the ground. It beat against the humble black houses and forced rain through gaps in their stone walls. Out of doors there was no life to be seen: even the seabirds had sought refuge from the storm. Murdo had returned to his roots, and now he lived with Miriam and Lexy in the wretched dwelling that had once belonged to Mad Bella. It had been very different when they had first arrived on Toronsay and taken up residence in Murdo's boyhood home.

On the long voyage from India, Murdo began to come to terms with the tragedy of Anjana. On good days his heart ached with pity for her. On bad days his terror of the hellfire he would have to endure for his part in her dreadful act of sati overwhelmed him and he cowered in his cabin, sick at heart. On those bad days he was consumed with guilt and sorrow. In the bitterness of his soul he could hate Anjana then; but he had loved Anjana dearly once, and as the rawness of the wound began to heal it was his love that brought him out of the darkness of his grief. During the long blue days at sea, and under the infinite night sky, Murdo learned to forgive Anjana. He knew that he would never be able to forgive himself, and his regret for her loss lay too deep for tears. Her death was his punishment for straying from the straight and narrow path that would have led to his salvation. His penance would be to devote the rest of his life to the service of the Lord.

Murdo's announcement within days of his homecoming that they were to move to Edinburgh so that he could attend the university there took Miriam by surprise, but it offered her a glimmer of hope. She had been shocked to the core by the change in Murdo. He had aged, and his eyes held a vague and distant look that shut her out. Far from sweeping Miriam into his arms after their long separation, Murdo shunned all physical contact. Unused to prying, Miriam tried on several occasions to muster the courage to ask what troubled him, but he had become so bleak and forbidding that she was frightened into silence. She guessed that he had become involved with another woman, but that was almost inevitable when so much time must be spent away from home. It was hardly something to cause a permanent estrangement, so Miriam could only hope and pray that a new life in Edinburgh would bring peace to Murdo, and that he would become once again the man she had married.

A few days before they left London, Murdo paid a visit to his lawyer. On board ship, when Murdo had gained a measure of acceptance for what was past, he had finally unwrapped the package Malati had given him and had been horrified to find an enormous wealth of jewels inside a sandalwood casket. Had he been in a position to do so he would have returned them forthwith, but by then it was too late. Now, in Ernest Frobisher's office, Murdo checked the drawers were securely locked and pocketed the keys before handing over the casket for safe-keeping. He then wrote on a piece of parchment, which he sealed and handed to the lawyer.

'Is there anything more I can do for you?' asked Ernest Frobisher.

Murdo nodded. 'I shall sell my shares in my uncle's partnership and invest the money. I would like you to draw up a will for me leaving everything to my daughter, and I want it tied up in such a way that it will be hers alone whether or not she marries. I want her to be free. We are moving to Edinburgh in a couple of weeks' time where I am going to study to become a minister in the Church of Scotland.'

Ernest Frobisher raised his eyebrows in surprise and Murdo gave a grim smile.

'It is what I was originally destined for so it's not as great a change in direction as you might imagine. I shall not come to England again and my days at sea are over.'

The lawyer nodded. 'I will have your will drawn up immediately. You may call in to sign it any time before you leave London. I wish you good fortune in your new life, Captain Nicolson.'

To Miriam's dismay the move did not bring about any improvement in her relationship with Murdo. They lived together, but they were isolated from one another. No harsh words passed between them and Miriam voiced no recriminations in spite of the despair in her heart. She devoted her time to Lexy whilst Murdo pored over his books.

Towards the end of his studies, the laird of Toronsay approached Murdo to offer him the position of minister on the island. It was unexpected and Murdo was surprised.

'Is there no minister there then?' he asked. 'What of my father?'

'Did you not know?' said Colonel Iain Henderson. 'Your father killed himself many years ago, and his replacement died last year. There's a missionary on the island just now.'

Murdo showed no reaction to the news of his father's death, nor to its manner. But in a gentler tone he enquired,

'And my mother?'

'She also went a long time ago,' said the laird. 'Some say that she died of a broken heart although I don't believe such things myself. I'm sorry you didn't know.'

Murdo sighed. He had known in his heart that his mother must have died, but the voicing of it saddened him. In his early years after leaving Toronsay he had sent occasional letters home, but he had never received a reply. He had last written shortly after his return from the Far East, which was a long time ago. Unexpected nostalgia washed over him, and he realised that he longed for the peace and wildness of the island. It was a place so far removed from the heat and passions of India that he believed he might recover there and learn to live again.

'What do you say to the appointment?'

'Yes, thank you,' said Murdo. 'I'd be glad to accept. It was kind of you to think of me.'

'Well, when I heard that you were at the seminary it seemed the obvious solution. Not easy finding a minister for Toronsay. Few people want to bury themselves in the islands, and there are not many who have the Gaelic.'

Murdo smiled. 'Mine is a little rusty.'

'Aye, well, it will come back quick enough. It's not an easy language to learn from scratch when you are an adult.'

Miriam had not wanted to go to the Hebrides. She did not want to leave civilisation behind to live amongst strangers who spoke an alien tongue, nor did she want Lexy to live the life of a country woman instead of gracing the ballrooms of society when she grew up. But she was Murdo's wife, and wherever he went she would have to go too; so she held her tongue whilst seeds of bitterness took root within her heart.

They sailed to Toronsay on a beautiful, calm day that emphasised only its good points. Morag opened the door to them. She had never married and still kept house at the manse. She welcomed them with a broad smile and fussed over Murdo.

'Come away in. Sure, I never thought to see you again. My goodness, how you've grown. And is this your wife and wee girl? I saw the boat, so I've got the kettle on.'

Murdo could not but laugh at Morag. 'Miriam, this is Morag, the angel of the manse. Morag, meet my wife Miriam, and my daughter Lexy.'

Miriam smiled at Morag. She had not understood a word of what had passed between her and Murdo, but the warmth of Morag's welcome together with the smell of fresh baking that wafted through the manse lifted her spirits. She sniffed the air, which set Morag off again.

'I've made oatcakes for you. I hope you will like them. They were always Master Murdo's favourites. I put them on the griddle as soon as I saw the boat, chust.'

'Thank you, Morag,' said Murdo. 'I'm sure they will taste even better than they used to after so long without any.'

'Go on with you,' laughed Morag. She bustled out of the room, breathless with delight.

As she listened to the exchange between Murdo and the angel of the manse, Miriam wondered if she would ever be able to learn the Gaelic with its unfamiliar pronunciation. She removed her bonnet and went to the window. The land sloped gently down to the sea and promised an ever-changing view from the parlour. She ran her hand over the polished furniture and stopped in front of a painting.

'Where is this?'

Murdo frowned. 'I've never seen it before.'

This was true inasmuch as he had not seen the painting before, but he recognised the scene as being the old cairn where his brother Finlay had come to grief. Finlay, and now he himself, and all for the love of a woman. What a mess we humans can make of our lives, he thought.

'Let me show you the rest of the manse,' he said. 'Don't worry too much about the Gaelic. You'll be surprised at how quickly you will pick it up when it's all you hear, and there are a few people here who speak English – at least, there used to be.'

Miriam was pleased with her new home. She sat with Lexy drinking warm, sweet milk and eating oatcakes whilst Morag looked on with a satisfied smile on her face. Murdo went out.

'I won't be too long,' he said. 'There is something I must do immediately, and I must go and see my brother and sister.'

Morag hurried after him, but she was too late, and Murdo was halfway up the lane before she reached the gate. Miriam did not ask to accompany him. She would meet his family in time, but for now she was content to let Murdo go and catch up on his past.

Murdo went straight to the kirk. Nothing had changed in there. It was as if he had never left the island, which was uncanny. Afterwards he went to the schoolhouse, only to find that Elspeth and Torquil no longer lived there. The present schoolmaster had only been in his post for three years and had no knowledge of the McBeths or their whereabouts, so Murdo made his way to Paddy McQuigg's house and knocked on the door. It was not Paddy who opened it, but a man a few years younger than Murdo.

'I'm looking for Paddy McQuigg,' said Murdo. 'I'm Murdo Nicolson, the new minister.'

'My uncle isn't here. You'd be wasting your time anyway as he wasn't a religious man.'

'Wasn't?' said Murdo, noting the past tense. 'Has something happened to him?'

'Who is it?' called a voice from inside the house.

'You had better come in. My aunt is here. I'm Seamus McQuigg.'

Murdo followed him into a clean, simple room with a peat fire burning in the centre of the floor. Smoke curled up through a gap in the thatch. A litter of children stared open-mouthed at the golden-haired stranger. Murdo stepped forward and clasped Catriona's hands in his.

'Ciamara tha?' she said. How are you?

'Ciamara tha?' replied Murdo. 'I don't know if you will remember me, and I apologise for my poor Gaelic. It's been a long time since I've had need of it.'

Catriona slipped easily into English. Paddy had never learned the Gaelic.

'Of course I remember you,' she said. 'It's good to see you again. Paddy often wondered what had become of you. We lost him last year. He didn't return from a fishing trip, so we assume that he drowned. Life sure is dull without his noise and bluster.'

Murdo looked stricken. 'I am so sorry, Mistress Catriona. How have you been managing?'

'We're all right,' she replied. She motioned to the oldest girl to pour tea for Murdo. 'Life's a struggle, but then it always was. You've become a minister after all then? Your father would have been pleased.'

'I didn't do it for him,' said Murdo. He reached into his shirt and pulled out the small pouch Paddy had given him years earlier. He passed it to Catriona. 'Paddy gave me this on the day he took me to Skye,' he said. 'I never had the need to use it and I wanted to return it to him. Now it is yours. Take it. It will help you.'

Catriona McQuigg looked inside the pouch and gasped. 'Paddy never had so much money in his life, Murdo. It is very good of you, but you must take it back.'

'You didn't know about it?' Catriona shook her head.

'Truly, it was Paddy's,' said Murdo. 'It was his good luck charm and it became mine, but I have no need of it now. Please take it and use it. Use it for the bairns if you won't spend it on yourself.'

Catriona took the pouch containing the gold sovereign. 'Fancy Paddy having such riches and I never knew,' she said. 'You are a kind and honourable man, Murdo Nicolson. Bless you.'

'Can you tell me where I might find Elspeth and Finlay?' asked Murdo.

'They aren't here any more,' said Catriona. 'When folk were being displaced to make way for the sheep, Elspeth and Torquil decided to emigrate to America with some of the others. Your mother had passed away by then. Oh, you probably don't know that Finlay married Sadie MacLeod in the end.'

'What?' gasped Murdo. 'He married Sadie?'

Catriona nodded. 'Their lives were made very difficult after the bairn was born. They were shunned. You know how narrow-minded folk can be. They married when their daughter was about five years old.

And believe it or not, they were happy together. Then, when Elspeth and Torquil decided to leave Toronsay, they threw their lot in with them. God knows if they reached America. There's been no word from them or any of the others and it's been a long time now.

When he left the McQuiggs, Murdo went to the graveyard. Someone had placed a simple marker at the head of Lachlan's grave. Murdo was unable to feel any sorrow for his death. Next to Lachlan's grave was that of his mother's.

Miriam found Murdo there, crouched on the spongy turf and gazing over the burial mounds to the sea. His face was etched with sadness. Miriam pulled her shawl over her head and waited. When Murdo rose and walked towards her Miriam saw the first trace in his eyes of the Murdo she had known: the faintest glimmer of a smile, but then it was gone; the seeds of bitterness in Miriam's heart, sown after Murdo returned from sea, began to sprout.

Murdo's arrival on Toronsay caused apprehension amongst the islanders. They remembered the stern approach to discipline favoured by his father and expected more of the same, but on the first Sabbath of Murdo's ministry his congregation was surprised to see a glaring emptiness where once the cutty stool had stood as a warning to all transgressors. Removing the stool of repentance and locking it away in a cupboard had been Murdo's first act on entering the place from which he had fled in distress as a boy. Even if the stool were to be brought out when occasion demanded its use, the removal of it from the sight of the congregation warmed the islanders to Murdo.

Lexy attended the parish school where she quickly learned to speak Gaelic. At home she helped her mother's struggles with the language, and Miriam tutored Lexy in French and German. The missionary had left a piano behind in the manse when he returned to the mainland, and this was a joy to Miriam and she taught Lexy to play. Their choice of music was severely restricted to the sheet music left with the piano. This consisted mostly of religious works, but there were a few sheets of Bach and Beethoven to provide some variety.

Occasionally they played host to travellers to the islands who strayed to Toronsay, and this was their means of learning what was happening in the world outside. Living on a small island far off the mainland it is easy to believe that the entire universe begins and ends with its own shoreline. By the time the eighteen-year-old Princess Victoria became queen of Great Britain and Ireland in June 1837, the East India Company had lost its trade monopoly, slavery had been abolished throughout the British Empire and the Palace of Westminster had burned down, but news of such events took months, sometimes years, to reach the Isle of Toronsay, by which time they were no longer news at all.

The Nicolson family lived its life on an even keel. There were no peaks of delight, but no troughs of deep unhappiness either. Murdo applied himself to his new calling with a stolid determination, doing penance for his sins, and Miriam learned to accept that she would never regain his love. Lexy was the one bright star of their existence. In the clean fresh air of the Hebrides she grew strong in body and mind, and as she grew she and Murdo had heated debates about his religion. She became a free spirit: different from Toronsay's own children, and without the life that they had known when they were young different from her parents too. She grew up watching the island's womenfolk work in the fields like beasts of burden, and her views on women's place in society were moulded here rather than in the parlours of the wealthy in London.

They could have continued like this indefinitely, but Murdo, used to a roving life of colour and excitement, became restless. He did not consider abandoning his chosen path, but he did begin to question the manner of it. There were two aspects of his ministry that caused him disquiet, and he allowed himself to be so eaten up with irritation over them that he became ever more morose.

Firstly, there was the question of patronage. In common with other ministers at that time, Murdo had received his appointment through the power of the laird. He had thought nothing of it at the time because this was normal practice, but thrust ever more inwards on himself, his intense introspection made him question this method of providing a parish with its minister. It seemed to Murdo that it was unjust to foist someone on a congregation without them having any say in who was appointed to be their spiritual guide. This meant, as in the case of his father, that a parish could find itself at the mercy of a man they could not abide and yet whom they were unable to dismiss.

Secondly, Murdo discovered that he was expected to preach that the *Clearances* were the will of God, when, in fact, God had nothing to do with it. He had no intention of becoming involved with such deceit and hypocrisy, and he became increasingly disenchanted with the Church.

In 1843 Murdo decided to attend the General Assembly in Edinburgh where the whole issue of patronage was hotly debated. Murdo joined with other Evangelicals behind their leader, Thomas Chalmers, all of whom stormed out of the meeting. The bitter row resulted in the Established Church being split, with the protesters forming the new Free Church. Murdo returned home with a clear conscience, only to discover that he and his family were to be evicted from the kirk and the manse. It was to his credit that his entire congregation remained loyal to him, but without an income the Nicolson's future looked bleak.

Colonel Iain Henderson was infuriated by Murdo's defection from the Established Church and he refused to give the islanders permission to build either a new kirk or a home for the evicted minister. The islanders stood by Murdo in spite of the laird. They laboured long and hard to clean Mad Bella's hovel, which had sat empty since her passing some years back. It was made habitable and life continued, albeit in severely straitened circumstances.

Miriam knew nothing of Murdo's wealth, although she did wonder what had become of the fortune he told her he possessed when they married, but something in Murdo's eyes prevented her from raising the subject. If Murdo remembered that he had a fortune salted away he gave no sign of it, and he used none of it to ease their situation. And the seeds of bitterness in Miriam's heart blossomed.

In August and September of 1846 blight destroyed the potato crop and the stench of rotting potatoes extended the length and breadth of the island. Typhus, dysentery and influenza struck the islanders down, and many died. Murdo was busy all hours of the day and night visiting the dying, praying with the bereaved, and issuing supplies of meal to prevent starvation.

The Free Church acted swiftly to limit the scale of the disaster. Emergency supplies of meal were ferried to the islands on board the schooner *Breadalbane*. Local clergy distributed these supplies to all those in need regardless of which church the recipients attended. Miriam and Lexy helped to minister to the sick, providing broth and what simple nursing they could perform. They were constantly hungry themselves, because Murdo insisted on giving a portion of the meal intended for their own consumption to those whom he considered to be in greater need. Miriam and Lexy often went to bed at night with empty, rumbling stomachs.

Lexy learned to hate her father and all he stood for, and they had many an acrimonious exchange of views.

'It's your fault that we are having to live like this,' railed Lexy. 'And it's your fault that we had to leave the manse.'

'I have to do what I believe to be right, my dear,' replied Murdo. 'I cannot preach what my conscience knows to be wrong. We must walk in God's way and obey His laws.'

'But you have added another commandment to the ten He gave us,' she cried.

Murdo raised his eyebrows and smiled. 'And what is the eleventh commandment, my little agnostic?'

'Thou shalt be miserable to the end of thy days,' said Lexy.

CHAPTER 19

On the eve of her twenty-first birthday Lexy sat indoors with her parents. Outside a storm was brewing, but in spite of the cold, wet evening the fire was not lit. It had been laid in preparation for the following day and provided cold comfort for Miriam and Lexy as they listened to Murdo read aloud from the Bible on his knee. Lexy paid scant attention. It was a nightly ritual and she knew the readings by heart after years of hearing them. She was restless and bored with her limited life on the island. Sometimes she recalled a place full of bustling streets filled with carriages, a place she remembered too clearly for it to be the stuff of which dreams are made. She was certain that she had been in such a place once long ago, and she ached to return there: to live somewhere that was alive and vibrant rather than the lonely and cheerless island that was her home.

On the opposite side of the fire from where she sat Lexy could just see her mother's face in the flickering candlelight. Although she was prematurely aged and careworn, there was no mistaking the fact that Miriam had once been a lady of quality. Years of heartache and insufficient food had rendered her pitifully thin, but they had not bowed her straight back or the proud tilt of her head. Lexy often wondered what kind of life her mother had had when she was young, and she marvelled that she had never heard one word of complaint or reproach from Miriam's mouth.

Miriam shivered and pulled her knitted shawl more snugly around her shoulders. However stoical she might appear, she was not impervious to the change in her circumstances. She was acutely aware of the grimy, soot-covered walls which the candlelight mercifully did not reach. Each evening after darkness fell, with just the candle to provide a glimmer of light whilst they said their prayers, Miriam could pretend to herself that she had not sunk so far, but it was a different matter in the cold light of day. Her only regrets were for her daughter. Lexy should be married by now, but Murdo had made no move to find her a husband, and there was no one suitable on Toronsay. Lexy should be having fun; she should be going to balls, dinners, tea parties and the theatre, and yet Miriam knew that 'fun' was a concept that Murdo had either lost or come to see as a sin.

In the candlelight Murdo was clearly visible, from the Bible on his lap to the lock of hair that fell forward onto his brow as he read aloud. He was still a fine-looking man, but he had become stern of countenance, and deep lines ran from either side of his nose to the outer corners of his mouth. He had grown thin like his wife and daughter, and his golden hair was faded and streaked with white. His face possessed no laughter lines, just furrows between his brows, but when ministering to those in distress his piercing blue eyes would become infinitely tender. Sometimes Miriam caught him in an unguarded moment when he would be lost in contemplation, his eyes betraying a haunted and tormented look, but she no longer cared to ask what caused him such sorrow.

There was a sudden pounding on the door and Murdo slammed the Bible closed in irritation. It was unlikely that anyone would be out of doors on a night such as this without there being an emergency, and Murdo guessed that he would have to brave the weather himself. When he opened the door, the wind blew the driving rain inside together with twigs blown from hardy shrubs. Fergus MacLeod stood on the threshold, drenched to the skin.

'Sorry to trouble you, Minister, but can you be coming at once? It's Wee Archie is dying just.'

'Is that so?' Murdo's voice was calm and quiet. 'Why, I was only sitting with him for a wee while this afternoon. He's dying, you say? Well, the Lord giveth and the Lord taketh away. The Lord's will be done.'

Murdo reached for his cloak and left the house, taking the candle with him and plunging Miriam and Lexy into darkness.

'Why did he have to do that?' Lexy's voice was bitter. 'What possible use is a candle going to be to him on a night like this? Why didn't he leave us the candle and let God light his way?'

Miriam gasped. 'Hush, child, don't mock God. Not ever, or you may have cause to regret it some day. Your father probably took the candle in case Fergus's family don't have one. You can't expect him to sit up all night in the dark.'

'Well, what are we supposed to do? No fire and no light. What sort

145

of a life do we have? I'm going to bed.'

'That's what people do when it gets dark, Lexy. We sat up later than most this evening. Your father is generous with the candles.'

'Yes, I know,' said Lexy, relenting a little. 'I sometimes wonder if he is afraid of the dark.'

'Perhaps he is,' agreed Miriam. She fetched a stub of candle from the cupboard. 'There's enough here to light us to bed,' she said. 'And I have something to give you for your birthday tomorrow. Go to bed and I'll join you in a moment.'

The bedroom, such as it was, was situated at the original entrance to Mad Bella's ruined black house. In those days her milch cow had occupied the room in winter with some of her hens. It was always cold in there, and wind whistled through gaps in the stone walls and cracks in the wooden door. Lexy and her parents slept on rough wooden cots with straw mattresses.

Lexy divested herself of her much-mended dress and crawled beneath an old patchwork quilt. She draped a woollen shawl around her shoulders and breathed under the quilt and blanket to warm her body. Miriam came into the room carrying something that was wrapped in a scrap of velvet.

'Move over,' she said. 'I'll get in beside you and we can keep each other warm.'

Lexy wriggled to the edge of the cot to make room for her mother. They tucked the quilt and blanket snugly around them, and then Miriam handed Lexy her birthday gift.

'This is the only thing of value that I possess, my dearest girl, but I give it to you with all my love.'

Lexy took the small package and ran her hand over the velvet, luxuriating in its silky softness and its tantalising glimpse of another kind of life.

'Go on,' urged Miriam. 'Open it.'

She watched as Lexy unwrapped the velvet to expose an oblong sandalwood box inlaid with ivory and semi-precious stones. Lexy feasted her eyes on it, never having seen anything so beautiful. When she raised the lid of the box she gasped with astonishment, for lying on a bed of black silk was a double strand of pearls with a diamond clasp.

'Oh, Mama,' she breathed. 'How beautiful. I don't know what to

146

say. Thank you so much. It's a wonderful present.' She put her arms round her mother and kissed her cheek. Miriam smiled with pleasure at Lexy's delight.

'It is long overdue that you have something like this,' she said. 'I hope the time will come when you will be able to wear the pearls, but for the time being you must put the necklace away and not let your father see it.'

'Why?' asked Lexy. 'Doesn't he know about them?'

'Oh, yes,' replied Miriam. 'He gave them to me. I don't quite know why he did, and I have a feeling that he would hate to see the necklace again. Don't ask me why because I can't explain.'

Miriam leaned back to rest her head on the wall. She stared at the flickering shadows for a long time, but then she began to talk, and Lexy heard a tale that she found almost impossible to believe in relation to her parents. She could not imagine her mother and father ever having been young once, much less having lived lives full of such drama. Miriam told Lexy how she met Murdo; how they had eloped and sailed to India. Lexy learned that the busy streets she sometimes thought about were where she began her own life, and she was astounded to learn that her father had once been a sea captain with the East India Company, but that he had left the sea for reasons unknown to follow a path he had earlier forsworn.

'My parents never relented. They refused to ever see me again and they never saw you, but I wish that my grandmother had lived long enough to see you. You are so like her to look at. You have the same foreignness, the same colouring, and you are just as beautiful as she was. If you ever saw a portrait of your great grandmother, you would know that I'm not exaggerating. I loved her so, Lexy.'

Miriam wept quietly and Lexy sat in silence beside her. She tried to picture her parents as young people so in love that they ran away together, but she failed. She could not imagine her father as possessed of any real feelings at all.

'Why did your parents cut you off? It seems so cruel,' said Lexy.

'They had far more important matters to concern them at that time to bother with their runaway daughter. My sister, your Aunt Alice, was about to be married, you see. But also, I had brought disgrace on the family and they would not forgive me.' Miriam fell silent again, lost in her painful memories.

Lexy's mind was in turmoil. 'You speak of Father as a happy, carefree man, Mama, but I have only ever known him to be morose and forbidding. I have never known him to be the least light-hearted.'

'But he was, my dear. He was so handsome, so debonair. Now that I have told you this much I may as well tell you the rest.'

Miriam paused and Lexy wondered what else was to come. Her mother had told her so much already, much of which she found hard to believe; what more could there possibly be?

'When you were two years old your father sailed to India again,' continued Miriam. 'We did not go with him because you were so young. It is a long and dangerous voyage, and India is not a healthy country for Europeans, so we stayed in London and he sailed without us.

'Perhaps we should have gone with him, I don't know, but when he returned he had changed so much that I hardly knew him. I thought that he would become his usual self after a while, but it was not to be. Gone was the happy, carefree man that I had married, and in his place was the man you know. I knew that I had lost him in spirit forever, and that is the cross I have to bear for my earlier, wanton behaviour.

'I can accept that I must end my days like this because I made my bed and must needs lie on it, but I do resent the way you are having to live. Sometimes I wonder what dreadful sin your father committed, or thinks he committed, on that final voyage that he should spend the rest of his life crying for forgiveness from his vengeful god: his God who shows no mercy.'

They became aware of footsteps outside as Murdo returned home. Miriam slid out of Lexy's bed and crossed the room to her own. The opening and closing of the front door created a draught throughout the black house, and the guttering candle spluttered out with a final, brave flicker. Lexy snuggled down in the darkness, but all desire for sleep left her as she lay for hours pondering the tale her mother had told her.

CHAPTER 20

After the gale of the previous night, the Sabbath day dawned bright and clear, but this swiftly changed to a surliness that promised rain. Murdo's parishioners gathered on the shore to hear him preach. During the winter months Murdo held his services in Old Fergie Gillies' barn. Old Fergie had been dead for several years and the barn now belonged to his son, but it was never referred to as belonging to Young Fergie. In the middle of May the congregation moved to the beach on Sabbath days. Dressed in black the islanders stood, like a parliament of rooks, facing Murdo. They would stand for a long time on this day because the ground was too wet for any but the most-foolhardy to sit on.

On the Sabbath, Murdo was transformed from a dour, but benign, man to one filled with religious fervour. He stood now and addressed his flock with a zealous light in his eye and an arm raised with a fist clenched as though in anger. He had to raise his voice to a shout in order to be heard above the thundering waves.

'Come, ye children, and hearken unto me. Remember the Sabbath day, to keep it holy. This is the day that the Lord hath made; we will rejoice and be glad in it.'

As he faced into it, the wind that whipped his hair from his face also snatched away his words from the people. They pressed ever closer to hear Murdo forewarning of the deep, dark, bottomless pit that awaited all sinners, and in their eagerness they pushed him backwards to the very edge of the waves.

Lexy watched her father with a pity tinged with contempt, and she listened to his words with scepticism. His message was always the same, the unchanging words repeated week after week. Only they were not his words; they were phrases taken directly from the Bible and uttered as if they were of his own making. Knowing what she now knew about him,

Lexy had the impression that her father lacked any conviction in what he preached. She wondered if he had any real faith at all. He certainly knew his Bible, but he gave no personal interpretation of it, as if he dared not. She thought of her mother's revelations of the night before and was filled with curiosity about her father. She wondered if he had indeed committed some unmentionable sin on his last voyage to India for she wanted to know if this man, so pious and holy, was human like any other. And she indulged in a moment of secret defiance against him and his uncompromising religion, for hidden discreetly beneath her high-necked dress she wore the pearl necklace.

The Sabbath seemed endless and deprived of activity Lexy could have screamed with frustration. When the rain came it was heavy but short-lived and the sun came out once more, but it was forbidden to venture outside. Murdo read from the Bible. Bored to tears Lexy twitched irritably in her chair and her father glared at her for the interruption.

In spite of Miriam's care the previous day the fire went out in the early evening. Standing on the shore that morning in the light drizzle had chilled them all to the bone and now, as the heat from the fire dissipated, their damp clothes became cold and they shivered. Miriam and Lexy huddled together to keep warm whilst Murdo read to them, but they went to bed early that night. Miriam's bouts of coughing kept Lexy awake and in the morning she was concerned to see her mother flushed with fever. In spite of her cough being worse and feeling unwell, Miriam insisted on preparing some broth to take to Effie MacDonald and her children. Never a robust woman, Effie had gone completely to pieces when her husband died unexpectedly some months earlier. She had a baby still at the breast and four other children whom she was neglecting to feed properly. Several of the islanders and her relatives had tried to help, but Effie refused to let anyone enter her black house. Miriam was determined that the children should be fed, but Lexy was concerned for her mother's own health.

'Let me take it, Mama,' she protested. 'You're not well and you should stay indoors with a cough like that. It's going to rain again.'

Miriam refused the offer. 'I'll be fine,' she said. 'Thank you for the thought. It won't take me long, and I don't know what I'll find when I get there so I'd rather you stayed away.'

Miriam picked up the pan of broth and went outside. It was only a short distance across spongy turf to Effie's dwelling, but the path was little better than a muddy stream after all the rain. In the few minutes it took her to walk there Miriam's feet and the lower half of her skirt were soaked. Shivering with cold she banged on the door. When there was no reply she put the pan of broth down and made her way round to the back. A few hungry hens scattered out of her way. Everywhere was a sea of mud and there were no other signs of life. Miriam returned to the door and knocked again.

'Effie! Effie!' she called. 'It's me. Mistress Miriam.'

The abnormal silence worried Miriam and she pushed at the door. It opened on to that part of the dwelling that was normally occupied by the animals. There were none there now, just a few chickens pecking in the dirt, but traces of animals remained, and Miriam trod carefully, although with her hands holding the pan of broth she was unable to prevent her wet skirts from trailing in the ordure.

Mad Bella's old home was a palace compared with Effie MacDonald's black house. Defeated by the soot-blackened interior, all efforts to maintain any degree of cleanliness had been abandoned long ago. No fire burned although partly cured herrings were suspended from the roof above the hearth. The room was cold and dark, and contained only a few items of rickety furniture. The three oldest children sat huddled together against a wall: two girls and a boy. All three were dressed in rags and looked as if they had not been near water for weeks.

'Where's your mother?' asked Miriam.

Three pairs of black eyes slid past Miriam and she turned to follow their gaze.

'Oh, dear God, no,' she whispered. She put the pan down on the table and moved to the corner where Effie lay on the dirt floor. She was wrapped in a tattered dirty blanket, and it was clear to Miriam that she was dying. Her two youngest children, a baby and a toddler, lay beside her, already beyond help.

'Calum,' said Miriam, raising her head. 'You go and fetch Hamish. And hurry.'

The boy had been sitting terror-stricken against the wall and he needed no second bidding. He fled from the black house. Inwardly cursing the absentee landlords whose hold over islanders' lives was such as to render them little more than slaves, Miriam knelt beside the dying woman.

'Effie, can you hear me?' Miriam stroked the matted hair from Effie MacDonald's forehead.

Her touch roused Effie and she turned to look at Miriam with dull eyes. A flicker of recognition crossed her face and her fingers fluttered on the blanket.

'My bairns,' she whispered.

Miriam gazed into Effie's defeated eyes. 'They'll be cared for, Effie,' she comforted. 'Don't fret. Help is coming, and the bairns will be all right. Be at peace.'

Miriam stayed at the dying woman's side for the last remaining moments of her life. When she had breathed her last Miriam closed Effie's eyes and laid her straight. She placed the two dead babies one on either side of their mother and covered all three with the blanket. Then she moved towards the two little girls who had not stirred from their places by the wall.

'Come here, you poor wee things,' she said, and held her arms out to them. They wept silently, and Miriam wept with them.

As soon as Calum returned, Miriam ladled broth into bowls for the children; they spooned it into their mouths so quickly Miriam wondered if they had been fed at all the previous day. Hamish groaned as he looked around the squalid room. He was a cousin of Effie's, a thin, middle-aged man who lived with his wife in the clachan by the shore about a mile distant from Effie's house. He and his wife had repeatedly tried to help Effie after her husband died, if only for the sake of the children, but she had always spurned their offers of assistance.

'Effie has passed away,' Miriam told him. 'Effie and the two babes.' Hamish sank onto a chair and buried his face in his hands. 'I want to ask if you will take the older children into your home and care for them.'

Hamish looked up. He had no living children of his own, all six Jeanette having borne him failing to survive infancy.

'Aye,' he said. 'Aye, that I will. We'd be glad to have them.' He nodded his head in the direction of the bodies under the blanket. 'What took them, do you think?'

Miriam sighed. 'Starvation and pneumonia probably. I don't know. They should not have starved, but it looks as if Effie has given little thought to food since Norman died. What a tragedy.'

'She turned us away,' said Hamish sadly.

'She turned everyone away, Hamish,' said Miriam. 'You must not go blaming yourself. At least you can help her now by caring for her bairns.'

When the pan was scraped clean of broth, Hamish rounded the children up with what little they possessed and took them away. Miriam trudged back home with a heavy heart to tell Murdo. A fine drizzle misted everything, and by the time she reached home Miriam was soaked through and chilled to the bone. Murdo left immediately he heard the news. Lexy fussed over her mother, helping her out of her wet clothes and draping them on furniture to dry. The steam that rose from the drying garments helped to ease Miriam's cough, but by the evening she had become very ill. Her face was hot and flushed, her breathing rapid and shallow.

That evening Miriam lay in her bed and Murdo sat beside her, dabbing perspiration from her forehead. He knew that she would die and then he would have her death on his conscience too. His eyes travelled around the miserable room and he appeared to see it for the first time – the abject poverty in which he had condemned Miriam and Lexy to live when he had the means to alleviate it. For himself it did not matter, but he had chosen not to see the reality in which Miriam struggled to make a home for them because he had not cared enough to look. In devoting his life to God in penance for his sins he had failed in his duty of care to his wife, and now it was too late to make amends. That sin which lay so heavily on his conscience was his sin not hers, and certainly not his daughter's, and yet he had punished them both as if they were equally to blame. They were innocent victims of his need to atone for the past, and he was ashamed.

He leant forward to brush a tendril of hair from Miriam's face. She stirred and opened her eyes.

'Can I fetch you anything?' he asked. She shook her head. 'Miriam, my dear,' he continued. 'I owe you an apology. I have been a poor husband to you for so long. Can you find it in your heart to forgive me?'

Miriam looked into his eyes. Her voice was weary when she answered him. 'The truth is, Murdo, that my heart is dead. I can feel nothing. There was a time when I could have forgiven you anything, but you could not love me enough to confide in me. I have watched you bear a heavy burden without ever knowing what it was, and I have never been able to understand what could possibly have caused you such torment.'

She was racked with another bout of coughing. When it was over

Murdo helped her to drink some warm milk, then he tucked the blanket around her to keep her warm because she was shivering.

'Have you stopped loving me?' he asked. 'I don't think I could bear that because it is only your love for me that has helped me through each grinding day.'

A tear trickled from the corner of Miriam's eye. 'I am your wife, Murdo, and I always loved you. I went on loving you even though when you returned from India I knew that you had stopped loving me. All these years I have known that your heart has throbbed for another whilst mine has bled for you drop by burning drop. Sometimes I wished that I could stop loving you for then I would not have had to suffer the daily torture of your presence, seeing the lack of affection in your eyes. I could have borne your lack of love for me if, just once, you could have spared me a little tenderness. Now it is too late, Murdo. I am sorry, but I have nothing left to give. My forgiveness would be meaningless, but I do pray for you. I pray that one day you will find peace.'

Murdo hung his head in sorrow and in shame. When Miriam drifted into a deep sleep he left the black house and went to the edge of the sea. How hard it had been to shake off his sense of belonging to the sea. How bitter his life had become. Mad Bella's prophecy came into his mind, and he realised with a shock that she had been right. Half his life had been good, but it had been the first half, the time when years flash past as though they were but days: the shortest half, the years full of vigour and life and love. But they had gone all too quickly, to be replaced with the tedious monotony of the second, much longer half of his life, when each day had dragged past, each one a year long in its sadness. He sat on the sand in the dark, his tears mingling with the rain on his face, and the sound of his sobbing blotted out by the wind and the waves.

All that night Lexy bargained with God for her mother's life. In the cold light of dawn, it seemed that her prayers had been heard for Miriam was a little better. Lexy scarcely left her side all day, dabbing her with a cool, damp cloth when the fever was high, and swaddling her in blankets when she shivered uncontrollably. That night Lexy sat beside her mother so that she was on hand should she be needed, but sleep overtook her in the small hours. Exhausted from the hours of tending and watching, Lexy slept deeply. When she awoke it was to find that Miriam was gone: claimed by the pneumonia she had been too weak to fight. Murdo was on his knees beside the body of his wife in an attitude of prayer but unable to find words for either his god or his daughter.

Lexy was filled with grief and guilt, blaming herself for her mother's death. She told herself that if she had not fallen asleep Miriam would still be alive; but she knew that this was not true, and she turned elsewhere to lay the blame. It had been her father's fault that Miriam had died. If they still lived in the manse their health would have been better and Miriam would have been strong enough to fight her illness. A monumental anger arose within Lexy's heart together with hatred for her father.

'How could you?' she stormed at him. 'How could you have reduced her to this after what she once was? Have you no shame?'

Murdo looked at her, his face haggard and drawn. 'I did what I had to do,' he said. 'I cannot tell you the reasons, so I don't expect you to understand.'

'No, I don't understand. I hate you,' Lexy yelled at him.

'You cannot hate me any more than I hate myself.'

Lexy wept bitter tears, and in the depths of her own grief she failed to see her father crumble before her. In his turn, Murdo sat and stared into space, sick in his soul at the futility of his penance, and oblivious to his daughter's distress. Because he shed no tears for Lexy to see she assumed that her father felt no sorrow, but she was mistaken. Miriam's death affected Murdo deeply, but he kept his pain to himself.

CHAPTER 21

The day on which Miriam was to be buried was one of those magical spring days with which the Hebrides can surprise and delight its inhabitants. The sun shone from a cloudless blue sky, the almost motionless sea was a deep blue and there was just the merest hint of a breeze. The machair teased with glimpses of the colour to come, and two grey seals basked on the rocks.

The coffin, draped with a black cloth, rested on two kitchen chairs beside the main door of the black house. Lexy, pale and still, kept vigil beside it. Her face was expressionless. The only way she could cope with this dreadful day was to pretend to herself that she was not really there, and yet she remained acutely aware of everything happening around her. Each time she thought that she had no more tears to shed, another bout of weeping possessed her. On this day there was more keening and lamentation than she could bear. Every man, woman and child on Toronsay came to pay their last respects to Miriam. She had been called upon for help and sympathy by almost every one of them over the years and they had never been left wanting. Miriam's kind heart and willing hands had endeared this very English woman to them all, and the entire island grieved for her.

The black house quickly filled with mourners and they spilled out onto the mossy ground outside. They were all arrayed in their best Sabbath black, which they wore to funerals, weddings and ceilidhs. It was Hamish's wife, Jeanette, who set about boiling water for tea as Lexy was in no condition to do so. While the women supped the tea, Hamish took a small gathering of men, all fortified with giggle-water, to dig the grave. Shona McRae tried to press an oatcake into Lexy's hands. Lexy shook her head, knowing that she would be sick if she tried to eat anything. Thoughts entirely unconnected with her mother filled her mind: why was Shona so stout when everyone else was so thin? And why did the minister from the Established Church shave his side-whiskers?

Shona's husband poured everyone a liberal dram of the local, illicit, whisky and there was more for those who wanted it. Such conversation as there was, was conducted in undertones. There was none of the usual jollity or wisecracking for which Hebridean funerals were noted, perhaps because of the shock of Miriam's untimely death.

Murdo prised himself from a chair in a dark corner and said a short prayer, but it was the minister of the kirk who conducted the short service before a procession formed to accompany Miriam on her final journey.

Six bearers were chosen from amongst the men present, and they would carry the coffin on their shoulders in relays, four at a time. The remainder of the men with Murdo at their head gathered behind the minister and the bearers, and slowly and sadly they made their way to the graveyard.

It was not the custom for women to attend a burial. They stayed behind to give support and comfort to Lexy. Tea flowed freely, and oatcakes and biscuits were wolfed down. Lexy scarcely noticed the subdued chatter or the clacking of knitting pins with which some of the women were busily employed, knobbed ends tucked securely into their armpits.

After the men returned and more whisky shared, they all drifted away to their own homes leaving Lexy alone. Murdo was nowhere to be seen. After a long, lonely while Lexy went to stand at the door and watched the sun as it sank behind Temptation Hill. The blackness of the hillside was softened by purple shadows, and the sea had turned to molten gold. Somewhere, far out to the west beyond the long island, the setting sun would drown in the Atlantic Ocean. Had it not been for Miriam's funeral it would have been a beautiful day.

Before darkness fell, Lexy pulled on her cloak and went for a stroll along the beach. She wondered vaguely where her father could have got to and wished that he would return home. The empty silence indoors was oppressive, and even Murdo's presence would be preferable to the bleakness of their home without Miriam. It was late when Murdo did finally come back and he was very drunk. He lurched into the room and tripped over a chair that was out of its normal place. He was singing one of the psalms they chanted on the Sabbath.

'Bow down thine ear, Oh Lord, hear me: for I am poor and needy.'

He broke off, hiccoughed and began to laugh.

Steeped in her own raw grief, and seething with anger, Lexy failed to recognise Murdo's drunkenness as an indication of his suffering. She directed her helpless rage towards him.

'You disgust me,' she cried. 'Look at the state of you, and Mama just laid to rest.'

Murdo, befuddled with whisky, gazed at the beautiful dark-eyed young woman before him. Buried memories were resurrected in his mind, which began to play tricks on him. Why was the love of his life so angry with him, he asked himself? He had never wanted to hurt her. He raised his arms to her.

'Anjana,' he whispered. His eyes filled with tears. 'Anjana.'

'What? What are you saying?' demanded Lexy.

Murdo did not reply. He was bewildered when Lexy turned on her heel and left him, taking the candle with her and leaving him in darkness. He shrivelled into himself in his confusion. 'Anjana,' he called after her.

Lexy lay awake and listened to Murdo crashing about in the unlit main room until eventually she heard the snoring of the very drunk. Her anger kept her awake for most of the night. The following morning, she kept herself busy by making gruel and a batch of griddle scones, whilst Murdo slept off the effects of the alcohol on the straw mattress he had put in the main room to sleep on after Miriam died. He woke once and got up to go to the midden a short distance away to relieve himself, then he went back to sleep. He stayed there all day, unkempt, unwashed and unshaven. His hair had turned white overnight, his cheeks were sunken and his eyes wild. The place reeked of stale alcohol so Lexy opened the door to allow some fresh air into the room although it was chilly outside. She was staring from the window in the late afternoon when Murdo startled her by calling out.

'Be merciful unto me, Oh Lord, for I will call daily upon you.'

Lexy turned and watched him with cold detachment. 'Yes,' she said. 'You do that. And whist you're at it you might ask His forgiveness for having killed Mama.'

Murdo rolled over and turned his back on her. He stayed in bed the following day and the day after that. He accepted a little gruel, but he rebuffed Lexy's offer of help to wash himself. Lexy alternated between tears and anger, but she also began to feel faint stirrings of fear. Murdo was silent most of the time, but sometimes he cried out and it was pitiful to hear him.

'Oh God, how can I live?' he called, followed by heartrending sobbing.

Two weeks after Miriam died it was clear that Murdo was losing his grip on reality and Lexy found this difficult to cope with. Had he had a physical problem she would have managed to care for him, but the difficulty in communicating with her father made her frightened of him. One evening when she tried to help him drink some tea he knocked the cup from her hand.

'Daughter, listen to me.' His voice was husky. 'It is better to put your trust in the Lord than to put any confidence in man.' He thrust his face close to hers and clasped her shoulder in a steely grip. 'Put not your trust in princes, nor in any child of man; for there is no help in them.'

Lexy pushed his hand away and jumped up in irritation. 'There you go again,' she said. 'More words straight from the Bible. Can't you say anything for yourself? Are you afraid to speak from your heart? Well, I don't want anything to do with your miserable God or your cruel religion. Look what they have done to you.'

Murdo shrank from her. His mind was muddled. Sometimes it was his daughter he saw beside him, sometimes it was Anjana; but whichever it was, she was always angry, and he could no longer endure it.

'It's all my fault,' he muttered. 'How can I live with this burden? The sinning was so easy, the living after it so crushing. Let me die. Oh God, please let me die.'

As Murdo let slip his hold on life Lexy was ashamed to feel so little sorrow for him. She felt only a mild panic as to what would become of her with neither parents nor husband to care for her. In her fear of being left alone she began to make great efforts to look after her father, but he had turned his face to the wall. Less than four weeks after Miriam died, Murdo followed her to the grave. Just before he breathed his last, he uttered a last prayer to his wrathful God before closing his eyes forever. Pressing his bony hands together he humbly begged forgiveness.

'Oh, remember not the sins and offences of my youth; but according to Thy mercy think Thou upon me, Oh Lord, for Thy goodness.'

Lexy sat on the straw mattress beside her father. His final plea stirred pity within her and she wondered what on earth he could have done to be so consumed with remorse that he was fearful of meeting his Maker, whom he had served loyally for many years.

Suddenly Murdo struggled to sit up. He opened his eyes and gazed unseeingly at Lexy's face. A radiant smile transformed his own. 'Anjana,' he whispered. He was dead before his head fell back onto the straw.

Once again Toronsay's entire population assembled for the funeral of a member of the Nicolson family. Lexy was astonished at the outpouring of grief for the passing of her father, but the distant and morose man she knew was not the same Murdo the islanders called on in their hour of need. To them Murdo was quiet and kindly, and their own hardships and sorrows were ever reflected in the understanding sadness in his eyes. They had felt and been encouraged by his sympathy; even his admonitions had been gentle, and so they mourned his loss.

On the day after Murdo's funeral Lexy squatted on the ground beside her parents' graves. It was a beautiful day and the sun imparted an appreciable degree of warmth. Her gaze travelled past seals frolicking in the sea until it came to rest on the distant, louring menace of the Cuillins. She had received several offers of a home with other families, plus four proposals of marriage, and she was trying to reach a decision.

'What am I to do?' she asked the barren mound of her mother's grave, willing her to reply.

The marriage proposals had been made in earnest, but none was suitable. Lexy knew that she should marry; in fact, she wanted to marry and raise a family, but not here, not on Toronsay. She wanted more than the life of a peasant. Somehow she had to find the means to make a new life for herself away from the island, away from the squalor in which she currently lived. If she married an islander her life would hardly change at all, and she wanted more than Toronsay had to offer.

She remembered her mother mentioning her sister in London. Aunt Alice was Lexy's only relative and she knew nothing about her. Perhaps this aunt would help. Encouraged, and with a sense of purpose, Lexy walked home with something approaching a spring in her step. She would write to her Aunt Alice and throw herself on her mercy. All she had to do was find her aunt's address.

Miriam had few possessions, so it did not take Lexy long to find what she was looking for. The address was written on a piece of paper that served as a marker in her mother's prayer book. Lexy was taken aback to see that her aunt was Lady Alice Wickham, not plain Mrs Wickham. Her mother had not told her that.

She turned her attention next to her father's sea chest. This had always been kept locked and Lexy had never been privy to its contents. After a lengthy search she found the key to the chest hidden behind Murdo's Bible. She inserted the key into the lock. Just as she was about to turn the key she suddenly froze in fear: she had the eerie sensation that her father was peering over her shoulder. She swung round, her eyes wide with shock. There was no one there, but Lexy knew without doubt that Murdo's *taibhse* was in the room with her. She could not see the taibhse, nor did she believe in ghosts, but she was no longer alone. Prickles of fear crept up her spine and the hairs on the nape of her neck stood on end. In her superstitious terror Lexy pictured her father standing there accusing her of intruding into the lives of her parents, uncovering their secrets and laying bare their private world.

Lexy lost all sense of time as she sat and tried to conquer her fears, but she gradually came to believe that Murdo's presence was benign. There was no sense of malevolence in the room with her and she had no reason to be afraid of the taibhse. She even had the feeling that it was watching over her, standing sentinel to protect her from harm. She drew an unexpected comfort from the presence, but why the taibhse should be that of the father she hated rather than of the mother she loved she could not understand.

She turned the key and opened the chest. Lying uppermost was Murdo's uniform. Lexy took each item out carefully and shook the uniform free of folds. Suddenly curious, she spread her parents' blankets on the ground and placed the uniform on top. Then she stood back and stared at it, trying to picture her father wearing his uniform. It was difficult as she could not imagine him as a young man, but there was something about the garments that stirred excitement in Lexy's heart. It was the only uniform she had ever seen, and she was touched by its aura of mystery and the tantalising glimpse of the life of adventure lived by a man wearing such a uniform. Oh, to be married to such a man! It was no wonder that Miriam had fallen in love with him.

She returned to the sea chest and removed a length of dark material that was wrapped around something light in weight. Lexy untied the ribbon that fastened it, folded back the cloth, and gasped at what was revealed. Gently she lifted up the most exquisite gown she could ever have imagined: gossamer-fine white georgette, trimmed with a fountain of lace, and in a style totally foreign to Lexy's eyes; there was no mistaking it as the gown in which her mother had been married.

Curious, Lexy stripped off her black skirts and put on the wedding gown. There was no mirror in which to see herself for mirrors were vanities, but Lexy did not need to look in a mirror to know that she looked beautiful. For the first time in her life she felt like a woman of some value: a woman a gentleman of quality might wish to marry.

'And, Mama,' she breathed. 'When I marry I shall wear your wedding gown.'

Lexy put her own clothes back on and folded the gown and uniform carefully. The only other item in the chest was a small lacquered box. She heated some broth and cut some bread to eat with crowdie, the local cheese, and then sat at the table with the box in front of her. She ate her meagre meal while she gazed at the box, wondering where it had come from. It was inlaid with a bamboo pattern in gold leaf, and Lexy guessed that it must have come from her father's voyage to China. When she finished eating, she opened the box. Inside it were two scraps of paper together with seven tiny keys threaded onto a gold chain. Then, with her heart pounding in her ears, she tipped a pile of gold sovereigns onto the table. She counted them – twice.

'Twenty-five sovereigns,' she gasped. 'Why, it's a small fortune.'

Her mind raced ahead. Now she had the means of leaving the island without having to ask for help from Aunt Alice – *Lady* Wickham. But her excitement quickly evaporated and she became bewildered, and then infused with fury as she realised the deeper implications of this hidden hoard. Her blood ran cold. She went to the window and looked out at a fragment of rainbow that drooped over the graveyard.

'You hateful, cruel old man,' she hissed. 'How could you have made us live like this, depriving us of sufficient food to eat and fresh clothes for our backs when you had all this money hidden away? How could you?'

Lexy buried her face in her arms and wept bitter tears of grief for her mother. By the time her weeping was done night had fallen, the fire had gone out and she was alone in the dark. She did not bother to light a candle but felt her way to the other room and went to bed. Bitterness kept sleep at bay, and she tossed and turned for hours.

In the morning she felt better in spite of the lack of sleep. Light rain clouds were dispersing, and the sun was warm. She dressed and forced herself to eat some gruel for breakfast, and then she turned her attention to the scraps of paper she had found in the lacquered box. One scrap was covered with columns of figures that meant nothing to her, but on the other scrap was written the name and address of a firm of lawyers in London. Lexy was rapidly learning that there was more to her father than she would ever have thought possible. She wished that she had asked him about himself when he was alive because there were so many questions she wanted to put to him now that it was too late.

Lexy found nothing for which the tiny keys could be used and was tempted to throw them away, but something stayed her hand. There must surely be a reason why her parents had kept the keys with their precious clothing and the sovereigns. She spent much of the day deep in thought, puzzling over the sovereigns, and finally came to the conclusion that her mother could not have known of their existence. Miriam would not have allowed them to go hungry if there were money for food. No, it was her father's secret hoard, of that Lexy was certain. She just wished that she knew why.

In the evening Lexy wrote two letters. Firstly, she wrote to her aunt to inform her of the deaths of Miriam and Murdo and stating her intention to come to London. She requested that she be permitted to stay until she found employment and accommodation for herself. The second letter was to Messrs Frobisher and Fosdyke of Chancery Lane, informing them of her intention to call on them when she reached London. The next day Lexy booked her passage on the next available steamship to Glasgow.

The number of islanders who came to wave goodbye to Lexy surprised and touched her. Shona McRae pressed a parcel of oatcakes into Lexy's hands.

'A wee bite for you on the journey just,' she said.

'Thank you, Mistress Shona,' said Lexy. 'I will miss you all. You have been so very kind to us.'

Jeanette MacDonald gave Lexy two knitted shawls and Lexy was so overwhelmed by everyone's concern for her future that she was almost tempted to stay on Toronsay with the people she knew rather than face an uncertain future in England. But she couldn't stay. Miriam's wedding gown and Murdo's uniform had opened the door on another, more exciting, kind of life, and Lexy could not ignore the eagerness in her heart. She had to go and find such a life for herself.

There was one final offering, which was of no material value but had a special poignancy. As the boat left the Isle of Toronsay for the Isle of Skye, Iain MacLeod stood on the shore and played his bagpipes. Lexy took the haunting, plaintive melody to her heart. She had turned down his offer of marriage, but she accepted his music as the finest treasure she could have been given.

CHAPTER 22

Lady Alice Wickham sat in her drawing room with Lexy's letter in her hand. She read it through several times before passing it to her husband. She knew that he would be far from pleased and she waited for the storm that would surely follow his reading of the letter. She did not have long to wait.

'No!' he roared. 'No, no, no, I'll not have it. That young woman cannot stay here and bring disgrace on my house. You must write to her immediately to inform her that she is not welcome.'

'That won't be possible,' said Lady Alice. 'My niece gives no address where I can contact her, and she must surely have left the Isle of Toronsay by now. I'm afraid we will just have to await events.'

Lady Alice and her husband stared at each other for a moment from opposite sides of the hearth before he tossed the letter into her lap. Lady Alice read it yet again. She felt a fleeting pang of guilt that her sister had died in that god-forsaken place whilst she enjoyed a life of luxury. She had moved from the protection of a wealthy father to that of an equally wealthy husband and was firmly of the persuasion that poverty was largely the fault of the poor themselves; but now that Miriam had passed beyond the reach of any bounty she might have bestowed upon her, Lady Alice felt embarrassed that she had never extended any help to her sister.

As plain Alice Garthwaite, she had been in earnest when she had told Miriam that she would be prepared to marry a title whatever the man was like. She had done precisely that almost as soon as she left the schoolroom. Sir Edward Wickham was not a pleasant man, but his title was the lure, so she had accepted his proposal of marriage without a second thought.

For Sir Edward the lure had been money. He could never have too much of it, although he only spent whatever was actually necessary; there were no little extras. When he made an offer for the heiress Alice

Garthwaite, he had not really expected it to be accepted. She was barely eighteen and he nigh on thirty-five, but no one else would have him, and he suspected there would be few who would want Alice Garthwaite, money or not, her being such a fool. Nevertheless, married they were, for worse rather than for better.

Sir Edward was of very short stature, a circumstance that had spawned a pugnacious disposition and a permanently discontented countenance. Constant efforts to prove his worth when he was a boy to counter the bullying to which he was subjected had left him bad-tempered, suspicious and overly sensitive to every slight, real or imagined. He comforted himself by overeating, and his clothes bulged with superfluous rolls of flesh. He sported bushy eyebrows above a pair of calculating eyes, and impressive side-whiskers, but he was as bald as a coot. Thanks to his father he was a gentleman of considerable independent means with a fortune earned in the tea trade with China, but he considered himself far from rich, hence his desire to marry money. He did not like women. That is not to say that he preferred men, but he could not bear the idle, inconsequential chatter of females and spent little time in their company.

In the first year of their marriage Lady Alice presented Sir Edward with a son. The following year there was a daughter, and in the third year another son. After James was born Sir Edward decided that he had done his bit for the furtherance of the human race and he no longer visited his wife's bed. Lady Alice was pleased to be relieved of the need to perform her marital duties and delighted when the ugly little man moved into another bedroom. They both got what they wanted from their marriage: Lady Alice had her title, and after her parents died Sir Edward took possession of the Garthwaite fortune; but much good it did them for theirs was not a happy household.

'I don't quite understand why you think that my niece would bring disgrace on our house,' said a petulant Lady Alice. 'Lexy may be poor, but we know of nothing untoward about her.'

'She'll be poor all right,' grumbled Sir Edward. 'And living in the back of beyond means that she is probably illiterate as well. She will have no idea how to conduct herself in civilised society. She'll make me a laughing stock.'

'How can you say so?' Lady Alice's cheeks reddened. 'She may have no experience of grand company, but I see no reason why she should not have been raised with a full sense of decorum. Besides, she implies that her stay with us will not be a long one. She only asks to be permitted to stay until she can set herself up somewhere.'

'Well, that's quite out of the question,' stormed Sir Edward. 'A young woman cannot possibly live alone. What would people think? A child of runaways, too. Bad blood will out, you mark my words. In any event, she won't be able to afford to live independently. The good reverend was a pauper, was he not?'

Lady Alice squirmed. 'Reading between the lines of my sister's letters I had the impression that life was difficult for them, but I never enquired into her circumstances, and she never elaborated on them. She never complained.'

'Well, I'm not prepared to have another mouth to feed. We'll have to marry her off quickly before she contaminates our daughter with her country manners.'

Sir Edward left the room, and when Lady Alice heard him send for his carriage she knew that he would not return until late in the evening. She hastily scribbled some notes to cancel the calls she had planned to make the following day, and then she set her mind to wondering whether or not she should go into mourning for a sister she had not seen for more than twenty years. On the whole she thought that she would not. Black did not suit her complexion.

The two Wickham boys were currently away from home. Charles, the oldest at nineteen, attended Cambridge University. He was a constant source of worry and exasperation to his parents. As the elder son he stood to inherit his father's estate in the fullness of time and saw no need, therefore, to exert himself in constructive occupation. He did just sufficient study to avoid being sent down, this being the condition set by Sir Edward if Charles expected his father to settle his gambling debts. Like Lexy, he appeared to have inherited his looks directly from his great grandmother, Zeinab Garthwaite, without them being diluted by the intervening generations. Lady Alice was devoted to her handsome firstborn son, and although she considered him tiresome at times, she always found a ready excuse for his licentious behaviour.

James would have to make his own way in the world and in preparation for this he attended the East India Company's military academy in

Addiscombe. Unlike his brother, James applied himself assiduously to the study of mathematics, surveying, fortifications and Hindustani. He was a serious boy, honest and straightforward. Sir Edward adored him, and scarcely a day passed when he did not wish that James had been born before that wastrel Charles. James was a son of whom to be proud.

Charlotte, the only daughter, was eighteen, and newly launched on London society. She had a pretty, heart-shaped face with dark blue eyes, dimpled cheeks and an English rose complexion. She was fortunate in that her blond hair curled naturally, thus sparing her the nightly torment of having it put in rag curlers. Lady Alice had ensured that Charlotte was equipped for a life of leisure rather than one of practical usefulness. She had not been educated beyond a basic level, it being considered that a learned mind was a drawback in the marriage stakes. In a rare display of unity, Sir Edward and Lady Alice agreed that no gentleman desired a clever wife with opinions of her own; wives merely needed to be decorous and be capable of overseeing the smooth running of a household. Charlotte read but little and was as empty-headed as her mother, and Sir Edward could never make the connection between the lack of education of girls and their consequent puerile level of conversation, which caused him such irritation when in their company.

There were two further members of the Wickham household – Evalina and Polly, Sir Edward's younger sisters, now in their mid-forties. Sir Edward had been obliged to provide them with a home under the terms of their father's will. Neither Evalina nor Polly was completely reconciled to their spinsterhood. Each harboured the fervent hope that one day they would be plucked off the shelf, and there was a tacit understanding between them that they would never refer to the possibility that they might remain forever unattached. It was not that they had lacked suitors; on the contrary, there had been many when they were young women, but their father had made it abundantly clear that he had no intention of making a marriage settlement on either of them for some unknown man to squander in the future, so the gentlemen had drifted away with regret, and Evalina and Polly remained at home to care for their mother during her final illness, and then run their father's household after her demise. He had been sufficiently grateful to leave each of them an annuity of one hundred pounds per year, paid in quarterly instalments, and a perpetual home with their brother.

Because of their nearness in age, Evalina and Polly had always been treated much as if they were twins. When they were young they were referred to as 'the girls', and now that they were in their middle age they were usually lumped together as 'the aunts'. Sir Edward often maliciously called them 'the maiden aunts', emphasising their situation and adding to their distress.

The Wickham family lived in a stuccoed house in Belgravia, a residential area that benefited from water supplies, drains and street lighting. Those who were sufficiently wealthy to live there did so in the grand manner. Sir Edward maintained his own carriage and entertained lavishly in an attempt to win friends, an enterprise worth spending money on.

Lady Alice left the running of the household to Mrs Baines, the housekeeper, who had been in her employ for many years, and whom Sir Edward suspected of cheating his wife over the household accounts because Lady Alice was too stupid to notice. Lady Alice did expect Mrs Baines to do her job satisfactorily, but on this particular evening it appeared that the housekeeper's eyes had been less than alert as Lady Alice was irritated to note that some of the silver adorning the dining table had not been properly cleaned. As the family were already gathering for the evening meal it was too late to attend to the matter, and Lady Alice could only pray that Sir Edward would not notice. They were not entertaining guests and dinner was to be a simple affair, but Lady Alice did expect the table to be laid, and the maid to be as immaculately turned out, as if they were expecting company. It was probably the fault of the new housemaid, fresh from Norfolk, but nevertheless, thought Lady Alice, Mrs Baines should have seen that everything was in order. Much as she hated having to confront her housekeeper, Lady Alice knew that it would have to be done. She sat down heavily and cast her eye around the room, searching for anything else that had been overlooked or carelessly undertaken.

There was little conversation while the Wickhams applied themselves to their dinner of Julienne soup, fillets of salmon and saddle of mutton with vegetables, but during the dessert of plum tart with cream Sir Edward asked a question.

'Have you heard any more from that niece of yours?'

Evalina, Polly and Charlotte looked at him in surprise.

'No, not a word,' replied Lady Alice. 'It's been several weeks now since her letter, so I can only suppose that she has changed her mind or that some accident has befallen her.'

'I didn't know that you had a niece, my dear,' said Evalina.

'She's my sister's daughter,' explained Lady Alice. 'My sister and her husband both passed away recently and Lexy wrote to say that she was coming south to visit.'

Charlotte frowned. 'Why have you never mentioned that I have a cousin, Mother?' She narrowed her eyes. 'There is a whiff of scandal about it if she has been kept a secret from us all.'

Sir Edward banged his spoon on his plate. 'That's enough of that, Charlotte. Watch your tongue.'

'Well, why have I never been told about her?'

'Because they lived on a remote island in the Hebrides,' said Lady Alice. 'I haven't seen my sister for more than twenty years and I never thought it possible that you would meet.'

'But you mentioned your niece coming to visit?' said Evalina.

'Yes. The poor girl is an orphan now, and to my knowledge we are her only family. She did say that her visit would be brief, but as she hasn't contacted me again I don't know what has become of her.'

'How old is this Lexy?' asked Charlotte.

Lady Alice counted on her fingers. 'She must be twenty-one, or thereabouts.'

'Twenty-one and not married!' exclaimed Charlotte. 'She must be very plain if no one wants to marry her.'

'That's a little unkind,' remonstrated Evalina. 'We know nothing of what life on a Scottish island is like. Perhaps there were no suitable gentlemen for her there.'

'Beggars can't be choosers,' said Sir Edward. 'Her father was a preacher so that might have something to do with it. A preacher and a pauper.' He stood up. 'I'll take my coffee in the library.'

After her father had left the room Charlotte turned to her mother. 'Do you think that Lexy is coming here to find a husband?' she said, anxious for her position as the desirable young lady of the house.

'I shouldn't think she will be much competition for you, dear, even if she is,' said Lady Alice. 'Oh, by the way, I forgot to tell you that our invitations have arrived for the Chisholms' summer ball. I have already sent a note to our dressmaker telling her to expect us next week, and tomorrow we will go to Peter Robinson's for material.'

The four women, only one of them young, became absorbed in the details of gowns and trimmings, and the conversation rapidly dissolved into the sort of trivia that drove Sir Edward so often from his home. Lexy Nicolson was completely forgotten.

Lord and Lady Chisholm's summer ball was an eagerly anticipated annual event at which some two hundred guests drawn from the aristocracy and wealthy patrons of the arts and industry gathered to see and be seen. In Lady Alice's morning room half a dozen ladies of quality sat on hard, straight-backed chairs discussing the frills and furbelows they planned to wear to this extravagant occasion. It was a Wednesday, and Lady Alice had established Wednesdays as her 'At Home' day when friends and acquaintances on whom she had called could return her visit. The cook laboured below stairs to provide endless pots of tea and plates of cakes, and the maid trailed up and down the stairs to keep the ladies of quality supplied with refreshments.

Maud Leighton replaced her bone china cup and saucer with a clatter on the occasional table beside her.

'You will never guess who I came across the other day at Gunter's Tea Shop,' she said.

Her statement was rewarded with a ring of intrigued faces turned in her direction.

'No, who?' asked Lady Jean Eastman.

'Mungo Sibley,' Maud Leighton announced triumphantly. She had scored a coup, as it appeared that no one else knew that he was in town.

There was an astonished silence whilst the ladies searched their memories. For some of those present the name held no significance, but a faint memory stirred in Lady Jean.

'Oh, surely not,' she said. 'Mungo Sibley? I have it on good authority that he passed over years ago. Dysentery, or something equally revolting, I believe.'

Maud Leighton was affronted. From above her pince-nez her piercing eyes bored into Lady Jean, and the feathers in her hat quivered as she refuted her statement.

'That's as maybe, Lady Jean,' she sniffed. 'But I can assure you that he was very much alive when I saw him at Gunter's. He was there with his sister.'

171

Lady Jean was flustered. 'Well, I'm quite certain that I was told that he had passed over. Perhaps I was misinformed.'

'Didn't he go to Africa or somewhere?' chipped in Ada Hollingsworth.

'India,' said Maud Leighton. 'This is the first time he has been back home.'

'Wasn't there some talk of an unfortunate affair?' asked Ada Hollingsworth.

'Yes, that's right,' said Lady Jean, determined to regain her place in the conversation. 'Goodness, it must be at least twenty-five years ago. You know, I am certain that I was told that he had passed over to the other side.'

'Do tell, Lady Jean. What unfortunate affair?' Evalina sat on the very edge of her chair. She found the whiff of scandal irresistible and, deprived of affairs of her own, she was obliged to live vicariously through the lives and loves of others.

'Well,' Maud Leighton interjected in conspiratorial tones. She had instigated this turn in the conversation and was determined not to be outdone. 'He fell in love with a countess and made rather a fool of himself.'

'Surely falling in love is romantic, not unfortunate?' said Evalina.

'But she was married,' said Lady Jean with a significant look.

Charlotte Wickham held her breath and prayed that her mother would not remember her presence. She rarely heard salacious gossip, and in common with most girls of her age was kept in ignorance of sexual matters, a fact that filled her with a dread of the unknown and a vague excitement fuelled by curiosity. What a disappointment then when Lady Alice, by way of a polite cough, a frown, and a nod in her direction, conveyed a reminder of her daughter's presence to the other ladies in the room. The scandalmongering was cut short before more than a titbit was divulged, and an awkward silence brought the gathering to an end with the elegant ladies departing in a rustle of taffeta and a wafting of eau de Cologne.

CHAPTER 23

With the summer ball of all-consuming interest to them all, Lady Alice, Charlotte and the aunts used the family carriage to take them to Peter Robinson, a linen draper in Oxford Street. They had no need of the store's own dressmaking department, but they took the opportunity of pouring over its designs for ball gowns and purloined some ideas to take to their own dressmaker. Fluttering and twittering like sparrows, they spent a great deal of money on fabrics and trimmings. They paid no attention to a petite, black-haired young woman who was also purchasing material in the store. For her part, Lexy could not fail to notice this bevy of females and she gave way to their noisy, self-assured manner, of which she felt in awe.

When Lexy arrived at Euston station at the end of the five-hour journey from Birmingham, she booked into the Victoria, the smaller of two hotels built beside the station, one on either side of the portico. The Victoria was little more than a dormitory providing bed and breakfast for a few shillings a night whereas the other hotel, the Euston, was altogether grander, and correspondingly more expensive. The first thing she did was to send a note to Frobisher and Fosdyke requesting an appointment for the following day. Then she ordered hot water and set about the task of making herself more presentable.

When Lexy arrived at the lawyers' establishment in Chancery Lane, she was ushered into a comfortably furnished office that smelt of leather, old books and pipe tobacco. A corpulent gentleman with an abundance of white curly hair heaved himself out of his chair to welcome her. A heavy gold watch chain stretched tightly across his ample stomach clunked against the buttons of his waistcoat as he extended his hand in greeting.

'Miss Nicolson, how do you do? How nice to meet you. I am Ernest Frobisher. Please come in and sit down.' He waved Lexy to a chair and then turned to the clerk who had conducted Lexy to the inner sanctum. 'Thank you, Timmins. Bring us tea, and then we are not to be disturbed.'

Lexy sat down, and removing her gloves looked around the office. Large, heavy tomes and smaller books filled every shelf, and the writing desk was littered with papers. A wooden cupboard stood in one corner spilling files and more papers onto the floor. It was an untidy, masculine room.

Ernest Frobisher sat at his desk and studied the young woman before him. She was not what he would have expected of a daughter of Captain Nicolson. He had been a handsome man, but the difference in their colouring came as a shock. Miss Nicolson was very dark and foreign-looking, beautiful too, in an exotic way. He wondered if she knew how much she had inherited; but, of course, she must know. Captain Nicolson could hardly have kept his wealth a secret all these years. He hoped that the young lady had someone to protect her, because she would be prey to every bounder in London without a guardian.

While they waited for Timmins to return with the tea they exchanged a few pleasantries about the weather and Lexy's journey from Toronsay, and she related the details concerning the deaths of her parents.

'I do wish to extend my condolences to you on your loss,' said the lawyer. 'I never had the pleasure of meeting your mother, but I knew your father well.'

'Mr Frobisher,' began Lexy. 'I hope that I am not wasting your time, but the reason I wanted to see you is because I found the name and address of your firm in my father's possessions, and I wondered what contact it was he had had with you.'

She sat calmly, straight-backed on the chair. She was dressed in a simple high-necked, full-skirted black dress and she wore no adornments. Her hair was tied back loosely beneath a black bonnet. Ernest Frobisher thought she looked lovely in black, a colour all the women of his acquaintance disliked because it made them look sallow. He leant his elbows on the desk, put his hands together to make a steeple of his fingers, and pursed his lips.

'I was your father's lawyer for many years when he was employed by the East India Company. Before you all moved to Scotland, Captain Nicolson entrusted me with something for you. Do you know anything of your inheritance?'

'Oh, yes,' said Lexy. 'I found it with the scrap of paper bearing your name and address. I'm afraid that I spent some of it on the journey here.'

Ernest Frobisher was nonplussed. He wondered what the girl was talking about. Was it possible that she knew nothing of her father's affairs? He cleared his throat.

'You do not need to account to me for your expenditure, Miss Nicolson. May I ask what it was exactly that you found?'

'Before my mother passed away she gave me her pearls, but after my father was gone I went through their things and found his twenty-five sovereigns hidden away. I was angry and upset at the time because we had always been so poor, but I was thankful to have the means to travel south.'

She fell silent. The lawyer waited for her to continue, but when it became clear that she had nothing further to add he realised that she had no idea about what he was going to tell her.

'Then you are not aware of anything else your father left you?'

'Anything else? How could there be anything else? If you knew the level of poverty we were reduced to after Father left the Established Church, then you would know that there was nothing else to leave to anyone.'

Ernest Frobisher reached for his pipe. 'Do you mind if I smoke?' When Lexy shook her head, he plugged the pipe with tobacco and lit it. Between puffs he peered at Lexy through the swirls of smoke.

'Well,' he said after a few minutes. 'There is more for you. Read this.' He handed Lexy a sheet of sealed parchment which bore her name in classical script.

Alexandra Nicolson
To be opened in the event of both parents being deceased

Lexy broke the seal with trembling fingers. Inside, in the same script was written: An inheritance may be gotten hastily in the beginning; but the end thereof shall not be blessed. Proverbs 20:21.

Lexy snorted. 'A quote straight from the Bible. How typical of my father. I wonder what lesson he is trying to teach me from the grave?' Her voice was bitter.

Ernest Frobisher sent for another pot of tea. After Timmins had brought it into the office and withdrawn, the lawyer rose from his seat, crossed the room and unlocked the cupboard door. He brought out a carved sandalwood casket and placed it on the desk in front of Lexy.

'This is for you,' he said. 'You will find the drawers are locked, but your father did not leave the keys with me. It would be such a pity to break the locks; I was hoping that he might have mentioned the keys to you.'

Lexy shook her head. 'He said nothing about them, but there are keys. I found seven tiny ones on a gold chain hidden with his sovereigns. I almost threw them away until I decided that he must have had good reason to keep them. I have them here.'

She rummaged in her bag and pulled out the bunch of keys. She stood at the desk and inserted a key into a lock but hesitated to open it.

'You will think me foolish, Mr Frobisher, but I'm almost afraid to look. My mother told me that my father was a very different man in his earlier years from the one I knew, and now I feel as though I am about to meet a stranger.'

'You don't have to open the casket here, Miss Nicolson. It belongs to you, and you are quite at liberty to take it away and open it in private.'

'I think I would prefer to open it here. I don't want to take it back with me to the Victoria in case it gets stolen.'

She turned the key and slid open the top left-hand drawer of the casket. The colour instantly drained from her face and she swayed on her feet so that Ernest Frobisher thought she might faint. Then just as suddenly her cheeks flooded with colour, almost as red as the rubies contained in the drawer. Without speaking Lexy closed that drawer and then she opened and closed all the others in turn before sitting down heavily, her heart pounding.

'I don't understand,' she said. 'We have been so poor these past five years. How could my mother have owned all these jewels when we went hungry for lack of money? It simply isn't possible, Mr Frobisher. There must be some mistake. The casket cannot have belonged to her.'

'There is no mistake, Miss Nicolson. After all, you have the keys in your possession. If it is any comfort to you, I can say that I don't believe that your mother knew of the existence of this casket or of the jewels it contained. Your father brought it here as soon as he returned from his final voyage, even before he went home. He could hardly bear to look at it and he shuddered after I had locked it away. It was as if he were afraid of the casket, melodramatic though that might sound.'

'Did he know what the casket contained?' asked Lexy.

Each of the seven drawers was crammed with rings, bracelets, necklaces, earrings, together with dozens of loose stones: diamonds, rubies, emeralds, sapphires and moonstones. Lexy did not want to believe that her father had allowed them to live in poverty knowing that he possessed such wealth.

'I am sure he must have done,' said Mr Frobisher. 'He handled the casket as if it burned his fingers; but of one thing I am certain, Miss Nicolson, your father will have bought the jewels himself even if he smuggled them into England. He was no thief.'

Lexy's mind was in turmoil, but before she could voice her confusion the lawyer spoke again.

'The casket is not all your father has bequeathed to you,' he said. 'There is more. He has left you the sum of one hundred and twenty thousand pounds.'

Once again, the colour drained from Lexy's face. She could not have been more shocked. 'How much?' she gasped. 'No, really, Mr Frobisher, my father was a minister of religion. He could not possibly have possessed such a vast sum.'

'Yes, but before entering the Church he was the captain of an East Indiaman and in a position to accrue a fortune. Also, he inherited his uncle's estate. More to the point, perhaps, he was a gambler – a very successful one.'

After a moment of astonished silence, Lexy threw back her head and laughed aloud. It was a gesture that her mother would have recognised instantly as the same one that had attracted her to Murdo when she was just eighteen.

'Then you really are mistaken, Mr Frobisher,' laughed Lexy. 'My father was a model of temperance in all things. He neither smoked nor drank. He did not dance or play cards or, in fact, do anything that might have been in any way frivolous, or even enjoyable. Gambling would have been quite out of the question because he would have deemed it an almighty sin.'

'Nevertheless, gamble he did,' persisted the lawyer. 'Not at the gaming tables, but on the Stock Market. He made some very shrewd investments of which you are now the sole beneficiary.'

Lexy could barely take it in. Had her mother known about this fortune? They must have been wealthy when her father was at sea, so how could she not have known? But why would her father have bought all these jewels and then not given them to her? Why was it all such a secret? Questions rolled around inside her head, and a monumental anger towards her father rose within her. She was convinced that her mother could not have known about the money or she would not have let them suffer. No, it was all his doing. Lexy hated her father's deceit, and she hated him for being prepared to sacrifice their lives for a secret. One day, she promised herself, she would find out what that secret was.

'Does the word "Anjana" mean anything to you?' she asked on a whim.

Ernest Frobisher frowned and shook his head. 'No, why?'

'It doesn't matter.'

'What do you plan to do now?'

'I don't quite know,' said Lexy. 'I had planned to try and obtain a position as a governess as that would give me employment and a roof over my head, but everything has changed now. I don't think I will ever be able to get used to the idea of being rich. I must write to Sir Edward and Lady Wickham. Lady Wickham is my aunt – my mother's sister. I was going to throw myself on their mercy, but now I don't need their charity after all. I don't want to go straight there because I need time to think first. You have taken the wind out of my sails.'

'Might I make a suggestion?' said the lawyer. 'How would you like to come and stay with my wife and me whilst you consider your future? Mrs Frobisher would be delighted to make a fuss of you, and it would give you time to have some clothes made so that you can go to the Wickhams looking every inch the wealthy, independent young lady you now are.'

Lexy glanced down at her shabby dress. 'Are the Wickhams very grand? Do you know them?' she asked.

'Not exactly. I was introduced to Sir Edward at my Club.'

Lexy looked at the lawyer through narrowed eyes. 'I get the impression that you do not like him.'

Ernest Frobisher smiled. 'Let's just say that I did not care to pursue the acquaintance. Now, what about my offer?'

'It is most kind of you,' said Lexy. 'If you are certain that I wouldn't be a burden on your wife, I would be delighted to accept.'

*

Myrtle Frobisher was born with an abundance of maternal feelings and Lexy was drawn to her at once. There was nothing striking about her appearance. She was of middling height, neither stout nor thin; her face was wrinkled, her hair white, but she exuded an air of such tranquillity and goodness that everyone noticed her. She was not an inquisitive woman; she asked no questions, and yet she knew everything about everyone because hearts were opened to her, troubles shared with her, and secrets divulged to her in the certain knowledge that confidences were safe in her ears. It was not long before Lexy wept the whole sorry story of her life onto Myrtle Frobisher's shoulder: her grief for her mother, her hatred for her father, and her utter bewilderment over her inheritance.

'I'm sorry to have made such a nuisance of myself,' said Lexy, dabbing at her eyes with a sodden handkerchief.

'Nonsense, my dear.' Myrtle Frobisher patted Lexy's arm. 'But that's all in the past now and cannot be changed. What matters is what you do now. In time the pain of your mother's passing will ease, and perhaps you will be able to forgive your father one day. I hope you will, because otherwise your hatred will destroy you. He must have had his reasons for doing what he did, but whatever the truth of the matter, he has provided for you to live in the grand manner. He has given you freedom and it is up to you what you do with it, but freedom is a heady thing and I hope his Calvinistic raising of you will enable you to use it wisely.'

Lexy smiled faintly. 'If I am to live in the grand manner, as you suggest, then I shall need new clothes. My wardrobe is sparse and totally out of keeping with London fashions. I feel very drab.'

'Then that's where we will start,' said Myrtle Frobisher. 'Tomorrow we will go to Peter Robinson – he's a draper – and then we will introduce you to London and what it has to offer.'

Lexy indulged in an orgy of shopping. She ordered day dresses and evening gowns, gloves, bonnets, and dozens of petticoats and pantalets. She chose silks, satins, crepe de chine, muslin, poplin and organdie, ribbons and lace. Then there were boots, shoes and pumps for dancing, hats and bonnets galore. When the shopping was done there were outings to the sights of London, the exhibitions, art galleries, the opera and theatre, and the zoological gardens. Lexy was overwhelmed and enchanted with it all, and the Isle of Toronsay seemed a lifetime away.

CHAPTER 24

Lexy's arrival at the Wickham residence in Belgravia did not take place in the manner in which its inhabitants had expected. She had sent a note to Lady Alice to apprise her of her arrival, and all four of the Wickham ladies took turns to peep through the lace curtains in nervous anticipation. Sir Edward had made it clear that Lexy was not to be admitted to the house, but he was out, and Lady Alice had every intention of seeing her niece for a few minutes before sending her on her way.

'I dare say she will be in mourning,' said Evalina. 'The poor girl must be terribly sad.'

'She will be easy to spot then if she's all in black,' said Charlotte.

'Yes, I expect so,' said Lady Alice.

'Are we to look for a carriage or a cab?' asked Polly.

'I shouldn't think so,' said Lady Alice. 'She is penniless. She'll be on foot, I daresay. I do hope she'll have the sense to use the tradesmen's entrance so that none of our neighbours will think that she's a visitor.'

Evalina frowned. 'How very uncharitable,' she said. 'She is your niece after all. Her poverty is not her fault.'

'Well, we are not supposed to receive her at all. You heard Sir Edward. If she had given me an address I would have written to her to beg her not to come. As it is, I will speak to her briefly, but that will be an end to it.'

'It seems very hard to treat a member of the family in such fashion,' said Evalina. 'I would feel humiliated if I were in her shoes.'

'I'm sure she will know her place,' said Lady Alice.

It was Evalina's turn at the window. She watched a carriage draw up outside. An imposing gentleman helped a young lady to alight, but Evalina did not make the connection between this impeccably dressed young woman and Lady Alice's impoverished niece so she did not draw anyone's attention to the couple. The first Lady Alice knew of her visitors

180

was when the butler entered bearing a card on a silver tray.

'Goodness,' she exclaimed. 'She's here already. Did you see her, Evalina? I'm sure I did not.'

Lexy and Mr Frobisher were ushered into the drawing room and the confusion on the Wickham ladies' faces was clear to see. Lexy had taken great pains over her appearance for this first encounter with her grand relatives. She wore a day dress of pale green batiste with a cream lace collar, cream gloves and a straw bonnet. She had parted her hair in the centre and tied it back with dark green ribbons. In her hands she carried the casket. Her eyes flickered over each person present until they came to rest on the lady she correctly guessed to be her aunt. She gave a small, but elegant, curtsey.

'Well, you have taken us by surprise,' said Lady Alice. 'What delightful manners. Dear me, you are not at all what we expected.'

Lexy smiled politely. 'Allow me to present my lawyer, Ernest Frobisher.'

'Lawyer? My goodness. You have a lawyer?' Lady Alice struggled to maintain her composure. 'How do you do, Mr Frobisher? Evalina, see that the maid brings tea. You will take tea with us, Mr Frobisher?'

'No, thank you, Lady Alice,' he replied. 'I have further business to attend to. May I have Miss Nicolson's chest brought in?'

Lady Alice nodded. She was so confused by the turn of events that she had forgotten Sir Edward's strictures that Lexy should be denied admittance.

Ernest Frobisher turned to Lexy. 'I'll have the rest of your belongings sent over tomorrow.'

'Thank you, Mr Frobisher,' said Lexy. 'You have been very kind.'

The lawyer was shown out and the four Wickham ladies stared at Lexy. Then Lady Alice patted the empty space beside her on the sofa.

'Do come and sit by me,' she said.

Lexy took her seat beside her aunt and Lady Alice completed the introductions. The maid brought tea.

'Have the blue room made ready for my niece,' Lady Alice instructed the maid.

Lexy smiled at the two older ladies.

'Do call us "Aunt", my dear,' said Evalina. 'I should like that very much, and what with me, Polly and Charlotte, if you keep saying

"Miss Wickham" we will never know which of us you are addressing.'

Lexy nodded her thanks. She was trembling inside, intimidated by the grandeur of the house and the poise of the ladies who sat and gazed at her with frank speculation. Lady Alice was anxious to know why Lexy was not the pauper she had expected to see, and yet she could not enquire directly into her circumstances for fear of seeming vulgar. She wondered if Miriam's letters had misled her. It was true that her sister had not spelled out her poverty, but she had certainly given the impression that the Nicolson family were in dire straits.

Evalina took an immediate liking to the dark, slender young woman, and she was inwardly amused at how Sir Edward would react when he arrived home. It was Charlotte who entertained the most conflicting emotions. Charlotte was vain. She had felt no more than a passing interest in a destitute cousin, but to see that same cousin sitting opposite her, not only beautiful, but also immaculately and exquisitely dressed, aroused in her the most bitter envy and resentment. Charlotte knew that she made a pretty picture in her flowered muslin dress with her hair a tumble of blond curls, but she was honest enough to admit to herself that she could never achieve the sheer elegance of her cousin. She was as jealous as only one woman can be of another.

Although this was her first season, Charlotte was determined that by its close she would have received at least one proposal of marriage. She was sufficiently young to nurse a starry-eyed notion of the wedded state, imagining that after the wedding ceremony a bride was carried off to a life of eternal romance. The daily challenge to this belief from her experience of her parents' far from happy marriage did not disabuse her of her dreams. Like all well-brought-up young ladies, she had no real idea of the nature of matrimony or the happenings of the marriage bed. The gossip of matron ladies was silenced at her approach, and it would not be until the eve of her own wedding that her mother would intimate, in hushed tones, the horrors she would be expected to endure. For the present, though, a husband was what Charlotte most desired, and now here was a young woman whom she could only view as a rival and a threat in the marriage stakes.

Lexy was uncomfortably aware that all eyes had drifted to the casket on her knees. She had dithered over what to do with it. If she had left it with the Frobishers they might have worried about being responsible for its safety, but if she had packed it in the sea chest it might have been lost or stolen. So she had carried it, and now the exotic carved sandalwood attracted curiosity. She guessed that it would not be long before one of them would ask what the casket contained. She was not disappointed.

'I take it that the box contains your mother's jewels?' said Lady Alice. 'Are we to be permitted to see them?'

Lady Alice was interested to know if her sister had possessed anything of real value. Lexy hesitated for a moment, but then she took the keys from her bag and opened the drawers of the casket. The four Wickham ladies gasped and stared open-mouthed at the array of wealth revealed. And at that precise moment, Sir Edward entered the room. So engrossed had they all been in Lexy's appearance, none of them had heard him return home. Lexy caught the look of fear that crossed Evalina's face and the fleeting look of alarm on Lady Alice's as Sir Edward strode towards her.

'I didn't know we were expecting a visitor,' he said. 'How do you do?' He ran his eyes appreciatively over Lexy.

'This is Alexandra, Edward. Lexy, my niece,' ventured Lady Alice, remembering too late that she was to be denied entry.

'Indeed?' Sir Edward raised his eyebrows in surprise. 'Allow me to extend my sympathy to you for the loss of your parents.'

Lady Alice, Evalina, Polly and Charlotte all stared at Sir Edward in astonishment. He ignored them, and his eyes fell on the jewels in the casket.

'Great heavens!' he exclaimed.

Lexy flinched as he reached into a drawer and pulled out a handful of diamonds.

'Were these your mother's?' he asked. He held one of the diamonds up to the light. 'How did your parents come by such jewels? I'll warrant it wasn't by honest means. Your father was a god-botherer, wasn't he?'

Lady Alice gasped. Lexy was furious. Shaken by her uncle's insolence, she leapt up and snatched the diamonds back, returned them to the casket and locked the drawers. Clasping the casket, she stood to confront her uncle.

'Whatever your opinion of my father and his calling, Sir Edward, his faith was deep and sincere. He would never have compromised his place in heaven for the sake of a few baubles. I am quite certain that neither of my parents, especially my father, ever did anything dishonest in their lives.'

She stopped abruptly, overcome with embarrassment for her outburst. She was confused as to why she felt the need to defend the father she hated against this awful man in whose house she was a guest. Determined not to show her fear of him, Lexy held Sir Edward's gaze, and she had the satisfaction of seeing his own falter.

Charlotte stared at Lexy in awe and admiration, her earlier envy forgotten. Personally, she had thought the Indian jewellery with its heavy gold settings perfectly hideous and totally out of place in an English drawing room, but it was a revelation to her that anyone would ever have the temerity to stand up to her bullying father. Evalina held her breath and waited for the outburst of rage her brother was certain to unleash on Lexy, but to her amazement Sir Edward merely grunted, turned on his heel and strode from the room.

'I see that you are not wearing mourning clothes, Lexy,' said Lady Alice, smoothly changing the subject. Although she had not felt the need to enter a period of mourning for her sister, she did think that Lexy should have donned black crepe.

'I have finished my outward mourning,' said Lexy. 'That does not mean that I no longer grieve for my parents, but I am sure that my mother would not have wanted me to wear black for very long, especially as it is the only colour I have worn for years without being in mourning for anyone.'

'I see,' said Lady Alice. 'In that case, if you are going to be staying with us for the summer, I wonder if you would be interested in attending a summer ball?'

Lexy's eyes shone. 'Oh, yes please,' she breathed.

'That's settled then. I will see what I can do. Now I'll send for Charlotte's maid and she will show you to your room. Annie will wait on you both for the time being. We will see you again at dinner.'

Lady Alice rang the bell and Lexy felt herself duly dismissed. As she followed Annie from the drawing room she knew that she was the subject of the animated conversation that erupted the moment the door closed behind her.

When she had dressed for dinner Lexy waited to be summoned to the dining room. She had no idea whether someone would come to fetch her or if a bell would be rung, so she sat on the bedroom chair and waited.

After a time, when no one came for her, Lexy opened the door and peered out. The landing was hushed and deserted. She tiptoed to the top of the stairs, and then crept down to the next floor. She lost her way and opened the door to Lady Alice's morning room. Her footsteps echoed on the polished floor before being silenced by a dark blue carpet. The walls of the morning room were painted cream. Dark blue curtains, matching the carpet, were tied back on either side of deep windowsills on which stood an array of potted ferns. Lexy's eyes travelled along a collection of blue and white porcelain on the mantelpiece. Then she looked into the mirror on the wall above and gasped. Reflected in the mirror was a portrait. She swung round, and her eyes opened wide in surprise for the portrait could have been one of herself. She stepped forward to examine it more closely.

'It's your great grandmother.' Lexy had not heard Evalina enter the room.

'Zeinab Garthwaite? My mother told me about her. She looks...' Her voice trailed away.

Evalina smiled. 'She looks alive in a way that ladies of today in our cold climate are expected to suppress. Your family were ashamed of her, but Lady Alice loved her, which is why she kept the portrait.'

'My mother loved her too,' said Lexy.

'My brother hates the portrait. He says that she brought bad blood into the family and that your mother inherited that bad blood, which is why she dared to flout her parents and elope with your father.' Evalina clapped a hand over her mouth. 'Oh, Lexy, I am sorry. I had no business to say such a thing. I am always letting my tongue run away with me.'

'That's all right, Aunt Evalina. Mama told me all about it. I am never upset by the truth.' Lexy stared at the portrait. 'My mother told me that I look like my great grandmother, but she is so beautiful, and she looks as if she had a wildness about her. I doubt if I would ever have the courage to flout convention in any way.'

'But you already have, my dear. You travelled a very long way without an escort or chaperon. Many people would say that that was unconventional. But your mother was right. You look almost exactly like your great grandmother, as does your cousin Charles, whom you may or may not meet some day. Come, we must not be late for dinner or my brother will be angry with me.' Evalina led the way to the dining room.

When Sir Edward saw Lexy a curious thing happened. The ugly

little man who did not like women was suddenly smitten by his niece and he wished he were twenty years younger. As he gazed at her in her gown of rose-coloured watered silk, he thought that she was the most exquisite creature he had ever seen, and he wondered how Murdo and Miriam Nicolson had produced such perfection. He searched his memory for an image of them both. Murdo he could not recall, but he had a vague memory of Miriam as being slim and dark. Neither of them had possessed the beauty of their daughter.

Sir Edward's previous interactions with the female sex had been confined to his mother, his nanny, a few prostitutes when a young man, his sisters, and his wife, whom he had married for her exceptionally generous marriage portion and the knowledge of her inheritance to come, not her appearance. There had been no women he had felt constrained to flatter, and most he had cursed. Now he stared at Lexy with lascivious intent, seeing in her petite, foreign looks a potential for unbridled sexual passion. His desire to possess her caused him physical pain.

Lexy was acutely aware of his gaze. She concentrated on the feast laid out before her and avoided eye contact with her uncle. The table groaned beneath the weight of an enormous quantity of food. The Wickhams did not reserve their best china and silver for entertaining, but used it daily, and Lexy marvelled at the resplendent formality of the family's evening meal. She toyed with the food on her plate, consuming little, and reflected that the amount of food on this one table would have fed her family for a week. She found the amount of food with which the Wickhams were cheerfully gorging themselves nauseating.

'Is our meal not to your liking?' asked Lady Alice.

Lexy blushed. 'Yes, it is delicious. You must forgive me, but my appetite is small.'

At that moment she raised her eyes and accidentally looked at Sir Edward. His smile was more of a leer and she looked away quickly.

'Have you made any plans for your future, my dear?' he asked.

'Not exactly,' she replied. 'On the journey from Toronsay I decided that I would become a governess, but my lawyer informs me that I do not need to seek employment after all, as I have been provided for.'

Sir Edward grunted. 'Am I to understand that your father, a penniless preacher, actually left you money, or do you mean to sell your jewels? They must be worth a tidy sum.'

Evalina was shocked at her brother's bluntness, but she was equally curious as to Lexy's financial standing. Even if her father had embezzled the collection money he could not have provided Lexy with sufficient funds to dress as she did, and where the jewels had come from Evalina could not imagine. She was none the wiser after Lexy answered Sir Edward's question.

'He left me sufficient to ensure my independence,' said Lexy. The lie came easily. She was uncomfortable with the fortune she had inherited, and she had no intention of revealing the extent of her wealth to the Wickhams.

'Well, you are very welcome to live with us,' said Sir Edward. His eyes wandered to the pearls at Lexy's throat. 'They are beautiful pearls, my dear. Most becoming. They suit your colouring.'

Again the leer, which made Lexy's flesh crawl. She fingered the necklace nervously. She could feel Sir Edward's eyes wandering lower and sensed he was undressing her in his mind. She did not know what to do, but Evalina noticed her distress and came to her rescue.

'Were they your mother's pearls?' she asked.

'Yes. I understand that my father gave them to her when he returned from his final voyage. Mama gave them to me for my twenty-first birthday.'

'Twenty-one!' Charlotte had kept silent throughout the meal, but now she had to speak. 'Are you really as old as that and still not married? Why, you are almost an old maid, Lexy.'

'Mind your manners,' said Sir Edward. 'You will treat your cousin with respect. Apologise at once.'

Charlotte blushed. 'I'm sorry, Lexy,' she murmured.

Lexy smiled at her. 'There was no one on Toronsay that I wished to marry although I did receive several offers. I've never had the opportunity to meet anyone else.'

'I dare say that gentlemen will come flocking to my door once your presence here becomes known,' said Sir Edward. 'But they will have to get past me first.' He hated the idea of some man other than himself having the liberty of his niece's tempting body, but he knew that she could not remain single. 'I'm sure I shall be able to find a suitable husband for you,' he added.

Lexy glared at him. 'I shall be the sole judge of whom I marry,' she said.

Sir Edward flushed, whether from anger or embarrassment Lexy could not tell. Evalina nodded a smile at her, and Charlotte wondered how this tiny cousin of hers was able to face down her father. Lady Alice rose from the table and the ladies followed her from the room in a rustle of silk and satin, leaving Sir Edward alone with his temper and his port.

CHAPTER 25

Two carriages drew up outside Lord and Lady Chisholm's mansion to join the other carriages that filled the sweeping drive. The jingle of harness provided background music to the excited chatter of the female guests. It was not yet dark, but hundreds of lanterns illuminated the gardens and terraces in the gathering twilight. To Lexy it was a scene of enchantment. She had travelled in the second, hired, carriage with Evalina and Polly behind the family carriage carrying Sir Edward, Lady Alice and Charlotte to the ball. When they reached the stone steps leading up to the main doors, a footman helped them down from the carriages and Evalina took hold of Lexy's arm.

'If you hold your head up high no one will know that you are scared inside,' she whispered.

'How did you know?' asked a pale-faced Lexy. She trembled with excitement and awe and felt very much the country cousin amongst such grandeur.

Charlotte crossed to Lexy's side. 'There isn't a single girl here tonight who can compete with us for the gentlemen's attention,' she said with a smug grin on her face. 'Just look at them. Fat ones, skinny ones, spotty ones. Our dance cards will fill the fastest.'

They joined the throng of guests as they made their stately progress up the imposing stairway. Polished wooden doors stood open to admit the elite who had been favoured with invitations to this grand occasion. It was thanks to Lady Alice's friendship with Lady Chisholm that she had managed to wangle an invitation for Lexy.

Lord and Lady Chisholm stood at the entrance to the ballroom to greet their guests as they were announced. A footman, resplendent in white powdered wig, blue brocade jacket with tails, and white brocade breeches took Sir Edward's card and faced the ballroom.

189

'Sir Edward and Lady Alice Wickham and Miss Charlotte Wickham,' he announced.

The three moved forward. Some young persons turned to wave to Charlotte and she left her parents' side to join her friends. She knew that she looked lovely in her white taffeta gown, which was looped up with forget-me-nots, but there had been a row with her mother over the style of the dress. Conveniently forgetting how she had felt many years earlier when denied her own choice of gown, Lady Alice insisted that Charlotte's modesty be preserved by a demure fichu and puffed sleeves. Charlotte thought it childish in comparison with the gown Lexy was to wear, but Lady Alice blithely subjected her to the same argument she had had with her own mother – Charlotte was too young to be allowed any say in what she wore. All Charlotte's friends wore similar gowns with only different coloured trimmings to distinguish one from another, and Charlotte had to trust that her beautiful hair and pretty face would make her stand out from the rest.

'Miss Evalina Wickham, Miss Polly Wickham and Miss Alexandra Nicolson,' announced the footman.

'Here we go, Lexy,' said Evalina. 'It's our turn. Chin up.'

They moved forward into the ballroom. The two aunts looked frightful but were ignorant of the sad truth. Both sported heads of frizzled hair after a sleepless night spent in rag curlers. Evalina's mauve gown and Polly's apple green one were unbecoming to their age and colouring and were of an unflattering design. Beside them Lexy was a vision of perfection. Heads turned to stare at her and there was a sudden buzz of interest.

When she had put on her gown of cream silk that evening Lexy had been filled with misgivings. Whereas Charlotte had thought her own gown too juvenile, Lexy felt semi-naked in hers. She had never worn a ball gown before and she was embarrassed by the amount of bare flesh above her tight-fitting bodice with its low décolleté. Anxious to cover herself she searched the drawers of the casket for something to spare her blushes. Her eyes lit upon an elaborate ruby and gold necklace, and the maid fastened it around Lexy's neck. It was so large and ornamental that it concealed much of her exposed bosom and she heaved a sigh of relief. The maid piled Lexy's thick black hair on top of her head and tucked a single red rose behind her ear.

The overall effect was dazzling. It was as if an exotic princess had suddenly appeared in the middle of London society. Who is she? was the question on everyone's lips. Gentlemen of all ages sought introductions so that they might sign her dance card, and many a restraining hand was laid on the arm of a gentleman as a reminder that he already had a partner for the evening. Not a few regretted that they were so tied and therefore unable to join the increasing throng which gathered around the unknown beauty.

Lexy was unaware of the impact she had on the assembled company. She gazed about her in awe. Enormous chandeliers were suspended from the ceiling for the entire length of the ballroom. Hundreds of candles in them caused the prisms of glass to shoot piercing gleams of colour onto the walls. There were gold velvet curtains tied back from five sets of glass doors opening onto the terraces, and vast porcelain vases filled with roses added their colours to the rainbow display of ball gowns. Here and there the flash of a scarlet tunic caught Lexy's attention and her heart skipped a beat. There was something about a uniform that attracted her like a magnet.

To one side of the room an ensemble of musicians played whilst the guests mingled, greeting old friends and being introduced to new acquaintances. Lexy smiled politely at each person Evalina presented to her but was too overwhelmed to remember anyone's name. She was besieged with requests for dances, and the little pencil attached by a gold tassel to her dance card was busily employed.

Sir Edward normally disappeared into the smoking room until refreshments were served but, on this occasion, he hovered beside his niece. When Lexy had drifted down the sweeping staircase in his home that evening he had been stunned, once more, by her beauty. Now he intended to put his name down against several dances for the chance of holding her close to him although it had been many years since he had taken to the floor. Lexy was frightened of the way he looked at her, but she did not know how to refuse him her dance card in front of all these people. Evalina hurried to her side.

'Now then, brother dear,' she said. 'To sign against more than one dance would be unfortunate, don't you think? Others might think you were making something of a fool of yourself.'

Sir Edward hesitated. Perhaps his sister was right. He would not want to make himself a laughing-stock, after all. He handed the card back to Lexy with a bow.

Lady Alice found a group of matrons each of whom was trying to impress on the others how much more beautiful their own daughter was compared with everyone else's. For some there was a hint of despair or desperation as balls came and went without a suitor being found for a daughter who was plain. Even those who were secure in the knowledge of their own daughter's charms felt increasing anxiety as they observed the interest Miss Lexy Nicolson had aroused. After her initial concerns, Lady Alice, looking at Charlotte and Lexy standing side by side, realised that they presented a formidable threat to any designing mother that evening. Lexy's dark foreign face beside Charlotte's blond curls and flawless complexion complemented and emphasised one another.

Evalina's attention was drawn to the dancing. She and Polly had joined a group of older ladies, spinsters like themselves, some of whom made spiteful remarks about the dancers in their own despair at being perpetual wallflowers. Although she would have loved to dance, and her feet tapped in time to the music, Evalina was no green-eyed monster. She had had her day; now it was only right and proper that the young should have theirs. Her face reflected her enjoyment and she did not notice a tall, thin, suntanned and middle-aged gentleman extricate himself from a group of people until he presented himself before her.

'Might I have the honour of signing your dance card?' he asked.

Evalina blushed like a girl and fluttered her fan. She dropped her dance card on the floor and the stranger stooped to retrieve it.

'You forget yourself, sir,' said an indignant Polly. 'As there has been no introduction you are forward in addressing my sister.'

'I do apologise,' he said to Polly. Then he turned back to Evalina and made a formal bow. 'Please forgive my boorish manners. I have been away from genteel company overlong. Allow me to introduce myself. I am Mungo Sibley of the East India Company, presently home on leave.'

'That will not do, sir,' snapped Polly. 'You must be properly presented.'

Evalina had no intention of losing this opportunity to dance for the first time in more years than she cared to remember. And this was Mungo Sibley of the unfortunate affair! She smiled at him.

'I am Evalina Wickham, sister of Sir Edward, and I would be delighted to dance with you. Thank you for asking me.' She handed him her dance card and he filled every space with his name.

'How can you?' spluttered Norah Blackwell. 'That was not a proper introduction. We don't know anything about this gentleman.' She glared at the stranger with suspicion.

'Stuff and nonsense,' said Evalina. 'And you are quite wrong. I do know something of Mr Sibley, and I am no sixteen-year-old to be guarded and protected. I shall dance with whomsoever chooses to dance with me.'

The maiden ladies were shocked by Evalina's brazenness and Mungo Sibley's effrontery as he extended his arm and led Evalina to the floor. They could only watch, open-mouthed, their indignation fuelled with envy.

Sir Edward and Lady Alice, at opposite ends of the ballroom, spotted Evalina on the dance floor at about the same moment. Expressions of horrified bewilderment crossed their faces. Sir Edward almost burst a blood vessel. What did the silly old fool think she was doing, he wondered. Making a bloody exhibition of herself, the stupid old trout. He glanced around the assembled company expecting to see scorn and laughter, but no one appeared to be paying any attention to the middle-aged couple. Thank God for that at any rate, he thought; but he was furious and embarrassed that his sister should so far forget herself as to be dancing like a young girl. It was grotesque, and he would have something to say about it tomorrow.

During the break for refreshments, Mungo Sibley stayed at Evalina's side, and after supper they strolled together in the gardens.

'Thank you so much for asking me to dance with you,' said Evalina. 'I have been a wallflower for so many years now that I had not thought that I would ever dance again, and I do love it so.'

'The pleasure was all mine,' said Mungo Sibley. 'But I must ask you something. You told your friends that you know of me, and yet we have not met before.'

Evalina blushed. She did not wish to give the impression that she indulged in spurious gossip even though it was true that she delighted in it. Mungo was amused by her confusion and gave a lopsided grin.

'Ah! I daresay that you have heard tell of a certain countess. Am I correct?' Evalina nodded. 'I thought so,' continued Mungo Sibley. 'I doubt if I will ever live that down.'

'I know very little of the matter,' said Evalina. 'It's really none of my business, so please don't concern yourself about it.' Hypocrite, she scolded herself. You are dying to know all the ins and outs.

'I should like to tell you. Just so that you know the real story and not some embellished fairy tale.'

'As you wish.'

'It all seems so silly now looking back, but when I was young and still wet behind the ears I fell in love with a married woman,' explained Mungo Sibley. 'I shall not give her name. Anyway, her husband learned of the affair and he challenged me to a duel. Being a coward, I ran away to India. It is only now that I know that he has passed away that I have dared to return to England. I never saw my countess again. I have no idea where she is now, or even if she is still alive. There, what do you think of that?'

'The heart does not always choose to love wisely,' said Evalina. 'But it must surely be better than never having loved at all. I think you were sensible not to fight that duel though, and no coward would go to India of all places, would they? It's a land of disease, isn't it?'

Mungo laughed. 'Indeed it is, but it's much more than that. It's a land of excitement, intrigue and enterprise.'

'And what do you do in India?'

'I am a lawyer, but don't imagine that that makes me some kind of intellectual. I have been lucky rather that clever. My progress owes more to my having stayed in the land of the living. So many young men die out there before they make their mark.'

They returned to the ballroom and continued to dance together until the evening drew to a close.

'Would you permit me to call on you at home?' asked Mungo as they said goodnight.

Evalina was flustered. She thought of what 'home' meant to her – a grace and favour existence in her brother's house. Although she had enjoyed Mungo Sibley's company and did wish to see him again, she shrank from the thought of entertaining him at home.

'How about meeting for an ice at Gunter's on Monday?' she said. 'We will be leaving for our country residence on Wednesday and I should like to see you before we go.'

'Gunter's it is then.'

Mungo returned Evalina to a dejected and lonely Polly whose spirits had sunk ever lower as the ball progressed. She had scarcely listened to the conversation being conducted around her as she watched her sister dance the night away. Quite what attracted the tall, thin man and the short, plump woman to one another was beyond her comprehension. She was consumed with envy, and she fed on her resentment throughout the night so that in the morning she could hardly bring herself to be civil to her sister.

'How could you be so selfish?' she complained. 'That was the first time an unattached gentleman of our generation has been seen at a ball for I don't know how long, and you kept him all to yourself. As he showed himself willing to dance, you should have shared him with the rest of us. It's too bad, Evalina, it really is.'

'But, Polly dear, he did not appear to wish to dance with any of you. He was at liberty to ask any one of you to dance with him, but he chose not to do so. Even if I had not danced with Mr Sibley, I doubt very much if he would have partnered you instead.'

Polly burst into floods of tears and Evalina was exasperated with her. 'Look,' she said. 'I am meeting Mr Sibley at Gunter's on Monday. Why don't you come with me?'

'Oh, how could you?' cried Polly. 'How can you leave me all alone again?'

'Don't be such a goose,' said Evalina. 'If you are left alone it is because you choose to be. Lexy is coming with me and you are welcome to come too. We are only meeting up to have an ice together. I'm not conducting some sort of clandestine affair, merely meeting a new acquaintance at Gunter's.'

But Polly stayed at home with a handkerchief pressed to her red eyes and nose.

Gunter's Tea Shop was a famous Mayfair rendezvous where the wealthy and well-connected gathered to eat ices and sorbets prepared from a secret recipe. It was always busy: carriages came and went, and the waiters dodged deftly between them as they delivered orders.

It was a beautiful summer's day when Mungo Sibley arrived for his appointment with Evalina. He leant nonchalantly against some railings and watched the world go by while he waited. Evalina and Lexy arrived in a hired carriage and parked in the shade of some trees. Mungo ordered their ices, and then jumped up beside them.

'I hope you enjoyed the ball, Miss Nicolson,' he said after Evalina had introduced them.

Lexy's eyes sparkled. 'Oh, I did. It was so thrilling. Only Aunt Evalina knows that I had never been to a ball before. I was quite out of breath with all the dancing. Scottish dancing is energetic, but at ceilidhs it is broken up by other impromptu entertainments like recitations or singing. I enjoyed the ball just as much as I enjoyed our ceilidhs, but it is impossible to compare the two.'

'You and the young Miss Wickham certainly eclipsed all the other ladies present, except for one,' said the gallant Mungo Sibley. 'Miss Evalina Wickham was the belle of the ball for me.'

Evalina blushed scarlet. 'Don't be silly,' she said.

'It's true,' said Mungo.

'Tell us about India,' said Evalina, fanning her red cheeks.

'Oh, yes please,' said Lexy. 'I should love to hear what you have to say about it. My parents went there before I was born. They never talked about it, so I don't know what part of India they went to.'

'What was your father's position?' asked Mungo.

'He was a sea captain with the East India Company.'

'That means he would have gone to Bombay, Madras or Calcutta.'

'Where do you live?' asked Evalina.

'I am stationed in Cawnpore. I sail from here to Calcutta, then go on a smaller boat up the Hooghly River to the Ganges and on from there. The journey takes forever. I work for *John Company* like your father, Miss Nicolson, but in nothing like as glamorous or dangerous an occupation. I began my career as a writer, but now I am a lawyer.'

'What is it like out there?'

'Unspeakably hot, unspeakably unhealthy, and utterly wonderful,' said Mungo. 'Of course, it's not what it used to be, and it was changing even as I went out there. In the old days we mixed more with the locals, and lots of gentlemen had Indian lady friends although I probably shouldn't be telling you that. However, now that European ladies are going there in ever greater numbers, and the Welsh missionaries are doing their utmost to convert the natives, we and the Indians are drifting apart.'

'What do you do with yourself in your free time?' asked Evalina.

'Sleep,' laughed Mungo. 'Sometimes it is too hot to do anything else but lie about all day. Actually, our lives are similar to life here. The ladies call on one another. We have a theatrical society, and there's always the pig sticking if you are so inclined – and I'm not.'

'Pig sticking!' exclaimed Evalina. 'How dreadful.'

'How much longer do you have here before you return?' asked Lexy.

'I have a few more weeks, but it will be some time in November when I go. That's the best time for the tides and the winds.' He turned to Evalina. 'I believe you leave London this week?'

'Yes, we are going to our house in Ramsgate until the end of September.'

'Would you permit me to visit you there?'

'Of course. That would be delightful.' Evalina scribbled the Ramsgate address onto a slip of paper and handed it to Mungo Sibley.

Lexy smothered a smile as she watched the two of them. It was clear to her that they were equally smitten with one another. She realised that Mungo Sibley must be important to her aunt because in entertaining him she would make two enemies for herself – her sister and her brother – but she was obviously prepared to risk their disapproval, and Polly was already well on the way to becoming enemy number one.

CHAPTER 26

The Wickhams' summer residence in Ramsgate was situated on the West Cliff in Royal Crescent and overlooked a harbour that teemed with fishing smacks. Servants had been sent on ahead to prepare the house for the family's arrival, and they had scrubbed and polished until everything gleamed. The ladies travelled down by the London, Chatham and Dover Railway, but Sir Edward preferred to use his carriage. He had no sympathy with modernisation and could not understand why his wife and daughter should be so enthusiastic about trains when they inevitably reached their destination with their precious clothes bespeckled with soot.

Lexy loved Ramsgate. The hurly-burly of London with its noise, gas lighting, cries of street vendors, shops and smart carriages had excited her, but Ramsgate was a haven of peace in spite of the hordes making trips to the seaside. What surprised her most was how different the sea was there compared with Toronsay. The Hebridean sea was wild, untamed and majestic in its isolation whereas in Ramsgate the sea and its immediate environs appeared so civilised. Here there were no frolicking seals, no thundering waves and no howling winds. Instead there were rows of fishing boats, uniformed nannies pushing perambulators along the promenade with young children in tow, and scarcely a glimpse of sand between the pleasure-seeking families and day-trippers on the beach. The contrast was stark and, for the first time since she left the Isle of Toronsay, Lexy was overwhelmed by homesickness.

After dinner on the first day of their stay in Ramsgate, Lexy excused herself and fled along the wide promenade before dropping down onto the sandy shore. She tugged off her shoes and walked and walked. Eventually she sat down at the water's edge and stared out to sea with tears streaming down her face. She was heedless of gulls screaming above her head, and she ached for her mother. She wanted to tell her of the fortune she had inherited, and she wanted her mother's advice on what to do about it. There was no one in whom she could safely confide, not even Evalina, but keeping it a secret, just as her father had done before her, made her unhappy and unsettled.

When she felt calmer Lexy jumped up, brushed the sand from her skirt and began to walk back the way she had come. Evalina met her halfway.

'Are you all right, my dear?' she asked kindly. 'I was worried about you.'

'I'm all right now,' replied Lexy. 'I just had to do battle with a few personal demons, that's all.'

They strolled back together, and then sat out in the garden as the sun went down with a pot of tea on the table beside them.

'I love it here,' said Evalina. 'I have come here every summer since I was born. It feels more like home to me than the house in London.'

'It is a more comfortable place,' agreed Lexy. 'It is less ostentatious.'

The Wickhams entertained less frequently and less lavishly in Ramsgate than they did in London, for which Lexy was grateful, but she quickly discovered that appearances had to be maintained and attendance at the morning Sunday service was obligatory for the ladies of the household. Lexy had a cavalier attitude to religion, considering most of it to be man-made mumbo-jumbo, but she did believe in God and had no strong objection to accompanying her aunts and cousin to church. She was inwardly amused at the Sunday observances of the Wickham family and knew that her father would have been mortified to think of her in such company.

Sir Edward's attitude to the Lord's day of rest was one of 'the better the day, the better the deed', and he usually went out riding rather than attend church. The ladies, however, always attended the morning service to get it over and done with for the day. When Lexy went with them on the first Sunday she was surprised to feel, for the first time in her life, a sense of reverence in the dignified medieval parish church of St Peter. The hushed tones, the organ music and the singing of hymns, none of which she knew, were in marked contrast to the disrespect and false piety she had seen in the kirk on Toronsay.

After the service, Lexy and Evalina wandered through the beautifully tended churchyard with its eighteenth-century tombstones whilst

Lady Alice and Polly chatted with the vicar, and Charlotte made sheep's eyes at the young organist. Then, with these sole observances of the niceties of the Sabbath behind them, the Wickhams conducted their lives as usual, and Lexy could not complain of being bored or idle.

Evalina blossomed that summer. She was frequently out in the company of Mungo Sibley, and sometimes Lexy joined them on long breezy walks along the cliffs or rambles in the country. Polly did not adapt to her sister's defection. She moped about the house, casting gloom and despondency all around her. She seldom ventured out of doors in spite of the glorious weather, but sat in a chair and wallowed in self-pity, alienating everyone who came into contact with her. She succeeded in making Evalina feel guilty, which was her intention, but the emotional blackmail she employed failed to have the desired effect: Evalina still walked out in company with Mungo Sibley.

One warm, sunny afternoon Evalina and Lexy strolled arm in arm along the promenade. The air was filled with laughter and the delighted squeals of children as they played and built sand castles on the beach. Evalina turned a pink face to Lexy.

'I rather think that Mr Sibley is going to ask me to marry him,' she confided.

Lexy stopped walking. 'How wonderful,' she said. 'Oh, I am so pleased for you. He is such a nice man. Will you accept him?'

Evalina looked thoughtful. 'I need your advice.'

'My advice?' said Lexy. 'Aunt Evalina, you must do as you please. It is not for me to advise you.'

'But I do need advice and I am turning to you because you have become as dear to me as a daughter. You see, it isn't just a straightforward matter of saying yes or no to becoming a wife. It is more involved than that.'

'Don't you want to marry him?' asked Lexy.

'Yes, I do. I can't think why he should want to marry me of all people, but he has made me so happy during these past weeks. I had long ago given up any hope of finding a husband. Now I hope that I'm not too old to change because marriage to Mr Sibley will be such an upheaval.'

'I'm not sure I understand,' said Lexy.

'I would have to make two major adjustments,' explained Evalina. 'The first is that of becoming a wife, of course. I dare say I shall be able to cope with that transition, but there is a much greater change that I should have to make – one that I have to admit does alarm me rather.'

'Whatever is it, Aunt Evalina?' said Lexy. 'You are trembling.'

Evalina looked at Lexy in some agitation. 'It's India, my dear. If I marry him I shall have to go and live in India.'

'India!' exclaimed Lexy. 'I had not thought of that, but how exciting that would be.'

Evalina sighed. 'Well, I have turned it over and over in my mind and I am terrified at the thought of it. Lexy, if I were to accept Mr Sibley's offer, would you come with us to India? I should feel so much braver with both of you beside me. Would you consider it?'

Lexy nodded, her heart pounding with the thrill of it. 'I will think about it seriously, but I would only consent to come with you if Mr Sibley is in full agreement.'

Evalina nodded. 'Thank you, my dear, I feel better already,' she said. 'Of course, I may be mistaken. He has yet to ask me to marry him, but if he does, then I am of a mind to accept him. But, Lexy, I would be grateful if you don't mention any of this to the others for the time being.'

'Of course I won't,' agreed Lexy.

Evalina dropped her bombshell the following week at the dinner table just after the dessert was served.

'I have received a proposal of marriage from Mr Mungo Sibley of the East India Company, which I have accepted,' she announced.

There was a moment of stunned silence. Lexy smiled encouragement, but the other three ladies quivered like mice before a snake as their eyes slid towards Sir Edward. None of them was prepared for his reaction, for he laughed. It started as a giggle, but his titter turned to laughter until it was a regular guffaw. His face reddened, and perspiration trickled from his forehead.

'By George, Evalina,' he gasped. 'That's rich. I didn't know you had it in you to be so funny. Ha! Ha! What a joke.'

'It is no joke, Edward, I assure you,' said Evalina quietly. 'Mr Sibley and I are to be married at the end of October.'

Sir Edward's expression changed to disbelief, and then horror, with the awful realisation that Evalina, that stupid dried-up old maid, was in earnest.

'Well,' he snapped. 'I won't allow it, and that's that and all about it.'

All her life Evalina had been in fear of her brother, but now the knowledge that she was soon to leave his house forever enabled her to stand firm and confront the bully.

'I do not need your permission or your approval,' she said.

'Don't be absurd,' shouted Sir Edward. 'A woman of your age? Why, it's obscene to even think about it. The man must be depraved. It is positively disgusting. What will people think?'

Evalina rose from her seat at the table and looked dispassionately at her brother.

'Now just you listen to me, Edward,' she said in a calm and controlled voice. 'I have been the butt of your sarcasm and your anger for as long as I can remember, but no longer. Mr Sibley is a gentleman. He treats me with courtesy and kindness, and I am never frightened of him as I have been of you. Far from swapping one bully for another as I did when Father died, and I became subject to your authority, when I am married I shall enjoy a measure of freedom such as I have never known.

'Yes, I know that I shall be my husband's property, but marriage to Mr Sibley will be a privilege for me, and by no means the degradation or obscenity you so indelicately suggest. I am prepared to share his life in India for as many or as few years as the good Lord sees fit to grant us.' She swept from the room in a rustle of silk.

Sir Edward stared at his plate and chewed his lower lip. Polly jumped up with a cry and fled from the room in pursuit of Evalina. Lady Alice, Charlotte and Lexy concentrated on their apple pie, not daring to speak or even look at one another. With a grunt Sir Edward gulped the last of his wine, and then stood up and glared at his wife. He had never felt so humiliated in his life.

'Have my coffee brought to me in the library,' he snarled before he strode through the door Polly had left wide open.

Evalina's private agonies as she debated with herself whether or not to marry Mungo Sibley had been considerable. As a girl she had viewed the prospect of marriage with excitement and pleasure, but from the viewpoint of middle age her eager anticipation was tempered by the sterile or downright miserable situations of some of her contemporaries. She reasoned with herself that she had more to gain from marriage than she had to lose – she would for the first time be mistress of her own household, and she would have a far superior position as a lawyer's wife in India than she had as an unwanted encumbrance in the home of her brother. But weighed against these advantages had to be two unknowns: how she would cope in India, and how she would be able to suffer the unmentionable torments of the marriage bed. She knew no one other than Mungo Sibley who had first-hand experience of India, so she only had his accounts to enlighten her; and on the subject of sex, she had never heard anyone have anything to say in its favour. Admittedly she had only heard occasional remarks from maiden ladies like herself, but there was no one to whom she could turn for advice. She certainly could not ask her sister-in-law, Lady Alice, so Evalina would be as ignorant as a bride of eighteen.

Finally, she asked herself why she was even contemplating marriage at her age, and it was the answer to this question that made the decision for her. Women married for many reasons: money, position, security; but she would not be marrying for any of these. She, Evalina Blanche Wickham, was going to marry Mungo Sibley because she felt a sincere and loving attachment towards him. Feeling that, everything else would fulfil her expectations, of that she was certain. She must look forward to her new future because it had to be better than the life she had lived so far. It only remained for Lexy to come to a decision about accompanying her to India.

Lexy relaxed in a cane chair in a corner of the garden. The air was heavy with the scent of the last roses, bees bumbled in and around the flowers, and butterflies flitted hither and thither. A garden was still a novelty to her and she revelled in the colours and variety of the flowers and shrubs. Ostensibly, she was spending time alone to consider whether or not to go to India with Evalina and Mungo, but that had been an excuse not to accompany Lady Alice and Charlotte who were repaying calls. Evalina was out walking with Mungo and Polly was in her room. Poor Aunt Polly had been seen less and less since Evalina's announcement of her forthcoming marriage. She had thrown sulks and tantrums in her bid to regain pride of place in Evalina's heart but had only succeeded in making herself intolerable company. Now she had withdrawn almost completely from society. She was rapidly sinking into deep depression, but she refused to see a doctor and rebuffed all friendly approaches.

'I just want to be left alone to die,' she wailed one day.

'Well, be quick about it, for God's sake,' Sir Edward snapped at her.

Evalina had no intention of giving up her prospect of marriage to appease her sister. Polly refused to speak to Evalina. She believed that her sister and Mr Sibley were conspiring to condemn her to miserable and lonely old age, but her self-pity and the mournful reproach in her eyes whenever she saw her sister alienated Evalina further from her. Even Lexy preferred to avoid Aunt Polly now rather than trying to cheer her up.

It was a lovely time of day to sit in the garden. Lexy's book lay unopened on the table beside her, and she closed her eyes as she thought about her future. There had never been any doubt in her mind that she would agree to Evalina's suggestion that she go to India. She had an overwhelming desire to do so: a romantic desire, and an intense curiosity to travel to the place where her parents had been young and in love. There was nothing and no one to keep her in England, and she revelled in the knowledge that unshackled to any man, and with her fortune, she could do whatever she pleased. She did not care what people thought of her.

During the brief time remaining to them Lexy and Evalina indulged in an orgy of shopping for their journey and their new life. Their personal baggage allowance was generous, more than they needed, and Mungo advised them that clothes more suited to the climate than anything they could purchase in London could be made in India by local tailors.

Mungo and Evalina were married in St Peter's church in Ramsgate. It was to have been a quiet family affair. Mungo's sister and her husband, who stood as groomsman, were the only members of his family present so the right-hand side of the church was almost empty, but this was more than compensated for by Evalina's friends who turned out in force to see her married.

Sir Edward had been coolly civil to Evalina since her announcement, but he did, much to her surprise, provide her with the one thousand pounds set aside for each of his sisters in their father's will on the unlikely occasion of their marriage. It brought tears to Evalina's eyes to think that her father had made this provision for her in his will when he had resolutely refused to do any such thing when he was alive.

Following a brief honeymoon, the lives of Mr and Mrs Sibley and Lexy were taken over by preparations for their departure. They had booked passage from Southampton to Calcutta with the P&O Company and were to travel by the overland route between the Mediterranean and the Red Sea, which meant that their journey would be much shorter than the one undertaken by Lexy's parents twenty-two years earlier.

They left London on a grey, drizzly November day with Evalina in a turmoil of excitement and regret. Polly was in deep depression, and the memory of her blank stare and lack of response when Evalina went to say her farewells caused her immense pain and would haunt her for the rest of her life.

No one went with them to wave from the dockside. Sir Edward flatly refused to do so, and he ordered Lady Alice to remain in London. Without an escort for the return journey Charlotte also had to remain behind, and Sir Edward turned a deaf ear to her pleas to be allowed to give the travellers a proper send-off.

'I envy you,' said Charlotte to Lexy. 'I wish I could come too.'

Lexy hugged her cousin. 'Perhaps you will visit us one day. Choose your husband with care. That way we may meet again, but I don't expect to ever return to England. I shall marry in India and make my life out there.'

Charlotte smiled. 'You look as if you belong there anyway. Put you in a sari and we would mistake you for a Hindu.'

'Goodbye, Charlotte,' laughed Lexy. 'I will write to you.'

'Goodbye, Lexy. Goodbye, Aunt Evalina and Uncle Mungo. Good luck.'

CHAPTER 27

Lexy stood at the rail of the steamer. She scarcely heard the wet thump of the paddles as they swished through the water and was not aware of the salt spray on her face or the light drizzle oozing its way through her cloak while she focussed on the faint smudge of England disappearing in the distance. As the final outline sank below the horizon there was a stifled sob beside her and Lexy turned to Evalina, who wept silent tears, her knuckles pressed to her mouth. The screams of seagulls, unnoticed a moment ago in Lexy's concentration, seemed now to mock Evalina's grief. Evalina knew instinctively that she would never return to her homeland, and the enormity of what she had undertaken hit her suddenly. Mungo, who had experienced similar regrets a quarter of a century earlier, put a comforting arm around her shoulders and Evalina turned to him, but in that motion of her head, her very unmaritime stomach rebelled. All thoughts of England were banished from her mind as she strove desperately, and unsuccessfully, to quell the seasickness that engulfed her. When the first spasms passed, Mungo led her to their cabin, but Lexy remained at the ship's rail.

It was not of England that she thought; she felt no pangs of regret for leaving a country she had known for so short a time. She watched the churning wake of the steamer with the gulls circling above and thought of that other, smaller island she had left – was it really only six months ago? What a funny thing time is, she thought. It seemed more like years. She bade a silent farewell to her mother, and then she ripped off her bonnet and threw it into the air, whooping for joy at the life she was leaving behind. The wind snatched at the bonnet, tossing it up and down until it fell into the sea with its scarlet ribbons trailing behind. Ignoring the astonished glances cast in her direction by fellow passengers, Lexy laughed aloud and danced a pirouette before skipping to her cabin.

As the ship pitched and rolled, an increasing number of passengers retreated to their cabins feeling very unwell. Mungo was unaffected, and Lexy suffered only a mild queasiness that she was able to control by remaining on deck in spite of the cold and the rain. She and Mungo took turns to minister to Evalina although Mungo did the lion's share, for which Lexy was grateful. She found the smell of sickness in the cramped cabin increased her own nausea, so she was always greatly relieved to flee the cabin and return to the fresh air on deck.

The passengers were a motley bunch. Lexy was soon on speaking terms with them as they left their cabins in dribs and drabs having finally found their sea legs. There were four unmarried young women travelling in the charge of a Mrs Chalmers. They spent most of their time giggling together and flirting with unattached gentlemen and officers returning to their regiments. Mrs Chalmers was an old hand and enjoyed frightening those travelling to India for the first time with exaggerated stories of life in that far-flung part of the world.

'Mind you don't fall ill out there,' she said to Lexy one morning. 'It's hard to say which would be the worst in such an event – to be ministered to by one of our own quacks or one of theirs. If you ask me, no doctor knows what he is doing. Our people die like flies out there and the Indians seem to have more than their fair share of cripples and open sores. My advice to you would be to keep out of the sun, although your skin looks as if it will tan easily. Not that a suntan is considered in any way attractive. Oh, and don't eat the fish.'

'Not eat fish?' queried Lexy. 'Why ever not?'

'Fish goes off in three days in England, but it only takes three hours in India for it to kill you, like as not.'

Lexy made a mental note to keep Evalina away from Mrs Chalmers and her scare stories – and not to eat the fish! What Mrs Chalmers said sounded reasonable, and there was no point in courting illness unnecessarily.

One morning Mungo nodded in the direction of some young children clustered about their mother's knee.

'The best way for you to learn some of the language would be to spend some time with them,' he said. 'They probably speak Hindustani better than they do English, and their vocabulary will be simple and straightforward even if their grammar leaves something to be desired.'

Lexy considered the family Mungo had pointed out to her. The mother was reading to a boy and girl of about five years of age. Their ayah squatted close by nursing a younger boy on her knees.

'Why don't you go and introduce yourself while I go and see if Evalina needs anything?' said Mungo.

Lexy moved towards the family. 'Good morning,' she said, and introduced herself. 'It is more comfortable on board now that the sea is calmer, isn't it?'

The mother nodded and smiled. 'Yes, it is. But it has been smoother than our journey to England earlier in the year. We had the misfortune to run into several storms. My name is Sophia Gardner. These are the twins, Jeremy and Ruth, and that is Conrad with the ayah.'

Conrad was fast asleep with his thumb halfway out of his mouth. His curly brown hair tumbled over his forehead, almost covering feathery eyebrows above his closed eyes. Jeremy and Ruth smiled shyly at Lexy and gazed at her through eyes the colour of cornflowers.

'Is this your first trip to India?' asked Sophia Gardner. Lexy nodded in reply. 'Are you visiting relatives out there?'

'No, I'm travelling as a companion to my aunt. She and her husband are on their way to Cawnpore.'

'Will you stay long?'

'I doubt if I will ever return to England,' said Lexy. 'There is nothing for me there and I am leaving no one behind. My parents passed away earlier this year and I have no brothers or sisters.'

'I find it hard to believe that you are leaving no broken hearts behind,' smiled Sophia. 'Are you hoping to find a husband in India along with the "Fishing Fleet" over there?'

'Fishing Fleet?' Lexy was mystified.

Sophia grinned mirthlessly. 'It's an unkind sobriquet applied to the bevy of unmarried girls and women who flock to India in the cool season with high hopes of hooking a husband. They are mostly relatives of people already out there. If they guard their pale complexions on the voyage there is always a chance that they will quickly land someone who has made his fortune. Sometimes romance blossoms on board the ship that carries them in search of their future happiness. Those that fail go back to England and are scornfully referred to as "returned empties".'

Lexy viewed the young women differently in the light of this newly gleaned information and felt sorry for them. 'How sad to be so desperate,' she said.

'We are all of us desperate to marry, are we not?' said Sophia. 'After all, what are we without a husband? Few women can say that they are not subject to some man or another, so it may as well be a man about whom one has some choice, as opposed to one that life has thrust upon one, such as a father or a brother.'

'That is true,' said Lexy, thinking of Evalina. 'But I can assure you that I am in no hurry to find a husband. What I did want to ask you is if you would permit me to borrow the twins for a little while each day. I am anxious to learn the language, and my uncle suggested that your children would be fluent.'

'They are indeed,' said Sophia. 'I would be delighted to lend them to you if you think it would help, but you don't really need more than a few words to deal with the servants. I manage with very little.'

'I hope to be able to speak it properly,' said Lexy. 'I have an ear for languages so hope to learn fairly quickly. I speak French and German, and I have the Gaelic.'

'The Gaelic? Are you from the Highlands? I had thought that you must be from warmer climes because you certainly don't look English. Pardon me if I seem impolite.'

Lexy smiled. 'My father was Scottish, my mother English, but my great grandmother came from warmer climes, as you put it, though I have no idea where. I have lived in the Hebrides for most of my life. That's why I have the Gaelic.'

'I see,' said Sophia. 'Well, you are welcome to borrow the twins whenever you like.'

'Thank you.'

Sophia Gardner watched Lexy as she rejoined her uncle. There may be no thoughts of marriage in that beautiful head at the moment, she thought, but Lexy Nicolson was going to be snowed under with requests for her hand within hours of her arrival at Cawnpore whether she liked it or not. She leaned back and closed her eyes, and her thoughts flew to her firstborn son, Julian, who was now settled into his boarding school in Hampshire. Julian had been her reason for travelling to England. She had rejected out of hand her husband's suggestion that the eight-year-old be put in the care of some unknown person travelling from India back to the Old Country and had insisted on accompanying him herself. Then she had fought tooth and nail for permission to take the younger children with her so that her frail and elderly parents could see them just once in their lives.

It had been a dreadful wrench to leave Julian behind in a strange school where he knew no one and had nothing in common with any of the other boys. She would not see him again for three years until she brought the twins on the same journey for their education. She had to keep reminding herself that she was fortunate to have this opportunity, since most parents were separated from their children from the day they left India for school in England at the age of eight until, with their school education completed, they returned fully grown. She was at least spared that, but it did not make the parting any easier. She had lived in India for the past ten years and had had enough of the dust and the heat, but she could not leave because her husband was stationed there. She would stay with him until he left, but she prayed that that day would come sooner rather than later.

Evalina did not put in an appearance until the steamer had sailed through the Straits of Gibraltar into the Mediterranean Sea. Pale and wan, with dark circles under her eyes, she gulped a huge lungful of air as soon as she came on deck. She was one of the last to emerge from the fetid cabins and she listened avidly to Lexy's gossip about their fellow passengers.

When they approached the coast of Egypt the excitement was tangible. Lexy stood at the ship's rail to watch the minarets of Alexandria loom ever closer. Major Robert Willoughby, who was en route to rejoin his regiment, and had been watching Lexy since the ship left Southampton, strode over to join her. He was a prominent member of the group that danced attendance on the 'Fishing Fleet', but his interest was more keenly employed in devising a plan of seduction involving the sultry beauty whose travelling companions seemed content to leave her to her own devices much of the time. A self-confessed connoisseur of women, Major Willoughby had originally intended an innocent flirtation to divert him during the voyage, but Lexy had an untouchable quality about her and had refrained from integrating into his group of officers and single ladies. Over the preceding days he had fantasised about being alone with her, and now that he saw her visibly relax in the warm sunshine, he determined to seduce her before they reached Calcutta.

'Are you travelling to India on holiday, Miss Nicolson?' he asked.

Lexy felt the familiar flutter at the sight of a uniform. 'No, Major, I am not,' she replied. 'I don't think that I would consider travelling so far in such discomfort for the sake of a holiday.'

'Ah,' said Major Willoughby. 'Point taken. You must be going to join the young man who is waiting for you to be his bride.'

'Not at all,' said Lexy coolly.

Major Willoughby was relieved. A mild flirtation or light-hearted love affair was easy to conduct on board ship, but his planned seduction could have fallen at the first hurdle if Miss Nicolson was already promised.

'Are your relatives taking you ashore at Alexandria?' he asked. 'If not, I would be delighted to escort you.'

Lexy raised an eyebrow. 'Thank you, but that won't be necessary.'

Major Willoughby decided to let matters lie for the time being and excused himself. 'Perhaps we will meet again this evening,' he said. 'It's our last night on this old tub and there's packing to do before I go ashore. Enjoy your sightseeing, Miss Nicolson.'

Lexy watched him go, and then turned back to the foreign fairyland she was about to set foot on. Across the sea came calls of the muezzins, one after the other, echoing over the city. Lexy felt the thrill of it and her heart quickened as if she were coming alive for the first time. It seemed that for the past twenty-one years she had not really lived at all: life had been a mere existence. Was it a reawakening of Zeinab's blood coursing through her veins that made her feel as if she belonged in the East, or was it an illusion? She did not know, but she was impatient to set foot on foreign soil, whereas Evalina's enthusiasm was tempered by a fear of the unknown.

'Thank you for coming with us, Lexy,' said Evalina as she joined her at the ship's rail. 'You seem so confident while I am trembling inside.'

'Just like I felt at the Chisholms' ball,' said Lexy with a smile. 'Our positions are reversed.'

'Are you all packed?'

Lexy nodded. 'Hours ago. I finished it early so that I could come and watch us arrive in Alexandria. Isn't it wonderful?'

Everywhere they looked the view was an alien one: mosques and minarets, whitewashed buildings, palm trees and cactus plants; Lexy was overwhelmed by the exhilaration of it all. Mungo laughed as he shepherded

Evalina and Lexy through the throng of hawkers peddling their wares on the quayside. He hired a carriage and they were driven through narrow twisting streets between high white walls. Ragged children chased alongside with their hands outstretched for baksheesh. Lexy delved into her bag.

'No, don't,' warned Mungo. 'We'll be inundated by every child in Alexandria. Wait until we get back to the quay, and then you can throw coins for them.'

That night Lexy sat in her cabin and wrote letters to Charlotte and the Frobishers. Her pen flew over the pages as she told of the sights and smells of Alexandria, her first taste of a foreign country – and India was still to come!

CHAPTER 28

The overland route from Alexandria to Suez shaved ten thousand miles off the sixteen-thousand-mile voyage from England to India by way of the Cape of Good Hope. This did not mean that the journey was any more comfortable than the seaborne route, but it was considerably faster. The first stage took them along the Mahmoudieh Canal from Alexandria to the Nile, and here they transferred to a small river steamer which conveyed them to Cairo.

Life along the banks of the River Nile was Biblical in appearance and had not changed for thousands of years. Lexy wished her father could have seen it. It was the first time that she had thought of her father with any kindness and it surprised her to do so, but she knew that he would have been deeply moved by this part of the journey. Water buffalo, giving free rides to the egrets on their backs, were partly submerged in the river; women and girls washed clothes, or fetched water in brass pots or terracotta jars; children frolicked in the shallows, and crocodiles lurked. Lexy could not get her fill of the exotic strangeness, and some of her excitement rubbed off onto Evalina.

In Cairo there was time for the passengers to stretch their legs and have a cursory exploration of the city. Major Willoughby discreetly attached himself to a group that included Mungo, Evalina and Lexy. They wandered through the colourful souks, bought shawls and lengths of cotton material, and stood in awe at the foot of the three great pyramids of Giza.

'They cut you down to size rather, don't they?' said Major Willoughby addressing Lexy. 'Here, modern, arrogant humankind is rendered insignificant by miracles of the past. I'm going to climb to the top. Would you care to come with me?'

'No, thank you,' said Lexy with a smile. 'I'll stay here and watch.'

The Major began to scramble up the side of Khufu's great pyramid where other officers and cadets were already struggling to pit their strength against the pyramid's deceiving height. Each time Major Willoughby reached another level he turned to wave to Lexy, and she happily returned the gesture.

Major Robert Willoughby had had many women, one of whom he had been forced to marry when she announced that she was with child. However there had been no baby after all, and unable to rid himself of his wife the Major had just accompanied her to England where he had left her with a small financial provision on condition that she did not try to rejoin him in India. He was a handsome man, fully aware of his sexual attraction, a schemer with a fund of amusing anecdotes which he used in pursuance of his aims. He spent sufficient time in Lexy's presence to keep him in her thoughts without being overly intrusive. He knew none of the other passengers and had kept his own counsel as regards his personal circumstances, so he felt secure in his intention to pass himself off as a bachelor.

Major Willoughby failed to reach the top of the pyramid, but he was undaunted when he rejoined Lexy.

'The view is better down here,' he said, gazing earnestly into her eyes.

Lexy caught his meaning and blushed. 'I must return to my aunt,' she said, leaving him staring after her and wondering how to penetrate her reserve. She was a prize well worth the chase.

The final eighty-four miles of the overland route, from Cairo to Suez, entailed a trek across desert lasting about twenty hours. The procession was an awesome sight. The one hundred and twenty passengers were crammed into twenty conveyances, known as vans, which were pulled along the track that served as a road by a series of horses and mules. Accompanying the vans was a caravan of three thousand camels which carried the luggage, provisions, water, the all-important mail, and coal for the ship they would board at Suez.

Mungo, Evalina and Lexy climbed into one of the vans, and Major Willoughby scrambled up beside Lexy. Members of the 'Fishing Fleet', whose faces became increasingly sour as they realised that the Major only had eyes for Lexy, claimed the remaining two seats. Lexy was flattered by his attentions and was acutely aware of his proximity to her, his leg pressed firmly against hers.

They set off by moonlight just after two o'clock in the morning, but there was no prospect of snatching any sleep. By the time they stopped for refreshments and a change of horses they were covered in dust and sand, and every muscle ached from being jolted and jarred. Lexy stepped down from the van to stretch her legs. The gallant Major immediately offered to escort her on a short walk.

'We won't go far, and we will stay in sight,' he assured Mungo and Evalina. 'I will bring her safely back to you.'

Evalina watched them go with some misgivings. 'Do you think she will be all right?'

'She won't come to any harm,' replied Mungo. 'There are too many people about for Lexy to be compromised in any way.'

The moon was low in the sky and its silvery light imparted a ghost-like quality to the desert. They walked as far as the camel train and Lexy stopped to gaze about her. There were camels as far as the eye could see, some standing, others lying with their legs folded beneath them. Here and there firelight flickered as meals were prepared for the camel drivers, and there was the quiet buzz of voices and occasional laughter. Bells jingled in the half-light, and the gaseous rumbles of camels' stomachs added their own music. Then, in the distance, as the first yellow streak of morning lit the horizon, came the distinctive call of a muezzin. Lexy caught her breath as camel drivers close to where she stood turned to face Mecca and began their ritual of morning prayer.

She wrinkled her nose at the sour smell of the camels and unwashed bodies, but knew that she was none too sweet either after the heat of the day and lack of facilities to wash on this part of the journey. She turned to Major Willoughby.

'I feel as if I have been transported on a magic carpet to another world,' she breathed. 'I can't believe that I'm really here.'

'You look as if you belong here,' he replied. 'I, on the other hand do not, and nor did I travel on a magic carpet. I ache in every bone already, and there's still a long way to go.'

'Are you glad to be going back to India?'

'A soldier goes where he is sent,' he replied. 'I don't much care where I live. India is as good a place as any and more tantalising than most.'

He moved closer to Lexy so that they almost touched. She lowered her eyes, but he put a finger under her chin and tilted her face to his, and then he kissed her softly and lightly. It was Lexy's first kiss, and it sent her heart pounding with a desire for more. She gasped and stepped back, but she did not protest, and the Major was encouraged.

'We had better return to your relatives,' he whispered. 'You are too beautiful to be so close to on a night such as this.'

He turned and led her back. Neither of them spoke for fear of breaking the spell. Lexy relived the feel of his lips on hers. Until now her heart had been unawakened, but Major Willoughby's kiss released a tide of passion that left her breathless.

From Suez they set sail for Calcutta. The days were hot, the nights sultry, and Lexy spent as little time in her cabin as possible. She enjoyed her time with the Gardner twins in the mornings and built up a considerable Hindustani vocabulary in a short space of time. Each new word learned she wrote down phonetically and practised its pronunciation again and again after she went to bed. But it was the afternoons and evenings that she lived for because that was the time she spent with Major Willoughby.

Late one evening they stood in the shadows on the deck. They appeared to be alone and Major Willoughby drew Lexy into his arms. His kisses and caresses became increasingly urgent and Lexy responded with a passion to equal his own. He knew that he had only to suggest it and she would invite him to her cabin, but part of the Major's pleasure was in the chase, and he was in no hurry to take her with so much of the voyage still ahead of them.

However, their intimacy had not gone unobserved, and the following day Sophia Gardner approached Lexy.

'I would like to talk to you privately, if I may,' she said. 'Would you come to my cabin?'

Lexy nodded in surprise. Sophia called to the ayah to take charge of the children, and then led Lexy below deck. The cabin was hot and stuffy, and smelled strongly of Conrad. There was little room to move as it was crammed with the many and varied accoutrements required by a family of three children on a long voyage. Sophia pushed a pile of clothing to one end of a cot, and they sat opposite one another.

'I want to speak to you as a friend,' began Sophia. 'I hope you won't be offended by what I have to say, but I feel I must say it.'

Lexy shifted uncomfortably. She wondered what she had done to upset her new friend.

'I know that this is none of my business,' said Sophia, 'but you have been such a help to me with the twins that I want to return the favour, even though you may not view it as such. I am not the only one to have noticed how much time you spend with Major Willoughby. Has your aunt spoken to you about it?' Lexy shook her head. 'Well, shipboard romances are common, but one does have to be on one's guard. What do you know of him?'

Lexy considered for a moment. 'Why, nothing,' she said in surprise. 'He has told me nothing of himself. Why? Is something wrong?'

'Hmm. I thought as much,' said Sophia. 'I have racked my brains as to where I have seen him before, and during a sleepless patch last night I remembered. I met him once at a reception in Delhi. He does not remember me, I know, and I cannot in all honesty say that I really know him. It is more his reputation of which I am aware, my dear. Forgive me if I am speaking out of turn, but he is well known in his regiment as being something of a roué.'

Lexy's cheeks flamed, but Sophia continued without mercy. 'I'm sure he must have kissed you in the moonlight, and I should imagine that he kisses with considerable expertise,' she said. 'And so he should, for apart from his flirtations and affairs, Major Willoughby is a married man.'

Lexy gasped in horror. She clapped her hands to her red cheeks, embarrassed and ashamed. 'He never said that he was married,' she gasped.

'Well, I don't suppose he would, Lexy dear. He wants to bed you, to put it baldly, and you are such an innocent that he could have almost succeeded before you were fully aware of his intentions, and then it would have been too late.'

The colour drained from Lexy's face. Her shoulders drooped, and her eyes filled with tears.

'I am sorry to be the one to tell you,' said Sophia more kindly. 'I'm only doing so in order for you to be able to protect yourself. Your good name is worth more than rubies in India. Don't give of yourself lightly or you will live to regret it. Only you can say if Major Willoughby is worth losing your reputation for. All I can do is urge you to be careful, for he will take what you give and then move on to pastures new.'

Lexy wept hot tears of shame and humiliation. Sophia felt sorry for her. 'You are a beautiful young woman,' she said. 'In India men, young and old, will cluster round you like flies. You will be highly desirable and will be able to pick of the best. Choose with care.'

'Thank you for warning me,' sobbed Lexy. 'What a fool I've been.'

'No, you haven't. You have been warned in time. And you have been lucky enough to test the waters. You will only be a fool if you fail to profit from the experience. I hope we shall stay friends?'

Lexy nodded. 'Of course, and I am grateful to you.'

'Enough said then. Dry your eyes and we'll go back on deck.'

Major Willoughby was bewildered. The instant he had caught sight of Lexy that morning he sensed something changed and knew from some indefinable quality in her that his planned seduction was at an end. She had assumed her mantle of untouchability again, and he cursed himself now for not having seduced her the previous evening.

CHAPTER 29

The heat of the Indian sun was like a furnace as the steamer travelled up the Hooghly River. They arrived at Calcutta in the blazing reds and oranges of a tropical sunset. Mungo heaved a sigh of relief and satisfaction – a traveller returned home – but Evalina was unable to conceal the fear and loathing that welled up within her. Lexy's smile of encouragement evaporated as Evalina suddenly laid a trembling hand on Mungo's arm.

'I shall die a horrible death here,' she whispered. 'I have such a premonition of impending disaster.'

Mungo frowned and patted her hand. 'Bear up, old girl,' he said. 'It's a culture shock for everyone at first. You're just tired and hot, but once we get home you'll feel better about it, you'll see.'

But Evalina stood tense and white-faced. She looked for all the world as if she had truly seen her fate.

They shed a goodly portion of their fellow passengers at Calcutta, but many remained on board to continue the long and arduous journey up the Hooghly and the River Ganges to destinations such as Cawnpore, Delhi and Meerut. Lexy sat beneath an awning on the deck of the river steamer and stared, enchanted, at the passing riverbank scenes: the temples, the huts with their thatched roofs clustered together in groves of tamarind trees, and the thickets of bamboo. Sounds of village women chattering on the bank as they washed clothes reached her across the water. Somewhere a temple bell rang, a pariah dog howled, and she could see limbs of trees swaying beneath the weight of vultures waiting for their next meal. She kept her excitement to herself, as nothing seemed to be able to draw Evalina out of her personal terror.

When they reached their landing stage, Lexy bade a tearful farewell to Sophia Gardner and her children. There were promises of letters to be exchanged and invitations for visits in the future. Major Willoughby

bowed to Lexy and as he straightened their eyes met. The Major smiled
and Lexy blushed. She was still confused about her feelings for him. Then
they parted company and waved handkerchiefs as the Delhi and Meerut
contingent continued on their way.

The cantonment at Cawnpore stretched for six miles along the south bank
of the River Ganges and consisted of both military and civil lines. Evalina
and Lexy were pleasantly surprised to find that Mungo lived in a spacious
bungalow with wide verandas sporting rows of potted chrysanthemums
and set in a lush garden.

'Mungo, it's lovely.' Evalina was cheered by her first real home and
bustled from one room to another.

'Well, don't get too fond of it, my dear,' laughed Mungo. 'This
is bachelor accommodation. We will have to move to something more
suitable. When I left here I did not expect to return complete with a wife
and niece.'

The whitewashed rooms opened off one large living area and were
sparsely furnished with cane furniture. There were two bedrooms, and
each had its own bathroom containing a hipbath, shower and earth closet.
Whilst Mungo went to catch up on business affairs before rejoining them
for dinner, Lexy and Evalina strolled in a splendid garden stocked with
unfamiliar plants – oleander, bougainvillea, hibiscus and frangipani.
There was a collection of huts at the far end of the garden. Lexy and
Evalina went towards them filled with curiosity, but when they saw natives
sitting outside they quickly retraced their footsteps.

'I will always be scared to death of them,' confided Evalina. 'I don't
know why. I can't really explain it. They look so graceful and gentle, but
they terrify me.'

'We'll get used to them,' said Lexy. 'Once you can speak some of
the language and can communicate with them I'm sure you won't feel so
nervous.'

'I hope you are right,' sighed Evalina.

Later that evening, folded up in the hipbath with her chin resting
on her knees, Lexy pondered the question of dressing for dinner. All her
clothes had been unpacked and neatly stowed away whilst she and Evalina
had lounged on the veranda drinking tea, but before her bath Lexy had
opened a closet to select a dinner gown and had been bewildered by the

quantity of clothes she had brought with her – and none of them really suitable for the Indian climate. Just looking at them made her feel hot and bothered. She wished she could slip into a simple white gown such as the one worn by her great grandmother in her portrait, but now it was the fashion to wear full skirts over a multitude of petticoats. A sari would be so much more comfortable, she thought, and so much more elegant.

She stepped from the bath and let the water evaporate on her skin. Now that she felt cooler she had even less desire to encase herself in stays, so she decided to abandon them for the evening, reassuring herself that no one would be any the wiser. Feeling shameless, she dressed for dinner minus her stays and one layer of petticoats. She piled her hair on top of her head to keep her neck cool and fastened her mother's pearls around her throat.

Evalina spotted her lack of undergarments immediately. 'Well,' she laughed. 'I seem to remember a certain young lady telling me that she would never have the courage to flout convention. It seems to me that you have made a very good start.'

Lexy blushed. 'I didn't think you would notice. How can you tell?'

'Just your general outline,' said Evalina. 'Your upper body is softer, and your skirts are a little less full. It is very difficult for one woman to fool another, my dear.'

They sat down to a simple meal of vegetable curry. 'Curry is a good thing to eat out here,' said Mungo. 'For one thing, and it's a very important thing, the *bobajee* knows how to cook it. I think one of the reasons I have rarely been ill is because I eat the local diet. I don't trust them to cook English dishes properly, but if you insist we might give it a try.'

'Actually, this is very nice,' said Evalina. 'I am happy to be guided by you.'

'So am I,' agreed Lexy. 'What else do we need to know?'

'Well, the huts you noticed at the end of the garden are the servants' quarters. One of them is the *bobajee khana*. I strongly advise you to keep away from there. It is very much the cook's domain, although you will certainly discuss our menus with him once you know some of the lingo. I will engage a *munshi* to come for an hour each morning to teach you. How much you learn is up to you, but I hope you will be good pupils and learn as much as possible. I dare say that Lexy will be fluent in no time, and now that the sun has browned her to an unfashionable colour, it will only be her clothes that will mark her out as being British.'

'Do I look as foreign as all that?' gasped Lexy.

Evalina nodded slowly. 'Yes, you do at a quick glance. Not if I look at you properly because your eyes give you away – the whites are too white. They are not Indian eyes.'

The hot weather closed in on them like a steel trap. Lexy and Evalina thought they would die of the heat. Mats of woven roots were hung across open doors and windows during the day to prevent even the slightest chink of sunlight penetrating the rooms. These tatties, as they were called, were kept constantly wet by one of the servants so that when the hot wind blew through them the dampness cooled the air inside. The tatties stank, but without them the heat indoors sapped their energy and left them prostrate and panting.

Because it was impossible to sleep indoors, their beds were moved out onto the lawns where they spent hot, but marginally more comfortable nights under the stars and their mosquito nets. They rose at five. Mungo left for work after an early breakfast, and Evalina and Lexy went for a stroll before the sun chased them indoors again. They had their language lesson with the munshi, and then their breakfast. In the heat of the day they sprawled on cane settees under the *punkah*, which stirred the hot air in the room. It was stifling, and there was no peace in the stillness. Only the raising of the tatties in the evening to allow a refreshing of the stale air inside brought a measure of relief. When it came, the darkness of the night was a minor miracle after the glare of the day, but the heat remained. All human activity was halted as each person bore the onslaught of the hot season as best he could, and even Evalina divested herself of most of her clothing in the privacy of her home.

The torment seemed endless. After living in the wet Hebrides Lexy would not have believed that she could long for rain to fall, but each evening she knelt beside her bed and prayed for the heavens to open. But all bad things come to an end just as do good things, and as they sat at dinner one evening Lexy looked up.

'What is that funny noise?' she asked.

There was an irregular tapping on the thatch. The tapping became a drumming, and then they could hardly hear themselves think as rain came down in torrents. Squealing with delight Evalina and Lexy ran outside and danced in it. They were drenched to the skin within seconds, and they coughed and spluttered with the force of the rain. Mungo stood on the terrace and laughed to see them playing like children. Within days the garden was a riot of colour once more, the parched lawns a lush green; but their relief was short-lived because with the coming of the rain the humidity rose to unbearable levels. Indoors they wore 'half a yard of nothing' as Evalina put it, to alleviate the prickly heat that plagued them both.

Then came the snakes and the insects brought out by the rains – mosquitoes, beetles, cockroaches and greenfly. Their clothes and shoes mouldered in the cupboards, and books became covered in mildew. Both women were filled with disgust and dread, but they remained in good health. Mungo supervised everything they ate and drank to protect them as far as he could from the fever and sickness that came with the rains. He refrained from telling them which of their neighbours had become ill or died so as not to frighten Evalina into remembering her earlier fears for her life in this alien land.

And then one day it ended. The Station came to life again, and Evalina and Lexy set about making the visits they had long deferred. Those who had gone to the hills to escape the hot weather returned to Cawnpore, and the social whirl was quickly resumed. When it became known that Mungo Sibley had brought from England not only a wife but also an unattached young lady, they were inundated with invitations to this or that tea dance or dinner party. Lexy was besieged with requests for dances, games of tennis (which she could not play), and carriage rides on the *maidan* in the afternoons. There were so many activities that she was never without company. All the bachelors seemed intent on gaining her for a wife, and there was much speculation amongst the old hands as to which one Lexy would accept.

She was not the only unattached young lady new to this season's social round. There were half a dozen members of the 'Fishing Fleet' immersed in their single-minded pursuit of gaining a husband. Lexy was aware of the hostility and envy she provoked amongst those seeking marriage partners, but she was at a loss as to how to direct the unwanted attentions she attracted to where they would be more enthusiastically and uncritically received.

Lexy hoped, and expected, to find a husband in India. Major Willoughby's kisses and the feel of his lean body against hers lingered in her memory, teasing her with erotic fantasies. Her body yearned for the fulfilment of marriage. She tried not to dwell on the fact that she was now twenty-two years old and would not be considered marriageable much longer, and she was disappointed not to have met anyone yet whom she wished to marry. Amongst the drunk, sickly, boorish or pathetic gentlemen who had been introduced to her there was not one to whom she was prepared to surrender herself; but she was not yet desperate, and the season was new. She could only hope that someone would arrive on the station who would sweep her off her feet before the hot weather returned next year. Meantime, she accepted invitations and waited for her life to begin.

CHAPTER 30

'Who are you coming dressed as?' This was the question on everyone's lips whenever two or more people gathered together.

'I haven't decided yet,' was the inevitable reply. This was a lie, of course, because everyone had long ago made up their minds as to how they would appear at the forthcoming fancy dress ball, but their outfits were a closely guarded secret. On every veranda a *derzi* sat cross-legged, his sewing machine whirring furiously, as costumes, simple or outlandish, came into being. The derzis possessed a magician's ability to conjure something out of next to nothing. Memsahibs presented their derzi with material and a picture, and an exact replica would be produced. Even Jean Tomlinson, cross as two sticks much of the time and scornful of the natives, would not be disappointed with the Madame de Pompadour dress being made for her after just one look at a miniature painting of the French king's mistress.

Evalina's nimble fingers were busily transforming lengths of black crepe and gold lace into a gown fit for Mary, Queen of Scots, and Lexy would not entrust her creation to anyone; besides, it was largely in existence already and only needed special adornment to make it complete. She had decided to attend the ball dressed as the Snow Queen. She already possessed a white satin, full-skirted ball gown, which merely required the addition of dozens of discs of *shisha glass* to be stitched onto it. Lexy and Evalina devoted hours to the task, neither of them having realised how long it would take. Their eyes ached; their backs ached; their fingers hurt and bled from needle pricks, but eventually it was almost done.

'I wonder if the Morleys will bring their visitor?' mused Lexy one evening as they stitched the final pieces. News of an unattached gentleman staying on the station had spread like wildfire.

'I would expect so,' said Evalina. 'I can think of several young ladies who will see him as a potential fish to be hooked, can't you? Poor man. I hope he has nerves of steel.'

'Have you seen him yet?' Lexy fastened off the end of a length of thread and picked up the spool of cotton. 'Do you know anything about him?'

Evalina shook her head. 'All I can tell you is that he is an old school friend of John Morley's. Jean Tomlinson is certain that he is a military man. It amazes me where she gets her information from, but I dare say she is right, as usual.'

'Really?' Lexy's interest was aroused. 'What regiment?'

'Heavens,' laughed Evalina. 'She didn't say. He can't be a young man if he was at school with John Morley. He must be nigh on forty.'

'It's odd he isn't married then,' said Lexy.

'Well, it's pointless our speculating about him. We'll know all we want to soon enough.' She broke off a length of thread. 'There, it's done at last.'

No one seemed to know anything more about the Morleys' visitor although it was confirmed that he was a military man. All newcomers, visitors and new residents alike, provoked a lively interest before their arrival, but rumour and speculation were often exaggerated, and the reality of meeting one of these strangers to Cawnpore could be a considerable disappointment. Lexy was curious about John Morley's school friend, but, like everyone else, she would have to wait and see what he was like.

On the evening of the fancy dress ball, Mungo, dressed under protest as Robin Hood, escorted Mary, Queen of Scots and the Snow Queen to the Club. Their entrance created quite a stir because they were the most impressively turned out of all the guests. Jean Tomlinson, as Madame de Pompadour, was piqued that her own elaborate outfit was outshone by the effective simplicity of Evalina and Lexy's gowns.

Lexy looked magnificent. Shisha glass discs flashed all over her white satin gown; Indian diamonds from the sandalwood chest sparkled in her hair, around her neck and wrists, and dangled from her ears. She seemed to be encrusted with ice, and everyone's eyes were riveted on her, but she was not the only one to attract attention.

'There he is,' said Mavis Brandon, pointing towards a stranger with her fan. 'The tall, fair-haired gentleman.'

They all craned their necks to look in the direction Mavis Brandon indicated, intent on catching a first glimpse of him. He had come dressed as one of the gods of Ancient Greece, and he exuded a health and vitality that was in stark contrast to many of the assembled company. He was not a young man, but neither was he an old one.

'Which is his regiment?' asked Jean Tomlinson. 'Does anyone know?'

'Oh, he isn't in one of the regiments,' said Flora Jenkins. 'I hear tell that he is Sanderson of Sanderson's Rifles.'

'No! Is he really? Goodness me.' All the ladies turned to gaze in admiration at the Greek god.

'What is Sanderson's Rifles?' asked Lexy.

'It's one of the Irregulars. You know – like Hodson's Horse. So romantic,' sighed Flora Jenkins.

'And not married, I understand,' said Mavis Brandon.

'What a waste of a magnificent man,' added Jean Tomlinson.

Lexy's interest was thoroughly whetted. The glamour and mystery of such a man drew her like a magnet. When he was presented to her, Colonel David Sanderson saw himself reflected myriad times in the Indian mirrored effect of the shisha glass. He bent to kiss Lexy's hand, and then gazed into her dark eyes as he straightened. Lexy's heart skipped a beat, and she felt the colour rush to her cheeks. And the old India hands nodded knowingly – Miss Lexy Nicolson had found herself a husband at last.

'You are as light as a snowflake,' said the Colonel as he and Lexy danced together. 'Your gown was well chosen. You are the Queen of Snowflakes.'

He smiled into Lexy's eyes, making her heart race, and he remained at her side for most of the evening. They danced together several times, and he escorted her into supper. Lexy was flattered by the Colonel's attentiveness and felt honoured to have been singled out by such a distinguished gentleman. Tongues wagged.

'I hear wedding bells,' said Jean Tomlinson to Evalina. 'Look at them. They are made for each other. What a striking pair they make. Like gold and ebony.'

Evalina's heart lurched. 'Do you really think she will marry him?' she asked Mungo when they had retired to bed that night.

'Goodness, my dear,' he said. 'They only met five minutes ago.'

'That's as good as a month here,' she replied sadly.

Evalina had known that the time must come when Lexy would marry, and it was only right that she should do so; but she had always thought that

Lexy would marry someone based in Cawnpore. It had never occurred to her that Lexy might leave her some day, and she felt the old irrational panic rise within her. She tried to take comfort from what Mungo said. After all, they had only just met, so why should marriage spring to everyone's mind immediately? But that was how things were in this strange country. Death and disease stalked closely beside each and every one of them, so opportunities were grasped with both hands whenever they presented themselves. When Evalina had watched the Colonel dancing with Lexy she too, like Jean Tomlinson, had heard wedding bells.

CHAPTER 31

David Bell Sanderson was a second son to whom his father had paid scant attention until the death of the firstborn a year earlier. Now his father expected him to return to England to assist in the management of the family estates, but the Colonel had no intention of doing as his father wished.

He had arrived in India in 1836 at the age of seventeen as a cadet in an East India Company native infantry regiment. He had seen active service on the North-West Frontier where he had distinguished himself by his bravery, and he had been so long in India that he had ceased thinking of himself as English. But he was an individualist rather than a team player, and he eventually received a special order from a local Maharajah to raise his own corps of rifles, something for which he was admirably suited. His right-hand man was a native Pathan who had fought at his side in Afghanistan. The Pathan was the nearest any man could be to being considered a friend of the Colonel. Colonel Sanderson had lived a mainly solitary life alongside his men and friendship was not a gift he bestowed with ease.

There was no inducement his father could offer that would tempt Colonel Sanderson to resign his commission. He was proud of his achievements, and his fair and open treatment of his *sepoys* earned him their respect and loyalty. His heart belonged to his adopted country and he vowed never to return to England.

John Morley had mentioned Miss Lexy Nicolson to the Colonel, and he had been surprised to learn that there was an English maiden who had survived several months in India without being snapped up by some man intent on gaining a wife. He decided that the young woman in question must be too old, too plain or too fussy, so when he was presented to the beautiful Miss Nicolson the Colonel was intrigued. She was clearly not one of those predatory women determined to secure a husband at any price, and her dark and sultry appearance captivated him. He decided on a whim that he was, after all, in the market for a wife himself, and this beautiful young woman was the only one who could fulfil that role.

After the fancy dress ball, the Colonel was constantly to be seen at Lexy's side. Their choices of entertainments were few: Lexy had never learned to play tennis, and nor did she play cards because her father had not allowed such tools of the Devil in the house. Their courtship, if such a term could be applied to their being together, was mostly confined to riding in the mornings, taking tea in the afternoons, and going for carriage rides on the maidan before dining with the Sibleys in the evenings.

Lexy did not know what to make of him. She was completely infatuated by him and dreamed of becoming his wife, although she had to admit that her sense of excitement about the Colonel was due more to his profession than to the man himself. She longed for him to take her in his arms, but he showed no sign of passion and she was confused and disappointed. She kept thinking of Major Willoughby's embraces, but then Major Willoughby had been no gentleman. Colonel Sanderson was most definitely an officer and a gentleman, and Lexy decided that that must be why he was so reserved. She had only Major Willoughby with whom to compare the Colonel, and although she ached for passionate kisses, she would only marry a gentleman, and it appeared that gentlemen did not kiss their lady friends.

'Has he asked you yet?' Evalina enquired one evening after the Colonel had taken his leave.

Lexy shook her head. 'Sometimes I don't think that he will,' she replied. 'I can't decide whether he is shy, or reluctant to give up his bachelor status, or whether he doesn't really want me after all. And sometimes I'm not sure that I want to marry him.'

Evalina leaned back in her chair. They were sitting in their favourite spot on the veranda. Moths bombarded the lanterns set at intervals along the terrace, and cicadas and toads filled the night with their love songs. She sighed, remembering how it felt to be twenty-two and still not wed.

'You should marry, my dear,' she said. 'If you don't you will face a life of loneliness. Believe me, I know. I am sure that he does intend to ask you to marry him, and you could do a lot worse than the Colonel.'

'You can also be lonely within marriage,' countered Lexy. 'There's something about the Colonel that scares me a little. Something unknowable. I can't explain it.'

'Are you saying that you don't want to marry him?' asked Mungo. 'You mustn't, you know, if you have any doubts. It's a simple thing not to marry, but a very difficult matter to end an unhappy marriage, especially for a woman. If you are going to marry him, be sure about it.'

'No, it's not that,' said Lexy. 'I have my doubts sometimes, but so does any bride. I shall accept him if he asks, and then I'm sure everything will turn out all right.'

'Well, marriage is a leap of faith,' said Evalina. 'You never really know anyone until you live with them.'

'By which time it is too late,' said Mungo, throwing a paper dart at her.

'Wretch!' laughed Evalina.

At the end of January, Lexy found herself the object of intense displeasure amongst some of the ladies of whose circle she and Evalina had become a part. After a buffet supper, a group of them had drifted onto the terrace. A bare-footed servant, immaculate in his starched white uniform with a dark red cummerbund and turban, offered them drinks from a silver tray. Jean Tomlinson, reaching for a glass, accidentally knocked against one of the others and the drink was spilled.

'You clumsy great oaf!' she shouted at the servant. 'Get out. Bring another drink immediately and clean up this mess.'

The servant bowed and withdrew.

'Honestly, they are perfectly useless,' she complained to the others. 'You can't trust them to do a single thing properly. They're no better than monkeys.'

Lexy drew in her breath sharply.

'Don't take on so,' soothed Mavis Brandon. 'We all know what they're like. We are living in a backward and heathen land after all.'

'They aren't heathens,' protested Lexy. 'They just aren't Christians. They have their own faith and their own gods.'

The sense of astonished outrage was palpable, and there was a sudden fluttering of fans. The servant returned with the tray of drinks and each lady helped herself to one absent-mindedly, as they were all focussed on Lexy.

'My godfathers!' exclaimed Mavis Brandon. An unhealthy redness crept upwards from her neck to her jowls. 'We have an Indian lover in our midst.' She pointed her fan in Lexy's direction. 'You cannot possibly place their religion on a par with our own.'

'You forget yourself, Miss Nicolson,' said Flora Jenkins, a thin, pinched-looking woman subject to bouts of fever that did little to sweeten her temper. 'And you forget that you are addressing your elders.'

'And no doubt you would also say my betters,' answered Lexy. 'Well let me tell you something about religious belief, ladies. I am sure that, as good Christians, you all expect to enter heaven in the fullness of time, but I have it on good authority that you will not.'

'Lexy!' gasped Evalina.

'I know what I am saying, Aunt Evalina,' said Lexy. She ran her eyes over the group of startled memsahibs. 'My father was a minister of the Free Church of Scotland,' she continued. 'A good Christian like yourselves, but he would have assured you in all seriousness, that of all the peoples in the world, only the Scots stand any chance of going to heaven. What is more, of the Scots, only the sinless of the Free Church will actually get there.

'I do not share my father's views, and it seems to me that religion is very much a manmade affair since there are so many varieties, but as for Christianity being superior to other religions, you only have to think of the crimes committed in its name by the Spanish inquisitors to give you pause for thought.'

Lexy turned on her heel, leaving the group of ladies stunned into silence. Evalina chased after her. Colonel Sanderson had been taking a turn of the garden beneath the terrace and, from his position behind an oleander bush, had been an unwitting eavesdropper; now he chuckled with glee. What a marvellous young woman she was. There was now no doubt in his mind that Lexy Nicolson would make him the perfect wife. He needed someone with unconventional views, and she was cast in a different mould from any other woman he had ever met.

After dinner the following evening, Lexy and the Colonel strolled together on the lawns at the rear of the bungalow. There was no moon, but their way was partially lit by the lamps on the terrace. How many times since her arrival in Cawnpore had Lexy walked this same path and imagined herself close in the shelter of her lover's arms? How many times had she relived the tingle of desire awakened in her by Major Willoughby and yearned to feel such passion again? How different reality can be from one's dreams! She knew with the unerring intuition of women that the man at her side was on the brink of offering her marriage, and yet not once had he shown her any hint of either love or passion. Perhaps it was always like this. Perhaps, in his desire to protect the honour of the woman he intended to marry, a gentleman restrained his natural ardour. Perhaps. All Lexy knew was that she wanted to be crushed to his heart, and to hear whispered words of love and professions of undying loyalty. Was it too much to ask for?

To distract herself from such thoughts Lexy crossed to the flowerbeds and plucked a white hibiscus flower from a bush. The Colonel followed her in the semi-darkness. His footsteps made no sound on the couch grass and his voice, so close behind her in the stillness of the night, startled her. She turned round, her eyes wide with surprise.

'I am sure you know what I want to say to you.'

'I can guess,' replied Lexy. She turned away from him to face the gurgling river below, a blackness in the moonless night.

Colonel Sanderson stood head and shoulders above Lexy. He did not look into the black emptiness: his eyes were drawn to the cleft between Lexy's full breasts, which were thrust upwards by her tight-fitting bodice. It was all he could do to prevent himself from clutching her breasts in his hands and squeezing until she cried out. He took a step back from her.

'Thank you for not playing the coquette with me,' he said. 'I am afraid I am not susceptible to feminine wiles. I appreciate your being straightforward.'

Lexy pulled a face in the darkness. 'If I am without feminine wiles as you call them, it is because I have had no experience of their use,' she replied.

She turned to face him. The Colonel's face was in shadow so that Lexy could not see his expression as he ran his eyes slowly over her body. He did not approve of the blatant manner in which the memsahibs flaunted their upper bodies in the evenings whilst shrouding their lower halves in vast and voluminous skirts. He thought the fashion misleadingly provocative since none of the ladies wished a gentleman to take advantage of the expanse of flesh she displayed, but there was something about Lexy that fascinated him. She looked beautiful in her low-cut gown and he loved her exotic appearance. Lexy felt a sudden chill and wrapped her shawl more closely around her naked shoulders; but the night was warm,

233

and it was the Colonel's presence that caused her to shiver. Because her gown was white Lexy was more visible in the lamplight than the Colonel. Of him, Lexy could only see the gleam of his blond hair like a halo, and flashes of brilliance as his movements caused his uniform buttons to catch the light.

'Would you do me the honour of becoming my wife?' he asked. And in the same breath, before she had a chance to respond, 'Should I approach your relatives?'

'That won't be necessary,' Lexy replied. 'I would never do anything to upset them, but they have no legal say over what I do with my life.'

'Then I will address you alone,' said the Colonel. 'If you accept my offer you will want for nothing and will lead a life of quality. I stand to inherit the family estates in Dorset in the fullness of time and should anything happen to me here I would hope that you would go there. But I must prepare you for the fact that my military duties demand that I am often away from home. I have neighbours, of course, and there are other European families close by. Could you bring yourself to live such a life?'

Lexy nodded. 'You have asked nothing of my circumstances,' she said. 'My parents have passed away and I have no brothers or sisters, but is there anything you wish to ask me?'

The Colonel smiled. 'I know more about you than you realise. I was privy to your spirited defence of the Indians last evening. That was enough for me to know what a perfect wife you would be for me.'

Still Lexy hesitated. There had been no mention of love, or even of affection. It all seemed so cold-blooded, but she forced her doubts to the back of her mind. She wanted to be married and there was no one else suitable. If she refused the Colonel she might never have another opportunity, and he was everything she had always wanted: he was secure in his position, he possessed the aura of danger and mystery a uniform seemed to bestow on a man, and he was handsome and healthy. As Aunt Evalina had said – she could do a lot worse. Thinking that she would feel passion in him when he kissed her, Lexy turned her face to the Colonel, inviting his kiss, but he remained motionless. She held her breath and waited for him to take her in his arms – surely he would? But he did not, and each minute of silence between them seemed like an hour.

'Would you do me the honour of becoming my wife?'

Lexy had not expected him to pose the question a second time. She thought that he would merely ask for her answer, and her 'Yes, Colonel' slipped out almost involuntarily. Immediately she had uttered the words she wanted to retract them, but it was too late. She had committed herself, and now she had dreadful qualms as to how little she actually knew of the man who was to be her husband.

CHAPTER 32

Only hours before the ceremony Evalina received a letter from Lady Alice that threw her into a tizzy. She locked herself into the room she shared with Mungo and swallowed hard to keep the tears at bay, determined to keep the news to herself until the evening. Her grief would have to wait, as she had no intention of donning black crepe and appearing as a black crow at Lexy's wedding. It took an immense effort of will, but Evalina knew that she could be strong if the occasion demanded; now the occasion demanded, and strong she would be. She folded the letter and placed it under her pillow ready to show it to Mungo after Lexy and the Colonel left Cawnpore later in the day.

Lady Alice's letter had been written weeks earlier, and Evalina felt faint to think how she had indulged in the social whirl oblivious to the tragedy unfolding in England. Cholera had swept through London and killed over fourteen thousand people, and amongst the first to die had been Sir Edward and Polly. Lady Alice and Charlotte had fled to the safety of the country where, at the time of writing, they were still in good health. Charles had assumed ownership of the Wickham estate, and Lady Alice, in a rare outburst against her darling son, expressed her concern that he was gambling heavily. The only good news was that James had received his commission and was on his way to India. Lady Alice omitted to say where in India he was posted, nor did she name his regiment, which showed the state of her mind when she wrote the letter.

The idea that James might already be in India cheered Evalina. She was sure that either Mungo or the Colonel would be able to discover his whereabouts, but she was concerned for Lady Alice and Charlotte. If Sir Edward had failed to make special provision for them, Evalina feared that they would be paupers before long because Charles would gamble everything away. She had no sympathy for Charles but wondered how

Lady Alice and Charlotte would cope when neither of them had ever had to do so much as pick up a dropped handkerchief for themselves. Well, thought Evalina, they will either sink or swim, and with youth on her side Charlotte would probably survive.

Evalina pushed her grief to the back of her mind and made ready for the wedding. The days were already hot, and Evalina knew that she would look like a boiled lobster in no time at all even though her gown was silk, which was supposed to keep one cool in the heat but never seemed to have that effect on her. Cotton was her preferred choice of material although too utilitarian to wear for a wedding celebration.

'What do you think?' Lexy twirled in front of Evalina. She had kept her wedding gown a secret, and now Evalina's eyebrows lifted in surprise.

The gown was of an age long past. There were no billowing skirts with umpteen petticoats, no layers of frills and no ribbons. Lexy wore the slim-skirted, high-waisted Empire style gown that she guessed had been her mother's wedding dress. Her thick black hair hung almost to her waist, and she wore her mother's pearls around her neck.

Evalina gulped. 'You look beautiful, my dear, but I fear that you will scandalize everyone.'

Lexy stopped twirling and her face fell. 'Really? Why?'

'Well, because by today's standards you look half-naked.'

'Oh.' Lexy's face reddened. 'This was my mother's wedding gown.'

'Then of course you must wear it,' said Evalina. 'Just don't be surprised when everyone looks shocked.' And then added with a grin, 'I'm sure I shall be able to cope with the outraged comments after you've left Cawnpore.'

Mungo entered the main room of the bungalow. 'Are you ready, ladies?' he asked. 'It's time to leave for the church.' He looked Lexy up and down with obvious approval. 'Well, my dear, if I didn't already have a wife I wouldn't be giving you away today for I would rather keep you for myself.'

Lexy smiled at Mungo. She had not known him long, but she thought him more of a father to her than her own had ever been. He was so even-tempered and generous of heart. Why are there so few men like him, she wondered? How will the Colonel compare? A shiver went down her spine and Mungo saw it.

'Cold feet, Lexy?' he asked gently. 'There's still time to back out if you want to.'

Lexy shook her head. 'No, I'm all right, Uncle Mungo.'

When the first notes of the Bridal March floated through the door of the church, Lexy took Mungo's arm and he led her down the aisle. Guests turned their heads to catch a first glimpse of the bride. There was an audible gasp from the memsahibs, who were every bit as shocked as Evalina had predicted, but that was offset by the frisson of delighted admiration, and envy of the bridegroom, which rippled through the majority of the male guests. As she moved, the soft silk whispering against Lexy's body suggested her form rather than revealed it, but it was all the more sensual for that.

Jean Tomlinson blushed a furious scarlet and pursed her lips in disapproval. 'The brazen hussy,' she hissed.

Other embarrassed ladies turned away, but most of the gentlemen stared in awe. Not one reaction escaped the Colonel's notice as he stepped forward to take his place beside his bride. He was entirely satisfied with the effect Lexy's appearance made on the assembled company. After all, this was the sole reason he was marrying her – to be envied by all other men.

'Dearly beloved, we are gathered here in the sight of God...' intoned the minister.

Lexy kept her eyes fixed on the floor. She was icy cold in spite of the heat trapped within the church from the burning sun outside and the crush of bodies inside. Her mind seethed with doubt, and she wanted her mother. She wondered what would happen if she were to turn and run from the church. She would be free, but that was not what she wanted. She wanted to be married, and there was no one else she would consider as a husband.

'I will,' said the Colonel.

With a start Lexy realised that the minister was now addressing her. This was her last chance to escape.

'Wilt thou have this man...?'

Run, run, a voice whispered inside her head. She heard someone say 'I will', and then realised that the voice had been her own. It was too late. She repeated the words she was expected to say, and her voice shook with each response. Then came the words that sealed the marriage contract.

'I pronounce that they be man and wife together.'

It was done. For better or for worse she had made her bed and must needs lie on it, come what may, just as her mother had done. Outside the church Lexy stood beside her new husband to receive the congratulations and best wishes of the wedding guests. She was able to recall none of it later. In her fear and confusion, she felt as if she had stepped off the world for a while, and only rejoined it when the reality of parting from Evalina and Mungo brought her sharply back to the present.

Evalina drew Lexy aside from the bustle and told her of Lady Alice's letter. Lexy was almost glad of the pain she felt for Evalina's loss because it took her mind off her own distress.

'Why didn't you tell me earlier?' she said. 'I feel so guilty that you have kept your grief bottled up just because of my wedding.'

Evalina hugged Lexy. 'I could not let anything spoil your day,' she said. 'Be happy, my dear, and keep writing to me. Your letters will cheer me up because I am going to miss you so. I look forward to hearing about your new home and your new life, and perhaps you will meet someone who knew your father. I do so want you to put aside your hatred of him.'

Lexy kissed Evalina's cheek. 'The hatred has dulled now, dearest Aunt Evalina. It was so long ago. But I will write, and you must write to me too, and then time will pass, and we will see each other again.'

'Christmas next year is such a long way off,' sighed Evalina.

'But it will come,' said Lexy.

'Yes, Lexy dear,' nodded Evalina. 'Now you must go. The Colonel is waiting for you.'

The honeymoon was to be spent travelling to the town south of Delhi where the Colonel was stationed. They travelled in gharries and spent the nights in *dak bungalows*. Although Lexy was filled with foreboding as to her future with her new husband, she did not fear her wedding night. In fact, she looked forward to it although she would sooner have died than admit it. Evalina had tried her best to explain to Lexy about her wifely duties, but she was overcome with embarrassment and Lexy thought that she had learned more from Major Willoughby's urgent kisses.

When she lay in bed on that first night waiting for the Colonel to join her, Lexy found that her curiosity was, after all, tinged with fear; but it was not the act of consummation that she feared: it was the man himself. She did not know why she feared him because he had always been a perfect gentleman but fear him she did.

The night was pleasantly cool, and the shutters were closed so that no filtering moonlight penetrated the enveloping darkness. A single oil lamp placed on the table between two beds cast a soft glow. Its flickering light pooled on the pillows and sheets as if emphasising that this was the only part of the room of any significance. The rest was in deep shadow.

As soon as he entered the room the Colonel put out the lamp, plunging them into total darkness. He did not speak, and the silent blackness had a sinister edge to it. Lexy felt him slither into bed beside her and her heart began to pump painfully. The bed was narrow and uncomfortable with little room for two people to lie side by side, and without further ado the Colonel pulled Lexy's nightdress to her chin, raised his nightshirt to his waist, and lowered himself onto her whilst she lay rigid and unresponsive. The Colonel did not make love to Lexy; rather, he performed a physical function, totally without passion and in utter silence. Deprived of sight and sound Lexy was left only with the sense of touch, and because he made no attempt to involve her in the act of consummation, she experienced only pain and frustration. There was no pleasure for her, nor she believed, for him. It was over quickly, and she lay bewildered and disappointed.

Was that all there was to it? Why, then, should the act of love be shrouded in so much secrecy? Why would any man or woman risk everything for it? Lexy could have laughed – or cried. She shivered at the thought of the life that stretched before her, devoid of any demonstration of love. There was no consolation to be had from the knowledge that it was her own fault, and that she should have listened to her instincts.

The Colonel misinterpreted her shivers as a sign of shock. He spoke softly in the darkness.

'I shall not trouble you very often, my dear,' he said. 'You will learn to accept your duty, but my needs are few.'

He rose from the edge of Lexy's bed and padded across the room to his own. Lexy wanted to tell him that she looked forward to him troubling her, but she did not have the words. She heard him tuck his mosquito net under his mattress and he was soon asleep, but Lexy lay and listened to his gentle snoring, sleepless till the dawn. The Colonel did not trouble her again throughout the journey.

CHAPTER 33

In the time it took to make the journey the hot weather arrived to torment them. The air was hot and heavy; to move was to swelter, and Lexy fervently hoped that it would be a long time before she had to stare at the back end of a horse again, for the smell and the flies were almost too great to bear.

If she had given any thought at all to the kind of place in which the Colonel lived, she had assumed that it would be similar to the bachelor accommodation lived in by Uncle Mungo, but Lexy's new home was very different and contrary to expectations. The Colonel's bungalow was huge, set in sweeping gardens and with extensive views over the *River Jumna*. Lexy was surprised, but pleased, to find that he did not live in the cantonment, but in an area beside a bustling bazaar. Her instant reaction was one of delight as she realised that she would now be able to experience more of the real India, as opposed to British India which left her unmoved, but having run up the steps into her new home she immediately froze to the spot. This was a woman's house. There was no mistaking the touch of a woman's hand in the choice of French furniture and exquisite chintz curtains and cushions. The whole bungalow was furnished in the manner of a woman accustomed to having only of the best.

The Colonel followed Lexy as she moved silently through the rooms, but when she approached one door he put out his arm to bar her way.

'This is my room,' he said. 'Yours is opposite.'

Lexy stared at the closed door for a moment, and then she crossed the passageway and entered a pretty room decorated in green and white: cool colours that made her think of an English summer. She looked at the Colonel, expecting an explanation, but none was forthcoming, and she was too afraid of him to ask questions.

He did not come to her that night either. In her loneliness, Lexy's thoughts strayed again to Major Willoughby. She was sure that marriage to him would not be like this, and she could not help wondering why the Colonel had married her. If he did not want to come to her bed, what did he want a wife for? It was not as if he needed her to care for him: there were servants to cater for his every whim. None of it made any sense to Lexy and she began to pine for the Cawnpore she had been so anxious to leave.

The Colonel resumed his military duties and Lexy left her card at various European houses. Once the hot weather eased she became a part of the European community, and although it was not quite what she wanted, it was preferable to the sterile atmosphere in the bungalow. There was no ready-made family circle of officers' ladies for her to join since the Irregular Corps possessed even fewer officers than the native regiments, and the Colonel's English officers were unmarried. Lexy's delight knew no bounds, therefore, when she met Sophia Gardner in the house of a local merchant. The two fell upon one another with glee.

'When we heard that Colonel Sanderson had married, you were the last person I would have expected to see as his bride,' said Sophia. She looked at Lexy intently. 'Are you happy?'

Lexy considered the question. 'I am not unhappy, if that's what you mean,' she replied, trying to be loyal to her husband.

'No, that's not what I meant, and you know it,' said Sophia. 'I would never have chosen the Colonel as a husband for you, and I doubt if you will be happy with him. Not that I know him well, but I would have chosen someone more red-blooded for you.'

Lexy sprang to her husband's defence. 'I don't know why you think him so unsuitable,' she said. 'He is a gentleman. He's a brave soldier and…' Her voice trailed away.

'And he's as cold as a fish.' Sophia finished for her. 'Isn't he?'

Lexy blushed scarlet and did not reply. The conversation turned to the Gardner children and nothing further was said about Lexy's marriage or her choice of husband. They parted with a promise to visit each other to renew their shipboard friendship.

Life took on a routine that seldom varied. Lexy and the Colonel rose at five o'clock each morning. They rode for an hour before the sun's heat became a burden. It was Lexy's favourite time of day because the Colonel was usually relaxed and in good spirits. They conversed in Hindustani at

Lexy's request until they returned home for breakfast, and in no time at all she was almost fluent in the language.

After breakfast, the Colonel left and Lexy attended to her own duties, none of which were either onerous or time-consuming. She consulted with the cook, arranged the flowers cut for her each morning by the mali, filled cigarette boxes, and put the laundry out for the dhobi who arrived each day on his donkey. The remainder of the day was Lexy's own to do with as she wished, and the hours stretched ahead, interminable and empty.

With little to occupy her constructively, Lexy became obsessed with gaining access to her husband's bedroom. She wondered what was in there that he did not want her to see. Several mornings in a row Salim, the Colonel's bearer, miraculously appeared from nowhere just as she put her hand to the door handle. He stood in front of the door to prevent her opening it.

'This is sahib's room, memsahib,' said Salim, shaking his head.

Lexy had always turned away, but one morning she replied to Salim in his own language.

'Yes, Salim, I know that, but I am sahib's wife and I intend to go into my husband's room. Stand aside and let me pass.'

Salim glided away on his bare feet with a troubled expression on his face and Lexy opened the door.

There were two beds, one draped with a mosquito net, the other with its net tied in a series of loose knots above the bed. Each of the beds was covered with exquisitely hand-embroidered linen. On the dressing table lay the Colonel's silver-backed hair and clothes brushes. Beside them were a tortoise-shell-backed hand mirror, brush and comb – a woman's possessions. But Lexy barely registered any of these details as her eyes were irresistibly drawn to, and held by, a small framed picture on the table between the beds. It was a photographic portrait of four persons: a young woman with an aristocratic face with her fine blond hair piled high on her head, a baby a few months old on her knee, and standing at her left side, a young fair-haired boy. It was the figure on this child's left which caused Lexy intense shock, as it was unmistakably the Colonel as a younger man. That they were a family was evident, and they exuded a sense of happiness that was almost tangible.

Lexy was numb with shock. Why had her husband kept this family a secret from her? She lost all sense of time as she sat on the bed beneath its knotted net, the framed portrait in her hands, so absorbed in her thoughts that she almost dropped it in fright when she heard the door close softly. She gasped when she looked up and saw the Colonel standing just inside the room. She had not heard him come in, and she could tell from the diffused anger on his face that he was in no mood to be humoured. They glared at each other across the room for a long moment before the Colonel stepped towards Lexy.

'So! You have opened Pandora's box.' His voice was ominously quiet. 'What are you doing in here? Salim had orders to keep you out.'

Lexy trembled and the framed portrait shook in her hands. Her face was pale as she wondered what he was going to do.

'Please don't be angry with Salim,' she begged. 'He did try to stop me, but I ordered him to let me pass. The poor young man had no choice but to obey me unless he physically dragged me away, and you know that he would never lay a finger on a memsahib.'

The Colonel gave a brief nod of acknowledgement. Lexy was right: Salim would not have thought that touching her was worth losing his caste for. Lexy held up the portrait.

'Who are they?' she asked.

The Colonel's eyes, cold and devoid of emotion, bored into Lexy's and her fear left her. She could not be afraid of him at that moment because all she could see was the emptiness in his soul. His anger had gone. Lexy held his gaze until he looked down at the portrait in her lap.

'They are my wife and sons,' he said.

'I thought I was your wife,' said Lexy.

'You are. My family died of a fever years ago.' Pain crossed the Colonel's face. He moved to the window and looked out so that Lexy should not see the tears in his eyes.

Lexy did not have the sense to let matters rest. She wanted to know more, and her persistence stirred the coals of passion within this man she had married, yet scarcely knew.

'Why did you not tell me that you had been married before?' she asked.

'You did not ask,' replied the Colonel. 'Would it have made any difference had you known?'

Lexy considered the question. She had thought it strange that a man of his age should not have been married, but he was right when he pointed out the fact that she had not asked him about his marital status.

'Would you have told me?'

'Of course,' said the Colonel. 'But I asked you if it would have made any difference.'

'Well no, it would not have prevented me from marrying you,' said Lexy. 'But it does make a difference now in as much that I cannot trust you. What else are you keeping from me?' She stood up and replaced the portrait on the table.

The Colonel turned from the window to face her. 'Nothing,' he said. 'Is that all?'

He looked so remote that Lexy's blood ran cold. The man seemed to have no feelings at all. 'You don't love me, do you?' she said.

'No.'

'Then why did you marry me? Why bring me miles away from the people I love if you didn't want me? I don't understand. What can I do to make you love me?' she pleaded.

'Nothing, my dear,' he replied. 'I married you for your looks alone. I wanted every man to envy me my good fortune in having such a beautiful woman at my side. I don't think you have any idea how beautiful you are. Might I ask why you married me?'

Lexy's heart sank with shame and misery. 'I wanted to be married,' she replied in a small voice. 'I wanted to marry someone with a good position, a man with a romantic aura about him. There was no one like you in Cawnpore, and all the women sighed over you.'

The Colonel laughed at her. 'Well, it seems we both got what we bargained for, so neither of us has any cause for complaint. I shall do my duty by you, my dear, but as for the trust you mentioned, I do not recall that word being used anywhere in the marriage service.'

Lexy was stung, and suddenly very angry. She ignored the fact that she had kept a secret from him, her inheritance, and rage loosened her tongue. She glared at him with her fists clenched tightly at her sides.

'Your duty?' she flung at him. 'I seem to remember from the marriage service that the purpose of matrimony is for the procreation of children. You appear to be failing miserably in your duty in that direction.'

The Colonel's face paled, and then reddened. Too late, Lexy realised that she had gone too far. He sprang towards her, grabbed her by the arm and dragged her to her room.

'Your duty, as you promised, is to obey me,' he hissed through clenched teeth. 'You will never enter my room again. Do you hear?'

Lexy nodded dumbly, but the Colonel had not finished with her. He kicked the door closed behind him. Lexy cowered before him, waiting for him to strike her, but he did not. Instead, in one violent movement, he took hold of her gown and ripped it from bodice to hem. She gasped in shock and clutched at her chemise. Sexually aroused by his violence, the Colonel tore at Lexy's clothes until she stood completely naked. She had never felt so embarrassed or humiliated but was powerless to resist him. Whilst he stripped off his own clothes Lexy trembled under his searching gaze as he inspected her body with a minuteness that made her attempt to cover herself with her hands. She screwed her eyes shut so that she did not have to watch him undress. With a snarl he pushed her towards the bed, pulling her hands away from her body, and pinned her down. Then he forced her legs apart with his knees and thrust at her brutally.

Lexy was too frightened to struggle, or even to cry out. She thought her ordeal would never end. The Colonel stayed with her, forcing himself on her time and again until he was exhausted. By the time he left her bed hours had passed and she was alone in a night as black as jet. Before the Colonel had attempted to win Lexy's love, he had taught her how to hate him.

Stripes of sunlight across her face woke her in the morning although she was not aware of having gone to sleep. For a moment she did not know where she was, but when she stretched her limbs, which were stiff from having lain motionless, she gasped with pain, and the horror of the night before came flooding back. She remembered every lurid detail, the humiliation and the shame of it. She curled into a ball and wept.

The following week, still bruised and shocked by the violence of her husband's assault, Lexy left for the hills with Sophia Gardner and her children to escape the hell of the hot season on the plains. When she returned in early October Lexy was solemn and withdrawn, and the beautiful garden, ablaze with colour and previously a source of delight for her, left her unmoved. She sat in the shade of a neem tree and mulberry bushes with a book on her lap, open but unread.

Lexy was pregnant, and neither she nor the Colonel could be described as being pleased about it. Lexy, who had looked forward to having children of her own, could only view the coming infant with resentment; whilst each time he looked at his wife, the Colonel was confronted with the memory of his vicious assault on her. He was ashamed although he could not bring himself to apologise to her.

The atmosphere in their home was coldly polite. The Colonel did not enter Lexy's room, and she took pains not to provoke his anger. They ate together in silence, and they no longer went riding in the early mornings. It was only the knowledge that Evalina and Mungo would be with them for Christmas that kept Lexy from going mad.

CHAPTER 34

November brought Diwali, the Hindu Festival of Lights. It seemed that in the whole town there was not a single window without its own little clay lamp flickering in the darkness. The river sparkled with the light from the lamps reflected in it like diamonds. Even Lexy's spirits could not fail to be lifted by the fairy-like beauty of Diwali and knowing that Christmas was almost upon them she managed to smile again.

To Lexy's astonishment, when Evalina and Mungo arrived they brought someone with them – none other than Charlotte Wickham. In her surprise Lexy forgot for a moment that Sir Edward had died earlier that year; but it seemed that Evalina's prophecy as to what would befall the Wickham family following his demise had been fulfilled. As Charlotte recounted what had befallen them, Lexy put aside her own misery to comfort her cousin.

'Charles left Cambridge the minute he learned that Papa had passed away,' explained Charlotte. 'He said that there was no point whatsoever in him pursuing studies for which he had neither interest nor aptitude. With nothing to fill his time he lived for the gaming tables and frittered everything away. Mama knew that he was a gambler, but even she was appalled at how quickly he ran through the fortune Papa bequeathed him. It was all gone in a matter of weeks. Even the houses.'

'What?' gasped Lexy. 'You don't mean it. It surely can't be possible?'

Charlotte nodded, dabbing her red eyes with a handkerchief. 'He lost our lovely house in Ramsgate on the turn of a card. Mama was distraught.'

'Whatever did you do? Where have you been living?' asked Lexy.

'Mama and I moved into rented rooms south of the river. Mama had to sell some of her jewellery to raise money. Then Charles found out where we were, and he came after us. He searched the rooms in which we were staying and stole anything of value he could find. There wasn't much, but

248

he took it anyway and gambled it clean away. Now he is in the debtor's prison, and there seems little likelihood of him ever being released. He has so many creditors it is frightening. We had to move several times before we felt safe from his pursuers. You can't imagine how dreadful it has been.'

Lexy regarded Charlotte with shock and pity. Charlotte had had such high hopes of making a brilliant marriage and yet, here she was, wearing clothes that had obviously been made over, and none too well at that.

'Whatever made you come to India?' asked Lexy.

Charlotte dried her eyes. 'Well, Papa left James just enough money for a commission in the East India Company but nothing extra, and nothing for me. Mama said that Papa would have expected Charles to take care of me, but I don't believe that. Papa knew what Charles was like. Anyway, Charles refused to put any money by for me to make a decent marriage, or to help James purchase his uniform and necessaries to take up his commission. Mama was in despair. She sold everything she had left to help James, but now he has to cope as best he can on his pay. There was nothing left for me, and Mama fears that she will end her days in the workhouse.'

'Could you not have found some sort of employment to help you?'

'What sort of work could I have done?' said Charlotte. 'I've never had to do anything in my life. I wouldn't have known where to start, and I don't have your education, so I couldn't have become a governess even if I'd wanted to. It was Lady Jean Eastman who suggested that I come to India. Do you remember her?'

Lexy nodded. 'She was the one who kept saying that Uncle Mungo was no longer alive even after she had talked with him.'

They all laughed, and everyone relaxed a little.

'Lady Jean thought my best option would be to come and stay with Aunt Evalina while I looked for a husband. It's humiliating to be reduced to this, but I don't see what else I could have done.'

'But is it what you want, Charlotte?' asked Lexy. 'To find a husband here in India?'

'It's all I'm fit for really,' sighed Charlotte.

'Yet you didn't find one in Cawnpore.'

'Neither did you,' replied Charlotte with a smile. 'After all, your husband was only a visitor there. To be frank, I didn't meet one gentleman that I would have taken willingly – except for one or two who were already spoken for.'

'So, you are not desperate?' laughed Lexy.

Charlotte grinned. 'Keen, yes. Desperate, no.'

The two cousins strolled into the garden together. Evalina stayed on the terrace and watched them with a sad and anxious face. Lexy could not fool her: she knew that there was something very wrong in the Sanderson household. There was no air of expectant happiness for the coming baby, which alarmed Evalina. For the present she would keep her own counsel, but if Lexy's mood did not lighten during the Christmas festivities she would not be able to stop herself from asking what troubled her.

Because of her advanced pregnancy, Lexy was unable to attend the balls and dinner parties, so the Gardners accompanied Evalina, Mungo and Charlotte to the social whirl on the station. Lexy's derzi altered some of her gowns to fit Charlotte, and a few new ones were quickly made. With all the entertainments Charlotte regained her zest for living, and she found the season in India during the cool weather every bit as exciting as that in London.

As was the custom whenever an unattached young woman arrived anywhere in India, Charlotte was quickly surrounded by gentlemen anxious to find themselves a wife, but she had eyes for only one of them. Sophia Gardner presented Captain George Cartwright to Charlotte Wickham and they gazed at each other in mutual admiration. At the ball held to celebrate the passing of 1851 and the dawn of 1852, Charlotte fell in love. Within days of meeting they were betrothed and were thrust into a flurry of wedding preparations.

Lexy's daughter was born when the New Year was barely a week old. The doctor who had agreed to attend Lexy should he be required had expected a disaster in view of her dainty stature. He was convinced that Lexy or the baby, or both, would fail to survive the ordeal of childbirth, but his fears were unfounded. Lexy may have looked fragile, but she was healthy and strong, and not only did they both survive, the birth was easy. Lexy felt ashamed at how little she had suffered, but when she looked at her baby she felt nothing for her.

Martha – or 'Mattie' as everyone called her – was the image of the Colonel and that, together with the manner of her conception, formed a barrier against Lexy's maternal feelings. When the ayah brought Mattie to Lexy to be fed, the baby squirmed and screamed the instant she left the ayah's arms. Each feed became a battle of wills and try as she might Lexy could scarcely believe that the red and wrinkled ball of temper had anything to do with her.

Evalina watched mother and baby with mounting concern. Mattie failed to thrive in spite of Lexy's ample supply of milk. Whenever Mattie was brought to her Lexy's face became pinched and hostile, and except for those times when Mattie was put to the breast, she would have nothing to do with her.

By the time she was six weeks old it was obvious that Mattie had inherited none of her mother's colouring. Her eyes had become the same clear blue as her father's and maternal grandfather's, and a fuzzy halo of golden fluff outlined her head. One evening, as she watched Lexy commence the inevitable, though lessening, battle of the breast, Evalina finally voiced her concerns.

'I don't know what the matter is, Lexy dear, but I feel that there is something very wrong. You don't have to tell me about it, but whatever it is, it is not Mattie's fault. You really mustn't hold her responsible for anything you are feeling because she doesn't deserve it.'

Evalina's words reduced Lexy to floods of tears. It was the first time she had cried since the day she was raped by her husband, and the relief was immense. She cried for herself; she cried for her mother; and she even cried for her poor unwanted baby. When her tears subsided Lexy poured out the story of her life with the Colonel and his savage assault on her. Evalina listened with mounting horror to the intimate details of another's marriage. She felt embarrassed and infinitely sad. She was so happy with Mungo that she found it hard to comprehend the married hell some women were forced to endure.

'It's all my fault,' sobbed Lexy. 'My husband doesn't love me or want me, and even the baby rejects me.'

'It still isn't Mattie's fault,' insisted Evalina. 'She did not ask to be born although I do understand that what happened to you affects your acceptance of her. But have you considered that Mattie probably senses your rejection of her, and that is why she fights you so? I'm no expert on babies, mind you, but from where I am sitting it seems as if open warfare has been declared on both sides.'

Lexy dried her eyes. 'She looks so like her father that I see him every time I look at her,' she said.

'Well, the Colonel is her father, after all. She cannot help which of you she takes after, and she is definitely not to blame for what happened. She is just an innocent baby.'

Lexy handed Mattie to the ayah and crossed to the window. 'I know,' she sighed. 'You are right, Aunt Evalina. I will try to feel more for her than I do. I promise that I will try,' she said flatly.

Eight weeks after they first met, Charlotte Wickham was married to Captain George Cartwright. The joy on the faces of the bride and groom was plain to see, and Lexy felt pangs of envy when she compared their delight in each other with her own loveless marriage. She wondered what it was that she lacked that caused her husband to have no interest in her other than showing her off as a prized possession at social gatherings.

A week after the wedding Evalina and Mungo left for Cawnpore. If Charlotte had not married and settled close by, Lexy felt she could not have borne this second parting from Evalina. When she had left Cawnpore as a new bride, Lexy had done so with a heart full of hope for the future. Saying goodbye this time Lexy had only the expectation of despair and misery to keep her company, but Charlotte's presence would comfort her in Evalina's absence. After Evalina and Mungo had gone Lexy felt utterly bereft, and she fed on the resentment in her heart.

One evening, shortly before Lexy left for the hills with Mattie, she and the Colonel sat on the veranda in the gathering gloom. Lexy studied him through half-closed eyes. He lolled back on a pile of silk cushions, wearing the loose *kurta* pyjamas of the Indians. Salim had prepared the Colonel's hookah and he puffed at it with pleasure, a self-satisfied smile on his face. Lexy resented his smug complacency whilst, at the same time, envying his physical comfort. She sat, tightly laced and stifling in her crinoline. She had been sworn to secrecy over the Colonel's evening habit of 'going native' because the days when this had been common and acceptable behaviour were long gone. Lexy smiled to herself to think of the outraged expressions on their faces should the po-faced memsahibs learn about her husband; but far from scorning his proclivities, she wished that she could emulate them. Much as she loved the newly fashionable crinolines, they were totally unsuitable for the Indian climate and Lexy wished that she too could wear native dress in the privacy of her home. She considered it ludicrous that the British thought it necessary to keep up their starched appearances in order to impress their superiority. If she had been Indian, Lexy would have regarded the British as mad as March hares.

In spite of her antipathy towards her husband, Lexy loved India. She loved the glittering colour, the beauty, the cruelty and the passion of it – the India of the Indians that is; for British India she felt little more than scorn, and aside from Sophia Gardner and her cousin Charlotte she kept herself aloof from the memsahibs. There were times when she could believe that she had been Indian in a previous life, but that would mean a belief in reincarnation, and she had not yet completely freed herself of her father's religion to accept that.

The following morning Lexy rode into the narrow alleys of the bazaars. Shopkeepers sat cross-legged at the entrances to their establishments, which were little more than small rooms off the street, and they made no attempt to sell their wares to Lexy, a memsahib who did not look like a memsahib, and had no business to be riding out alone. If she had not chanced to see lengths of sari silks and jamas on display Lexy would not have reined in her horse, but the jewel colours of the silks and the memory of her resentment at the Colonel's comfort the previous evening brought her to a halt outside one of the shops with mischief in her mind. She did not dismount. The merchant was so surprised to be addressed fluently in his own language that he allowed her to haggle a lower price than he would normally have done for a memsahib; not that a memsahib had ever favoured him with her custom before.

Smiling to herself over what she planned to do, Lexy made her way back through the alleyways but was brought up short as the sound of piercing screams rent the air, startling her and her mount alike. Instinctively she turned in the direction from where they came. As she approached, she heard the shouts and distressed cries of adults and children, but above the hubbub rose earth-shattering screams that made her blood run cold. She came across a crowd of people following a woman who carried a badly burned child. Lexy joined the procession, and when they reached their destination the woman carried the child into a small building. Lexy dismounted and handed the reins of her horse to a boy to hold for her. She followed the woman into a clean, sparsely furnished room. An Indian dressed in immaculate white muslin ushered the leading group into an inner room and the mother laid her child on a well-scrubbed table. The doctor bent over the charred and blackened child who continued to scream in agony. Lexy plunged her hand into her bag and pulled out a bottle of laudanum.

'Will this help?' she asked. 'It's tincture of opium.'

'Yes, thank you, memsahib.' The doctor took the bottle and read its label before turning to speak softly to the boy's mother.

'The memsahib has offered something to ease his pain,' he said.

The mother turned anguished, frightened eyes to Lexy and nodded. The doctor gave the boy some of the medicine and they waited for it to take effect.

'Will he survive?' asked Lexy in English, not knowing whether or not the doctor would understand.

'No,' he replied. 'I can do nothing for him. His mother knows that I cannot save her son. She will be grateful that his pain leaves him. That is all she can hope for.'

Lexy looked at the burned child. 'Whatever happened to him?'

The doctor sighed. 'He fell into the cooking fire. It is a common enough occurrence, I'm afraid.'

The boy's mother stayed at his side until the laudanum took effect and he slept. Then she went and crouched against the wall in a corner of the room. Lexy sat on the floor beside her. All they could do now was wait for nature to take its course. A char-wallah brought tea and Lexy, the doctor and the boy's mother sipped their drinks in silence. The door was closed firmly against the crowd outside.

It seemed a lifetime of waiting, but in reality no more than an hour passed before the boy awoke. He searched with his eyes for his mother and she went to his side. She crooned to him softly, and after a little while he died. His passing was peaceful, yet the crowd outside knew of it somehow. A clamour of wailing shattered the silence inside the hot, stuffy room.

'Is there anything else I can do?' asked Lexy.

'No, thank you. You did more than the mother would have expected. Thank you for the laudanum.'

The doctor held out the bottle for Lexy to take, but she shook her head. 'You keep it,' she said.

The doctor put the bottle into a locked cupboard, and then he opened the door to speak to the people outside. A man entered and lifted the dead child in his arms. At the doorway the mother turned back and spoke to Lexy.

'Thank you, memsahib, for showing honour to my son.'

'She thanked you for your kindness,' translated the doctor.

'Yes,' said Lexy. 'I understand your language.'

Lexy left the building, paid the boy who had held her horse, mounted, and rode slowly home. It was impossible to rid her mind of the tragic child and the manner of his death. As soon as she reached home, she rushed to Mattie's side to reassure herself that all was well. It was the first time she had thought of her with any motherly concern.

CHAPTER 35

After her bath that evening, Lexy dressed in some of the garments she had bought in the bazaar. If the Colonel enjoyed being free of his uniform, then she was going to enjoy an evening free of the tight lacing, hooped petticoats and crinolines fashion dictated must be worn by the upright, morally-superior memsahibs. She was still preoccupied with thoughts of the morning's tragedy and did not stop to consider the effect her appearance might have on her husband. It was not until she entered the dining room to join her husband for their meal and saw the shocked disbelief on Salim's face, that it occurred to her that the Colonel might be furious. It was one thing for a sahib to repeat history and 'go native', albeit in secret now that times had changed, but how many memsahibs dared to dress so?

In the event, far from being displeased, the Colonel rose to greet her with frank admiration in his eyes. He turned to Salim.

'You will not mention what you have seen,' he ordered.

Salim's eyes were veiled. 'No, sahib,' he murmured.

When the bearer left the room, the Colonel gazed at Lexy. 'My dear,' he said. You look wonderful. Turn around and let me look at you.'

Lexy did as he asked. She was wearing loose silk jamas of a sea-green colour with a short-sleeved bodice to match, richly embroidered with gold thread. Over this she wore the kurta, a gauzy transparent garment that reached her hips. A dupatta was draped over her head and shoulders, and round her neck she wore her favourite emerald necklace from the sandalwood casket. The Colonel regarded her appreciatively.

'The memsahibs will be shocked when they learn of your outrageous behaviour,' he said with a smile of satisfaction.

'How will they know unless you tell someone?' Lexy asked. 'Salim will not disobey you.'

'My dear girl, nothing remains secret here for more than five minutes.

I shan't say anything, of course, but your ayah will tell someone else's ayah, who will tell her mistress, and I would wager that by this time tomorrow everyone will know how badly you have let the side down.'

'Oh dear,' said Lexy. 'I didn't think. I only wanted to be more comfortable. Our clothes are so hot, but I'll go and change at once.'

'No, please don't,' said the Colonel. 'I like how you look tonight. It is disturbing in a very nice way.'

Lexy blushed, and that evening was passed in an atmosphere very different from any other Lexy had spent with the Colonel. It was an evening of companionship charged with sensuality, and that night, for the first time since he had assaulted her, the Colonel came to Lexy's room.

He entered without knocking. Lexy had dismissed her ayah and sat at her dressing table brushing her own hair. She was still wearing the kurta pyjamas. The Colonel crossed the room and stood behind her. He bent to kiss her neck, and then gazed at her reflection in the mirror. Lexy could feel his hot breath on her head, and she could feel her old fear of him creeping back.

'Stand up,' he said suddenly.

She did as he ordered and darted a frightened look over her shoulder.

'Don't turn round. Face the mirror,' said the Colonel. He kicked the dressing stool away and pressed himself against her back. She could feel his every muscle and she began to tremble.

Two candles lighted the room. There was one beside the bed and one on the dressing table. In the wavering light from this candle, the Colonel's eyes wandered up and down over Lexy's reflection in the mirror. The contours of her body were clearly visible through the flimsy material, but her long black hair had fallen forwards over her shoulders and covered her breasts. The Colonel brushed her hair back with his hands, and then he ran his fingers lightly over her breasts until Lexy's nipples thrust against the fabric.

Lexy's breath came faster, partly through desire, but mostly because she feared another assault. She tried to move away, but he held her fast.

'Keep still,' he whispered. 'I don't want you to move.'

Too frightened to cross him, Lexy stood rigidly whilst the Colonel peeled her garments from her one by one. She turned her face away from the reflection of her naked body, deeply embarrassed by the Colonel's scrutiny. He pulled her hair to force her to face the mirror, so she closed her eyes.

'Open your eyes,' he ordered.

'No,' she squirmed.

He took hold of her breasts and squeezed until she gasped with pain. 'Open your eyes. I want you to watch.'

Mortified, Lexy opened her eyes and was forced to watch as the Colonel slowly fondled and explored every part of her. She could feel his mounting excitement, but the faint stirring of desire he had aroused in her was swiftly changed to terror and disgust by the element of coercion he exerted. Without warning, the Colonel picked Lexy up and took her over to the bed where he continued to probe and push, and the more she tried to twist away from him, the more excited he became. When he entered her she lay completely still, remembering just how much pain he was capable of inflicting; and then he suddenly lost interest. He left her abruptly for his own room.

After he had gone Lexy pulled the sheet over her and lay awake for a long time trying to make sense of the man she had sworn to love, honour and obey for the rest of her life. The admiration that she had once felt for him he had successfully extinguished, and she knew now that she would never be able to love him.

Her fear of the Colonel meant that she would keep her promise to obey, but she could not honour such a man for he was a man without honour. He had no regard for her, and he had left her feeling tense and unfulfilled. She felt used, cheapened and resentful.

Several days later the Colonel and Lexy sat on their veranda spending the last evening together before Lexy and Sophia departed with the children for the hills to escape the hot season. They both wore native dress and the Colonel was enjoying his evening pull on his hookah. He watched Lexy through a haze of smoke.

'You are not like a memsahib,' he said. 'You don't really look British. In fact, you don't really look European at all, especially dressed like that. Was your great grandmother an Arab?'

'I don't know,' replied Lexy. 'I don't think my mother knew. At least, she never mentioned where her grandmother came from. We never ask our parents about their lives, do we? There was so much about my parents that I did not know about until shortly before they passed away.'

'Mmm. Well, I'm glad she came from a country where skins are darker than ours because yours has turned nut brown under this Indian sun and that, together with your knowledge of Hindustani and your wearing of native clothes, could save your life one day.'

Lexy looked up sharply. 'Save my life? What do you mean? Am I in danger?'

'Not at the moment, my dear, but I am concerned for the future.'

'Why? What has happened?'

'There have been a good many instances of British stupidity over the years, but I fear things are getting out of hand. We have always been a manipulative lot, protecting our own interests – you know the sort of thing.'

'But if it has always been like that why are you so concerned now?'

'Because we are tampering too much with Indian laws and customs. It started years ago when Bentinck made widow-burning illegal, and now we fuel the growing discontent by refusing to accept the custom of the adoption of a son where there is no natural son born to a man. No good will come of it.'

'You surely don't believe sati to be acceptable?' Lexy was appalled.

'No, of course not. It's barbaric. My point is that these are their customs, and if we interfere too much we will do so at our own peril. Now we've got memsahibs here in ever greater numbers and they frown on the taking of Indian mistresses by European men, and the Welsh missionaries are intent on converting the natives to their own particular brand of Christianity. Sometimes I have detected a shifty look amongst the sepoys.'

'I thought you trusted them,' said Lexy. 'You told me that the sepoys' loyalty to you and to Sanderson's Rifles would supersede their loyalty to caste. You have always been proud of them.'

'I am proud of them and I do trust them, but only up to a point,' said the Colonel. 'I am neither blind nor stupid. They are a superstitious race of people who could easily be panicked. And although they are docile for the most part, one day the worm could turn. Wouldn't we resent it if a Hindu, Musselman or Buddhist set about mocking our religion and attempted to forcibly convert us?'

'I am the last person to ask,' said Lexy. 'Frankly, I have no time for religion of any description, shocking as that must sound. I don't care what beliefs people have, but I do think they are entitled to have them and should be left in peace.'

'Father O'Brien would call you a heretic, my dear,' laughed the Colonel. 'He would feel the need to visit you every day, I'm sure, if he knew how you felt. He would want to save your soul.'

'Well, I'd be a good match for him,' said Lexy. 'I grew up having heated debates with my father on the question of religion.' She laughed mirthlessly.

'Coming back to where this conversation started,' said the Colonel, 'you are not in any danger at the moment, but if the time does come when the worm turns, we are few in number and will be at their mercy. Your appearance could save your life, but I fear for poor little Mattie.'

The Colonel was not expecting Lexy to return until the middle of October, so he was not in when she came home at the end of September. It had been a dreadful time in Simla: baby Conrad Gardner became ill and died suddenly. Sophia was strangely calm, but she could not bear to stay in the hills. She needed the comfort of her husband, so they all returned early.

Lexy was surprised to find that she was looking forward to seeing the Colonel. Their last evening together had been pleasantly relaxed, and she hoped that the strained relations between them might improve. She knew that he would be pleased to see how much more lively Mattie was after spending time in the cool air in Simla. The child had grown and seemed less unhappy.

Assuming that the Colonel was attending to his military duties, Lexy was not concerned that he was not at home until he had still not returned in time for the evening meal. Salim assured her that the Colonel was not away with the Corps so she ordered hot water for a bath to soak off the long journey, and sat down to wait for him. When the Colonel did not appear, she ate her meal alone.

By midnight Lexy wondered where he could be. She knocked on his bedroom door, and when there was no reply she peeped inside. The room was empty, and the bed had not been slept in. She was disinclined to go to bed, so she wrapped a light shawl around her shoulders and wandered into the garden. The days were still very warm, but the nights were cool. Lexy stood for a while in the darkness and breathed in the heavy perfume of jasmine. A pariah dog barked somewhere in the distance, and a toad croaked close to where she stood. The moon was on the wane and shed little light, but Lexy preferred the darkness to fetching a lamp, which would only attract the insects she loathed.

As she stood and listened to the noises of the night she became aware of another, muffled, sound. She moved towards it and realised that it was music. Then she heard a deep-throated laugh and knew it was her husband. The sounds came from behind a hedge of hibiscus and oleander bushes. Lexy had to make her way along its entire length to find a way through to the other side. When she squeezed through the gap she found that she was at the rear of a small single-storey building of which she had previously been unaware. It was in a poor state of repair: paint peeled from the walls and shutters, and some plasterwork had crumbled away. She made her way across flagstones with weeds sprouting in the cracks between them. When she reached the corner of the building the music stopped and Lexy froze to the spot. There was total silence from the building now.

She placed a hand on the wall, which still radiated heat from the sun, and peered round the corner. Light filtered from a window where a shutter had been left open and formed a pale yellow oblong on the terrace. She inched forward cautiously and peeped round the shutter into the room. She stayed there only a moment before, hot with shock and embarrassment, she fled back the way she had come to the safety of her own room. She kept a hand clamped over her mouth to prevent any sound from betraying her presence, but in that brief moment the scene to which she was an accidental witness was imprinted on her mind in every detail and would remain with her forever.

From its exterior the building gave no hint of the sumptuousness of the room Lexy had glimpsed. The floor was richly carpeted, the walls painted with murals of birds and flowers and fountains. A woman sat cross-legged on a cushion in one corner with a musical instrument resting on her lap, which she had stopped playing so that she could watch the scene before her.

In the centre of the room stood a raised dais liberally strewn with cushions and bolsters. At each corner of the dais a carved pole rose towards the ceiling to support an elaborate canopy of brocade with heavy gold fringing and tassels. There was a dainty Indian girl beside the dais. Her naked body was visible through the gold-bordered, but otherwise transparent, gauzy fabric draped around it. Pearls dripped from her earlobes, along her parting and around her hairline, and a huge, fine hooped ring pierced her left nostril. Lexy could hear the gentle clink of her leg and arm bangles as the girl moved slowly, gently, rhythmically.

Lying face up on the padded dais, spread-eagled with each arm and leg tied to one of the four posts that supported the canopy, was the Colonel. His eyes were closed and on his face he wore a beatific smile. It was all he wore, for the Colonel was otherwise stark naked, while the girl expertly teased and inflamed him to the highest degree of sexual arousal.

CHAPTER 36

Colonel David Sanderson had not regarded himself as a highly sexed man when he was young. He lost his virginity at a debauch as his training at Addiscombe came to an end, but it had been a sordid affair and he had not dabbled further until he married Eleanor Frampton. Eleanor had been born in India and had just returned to her parents on completion of her schooling in England when they met. David Sanderson recognised that Miss Frampton would be an asset at his side as he forged his career, and she saw a well-positioned future for herself as his wife. His lack of sexual experience combined with her distaste for that side of married life made his visits to her bed a less than enjoyable affair, so they came together infrequently; but David Sanderson loved his wife and she adored him. That they had two sons together was a cause for surprise and celebration, and when Eleanor and the boys died from the intermittent fever, the Colonel was overcome with grief. He sat for hours at their graves on each anniversary, and nearly two years passed before his pain eased sufficiently for him to pick up the threads of his life again.

One evening, as dusk fell and the air was deliciously cool, the Colonel went for a walk. He strolled aimlessly at first, but his footsteps led him to the rear of a large mosque. He turned at an angle from the mosque and walked to the bazaar. He had heard about this place from fellow officers but had not visited it before. Now he walked along its length and gazed at the upper storeys of the buildings where balconies with columns supporting decorative Mughal arches formed a stage on which girls laughed and giggled together as they pointed at passers-by in the street below.

On a whim the Colonel crossed the street and entered one of the buildings. He walked into a richly carpeted room. There was no furniture, but cushions and bolsters lined the walls. Already men lounged against them; mostly they were Indians, but there were a few Europeans amongst them. The Colonel sat down and shrank into a corner.

Three musicians came into the room and began to play in a hypnotic rhythm. A singer entered and added her nasal tones to the music, and then came the dancers. The Indian music soon began to grate on the Colonel's nerves and he decided to leave, but as he made a move to get to his feet a young girl glided into the room. She could not have been more than twelve or thirteen years old. The Colonel drew a sharp intake of breath, overwhelmed by the sheer grace and delicacy of the girl. He thought her the most beautiful creature he had ever seen.

She wore full, flowing, dark blue satin trousers with a dark blue veil edged with gold. Bangles extended from her wrists almost to her elbows, and anklets of bells tinkled and jangled with each movement. She danced in a slow circle while the other nautch girls clapped their hands in time with the music. Some members of the audience began to nod and sway their heads as though in a trance. The pace of the dance quickened and the bells around the girl's ankles rang as she stamped her feet harder and ever faster.

The Colonel watched spellbound, and he felt a surge of desire such as he had never known. He swallowed hard and tried to look away: she was, after all, only a child; but it was partly the forbidden nature of his desire for one so young that hypnotised him into thinking the unthinkable. This child ignited his long repressed, and always denied, sexuality. When the dance came to an end and the young girl glided from the room, the Colonel wanted to shout for her to come back; although he had not even considered patronising one of the many brothels in the bazaar when he had strayed into the area, he now knew that he would be doing so. He had never felt so desperate for sexual release.

For several days the Colonel could not rid his mind of the young dancer and he decided to return to see her again. As he watched her graceful movements increase in tempo to a wild abandon, she inflamed him once more. He wanted her with an unbridled passion, but she danced, not in one of the brothels, but in a genuine place of entertainment. She was not available for casual sex, and there was no prospect of going into one of the rooms upstairs. The only way the Colonel could possess the girl would be if he bought her, and she might not be for sale.

He sent Salim to make enquiries about the girl and her parents, and he returned with the information that they were poor people who might be persuaded to part with her if a suitable offer were made. The Colonel went to visit them in their mean hut on the edge of a shantytown. They drove a hard bargain whilst the girl looked on with frightened eyes, but everything has its price, and the truth is that the Colonel would have given everything he had to possess the dancing girl. Three days later he installed her in the *bibi khana* in the grounds of his house.

Savita possessed a sexuality and knowledge of sexual pleasure beyond the Colonel's wildest dreams. He did not ask where she had learned her arts but was content to spend hours with her, immersed in heights of physical arousal bordering on pain; and he relished this pain she inflicted so lovingly. She knew how to prolong his excitement until the ecstasy of gratification was exquisite torture. And the more Savita gave him, the more he craved, with no lessening of his desire with the passing of time.

When the Colonel married Lexy he had no real interest in the intimate side of their life together. With her foreign appearance, he wondered if she might be different from other memsahibs, but she knew nothing and could not give him what Savita could. His tragedy was that he believed that no European woman could truly pleasure him, and intimacy for the Colonel was a matter purely of receiving pleasure. It did not occur to him to give pleasure in return. He had been brought up with the understanding that decent English ladies loathed, and simply endured, their marital duties, and could never be so base as to find enjoyment in them. And that was Lexy's tragedy: her body cried out for a fulfilment of which she was too ignorant and inexperienced to make known to him, and he was too selfish to help her. Their marriage was condemned to emptiness.

After witnessing the scene in the bibi khana Lexy spent a sleepless night during which she alternated between anger, despair, contempt and, she had to admit, envy. She had thought her husband cold and incapable of emotion, but she had seen a passion between him and the Indian woman that she had not dreamed existed. When she rose for her customary early morning ride, there was no sign of the Colonel, so she rode alone. When she returned for breakfast he was still not at home. She waited briefly, but then started without him. She was drinking a second cup of coffee when the Colonel joined her.

'Good morning, my dear,' he said. 'I did not know you were returning so soon. If you had sent word I would have been here to greet you. Did you have a good time?'

'No,' she replied shortly. 'Conrad Gardner passed away. That's why we came back early.'

'Good Lord,' exclaimed the Colonel. 'What happened? Was there an accident? How awful for the Gardners. I know how they will suffer in their loss.'

'He collapsed suddenly after a bad chest cold.'

'I'm sorry. And you and Mattie? Are you both well?'

'Yes, thank you, quite well.'

Lexy's voice was stony and the Colonel glanced at her with uncertainty. 'Are you recovered from your journey? Did you manage to sleep last night?'

'No,' she replied. 'I couldn't sleep so I strolled in the garden for a while and I heard music. I know about the house beyond the oleanders. It is well hidden from us here.'

There was a deathly hush. The Colonel reddened to the tips of his ears, and then he turned white. Lexy was gratified to see how discomfited he was. He pushed his plate away and wiped his mouth with his table napkin, but he did not speak. Lexy stared at him dispassionately, like a cat playing with a mouse.

'You really should close shutters at night, you know,' she said. 'From the darkness outside a lighted room has every appearance of a theatrical stage. The play being performed last night was instructive, to say the least.'

The Colonel gasped, and then he laughed. 'Well, we must find out what you have learned, my dear.'

Lexy glared at him. 'You will keep away from my room,' she said. 'At least I now understand the reason for your reluctance to fulfil the role of a husband.'

She rose from the table and swept from the room leaving the Colonel to sit alone and meditate over his unseemly exposure to his wife, but he smiled to himself as he decided to do as he had suggested and find out what, if anything, Lexy had learned.

CHAPTER 37

Shrieks and yells of delight pierced the air as a collection of children chased each other around the garden under the watchful eyes of their ayahs. It was Mattie's fourth birthday, and a party was being held in her honour. She was a quiet, self-contained little girl who rarely played with other children. She stood now, on the sidelines as usual, and gazed at the antics of those who were making all the noise. It was almost as if she did not belong in the same world as they; as if it were utterly beyond her comprehension that children could derive any pleasure from such abandoned activity.

Charlotte's son, Benjamin, stood beside Mattie and she clutched his hand, fearing that he might leave her side and join the others. Other than her ayah and the Colonel, Benjamin was the only person to whom Mattie seemed to be able to relate. From the moment of his birth she had regarded him as her own personal property. As soon as he could crawl, Benjamin followed his cousin everywhere like a faithful puppy. Each hated to be parted from the other so Mattie frequently stayed with her Aunt Charlotte and Uncle George in the cantonment, and Lexy was more than happy with this arrangement. She found her daughter's piercing, almost accusatory gaze unsettling. Lexy had never learned to love Mattie in the way she had been loved by her own mother, and she felt sufficient guilt about this without Mattie's sad and anxious face constantly reminding her of her shortcomings. Charlotte was delighted to have Mattie to stay as a playmate for Benjamin as she thought the girl an endearing surrogate big sister for him. It was clear to her that Mattie lacked her mother's love and she could not understand the reason for it, but the Colonel did love his daughter, and now Charlotte laughed to see him crawl on all fours with Mattie and Benjamin on his back.

To an outsider, the life shared by Lexy and the Colonel appeared unremarkable. They entertained and were entertained by others, and on those social occasions no fault could be found with the scrupulous attentions the Colonel paid to his beautiful wife. There were whispers that the couple 'went native' in the privacy of their own home, but they had never been seen in anything other than impeccable English dress, so little weight was attached to the rumours.

Whatever the state of their marriage in public, relations between them were strained in private. After dinner each evening, the Colonel bade Lexy goodnight and took himself off to the bibi khana. He ceased to trouble Lexy with his sexual advances, and as a result there was little prospect of a brother or sister for Mattie.

The fact that he loved his daughter and his sepoys was perhaps the Colonel's only redeeming feature. When he had first peered into the cradle and seen Mattie lying there like a cherub, he had finally been able to lay to rest the ghosts of his dead family. He delighted in his daughter, and as she grew he thought it comical how like him she looked.

'She doesn't even have your brown eyes,' he had marvelled one day when Mattie was a few months old. 'There doesn't appear to be anything of you in her.'

'Perhaps that has something to do with the way her life began,' Lexy had snapped in reply.

The Colonel's face reddened at the first allusion Lexy had ever made to his assault on her. He hastily excused himself and fled from her unwelcoming presence, confused by the conflicting emotions of appeal and hate she aroused in him.

When they met in Cawnpore the Colonel had seen in Lexy's dark beauty the promise of a sensuality he had known only with his Indian mistress, and he had congratulated himself on his good fortune to possess two beautiful women to pleasure and delight him, but Lexy was, after all, an innocent, raised to be modest and virtuous, and her maidenly blushes spoiled his fun. He found with his wife that he had to be cruel in order to perform at all, and he blamed her totally for this. If she would only abandon herself to his personal tastes he might love her; as it was, he despised her for her fear of him.

Lexy was not insensible to the hard shell that slowly encircled her heart. She wished that she could be rid of her husband, but divorce was out of the question. She knew that the Colonel would not divorce her even if she deserted him, and she had no grounds to divorce him other than that of cruelty, but his cruelty only occurred behind the closed door of her bedroom, and nothing on this earth could bring her to reveal her shame. Also, if she decided to leave the Colonel, she would have to leave Mattie behind for the law held that the child was his absolutely, and circumstances would have to be exceptional for Lexy to be able to claim her. Lexy recognised that she was a poor mother to her daughter, but that must be better than Mattie having no mother at all. Not once did it occur to Lexy that she possessed the financial wherewithal to leave her husband. She had forgotten that she was a wealthy woman; but even if she had remembered, there was still the matter of Mattie's future, and Lexy had no wish to desert her.

On a cool morning with a slight mistiness in the air, Lexy rode without any particular route in mind, enjoying the freedom of riding in the winter's chill. She smiled as she recalled how shocked some of the memsahibs had been when they discovered that she had taken to riding alone, but they were used to her eccentricities now although they did not condone them.

When she realised where her aimless riding had led her, she reined in her horse. She was in the lane where the poor burned child had been carried to see the doctor. Two old men squatted on their haunches against the building, their greasy hair adding more depth of colour to the broad grubby stripe on the wall behind them, created over the years by countless heads before theirs. Lexy dismounted and greeted them. They stared at her, expressionless on the exterior, but inwardly affronted by the brazenness of the unusual memsahib with her uncovered face. One of the old men, with ill-concealed contempt, spat a stream of betel juice onto the ground before nodding a grudging reply. The juice had stained his mouth and few remaining teeth red, and Lexy shuddered with the thought that he would look just so had he been drinking blood.

The sound of women engaged in heated argument could be heard in the distance, and the lane stank with the pungent odour of human and animal excrement. While Lexy hesitated, uncertain whether or not to leave, a Brahminy bull ambled past with scraps of vegetation dangling from its mouth and marigold flowers twisted around its horns. The door of the building opened and out through it tottered an ancient man on spindly legs. The fresh dressing applied over his left eye was starkly white against his grimy, wrinkled skin. The two old men who had been waiting for him rose with creaking joints, and all three hobbled crookedly down the lane with Lexy gazing after them.

The doctor peered out of the door and saw Lexy standing alone. The two stared at each other in silence for several moments, the doctor unsure what the memsahib could want with him.

'Come in,' he said finally.

Lexy dismounted and followed the doctor inside, blinking in the dimness of the room after the glare of the sun outside now that it had burned away the mist.

'Sit down, please.' He indicated a wooden chair and Lexy sat on it. He perched on a stool opposite her. 'What can I do for you, memsahib?'

Lexy studied the doctor. She had forgotten, or not had time to properly notice, what a good-looking man he was. His features were regular with a finely chiselled nose and almond-shaped eyes of velvet brown. Her overwhelming impression of him was one of grace and gentleness.

'I don't really know,' she replied. 'I didn't come here on purpose. How is the mother of that poor little boy?'

'Grieving, of course. The loss of a son is a loss indeed.'

Lexy nodded. She felt herself relax in the presence of the Indian doctor and she lowered her usual defensive guard.

'My name is Rakesh,' he said. 'Rakesh Chatterjee.'

'My name is Lexy Nicolson. Er, I mean, Lexy Sanderson.' She blushed at her error.

'Ah!' Doctor Rakesh Chatterjee nodded his head in the up, down, roundabout manner of his race. 'You are a new bride and not yet used to your married name.' He spoke in English.

Lexy looked down at her left hand, which bore her wedding ring. 'Actually, I have been married for several years and I have a daughter.'

The doctor raised his eyebrows in surprise and looked hard at Lexy, studying each fleeting expression. He would be ashamed to possess a wife who looked so untouched, virginal.

'What do you feel about your life here in India? Were you born here?'

Lexy frowned and her eyes filled with tears. 'I don't know what I feel,' she sighed. 'I was born in England, but I feel as if I was born into the wrong skin or born at the wrong time. I would have been happier if I had lived here in the days when our races mixed more freely. I don't seem to fit in to today. I belong more to yesterday. But I don't expect you to understand.'

She lowered her lashes, which caused her tears to fall, but she made no attempt to brush them away.

'Tell me about your husband.'

Lexy's face closed immediately. 'He doesn't want me,' she said.

'Well, he is a fool to neglect you and doesn't deserve to have you. We believe that it is a husband's duty to ensure his wife's happiness. I would say your husband is no proper husband to you.' He stopped abruptly, as if he had perhaps gone too far, and glanced awkwardly at Lexy. But Lexy just gave a faint nod and sighed.

'Are you married?' she asked.

Rakesh Chatterjee shook his head. 'Betrothed only. The astrologers have set a date for my marriage at the end of next month. The girl has waited a long time for me to complete my training and establish my medical practice. She has been very patient and I have no more reason to cause delay. My parents are losing patience with me.'

'You sound as though you don't wish to marry the girl,' said Lexy.

He shrugged. 'It's not a question of choice. These matters are arranged for us. When you say that you feel you were born at the wrong time in history, I understand exactly what you mean. I, too, feel like that. My parents will have chosen wisely for me and my marriage will unite two wealthy families, but I have no appetite for it. There are times when I feel smothered by tradition and convention. What I wish for is probably madness, but that doesn't stop me: freedom of choice, equality of opportunity and education for all are what I want. You feel that you were born too late, but I know that I was born ahead of my time.'

Lexy smiled. He was friendly and easy to talk to. 'I'm glad that we were born into the same time or we would not have met.'

Rakesh talked some more of his aspirations and hopes for a better and fairer society, and Lexy listened intently, her liking of this thoughtful man growing by the moment. She could have stayed all day, but he had patients to see and she knew she must be heading back.

'I feel so much better now than I did when I arrived here. It was good of you to spare me some of your time. Thank you.'

She rose to take her leave, and Rakesh opened the door for her. 'Will you come again?'

'Yes,' said Lexy. 'I should like that.' She mounted her horse and rode away without looking back.

Rakesh watched until she disappeared from view. He had not had any previous contact with European women, although he had often seen them in their carriages when they paraded along the maidan in the evenings. Their brash voices and whinnying laughter grated on his ears and their pale, pasty skins reminded him of raw, plucked chicken. Mrs Lexy Sanderson turned his perceptions on their head. She did not conform to his mental image of a memsahib; there was an Indian stillness about her.

Although the very idea was preposterous, Rakesh felt a strange attraction to Lexy. He could not account for it, but it was important to him that she would come and see him again. He wondered what sort of a man could be married to her without realising or appreciating what a precious gem she was. It astonished him that any man could feel anything but pleasure and desire that such a woman should have gone to him of her own free will. He would give anything to have such a wife. This unusual memsahib had touched his soul, and he felt blessed that the gods had led her back to his humble surgery. He wished they had set a date for her return.

As she rode away Lexy was conscious of Rakesh's eyes on her back like a caress, and she blushed as she remembered unburdening herself to him. For so long now she had had no one in whom to confide. Evalina was miles away in Cawnpore and letters between them took so long that the immediacy of need was rendered useless. Sophia Gardner had returned to England with the twins, leaving her husband to soldier on alone. That left Charlotte, but it would have been futile and unkind to share her unhappiness with her cousin. Charlotte would not have understood, and Lexy would have shrunk from exposing her marriage to her. Telling her troubles to a stranger who was not in a position to repeat them to the European community had been a blessed relief. Not that Doctor Rakesh Chatterjee had seemed like a stranger: Lexy had the odd impression that they had always known one another. It was a comfortable feeling, and the peace she felt following their encounter began to melt the ice in Lexy's heart.

That evening as Lexy and the Colonel sat quietly together he watched her through a haze of smoke from his hookah. It was cold and a log fire burned in the grate. Carpets had been laid on the marble floor and extra blankets were piled on the beds. The smell of local tobaccos blended with molasses and cinnamon swirled through the air with the smoke, and the Colonel heaved an intoxicated sigh as he studied his wife.

Lexy wore a dark red crinoline trimmed with jasmine from the garden with a Kashmir shawl draped round her shoulders, and she held a book in her hands. The Colonel thought that there was something different about her that night, something indefinably different, but he was damned if he knew what it was. He sighed again, more loudly this time, but Lexy continued to ignore him.

'You are very quiet this evening,' he said.

She raised her eyes from her book. 'Am I?'

'Mm. It's as if you are in another world altogether.'

Lexy was glad of the semi-darkness which concealed her blush as she had been thinking of the Indian doctor and what it might be like to be held in his arms.

'Well, I am reading,' she said. She laid the book aside. 'What would you like to talk about?'

The Colonel shook his head. 'Nothing.' Damn it, he thought. What was it about her tonight? And he cursed the cold weather for preventing Lexy from wearing native dress. He preferred her when she wore the local garb; she was more desirable when she looked as erotic as his Savita. Perhaps her gown was new, but he thought not. This was driving him to distraction; he put his hookah down, irritated that it had not relaxed him sufficiently to ignore his wife. Her composure and the faraway look in her eyes aroused his anger, and when she rose to go to her room he followed her. At her door Lexy turned and held up her hand.

'No,' she said. 'Go to your *bibi*.'

It was a mistake, for he grabbed hold of her and pulled her roughly towards him. If Lexy's thoughts had not been filled with the Indian doctor she would have endured her husband's embraces, always hoping for something unknown to her that was never forthcoming, but the thought of him in her bed tonight filled her with disgust and she struggled against him. He yanked her head back with his hand in her hair and bruised her mouth with his own. He enjoyed her struggle: it heightened his desire for her. He pushed her into the room and onto her bed, but as he forced himself upon her she suddenly went limp, fearing the pain he had inflicted on her before.

'You bitch,' he snarled. 'You belong to me and I'll have you when I want.'

'Then I thank God that you do not want me very often,' she whimpered.

The Colonel struck her across the face and left the room. Lexy ran to her bathroom and vomited into the sink, and then she rinsed the blood from her cut lip. When she had bathed her battered face and black eye, she crawled between the rumpled linen sheets and lay staring into the blackness of the night.

In the morning she stayed in her room until she heard the Colonel leave. She dressed and ate a hasty breakfast before ordering the syce to bring her horse. She knew where she was going, and she knew that by going to Rakesh she would be a pariah amongst her own people should it become common knowledge, but she felt a desperate need to erase all memory of her husband from her mind. It was unthinkable that a memsahib should stoop so low as to take an Indian lover, and Lexy was aware that if they embarked on such a relationship Rakesh had as much, if not more, to lose than she did because he would lose caste, and this was every bit as unthinkable in Indian eyes, and less easily forgiven. Lexy did not set out that morning with the intention of starting an illicit affair, but she felt a deep affinity for this man and was prepared to risk whatever censure came her way just to be with him.

The door was opened immediately to her knock. Rakesh ushered her inside and pulled a curtain across the door after he closed it, so that anyone else who came to him would know that he was not to be disturbed. Without a word he led Lexy into the inner room and sat her down. He poured some lotion into a small bowl and dabbed at the dried blood on her mouth, and once the wound was clean he applied a cooling salve. She was on the point of explaining what had happened to her when he laid a gentle finger on her lips.

'Don't speak of it, flower of my heart,' he said. 'I can feel your pain without you putting it into words.'

Rakesh was shocked to see Lexy's bruised face. It was common for wives to be beaten, of course, but to see her so roughly used flooded him with pity. He knew why she had come to him and knew that it was not just to have her injuries treated. He had prayed for her to come and seeing her looking so forlorn and vulnerable sent a flood of desire coursing through his veins; it was a desire to have her belong to him, forever, and his desire was tempered by fear of the consequences. At the very least they would both be outcasts; and at the worst he could be executed for rape, because it would never be believed that a white woman had come to him willingly.

Then their eyes met, and each saw their own unbounded love reflected in the eyes of the other. Their fates were sealed. Rakesh held his arms towards her, and Lexy stepped into his embrace.

Following Anjana's act of sati, Vijay and Malati Chatterjee left Calcutta in a hurry. In 1827 Lord William Cavendish Bentinck, the first Governor-General of India, had outlawed the custom of widow burning in the first direct attack on Indian religious beliefs. The Chatterjees were now in breach of the law. They fled to a town on the banks of the River Jumna and established themselves in a large haveli set in extensive gardens just outside the north gate of the old town walls. Rakesh had fleeting recollections of his early years in Calcutta, but in spite of his persistent questions he had never been able to discover the reason for the move, other than that there had been a family tragedy.

The Chatterjee family lived in a degree of luxury that, in Rakesh's eyes, contrasted offensively with the poverty and squalor within the old town. His brothers laughed at Rakesh's misplaced sentimentality, and Vijay wrung his hands in despair at the strange, sensitive son he had produced. Whilst his brothers learned the intricacies of the gem trade at their father's knee, Rakesh roamed the streets. He talked with the poor, the sick and the crippled, and as he grew he knew that he wanted to do something to help them when he reached adulthood. There were bitter rows with his parents when he suggested they distribute some of their wealth to the disadvantaged in society. After years of alternating bouts of pleading and temper, Vijay Chatterjee bowed to the inevitable and agreed that Rakesh could follow a different calling. Rakesh was sent away to train as a doctor. Overnight he was transformed from a boy whose daydreaming formed his only defence against his angry father and derisive brothers, into a young man whose enthusiasm for his vocation gave him the self-assurance he had always lacked.

When his parents announced that they had found a bride for him, Rakesh had no stomach for further battles with his father, and astrologers were consulted for an auspicious date for the marriage to take place. Rakesh accepted his fate with resignation, but now, far from either looking forward to or being indifferent towards the marriage, he viewed it with dread. As he and Lexy lay together after their first act of surrender Rakesh tried to blot his approaching marriage from his mind. The thought of betraying this woman with whom he had fallen deeply in love, with another of his parents' choice filled him with dismay.

His eyes travelled the length of Lexy's body as she lay sleeping beside him, wanting her again. She woke to his touch and her languid eyes sought his. The gentle caress of his cool fingers thrilled her and she smiled at him. In full recompense for her years of frustration and loneliness, she drew him to her.

CHAPTER 38

Colonel David Sanderson never failed to feel a deep sense of pride each morning as he inspected his men, but today he had left home in a bad mood, and on parade there had been one or two incidents which had served to increase his ill humour. The men appeared ill at ease. He noted the sideways slide of a pair of black eyes that would normally have met his gaze unflinchingly; and a sepoy stood to attention with something less than full military precision. They were small details, but no less troubling for being so, and the Colonel knew he would have to discover the reason for the change in his men so that he could nip any trouble in the bud before it had time to fester and infect others. At the end of the parade he ordered his native officers to his headquarters.

It was clear that something was wrong. The officers glanced quickly at one another, but none would meet the Colonel's eye. Colonel Sanderson regarded each one in turn before speaking.

'Good morning, gentlemen. I want to keep this meeting informal and none of you will suffer by speaking freely. On parade this morning I detected an evasiveness, a feeling of discontent here and there amongst the men. I am relying on you to explain the reason for it.'

The native officers shifted uncomfortably, but none spoke.

'*Subedar* Khan, have you anything to say?' asked the Colonel.

The officer stared at the ground for a moment before looking up at his commanding officer. 'The ill feeling is not directed towards you personally, Colonel.'

'Then to whom?'

The subedar looked at his fellow officers, some of whom nodded. It seemed they had already nominated him as their spokesman. He cleared his throat.

'Some of the sepoys are unsettled by the threat posed to their religious beliefs by one of your British officers, sir.'

'Threat?' demanded the Colonel. 'What threat? What are you talking about?' He was genuinely surprised.

The subedar's distress was plain to see. He and the Colonel had campaigned together for fifteen years, fighting side by side on the Northwest Frontier in the Sikh Wars. He was deeply ashamed that there should be any disquiet amongst the sepoys in Sanderson's Rifles.

'The sepoys are loyal to you, sir.'

'But what is the threat you speak of?'

Subedar Khan sighed. The winds of change were blowing across his country. They came with the memsahibs and the missionaries, and he feared the storms that would surely follow. In truth, change had begun long ago in isolated gusts, but those gusts had become a steady breeze, which, with nothing to hinder it, had gathered strength until the beggar at the temple and the peasant in the field felt it blow into their lives just as keenly as a dispossessed maharajah felt it blow into his. The maharajahs might lock horns with the East India Company where matters of land, money and policy were concerned, but it was the rank and file of India who would light the touch-paper of disaster if they chose to do so. And there would be no stopping them.

'I'm afraid that one of your British officers is trying to convert the sepoys to Christianity,' he said finally. 'Naturally they resent it.'

There was a murmur of agreement amongst the other officers. The Colonel's blood ran cold. Like all the native regiments, the British serving with Sanderson's Rifles were heavily outnumbered and relied heavily on the obedience and goodwill of the sepoys. It only required one of his British officers to step out of line and his life's work could be destroyed. He searched each face before him for any sign of hostility but saw only a concern to match his own.

'Very well.' The Colonel tapped his riding crop against his boots. 'You can assure the men that they are free to practise their faiths without let or hindrance from me. I will deal with the matter and they will not be approached again. Thank you, gentlemen.'

The native officers shuffled out and the Colonel could hear them talking quietly together as they headed towards the parade ground. They walked towards the sun, casting long thin shadows on the parched earth behind them. It was already hot; the Colonel flicked flies from his face.

He sat at his table and mentally reviewed which of his officers might be involved. He had three British officers altogether. These included old 'Sawbones' McKinley, but he was an unlikely culprit being a self-proclaimed atheist who maintained loudly, when he was in the mood and 'in his cups', that any god worth his salt would either not permit such disease and deformity as afflicted this brutal world, or else doctors and surgeons would be granted the skills and wherewithal to prevent them.

So, it had to be one of the other two, the most likely of whom was young Lieutenant John Piggott. He had only been with Sanderson's Rifles for a few months and had failed to live up to the promise he had shown when the Colonel had picked him to join the Corps. Anxious not to give him any further opportunity to upset the sepoys, Colonel Sanderson summoned the officer to his presence.

Lieutenant Piggott was a young man in his mid-twenties. He had no wealthy family behind him, so he had to manage on his army pay. Lacking the funds required to purchase a commission in the Queen's army, he had chosen the brighter prospects offered by the East India Company. His boyhood had been spent in the wilds of the Welsh borders where attendance at chapel on Sundays was mandatory, and where he had absorbed great tracts of the Bible from an early age. However, when he reached India and saw its glitter and beauty, and the inside of a brothel, all his religious scruples and education were thrown out the window. He attended church parades with everyone else, but his mind was usually in the cesspits and pleasure houses of the bazaars until, that is, he faced his first real danger when he was sent to put down a minor skirmish.

Faith and alcohol loomed large in the hearts of men who went to war. Faith, with or without alcohol, imbued officers with a sense that divine right was on their side; and alcohol, with or without faith, dulled the senses of the men who must obey orders without question. Lieutenant Piggott's faith was put on the backburner although he did not replace it with overindulgence in alcohol.

Lieutenant Piggott was shot during that skirmish. The wound in his upper arm was superficial, but the young officer thought that he was going to die. A dying soldier wants two things – his god and his mother. Lieutenant Piggott called for both, and when he did not die from his wound he knew that it was God who had saved him. Now he wanted to save souls as his way of thanking Him. He put his sinful life behind him – something that is always easier to do when one has already wallowed in the gutter – and set to work on the heathen sepoys.

When Lieutenant Piggott was shown into his office, the Colonel pointed silently towards a chair and carried on writing the report in front of him. The Colonel wanted the young officer to stew for a while, but he did not want to give him a formal dressing-down or he would have had him stand to attention until he was ready to deal with him.

The Lieutenant was at ease. He could think of nothing he had done wrong and thought the Colonel wished to speak to him on some minor matter. When the Colonel challenged him, he was surprised.

'But, Colonel,' he protested. 'It is our duty as Christians to convert the heathen.'

The Colonel was furious. 'Do you mean to admit to me that without my knowledge or permission you are actively engaged in thrusting Christianity down the throats of my men?'

'It is our duty,' repeated the Lieutenant.

'And just how are you carrying out this so-called duty?'

'Well, I read to them or quote passages from the Bible.'

'Then you are a young fool,' snapped the Colonel. 'I am going to give you the benefit of the doubt and can only assume that you have no idea of the implications of what you are doing, but you are treading on dangerous waters. Exactly what would it take to convert you to Hinduism or Islam? How would you feel if the tables were turned?'

Lieutenant Piggott stared uncomprehendingly at the Colonel. 'It's not the same thing at all,' he said. 'They are heathens. Infidels.'

The Colonel snorted. 'As far as the Musselmen are concerned it is we who are the infidels. And as far as the Hindus are concerned Christianity threatens their entire way of life. Equality is anathema to them. If Hindus were all equal, who would be their sweepers, their attendants of the dead, their leather workers? Who would do the unclean work of the untouchables? They are not ready for equality of all people in their land. Perhaps they never will be, but in any event, it will not happen in our lifetime and we meddle at our peril.'

The Colonel sighed, and his voice became more conciliatory. 'Look here, Piggott, I will give you one more chance, but if I hear that you have been preaching and sermonising to my sepoys again you will be out of

Sanderson's Rifles before you can blink. Do I make myself clear?'

Lieutenant Piggott nodded. 'Yes, sir.'

'You must bear in mind that we rely on the sepoys to protect us and our families and the interests of the East India Company. They vastly outnumber us, and if we alienate them we will lose their loyalty and their trust. And, God help us, on the day that happens we will probably also lose our lives. I suggest you spend some time thinking about the risks to which you are exposing us all. That will be all.'

Lieutenant Piggott saluted and left. The Colonel sighed deeply. Was he the only one who felt concern for the future? Does no one else see the catastrophe that awaits us if we are not careful, he wondered? In his opinion there were too many gods and too many religions, and Colonel Sanderson cursed them all for the wars fought in their name.

He went home in a choleric frame of mind, which was increased when he caught sight of his wife. Lexy had waited for him to return for *tiffin*. She wore a plain day dress that he had seen many times before, but today her radiance gave it an unfamiliar appearance. She rose as he entered, her blue-black hair shimmering like silk, her cheeks aglow and her eyes sparkling. He had never seen her look like this, and in his angry mood all the Colonel's senses were heightened. He was suspicious of the vitality emanating from his normally withdrawn wife, a vitality she could not hide, and his eyes narrowed. There could only be one reason for such a change in her, and his own guilty conscience screamed it into his mind.

'Have you taken a lover?' he snapped without hesitation.

Lexy's mouth dropped with astonishment. The unexpectedness of the question made her blush, only partly from guilt, and her look of surprise was so genuine that the Colonel was immediately contrite.

'Do forgive me, my dear,' he said. 'It has been a very trying morning.'

Without taking tiffin, the Colonel turned on his heel and left the room leaving Lexy trembling with uncertainty.

CHAPTER 39

In the days leading up to his marriage, Lexy visited Rakesh as often as possible. As a way of diverting suspicion, she had instigated a weekly welfare clinic at his surgery. The Colonel had given his blessing to this enterprise as she was not the only memsahib trying to teach the basics of hygiene and nutrition to the poor in the old town, but he had extracted his pound of flesh in return. Lexy had had to agree to him coming to her bed once a month and, having made her husband promise that he would never again use force, she yielded to his demand because her need to be with Rakesh was greater than her need to keep the Colonel from her bed. In the event, the Colonel rarely visited her because he preferred to be with Savita, but he did not use force on those occasions when he did decide to exercise his right.

When they met for the last time before she left for the cool of the hills, Lexy and Rakesh clung to each other, fearing to let go. It would be months before they saw one another again, and when they did Rakesh would be a married man. Lexy was terrified that she was about to lose the man who meant more to her than life itself. She was afraid that Rakesh's bride would be skilled in the arts of love and would seduce him from her, just as Savita's siren song had ensnared the Colonel. Her insecurity increased the dread and pain of parting.

Rakesh read her thoughts. 'Don't think of it, flower of my heart,' he comforted. 'Our lives are only real when we are together. All else is *maya* – illusion – and it doesn't count at all. Think of me during your difficult times, and I will think of you during mine.'

Lexy and Mattie travelled to the hills with Charlotte and Benjamin at the end of May. It was their first time in Simla without Sophia Gardner and the twins, but they were very present in their thoughts. Rupert Gardner had decided to resign his commission and return to England.

The twins were settled into school there and Sophia had refused to ever set foot in India again, so Rupert Gardner's choice was stark – his career or his family. He chose his family, and he asked Lexy to place a simple cross at the head of his son's grave for him because he saw no prospect of being able to do so himself before he left India.

Lexy and Charlotte did as he asked, and as she stood beside Conrad's final resting place Lexy wept for the beautiful child whose life was snuffed out before it had really begun. But there was to be a new life, and Charlotte was blissfully happy as she awaited her forthcoming baby in spite of a difficult pregnancy. Although Lexy was untouched by it, the harsh Indian climate was taking its toll on Charlotte's health and looks. She tired easily and was often listless. Her blond curls had faded, and her face was drawn and sallow, but her love for her husband and son overflowed to embrace the world in general, which gave her an altogether different kind of beauty.

By the time her pregnancy came to an end Charlotte's face and hands were puffy, and her feet and ankles swollen. She spent much of her time resting on her bed and telling stories to Benjamin and Mattie. When her time came, her labour was long and difficult. Lexy sat beside her and sponged the perspiration from her face and body. She took on the role of nurse to her cousin, insisting that the ayahs care for the children and only come into Charlotte's room with fresh linen, hot water and simple meals.

Lexy feared that Charlotte would die in childbirth, and it wrenched her heart to hear her crying out for her husband, but Charlotte was determined that this new life was going to be born.

'I can do it with your help,' she whispered between her pains. 'It's not so bad. We'll manage together.'

But it was bad, and it seemed endless. Charlotte battled to bring her baby into the world, and when she finally did so, all memories of her ordeal vanished in an instant as she held her infant daughter in her arms.

'What will you call her?' asked Lexy, plumping the pillows and helping Charlotte to sit up after she had slept for hours.

'Clara May,' replied Charlotte. 'George chose her name before we left home. Bless you for all you did for us, Lexy. I couldn't have done it without you.'

'You did all the work,' said Lexy. 'Would you like me to fetch Benjamin for you?'

'Yes, please.'

When Benjamin stood beside the bed Charlotte pulled the shawl away from the baby's face so that he could see her.

'Look, Benjamin,' said Charlotte. 'I promised that you would have someone to play with, and here she is. This is Clara May, your new sister.'

Benjamin stared solemnly at the baby for several minutes before he removed his thumb from his mouth.

'That?' he said scornfully. 'I can't play with *that!*' He ran from the room to return to his beloved Mattie.

Charlotte looked stricken and then burst into tears, but Lexy laughed.

'He'll get over it,' she said. 'When Clara May grows a bit and Benjamin finds that he can play with her after all, it will be all right, you'll see.'

Clara May proved to be a healthy and contented baby, and Charlotte slowly regained her strength. When they returned home at the beginning of October, George Cartwright was thrilled with his infant daughter and overjoyed to have his family safely home again. Lexy said her farewells and then took Mattie to the sad emptiness of their own house on the banks of the river close to the bazaar.

Lexy and Rakesh's passion for one another was as fierce as ever. Neither of them mentioned his marriage, and Lexy could almost believe that he had no other life but the times they shared, screened from the eyes of the world and drowning in each other's embraces. The thrill of the touch of Rakesh's almost too slender body against hers stirred her whole being, and she yielded herself to him body and soul.

By the middle of December Lexy knew that she was pregnant, and she was thrown into a panic. In spite of the Colonel's occasional nocturnal visits to her bed there was no doubt in her mind that Rakesh was the father of the baby, and she knew that it would not be possible to pass it off as her husband's child. She calculated that the baby would be born in June and for a time she kept the knowledge of her pregnancy to herself, thrilled to be carrying Rakesh's child, and yet terrified of what would happen when the Colonel discovered the truth. It seemed inexplicable to her now that she had not considered pregnancy as a probable outcome of her adultery.

At the end of December, the Colonel came to Lexy's room. She was so horrified that she blurted out the fact of her pregnancy to him. The Colonel stepped back and looked at her with narrowed eyes.

'Are you certain?' he asked. 'I have only lain with you once since you returned from the hills.'

'Once is enough if I remember correctly from last time,' Lexy replied.

The Colonel hesitated. 'Very well,' he said. 'I will not trouble you until after the child is born. I must say that I am surprised, but it will be good for Mattie to have a brother or sister to play with. Perhaps she will stay at home more. Goodnight, my dear.'

In the New Year they hosted a lavish dinner party and the meal was followed by drawing room entertainment provided by themselves and willing guests. The Colonel had a talent for quoting yards of Shakespeare, and he regaled them with speeches from 'Hamlet' and 'Twelfth Night'. Lexy played the piano while George and Charlotte sang duets. The evening ended with a game of charades, but before the guests took their leave the Colonel held up his hand and called for silence.

'I beg a moment's indulgence,' he said, and then hiccoughed. He was the worse for wear and unsteady on his feet.

Lexy caught Charlotte's eye and pulled a face, but everyone had drunk several glasses of wine and soon they were all laughing.

'Permit me to speak once more.' The Colonel swayed on his feet. He leant on the mantelpiece to steady himself, and the expression on his face was one of elaborate gravity.

'I will hereupon confess I am in love,' he said solemnly. 'Pray silence. I have something to add to the evening's entertainment.'

Charlotte tittered, and the Colonel held up his hand again.

I will hereupon confess I am in love
But love is blind and lovers cannot see.
Love is a smoke raised with the fume of sighs.
Alas, how love can trifle with itself.
Ay, every dram of woman's flesh is false –
Her children not her husband's.
I do believe her though I know she lies.

The Colonel looked directly at Lexy as he spoke the last line, and she unthinkingly placed a protective hand over her abdomen. Her heart hammered in her breast, and she held her breath. He knows, she thought, swallowing hard. She felt faint and wondered what he would do; she had no doubt that he knew the child she carried was not his.

George broke the hushed silence. 'Well done, sir,' he said. 'Who was the poet?'

'The Bard, dear boy,' said the Colonel, turning to him. 'Who else?'

George laughed. 'Not the Bard, dear fellow. I know my Shakespeare, and that was new to me. What's it from?'

'Several of them.' The Colonel hiccoughed again. 'They were just odd lines I remember from several of his works. I just strung them together. Was it any good? I can't recall a thing I said.'

'Not really,' said Charlotte, who knew no Shakespeare. 'But whose children are not her husband's? Anyone we know?'

She began to giggle. Lexy struggled to maintain her composure; she could not get rid of her guests quickly enough. But when they were alone the Colonel made no mention of his poem and Lexy breathed more freely. If he suspected her of infidelity, he would have provoked a scene. For the time being, at any rate, she and her baby were safe, and she would worry about the Colonel's reaction to it after the child was born.

When she told Rakesh that she was carrying his baby he was more concerned than pleased. There was an initial flash of delight in his eyes, but almost immediately he frowned.

'Aren't you pleased?' asked Lexy.

The colour in his face deepened. Their eyes met, but then he looked away. Lexy winced, and her heart sank.

'You are angry,' she said.

'Angry? No, I am not angry.' He took her in his arms. 'How could I be angry? I fear for him though. I fear for us all.'

The differences between them that had seemed so insignificant at first now suddenly loomed large and Lexy trembled with uncertainty.

'I don't understand,' she said. 'You have nothing to fear. I am the one who has cause to fear. When it becomes known that I have borne a child that is clearly not my husband's, I don't know what will happen to me.'

Rakesh sighed. 'It is you who doesn't understand, flower of my heart. Our son will be neither one thing nor the other. Neither the British nor the Indians will accept him. You know how half-castes are sneered at by both our countrymen.' He put a finger under Lexy's chin and raised her face to his. 'But for myself, I am happy, and my arms ache to hold our son.'

Lexy buried her face in his shoulder, not wanting to believe what

Rakesh said, and yet knowing that it was the truth: their child, be it a boy or a girl, would fall between two stools and its future would be uncertain. When she left him, Rakesh sat for a long time with his head in his hands. He and Lexy had lived too long in their private paradise and now he was plunged into a sudden and silent grief. It was like a terrible dream, and he had never known such pain.

After a while Rakesh poured some water into a bowl and splashed some of it over his face. Then he changed into fresh linen and left his surgery. He made his way past stalls where he bought some sweets covered in silver paper, and then he turned into a wider lane filled with the heady smells of spices and incense. He pushed through the crush of people, looking neither left nor right, until he came to the temple he sought. It had been a long time since he had been there because his family usually said prayers at the shrine in their home, but now Rakesh needed the anonymity of the temple.

He paused to buy some sacred marigolds before climbing the temple steps. He ignored the filthy, whining beggars who sat on the steps, most of whom were capable of doing a day's work, but he paused at the top and fumbled in his pocket for a couple of annas, which he dropped into the bowl of the blind beggar.

All around the temple were rows of brass bells, and Rakesh put his hand to one of them to alert the god to his presence. He slipped off his sandals and went inside. It was hot and stuffy in there. Worshippers came and went, each with their own hopes and fears. Rakesh laid his offerings at the feet of Ganesh, the elephant-headed god of wisdom, and after a few silent minutes of blankness, he began to pray.

'Ganesh, Oh Wise One, keep them safe. Let no harm come to them. If tragedy is to befall, let it rest on me alone. I take all blame upon myself.'

CHAPTER 40

Subedar Khan could not sleep. Twice his restless tossing and turning had disturbed his wife and she had complained to him to lie still. Eventually he decided that a walk might ready him for sleep, so he dressed and left the hut that he shared with his large family. The hot weather was fast approaching and already it was only marginally cooler outside at night than it was indoors. He strolled along the outer perimeter of their camp but came to an abrupt halt when he heard the murmur of voices. It was unexpected, and there was something about the subdued tones of the main speaker that put the subedar on the alert. He inched closer until he caught sight of a shadowy group of sepoys who squatted on their haunches in front of an unknown civilian clad in a dirty dhoti. There was little light so Subedar Khan was unable to distinguish individual faces, and he listened to the speaker with mounting unease.

'I'm telling you,' said the stranger. 'The chapattis mean that there is great trouble coming. The *chowkidars* in the villages are each receiving a chapatti with the command to make four more and distribute them. Every village in India is finding a chapatti at the door of their chowkidar. It is a message telling us to prepare. I have come to warn you so that you will be ready.'

A ripple of movement stirred the gathering and there was a low grumble of voices.

'How do you know it is a sign of trouble? It could be a magic symbol to ward off trouble,' came a voice from amongst the group of sepoys.

'I've heard that the chapattis are offerings to the gods to spare us from a cholera epidemic,' said another voice.

Subedar Khan edged closer, but he could not get near enough to see the stranger's face without revealing his presence.

'No, no, that's not it at all. Offerings to the gods are left at the temples,' said the stranger, bobbing his head up and down. 'And there's more to it than the chapattis. The British Queen has sent Lord Canning here especially to convert us all to their faith.'

There was a collective gasp followed by rumblings of anger, together with one or two protests of disbelief.

'I don't believe you,' said a voice in the darkness. 'The British wouldn't be so stupid. They know they rely on us to fight for them, so why would they deliberately set us against them?'

'It's true though,' said another voice. 'And I've heard that we are to be sent overseas to fight. That means we will lose caste.'

The group muttered amongst themselves, some convinced, but others uncertain. The stranger let them feed on each other's insecurities for a while. Subedar Khan wished that he could see the man's face. He wondered if the stranger was known to any of the sepoys and had been invited to address this meeting, but perhaps he was just a stranger who had come to stir up hatred for the British. The sepoys stopped grumbling and the stranger began to speak again.

'Then there's the new cartridges,' he said. All eyes stared fixedly at him. 'Have any of you handled the new cartridges yet?'

There was a general shaking of heads and the sepoys looked puzzled. 'That's just as well,' continued the stranger. 'I've been told that they have been greased with beef and pork fat. When you bite the end off the new cartridges, where will your caste be then, eh?'

Subedar Khan crept silently away, all hope of sleep banished from his mind. He had heard these rumours himself and he had reported them to the Colonel, but this was the first time he was aware of a deliberate attempt to inflame their sepoys on a personal level. Early the next morning he took his concerns to Colonel Sanderson and told him of the night visitor.

'And you have no idea at all who he might be?' asked the Colonel.

Subedar Khan shook his head. 'It was too dark to see his face clearly from where I stood.'

The Colonel drummed his fingers on the table. The subedar cleared his throat.

'It's not true about the cartridges, is it?' he asked.

The Colonel frowned. 'I wish I could say "certainly not", but the fact is that I am as concerned as you are. It is most unlikely, though, and at least we don't have any of the new ones here yet.'

'And the chapattis?'

The Colonel shrugged. 'Your guess would be better than mine. Have you any ideas?'

'No, but rumour is rife that the British have added powdered cow bones to flour so that even civilians will be contaminated. Even if these things are not true, they are beginning to cause serious disquiet amongst the men. We Indians are a superstitious race.'

The Colonel smiled. 'So are we, so are we. Rest assured that I shall take this further and find out what I can.'

He wasted no time. The following evening a dozen British officers from native regiments and their wives were invited to dinner. During the meal the conversation was kept to general topics, partly so as not to frighten the ladies, and partly due to the number of servants present. As soon as Lexy led the ladies from the dining room, port and cheroots were distributed amongst the guests, and then the Colonel dismissed the servants.

'What's the old boy up to?' whispered one of the officers. 'He's surely not going to wait on us himself, is he?'

There was a muffled titter, which was quickly stifled when the Colonel wasted no time beating about the bush.

'There's talk about the new rifle,' he began. 'Has anyone heard anything about it?'

'The Enfield rifle?' queried a major. 'What about it?'

'There's a rumour that the cartridges are wrapped in paper that has been oiled with beef or pork fat.'

Some of those present laughed, but the Colonel was not the only one to be concerned.

'They can't be,' said one. 'The sepoys have to bite the end off the cartridges. They can't possibly be using animal fat on them, can they?'

'I've heard that rumour, too,' said a rotund captain. 'I don't believe it myself. They'll be greased with tallow, not pork fat. Stands to reason. It's just some tall story to incite the natives.'

'Then it is proving to be very effective,' said the Colonel. 'I have noticed the occasional incident bordering on insolence amongst some of my own sepoys so I, for one, am taking the matter seriously.'

Major Chalmers spoke. 'I understand that the cartridges are being manufactured here in India.'

'I've heard that, too,' said another. 'And worse – they haven't been given any specific instructions about what lubricant is to be used.'

'No wonder the sepoys are suspicious,' said the Colonel.

'I believe that some of the regiments have already taken action,' said Major Chalmers. 'They are teaching a new drill. The sepoys are to tear off the end of the papers on the cartridges instead of biting them. That way it won't matter what they are greased with.'

'That sounds like a good idea,' said the Colonel. 'Are any of your sepoys being taught the new drill?' Most of the officers shook their heads. 'Well, I shall teach my men,' said the Colonel. 'Even though we don't have the new cartridges yet I see no point at all in giving the men something to rebel over.'

He stood up and they went to join the ladies, but the mood had become sombre and the party broke up early. The Colonel was worried, not only about possible unrest amongst the sepoys, but also because of the lack of any real concern amongst so many British officers. He informed Subedar Khan that he would be ordering a parade to teach the drill for handling the new cartridges, but before the parade took place he had an unexpected visitor. Salim woke him in the middle of the night.

'Colonel, sahib, you must wake up.'

'What is it?' yawned the Colonel.

'A thousand apologies for disturbing your sleep, Colonel sahib, but my brother has come from Meerut. There is trouble there.'

The Colonel sat up, instantly alert. 'What kind of trouble?'

'My brother says that there was a firing parade with a new rifle and the sepoys refused to touch the cartridges.'

'Refused? All of them?'

'He says that all the sepoys refused except for the non-commissioned officers. My brother says that they were told that the cartridges were of the old type, but the sepoys did not believe it.'

'What happened to the sepoys?'

'My brother does not know. He came here straightaway because he says there is talk in the bazaars of big trouble brewing.'

'Thank you, Salim,' said the Colonel. 'Thank your brother for me and see that he is fed.'

So, he thought, it begins. He hoped that the unrest would remain confined to Meerut, but he would have to consider protection for Lexy and Mattie in case the trouble spread. Later in the day, the Colonel learned that a Court of Inquiry was to be held into the protest, and he tried to feel confident that common sense would prevail and the whole thing would blow over.

That evening, mildly intoxicated by his customary pull on his hookah, the Colonel wondered how best to prepare Lexy for the possibility of an uprising without causing her unnecessary alarm. She needed to be told. Because she was heavily pregnant Lexy had decided not to go to the hills this May, which she had always done in previous years as a means of blessed escape from her husband as well as the heat. The Colonel did not hold with the belief that ladies should be shielded from all matters unpleasant as their reliance on bazaar gossip in place of proper information only caused more distress in the long run, but Lexy's delicate condition could make her react badly to any news of mutiny amongst the sepoys.

It was hot on the plains and Lexy had taken to wearing native dress whenever she was at home. Stays and crinolines were unbearable in her state, and she was thankful that the Colonel was happy for her to 'go native' with him. She watched her husband through half-closed eyes. It was clear to her that he was steeling himself to speak and she dreaded him making any comment about the forthcoming baby, but the Colonel was too concerned about the military situation to speculate on whether Lexy would give him a son or another daughter. He spoke softly to her in the semi-darkness of the terrace.

'I know that you think me a poor husband, my dear,' he began. Lexy was too startled to either agree or disagree. 'But even though I have never been able to love you, I do owe you a duty of care,' he continued.

Lexy's expression turned to one of scorn. Being treated by her husband with a British notion of what was right was demeaning. He made her feel of less worth than a pet dog, and she would have found his hatred easier to bear.

The Colonel raised his eyes and held her gaze. 'There has been a problem of disobedience amongst the sepoys in Meerut,' he said. 'A court martial is in progress, but I fear the outcome whether or not they are found guilty. I want to take measures to protect you and Mattie should the need arise.'

'Why should events in Meerut be a threat to us here?' asked Lexy. 'Meerut is forty or fifty miles away.'

'That is true, and nothing may come of it, but I want you to be prepared should the trouble spread here.'

'Do you think it will?'

'I don't know, but I rather think that it may. I suspect that we are about to reap what we have sown over the years. I have a sinking feeling that the bonds between the British and the Indians are about to disintegrate like ropes of sand. I fear that we will be torn between our duty to defend the towns and cities, and our duty to protect our women and children. God help us, we are too thinly spread to do either. My duty as a soldier must come first and I may not be here to look after you and Mattie, so I want to talk to you about keeping yourself and Mattie safe.'

Lexy felt the first stirrings of fear. The situation must be truly serious for the Colonel to discuss it with her, and yet it was the first she had heard of it.

'I haven't heard anyone else express any concern,' she said.

'No, I don't suppose you have,' said the Colonel. 'Most of the sahibs will not want to worry the ladies' pretty little heads, as if ignoring trouble will prevent it coming.'

'You have obviously formed some sort of a plan,' said Lexy. 'What is it that you want me to do?'

The Colonel took a long pull on his hookah. Lexy was not going to like what he was about to say, but there was nothing else for it.

'I want you to carry on wearing native dress. I've told you before that you look more like a local than a European when you are dressed like that. Don't go out at all unless it is absolutely necessary, and I can't think of any reason why it should be as long as our servants don't run away. Lastly, I want you to move into the bibi khana.'

'What?' Lexy was shocked to the core. 'Never! I will not set foot inside your whorehouse. How dare you even think of it, much less suggest it?' She could scarcely believe her ears.

The Colonel laid his hookah aside and leant forward with his elbows on his knees. 'I am not asking you to do this, Lexy. It is an order. Think of Mattie's safety even if you have no care for your own.'

'Then I must disobey you.' Lexy's voice was icy. 'I shall never set foot inside that place where I saw you so – so – so indecently exposed with your woman.'

'You will, and you must, do as I say.' The Colonel raised his voice

293

in anger. 'For goodness sake, do you think I ask this of you lightly? You and Mattie would be safe there. No Indian, Hindu or Musselman, would violate women's quarters. This is the only way you have to save your lives if the trouble flares and spreads, which it well might.'

Lexy sat in silent fury. It would be the ultimate degradation at his hands if she did as the Colonel ordered. She was determined to defy him. 'No, I refuse to do it.'

'Don't you care about Mattie or the child you carry?' he said. Instinctively Lexy put a defensive hand over her bulge.

'Ah, no, of course not,' he said with sudden insight. 'They are my children. You could not care less about them, could you?'

Lexy blushed for shame. She did care. She cared deeply about Rakesh's child, and she was surprised to find that she cared about Mattie's safety too.

'There's something else I want you to do,' said the Colonel. 'Send the ayah to the bazaar for some dye to change the colour of Mattie's hair. She'll never pass for anything other than a European, but it might buy you some time if her hair is dark.'

The Colonel was so proud of Mattie's golden hair that Lexy realised that the situation must indeed be perilous if he should want it to be disguised.

'How long will the court martial take?' asked Lexy. 'How much time do you think we have?'

'The simple answer is that I don't know, but my guess is that it is only a matter of days.' The Colonel looked at his beautiful wife with regret. 'If anything happens to me I would hope that you will take the children to my father in Wiltshire. There is no one else to inherit the family estates.'

Until the possibility of the Colonel's death was mentioned the whole thing had seemed academic, but now Lexy's mind was brought sharply into focus.

'I will do as you say up to a point,' she conceded. 'I will wear native dress and I won't go out. If trouble does come here I will move in with your woman, but only if Mattie's life is in imminent danger.'

And the Colonel had to be content with that.

CHAPTER 41

At the court-martial in Meerut, all eighty-five sepoys involved in the protest were found guilty, and this verdict was returned by all but one of the fifteen native officers who had tried them. They were sentenced to ten years imprisonment with hard labour, and on Saturday 9 May the sentence was carried out. The protesters, on parade, were stripped of their uniforms, shackled together, and led off to gaol. European troops, and those sepoys who had not been involved in the protest, were on parade to witness this public humiliation. The disgraced sepoys did not go quietly: they cursed and threw boots at Colonel Carmichael-Smith. Some of the sepoys were old and much decorated by the British for their bravery in earlier battles; they would lose their pensions along with their livelihoods. The situation was tense, but any suggestion that a mutiny might result from what had occurred on that day was dismissed.

The following day began with the usual early morning church parade. Although there had been minor incidents on most nights since the arrest of the sepoys, it seemed quiet in Meerut that morning. The day was oppressively hot and the British community sought refuge indoors. Because of the heat the evening church parade was delayed from half-past six until seven o'clock, and when the British emerged from their homes to attend church that evening it was to find that the native infantry lines were on fire. Not all the sepoys mutinied, but hooligans from the bazaar, who burned and looted as they went, joined those who did. Earlier that afternoon the telegraph wires had been cut so it was impossible to send a warning to the capital and, after an orgy of killing and looting, the rebels left Meerut under cover of darkness to march on Delhi.

In the early hours of Monday 11 May, the mutineers crossed the bridge of boats over the River Jumna, heading for the Red Fort, their rallying point and home of Bahadur Shah Zafar, King of Delhi, a descendant of the Mughal Emperors; they had come to ask the emperor to give his blessing to their mutiny. Captain Douglas, the commandant of the Palace Guard, ordered them away from the Red Fort. Bahadur Shah asked Captain Douglas to have all the gates into the palace and the city closed, but it was too late. The mutineers and the rebels had already entered the city through the Rajghat gate, and the killing and plundering were renewed.

It was late morning on 11 May when news of the mutiny in Meerut reached Colonel Sanderson. Many lives had already been lost: both Europeans, and Indians in any way connected with them. The Colonel immediately rode home to warn Lexy, and as he went he could see signs of unrest in the bazaars. News had reached the locals too, and it was not just the Europeans who were frightened. One or two fires had started and smoke from these rose into the air to mingle with the innocent smoke from cooking fires. Indians slunk along in the shadows, and Europeans were making ready to flee in buggies and carts. The Colonel knew that his corps of rifles would be involved in putting down this insurgency, but first he had to make sure that Lexy had taken Mattie into the bibi khana.

She had not. She had just stepped from her bath when the Colonel burst into her room. She had lingered in the tub longer than she normally did, enjoying the feel of the cooling bath water on her hot body. She gasped with shock when her husband strode into her bathroom without knocking. She hurriedly pulled a towel round her to hide her nakedness from him and saw a glint in his eyes as he ran them over her body. But it was not lust that made them shine – it was fury.

'Why aren't you in the bibi khana?' he roared. 'The sepoys in Meerut have mutinied. Delhi will be next. There's trouble brewing in the bazaar; you must have heard it and seen the fires.'

'Well, I haven't,' said Lexy. 'I've been having a long soak in the bath. Anyway, I can't believe that women and children are in danger.'

'I wish I could say that you are right, but you're not. Lots have been killed in Meerut and it won't be long before there is bloodshed here as well. You could be next if you don't do as I say. There's no controlling a murderous mob and I can't stay here to protect you. Where's Mattie?'

The colour drained from Lexy's face. 'She's not here,' she gasped. 'Where is she?'

'Charlotte collected her yesterday. It's the Lawsons' boy's birthday today.'

'For God's sake, Lexy,' shouted the Colonel. 'I warned you. I know I was a lone voice in the wilderness, but you can't say you weren't warned. Didn't you listen to a word I said? You agreed to go into the bibi khana and that's where you must go. Right now. I'll go and fetch Mattie and bring her to you. I only hope I'm not too late.'

He turned on his heel and hurried away just as a spatter of gunfire sounded in the distance. Until she heard the guns Lexy had not been unduly concerned for her safety, but now she was spurred into action. She called for the ayah to cram some things into carpetbags whilst she donned the cool Indian cotton clothes that had become her preferred manner of dress as her pregnancy advanced. She took her favourite moonstone necklace from the sandalwood casket, but as she fastened it around her neck she was frightened into immobility by someone pounding on the front door. Lexy peered from her bedroom and saw Salim edge towards the door.

'Who is it?' whispered Lexy.

Salim shrugged and shook his head. The pounding continued.

'Open it.'

Salim turned the handle and the door suddenly crashed open. Lexy's heart lurched with fear, and when Rakesh stepped into the hall she almost collapsed with relief. He turned immediately to the ayah.

'Bring some of the memsahib's clothes,' he ordered.

The ayah scuttled away and returned with the carpetbags. Rakesh turned to Lexy.

'You must come with me,' he said with urgency in his voice. 'Don't ask questions. Your life is in danger. I'll explain later.'

He grabbed the bags from the ayah and led Lexy from the house. She followed as he led her through the streets. He moved too quickly for her in her state of pregnancy, but she dared not ask him to slow down. The worry on his and the Colonel's faces made her realise that the situation really was serious. As they hurried along the streets and lanes, Lexy darted frightened eyes in the direction of smoke billowing from shattered windows of looted buildings along the way, and she flinched at every burst of gunfire.

When Rakesh went through the gates of the cemetery she shivered, not wanting to go any further.

'Come,' said Rakesh. 'We're nearly there. I have somewhere safe for you to hide. We must hurry. Anything can happen when the devil gets hold of a mob.'

She followed him past lines of graves that marked the passing of Europeans: victims of the climate, disease or overindulgence. When Lexy stepped into the shadow cast by the outstretched wings of a white marble angel she cried out, surprised and shocked. The angel stood sentinel over a large central sarcophagus that was flanked on either side by a much smaller one. The inscription reduced Lexy to tears.

My Only Beloved
In This World And The Next
Eleanor Sanderson 4.3.1822 – 6.8.1847
Wait For Me For I Will Come To You

The two small sarcophagi bore the inscriptions of the boys' names: Oliver aged 4 years, and James aged 6 months.

Lexy's face was as white as paper as she stared transfixed at the Colonel's public declaration of love for his first family. Her heart sunk. With the turmoil of the uprising burgeoning around her, she understood in an instant the Colonel's inability to lose himself to love ever again. Having lost all that he held dear, it was little wonder that he had wrapped an impenetrable shield around himself.

Rakesh called to her from the far corner of the cemetery. 'Come Lexy, quickly.'

She dashed the tears from her eyes and hurried towards him. He had moved a heavy flagstone to one side, revealing a flight of steps that spiralled downwards into the blackness. A dank, primeval smell emanated from the hole in the ground.

'We must go down there,' said Rakesh.

Lexy drew back in horror. There was something repellent about having to descend the shaft: like stepping into one's own grave. She shuddered.

'I can't.'

'You must,' said Rakesh. 'I'm coming with you. You won't be alone. It leads to a secret underground room. We'll be safe there, but we must hurry. If anyone sees us it will be a secret no longer.'

Lexy had no choice but to trust him. Gingerly she lowered herself over the edge and climbed down a dozen or more steps. Rakesh climbed into the shaft and pulled and tugged the flagstone back into place.

'Stay still a moment,' he whispered. 'I have a lamp hidden here.'

Lexy could not have moved even if she had wanted to. It was dark and smelly, and she was petrified. Rakesh fumbled about until he found the lamp. It was a relief to them both to have some light. They made their way down the steps and along winding passages, their shadows dancing on the walls beside them. The further down they went the colder it became, until it was difficult to remember the intense heat above ground they had felt only a few minutes earlier.

They entered a domed chamber. Long ago it must have been a place of beauty, but now paint peeled from the murals on the walls and water dripped from the ceiling, making green slimy patches on the floor.

'What is this place?' asked Lexy.

'It's part of a *tykhana*,' said Rakesh.

He led her along another passage until they came to a well-preserved vaulted room. Its marble walls still retained much of their original splendour with designs of birds and flowers still largely intact.

'In the old days,' explained Rakesh. 'This is where the owners of the haveli above would have spent the hot season.' His voice echoed and Lexy felt constrained to whisper in reply.

'Does anyone live up there now?'

Rakesh nodded.

'Why don't they use it anymore?'

'They don't know about it,' said Rakesh. 'Above is my family home. We have lived here ever since we moved from Calcutta when I was just a boy. I found the tykhana by chance, and I used to come and hide down here where my brothers couldn't find me.'

'We seem to have come a long way underground. Why is there a passage from here into the town?'

'I don't know, but it's lucky for us that there is. I know of four passages altogether. There's the one we used, the one that leads to the garden above, one that leads to a water gate, and one that is completely blocked.'

Lexy shivered in the chill of the underground room. Rakesh handed her the carpetbag.

'Here, wrap yourself in something warm. I must go and tell my mother that you are here because you will need food and blankets. I won't be gone long. Don't be frightened.'

'Promise you will come back,' said Lexy.

'I promise,' said Rakesh. 'All I want to do is keep you and our son safe from harm.'

He left by way of one of the other passages. For a few moments she could see the lamplight flickering on the walls, and then he was gone. In the silence Lexy took stock of her surroundings. She was beginning to adapt to the coolness of the tykhana and had stopped shivering. On the outer wall, too high for her to see through properly, was an arched window with stone tracery. It had been well-designed and allowed sufficient light into the underground room whilst keeping out the worst of the sun's rays.

Everything had happened so quickly that it was only now that she was alone that Lexy remembered Mattie. She gasped with shock when she realised that her little daughter had been completely forgotten. The Colonel must have brought her home by now and he would be furious when he discovered that Lexy had disappeared. He would have had to leave Mattie with the servants or, even worse, with his woman in the bibi khana. The Colonel had warned Lexy that he would not be able to stay to protect them, but she had not really listened, and now Mattie's life was in danger because of her. As soon as she heard footsteps in the passageway, Lexy sprang towards Rakesh in panic.

'Rakesh. Oh, Rakesh,' she cried. 'I've left my daughter behind.'

The colour drained from Rakesh's face. 'Where is she? I'll find her and bring her here.'

'I'm not sure.' Lexy burst into tears. 'She was staying with my cousin in the cantonment, but they were going to a birthday party at the Lawsons. My husband went to fetch her. He may have taken her home. I don't know. What am I going to do?'

'Hush,' said Rakesh. 'Where in the cantonment was she staying?'

'At Captain George Cartwright's house.'

'What is her name?'

'Mattie.'

'I'll try and find her.'

'I'll come with you.'

'No,' said Rakesh. 'You must stay here. It's not safe for any Europeans out there at the moment. Give me the two addresses. I'll be as quick as I can.'

Rakesh hurried away and Lexy turned to the woman who had come into the tykhana with him. Malati Chatterjee stepped from the shadows into the pool of light cast by the unglazed window. She placed a rolled-up blanket on the stone seat and then faced Lexy. She had summed up the situation in a single glance.

'My son is the father of the child you carry, isn't he?' she said.

Lexy blushed. 'I am really sorry for putting Rakesh in danger. He has been very good to me.'

Malati tutted and shook her head from side to side. 'Whatever were you both thinking of?' she said.

The two women eyed each other warily. Suddenly Malati gasped. She leaned forward to peer more closely at the necklace Lexy wore. Her hands flew to her throat.

'I don't believe it. You must be Lexy, Captain Nicolson's daughter,' she whispered.

The words echoed round and round the chilly marble room. It was Lexy's turn to be shocked. She thought she would faint.

'How do you know who I am?'

Malati sank down onto the marble seat that jutted from one of the walls. She unwrapped the blanket beside her and patted it for Lexy to sit with her.

'I know who you are because you are wearing my sister's favourite moonstone necklace,' she said.

Lexy put a hand to the necklace. 'I don't understand,' she said. 'Did you know my father?'

Malati nodded slowly. 'I have thought of him often over the years. Tell me about him. Is he still alive?'

Lexy shook her head. 'It must be nine years now since my parents passed away.'

'Did he have a happy life?'

Lexy reflected for a moment and frowned. 'No, I don't think I would describe it as having been a happy life. There was an aura of tragedy about him. After his last voyage to India he left the sea and became a minister of religion, which appeared to bring him nothing but misery. No doubt you will think badly of me for saying so, but I thought he was a mean-spirited man. I'm sorry to say that I hated him.'

Malati's shrewd brown eyes bored into Lexy's as she wondered how much of Captain Murdo Nicolson's story she should reveal, but once she

301

began the telling of it she could not stop. She told Lexy everything – the story of a forbidden love and its dreadful consequences. She poured out her own grief over Anjana's tragic act of sati, and the utter desolation of a man's soul.

In the semi-darkness of the underground room, Malati held Lexy in thrall with her recounting of the past. They were lost in a world of times gone by, completely unaware of the nightmare raging in the streets above their heads.

CHAPTER 42

When he left Lexy, the Colonel rode furiously to the Cartwrights' house, only to find that Charlotte and the children were not there. Frantic with worry and anger he pounded on the door of the house next door.

'They've gone to the Lawsons in the civil lines. It's their son's birthday,' he was told.

The Colonel did not stop to talk, or even to warn of danger, he simply mounted at once and rode back in the direction he had just come, cursing his wife all the way.

Neville Lawson was a wealthy merchant with a shop in the walled town. He and his wife had lived in their haveli for seven years and were well known in both the British and Indian communities. He was taken aback when Colonel Sanderson rode into his garden in a cloud of dust.

'Where's Mattie?' gasped the Colonel, almost throwing himself from his horse.

Neville Lawson gestured behind him. The whole family were collected together at the rear of the house. The Colonel rushed inside.

'Mattie must go home immediately,' he said to Charlotte, trying not to alarm the ladies.

Charlotte raised startled eyes. 'Whatever is wrong?' she said.

'There's trouble in the town.'

As if to emphasise the point there was a sudden burst of gunfire. The Colonel hesitated. There was no time to get Mattie home after all. He hurried to Neville Lawson's side and spoke softly to him.

'I can't stop as I have to join my men. You must keep everyone inside and bolt the doors. Close all the shutters and blinds and arm yourself. Try and keep the ladies calm so as not to frighten the children. Hurry, there is trouble on the way and none of us is safe.'

He rode off at speed, terrified for the safety of his daughter, but having to obey the call of duty above all else. He had delayed long enough. God, protect her, he prayed as he went. As they watched the Colonel gallop away, Neville Lawson spoke in tones of disbelief.

'I think the old boy must have a touch of the sun,' he said to his wife. 'He is the last person I would have expected to panic over nothing. It's quite extraordinary. I can't imagine what has got into the man.'

'You are not inclined to believe him then?' queried Grace Lawson. 'Like you, I would not have expected Colonel Sanderson to spread alarm without reason, but it wouldn't do any harm to do as he suggested. Better to be safe than sorry, as they say.'

'Nonsense, m'dear, of course I don't believe him. We've no reason to suppose there will be any trouble here. The gunfire is probably a wedding celebration. In any case, even if there were trouble we would not be harmed. We're too well known.'

The Colonel's flying visit caused a flutter of alarm amongst the ladies and they drew their children to them whilst the Lawsons went to the front gate to peer down the road. The servants brought tea and lemonade, and the ladies huddled together beneath the punkah trying to keep cool. Charlotte, never one to think too deeply about anything, was lulled into a sense of false security by Neville Lawson's complacency, and she decided to take Mattie home later in the evening after the heat of the day had passed, any trouble there might be probably having died down by then. Whilst they languished and chattered desultorily indoors, the anger in the streets and bazaars spread like wildfire; but the sporadic sound of guns came no closer.

When he reached the streets of the old town, Rakesh was horrified at the chaos everywhere. The whole town appeared to be in revolt and the noise was deafening. There was no reasoning with a mob such as this – a mob containing amongst their number many who believed that killing an infidel would ensure their place in paradise. The crowd screamed, yelled, fired guns and slashed out with knives as they descended on properties inhabited by *feringhees,* sacking and looting as they went, and killing indiscriminately – men, women and children, both Europeans and their Indian servants. Ayahs and bearers fell with their masters, and little children were easy prey for the dark-skinned assassins because they had always trusted the natives who were responsible for the greater part of their care. A wild-eyed Indian fleeing past their house shouted at Neville Lawson.

'Run, sahib, run. The mob is coming.'

'Mob? What mob? Get a hold of yourself.'

'They are coming up the road from the bazaar,' said the frightened man over his shoulder as he ran on.

Neville Lawson shaded his eyes and looked down the road. He could hear shouts and gunfire in the distance, but still did not fully appreciate the danger they were in. Meanwhile, thoroughly alarmed by the guns, the party guests decided to go to their homes and were dispersing in disarray. Charlotte grabbed Benjamin and Mattie by the hand and ran with them down the steps onto the lawns at the rear of the haveli. The terror she felt sent her into a blind panic. All she could think of was that she had to save the children. Running from the building she met the Lawsons' cook fleeing in the opposite direction. He faltered when he saw the memsahib with two small golden-haired children.

'In there, memsahib,' he panted, pointing behind him. 'Hide them in there. They will not be found.'

The cook pointed to a rough hut that was almost totally obscured by greenery. It was situated at the far end of the garden at a short distance from the servants' quarters. Charlotte ran to it, flung open the door, and pushed the children inside. It was the servants' latrine, a noisome place, but Charlotte did not hesitate.

'Promise me that you won't move and you won't make a sound,' she said.

The children nodded. Benjamin's thumb went into his mouth, and both he and Mattie stared at Charlotte, wide-eyed and sensing her terror.

'Good,' said Charlotte. 'I'm going to fetch Clara May. I'll come straight back to you. I won't be long.'

She fled back to the house, raced up the steps onto the terrace and disappeared inside. Once indoors she could hear the mob as they reached the gates to the grounds of the haveli. She ran up the stairs, clutching her skirts above her knees so that she would not trip over them, and hurried to the bedroom where Clara May was asleep in a cot. She grabbed the baby and ran to the top of the stairs. Then she heard the first scream. Her first impulse was to hide in one of the cupboards in the room she had just left, but then she thought of Benjamin and Mattie. She could not leave them all alone to face whatever might come their way. She had to go back down the stairs.

Swallowing the gorge rising in her throat, and not daring to yield to her desire to scream, thereby betraying her presence, Charlotte crept down the stairs as far as the window on the lower landing. She inched forward and peeped into the garden. Frozen with fear she saw Neville Lawson fall. Grace Lawson began to run, which spurred the mob to laughter. Their son, who was celebrating his fourth birthday, stood stock-still and screamed. Charlotte watched with horror as one of the rebels walked calmly up to the boy and killed him with one swipe of his *tulwar*. Then they turned their attention to the boy's mother.

The sudden silence as the boy's screams stopped abruptly galvanised Charlotte into action. When the mob was finished with Grace Lawson they would come inside to loot and destroy, and they would find her there. Desperate to save Clara May, she kicked off her slippers and fled down the remaining stairs, ran across the hall, through the drawing room, onto the veranda, and down the steps onto the lawns. As she ran she heard a shout of triumph behind her: the mob had come through the haveli and caught sight of her in the garden. They were in no hurry as they followed Charlotte. She could not escape them; her fate was sealed.

Charlotte ran towards the servants' latrine, but suddenly realised through her terror that she was leading the murderers straight to Benjamin and Mattie. At the last moment she swerved to change direction, but as she did so she tripped over her long skirts and sprawled headlong. The mob roared with laughter. Some hissed and jeered, others bayed for her blood; and then they set upon Charlotte and Clara May with their knives.

Inside the latrine Mattie and Benjamin watched through the narrow gap on the hinged side of the door. They watched as Charlotte and Clara May were cut to ribbons. They watched as the paraphernalia of the birthday party was smashed to smithereens on the grass; and they watched as items were brought from the house and set on fire. They watched it all, and yet they made no sound because they had promised Charlotte that they would not.

The mob did not stay long, nor did they go near the servants' quarters, preferring instead to go in search of further European victims, so the two children were not discovered. When she could no longer see or hear anyone, Mattie turned her beloved cousin towards her so that his face was buried in her shoulder. He could not see his mother and baby sister any more, but Mattie's horrified gaze remained fixed on their bloodstained bodies. She made no attempt to lead Benjamin from the awful place in which Charlotte had hidden them. She did as her aunt had said, and they stayed huddled together in shocked silence.

The Sandersons' residence was intact but deserted. Rakesh wasted no time there but hurried towards the civil lines in search of the Lawsons' house. Most of the rebels had left the bazaars now and were swarming through the civil and military lines. The regiments had mounted a determined defence, but if the sepoys mutinied and joined the mob it would only be a matter of time before they were overrun. Fires burned in the lines and smoke swirled in the air, dimming the brightness of the sun. Bodies lay where they had been cut down and looters filled the streets.

Rakesh found the address Lexy had given him and entered through the broken gateway. He picked his way over the ornamental gates lying on the ground; one glance told him that he was too late, but he had to know what had happened to Lexy's daughter. Several bodies lay between the gateway and the building. They lay in grotesque attitudes in pools of blood. Rakesh's nostrils flared with the smell, but he threaded his way amongst them, Europeans and Indians alike, looking for signs of life and searching for Mattie. Flies already swarmed over the dead and Rakesh shuddered with disgust. Slowly his mind registered the fact that there was no little girl's body amongst them. Mattie was not there.

Ashen-faced, he walked mechanically towards the haveli. His feet scrunched on the glass from broken windows. When he went through the front door he could see that the place had been ransacked and the rear of the building smouldered. A door hanging drunkenly from one hinge creaked, and Rakesh flinched at the sound. He went upstairs and into each room but found no one. He went back downstairs and into the rear gardens. Flowers and shrubs, already half-dead from the heat, had been trampled to the ground by stampeding feet. A pile of books and clothes burned on a bonfire of tables and chairs.

He crossed the parched lawns and moved towards the servants' quarters at the far end of the garden. A slight movement of white caught his eye and he froze to stillness. The fractional movement of white occurred again and Rakesh crept towards the hut that stood behind the hibiscus bushes. Someone was in the hut, and Rakesh could smell his own fear as he stopped outside the door.

'Who is there?' he asked softly.

He waited in the silence. There was no reply, just a quiver of white through the crack at the side of the door. Gaining confidence from the lack of reply Rakesh moved closer. He reasoned to himself that if it had been one of the rebels in the hut he would have already burst out and attacked him. He tried again.

'Is your name Mattie? I am looking for Mattie Sanderson. If you are Mattie, I can tell you that your mother is safe. I am a friend.'

There was still no sound from inside the hut. 'I am going to open the door now,' said Rakesh. 'Don't be afraid. I am not going to hurt you.'

Tentatively Rakesh opened the door and peered inside. He had hoped to find one child; instead there were two, and they stood rigid with shock. It had been a shiver of Mattie's white party dress that had caught his eye. Neither of the children looked at him. The little boy's face was buried in the girl's shoulder, and the little girl stared fixedly past Rakesh. He turned to follow her gaze and sucked in his breath sharply when he saw the bloody mess on the flowerbed. Rakesh had not seen the bodies of Charlotte and Clara May when he approached the hut because they had been hidden by the dense hibiscus bushes. The memsahib lay in a blood-soaked bundle, still clutching her baby to her bosom. Rakesh strode towards the bodies. Not knowing what else to do, and anxious to cover them so that the children would no longer be able to see them, he bent down and pulled the top layer of Charlotte's crinoline dress over the stump of her neck and her severed head.

'I am sorry, memsahib,' he whispered.

He hurried back to the children, who had still not moved or uttered a sound. 'Stay here quietly,' he said. 'I'm going to find something I can hide you in to take you to your mother.'

He ran across the garden to the mali's hut and found what he was looking for. The handcart was partly broken, but it would serve Rakesh's purpose. He put some bits and pieces of blanket left by the looters into the cart and hurried back to the children. He lifted them one by one into the cart and covered them.

'Stay under the blanket so that no one sees your beautiful golden hair,' he urged.

He pushed the cart out through the broken gateway and into the street. He had to force himself to walk normally through the gathering dusk. He dared not run. He could only save the lives of these two children if he became just another of the many looters, blending and melting into his surroundings.

In the tykhana Lexy listened to Malati in stunned silence, overwhelmed by the tragedy of her father's love for Anjana, and her sacrifice for him. She was moved to tears by the heavy price they paid for breaking the rules. She remembered the bleak and haunted look in Murdo's eyes and understood why he had held the world at arm's length.

'My father would never have been able to forgive himself for causing your sister's death,' she said. 'In fact, now I know about the secret burden he carried, I would go so far as to say that he spent the rest of his life immersed in guilt.'

Malati sighed. 'That is a pity because it was not his fault. I must admit that for years I did blame him for Anjana's death, but as the grief faded I realised that I was wrong. Anjana made her decision of her own free will, and she would have followed the same course even if she had never met Captain Nicolson. Loving him as she did simply made it easier for her; you must believe me when I tell you that she would have become sati anyway. She was not happy in this world until she met your father, and she went to him of her own free will. Captain Nicolson was a gentleman. He did not chase after her; he was not to blame in any way.'

'Your sister's name was on his lips as he died,' said Lexy. 'I didn't know what he meant at the time, but now I realise that he thought that he saw her as he died. He never stopped loving her.'

Malati wiped tears from her eyes and patted Lexy's hand. 'Now we must let the past bury its dead. It was tragic, but they are both at peace now.'

They looked up as Rakesh came along the passage with a child in each arm. As soon as he appeared at the entrance Lexy leapt to her feet and rushed forward, arms outstretched.

'Mattie! Benjamin! Thank God you are safe.' She took Mattie from Rakesh and hugged her close. 'Thank you, Rakesh. Thank you for finding them. Where were they?'

'They were in the civil lines. It's a nightmare up there. The children are in shock and I must get them warm drinks. Here, take the boy and wrap them both up warmly.'

Both the children's faces wore blank expressions. Despite having been curled up in the cart beneath a pile of blankets their clothes were still immaculate, in stark contrast to Rakesh's smoke-smeared appearance. His clothes and hair were covered with dust and ash from the streets and fires. Lexy sat with Mattie on one side and Benjamin on the other. Malati tucked blankets around all three, clucking her tongue and shaking her head.

'When is your baby due?' she asked.

Lexy felt herself blush. 'In a month's time.'

Malati pursed her lips. Lexy and the children could not stay in the tykhana without arousing suspicion in the house above, and yet she would not be able to travel far so near her time; but it would be impossible to provide meals without their presence becoming known, and it would be useless to expect Vijay to help to keep them hidden because he had never forgotten or forgiven the affair between Anjana and Captain Nicolson. He no longer trusted Europeans, and he would cast Rakesh out for having an affair with a memsahib.

Rakesh returned with warm sweet milk, which he made the children drink. He looked from Benjamin to Lexy and spoke softly.

'You did not tell me that you have a son,' he said.

Lexy smiled and shook her head. 'Benjamin is not mine. He is my cousin's son,' she explained. 'When you found the children did you see a fair-haired memsahib with a baby girl?'

She saw a shadow cross Rakesh's face and knew from the pain in his eyes that Charlotte and Clara May were dead.

'The baby too?' she gasped.

Rakesh nodded. 'There are many dead. Houses and stores have been ransacked, looted and torched. The mob has gone mad. They are even killing our own people. I saw ayahs and bearers shredded to ribbons.' He shuddered. 'I can't believe the horror of it. How can such a disaster happen so quickly?'

Suddenly Benjamin spoke. His voice was flat, matter-of-fact, and his words stunned them all. 'They cut off Mummy's head.'

Before Lexy had time to register his words Mattie screamed. The piercing shriek released something within Benjamin and he, too, began to scream. Lexy rocked them back and forth, holding them firmly to her and humming a lullaby. As the medicine Rakesh had added to their milk took effect their screams subsided to sobs, their sobs to a quivering quietness, and then they slept. Lexy and Malati laid them on the marble bench, shrinking from the hideous magnitude of what the children had witnessed.

Colonel Sanderson's belief in himself and his life's work crumbled to dust that day. The speed with which violence erupted in the bazaars was beyond his comprehension. The old town had seemed an unexceptional place, and yet there must have been an undercurrent of tension hidden beneath its calm exterior. Hatred, mistrust and festering grudges had flared like a tinderbox. Even he, with his vague concerns for the future of Europeans in India, had failed to anticipate such a degree of bloodlust. He was irritated by Neville Lawson's blank disbelief that they could be in danger, but he had no time to argue. His personal responsibilities were secondary to his responsibility for the defence of the town. Convincing himself that Charlotte would take Mattie home before it was too late, and that Lexy would take their daughter into the bibi khana, the Colonel rode away from the civil lines to rejoin his men.

News of the uprising had spread, and a flustered Lieutenant Piggott was waiting for him.

'Sir,' he said with a quick salute. 'Are you going to give the order to disarm the sepoys? That's what is happening in some of the regiments.'

The Colonel stared at him. 'Disarm my own men? Never!' he barked. 'I will not show any loss of faith in the Corps just because some misguided sepoys have decided to mutiny.'

'But they could turn their weapons on us,' protested the young officer.

'Yes, they could,' agreed the Colonel. 'But they show no sign of disorder at the moment, and the act of disarming them could well provoke the very unrest I hope to avoid.'

'Well, I hope your trust is not misplaced. Perhaps it will prove to be a storm in a teacup after all,' said Lieutenant Piggott. 'A few days of insubordination from the sepoys and rioting in the bazaars and that will be an end of it, I daresay.'

'I don't agree,' said the Colonel. 'You haven't seen what is happening within the walls. I think we are close to a disaster. God knows, I can't say I blame them, but I trust my men and will not disarm them without cause.'

The Colonel brooded. He knew that he was not, and never could be, Indian. Hindus were born, not made, and yet he had lived so long amongst them that he was Indian in his heart and no longer belonged to his own people. But his Indianness was within him, hidden from view, and he was well aware that it would be his fair-haired, blue-eyed European exterior that would determine his fate.

Lieutenant Piggott regarded his Colonel thoughtfully. If anyone understood how the native mind worked, the Colonel did, but he was of the opinion that the old man was making something out of nothing. Lieutenant Piggott had to cling fast to his belief that there was nothing seriously wrong because he was afraid – if the Colonel's assessment of the situation were correct, and they faced disaster, where would that leave him? He had never shared the Colonel's regard for Indians, and his zealous attempts to make Christian converts amongst them would not go well with him if they lost control of the men. He offered up a silent prayer for his survival, and then turned to the task of calling Sanderson's Rifles to order.

They set off to deal with the rebels within the old town. The narrow alleys of the bazaars were choked with people – rebels, and those fleeing for their lives. The Colonel led his men, forcing a path through the crowds and shooting identifiable assassins and murderers. Wine flowed from looted bars and many of the *badmashes* were drunk – drunk from the effects of alcohol and the smell of blood on their hands.

A stray bullet grazed Lieutenant Piggott's temple and he fell from his horse. He struggled to his feet with blood streaming down his face, but before he could orientate himself and remount, he was set upon. Hurt, dazed, but fully conscious, he endured many bayonet thrusts before he died. The Colonel ordered some of his sepoys to the Lieutenant's defence, but they were half-hearted in their response and the young officer was killed by his own men.

Colonel Sanderson and Subedar Khan fought shoulder to shoulder. The Colonel fired his pistol with deadly effect, but they were outnumbered and even as he fought, the Colonel knew that he wouldn't be able to hold out much longer. The subedar was killed first, vainly trying to protect the Colonel with whom he had faced and overcome many dangers. Moments later Colonel Sanderson lay on the ground beside him, and the rebels continued to slash their bodies long after death had claimed them.

CHAPTER 43

Malati came to a decision as darkness gathered outside the underground room.

'We must return Lexy to her own people,' she said. 'It will be impossible to keep her presence here a secret. Had it just been Lexy we might have tried, but with the children as well it simply won't be safe for any of us.'

'But it's not safe out there either,' protested Rakesh. 'It's better to keep them here and manage as best we can than expose them to the mob in the street.'

Malati shook her head. 'If they stay here we risk all our family and I cannot allow that.'

'Were would I go?' asked Lexy. 'I don't want to put any of you in danger, but where can I go with the children?'

'To Meerut,' said Malati. 'If that is where the trouble started it will be quiet there now, and they can't have killed all the Europeans.'

'But it's fifty miles away,' said Rakesh. 'How can they travel so far in safety?'

'I have thought of that,' said Malati. 'You will travel together as a family as if you were going to visit relatives in one of the villages. Chhaya will go with you.'

Rakesh gasped. 'No, I don't want her with us. I'll take them on my own.'

'You will need her,' argued Malati. 'Lexy might pass as one of us at a distance, but you will need an Indian woman with you to go into the villages for food. Besides, Chhaya has relatives on the other side of the river and she can ask them for help.'

'Who is Chhaya?' ventured Lexy. Rakesh looked uncomfortable.

'Chhaya is Rakesh's wife,' said Malati.

Lexy's heart lurched. She had pushed the fact of Rakesh's marriage so far to the back of her mind that she had all but forgotten that he had a wife. As long as she was not mentioned Lexy could almost believe that she did not exist. To have her as part of the rescue plan filled Lexy with foreboding, but she was powerless to protest. She was in Malati's hands, and she trusted her.

'I will go and fetch Chhaya and we will provide Lexy and the children with some fresh clothes. We must hurry because I want you to set off now so that you can be as far away from here as possible before morning comes.'

When Chhaya arrived in the tykhana Lexy was shocked to see that she, too, was pregnant, and she was forced to confront the fact that the man she loved, and who professed to love her, had an intimate relationship with another woman. She had of course known of Rakesh's marriage, known that it must be consummated, but had somehow never allowed herself to believe it. Now it stared her in the face. Rakesh belonged to another woman just as she belonged to another man, and the full impact of her own conduct was brought home to her in all its impropriety.

The instant Chhaya entered the tykhana and saw Rakesh and the memsahib together she knew that her husband had fathered the child the white woman bore. The jealousy on Lexy's face was mirrored in her own as the truth dawned; she could now make sense of Rakesh's lack of ardour towards her.

Chhaya knew that she was plain because her sisters had often told her that her lack of beauty meant that she would never be married. When her parents had informed her that she was to be betrothed to Rakesh Chatterjee she could scarcely believe her good fortune. She had known Rakesh for most of her life, and as they grew up she had worshipped the handsome boy, never contemplating for one moment that her dream to be his wife could ever come true. She did not know that both sets of parents saw a marriage between Rakesh and Chhaya as a way of solving the difficulty of marrying off a very plain girl and an odd loner of a son, and Chhaya's parents were taken aback at her obvious delight in their choice of husband for her.

To begin with Rakesh's aloofness towards Chhaya following their wedding had caused her only passing concern. She assumed that he was

315

disappointed in her ugliness, so she devoted herself to ensuring that that would be the only fault he could find in her. Now she understood the real reason: he loved another woman, and a white woman at that. A dark memsahib she may be, but the forbidden nature of that love could not fail to add to their mutual intoxication, and Chhaya knew that even if she had been beautiful she would not have been able to compete with this woman for Rakesh's affection.

When Malati told Chhaya that she was to assist a memsahib in her escape she had wanted no part in it, but now, seeing Rakesh and Lexy together, she was prepared to do anything to be rid of her. She handed the clothes to Lexy in resentful silence, and then Malati sent her back to the house for food to take with them on their journey.

'I cannot order anything hot for you,' apologised Malati. 'The cook would be suspicious, but Chhaya will bring bread and yoghurt, and perhaps some cold rice.'

Rakesh disappeared down one of the passages while Lexy changed into simple white muslin garments, and when he returned he had some good news.

'This passage leads to the water gate and there is a small boat tied up a little further along the bank. We can use that to get across the river. It will take two crossings though because the boat is too small to take us all at once.'

Chhaya returned with the food. Rakesh ignored her. He spoke to Lexy.

'Do you think you will be all right? We have a long walk ahead of us,' he said.

'It's surprising what one can manage when one's life is threatened,' she replied with a wry smile. 'But the children won't be able to walk far without stopping to rest.'

'We will take the cart with us,' said Rakesh. 'It's not very sturdy, but we can use it until it falls to pieces, and then Chhaya and I will carry the children.'

Chhaya darted a venomous look at Lexy. She was at about the same stage of pregnancy as the memsahib, but her husband had paid no heed as to whether she would be able to carry one of the well-padded feringhee children in her condition. She hoped the rebels would find them and kill the memsahib. In fact, she hoped they would all be killed, for what was the point of her life if Rakesh could not bring himself to acknowledge her existence?

They wasted no more time. Malati accompanied them along the passage to the water gate. Rakesh slunk along the water's edge to steal the boat. While they waited for him, Lexy removed Anjana's moonstone necklace from around her neck and handed it to Malati.

'This really belongs to you,' she said. 'I want you to have it. It will be safer with you than with me.'

Malati fastened the necklace around her own neck, and the two women clung to one another in the darkness. The waters of the River Jumna lapped against the bank with a sucking sound as Rakesh rowed the boat to the water gate. Lexy stepped gingerly into the boat and crouched down in the bottom. Malati handed the children to Rakesh one by one.

'I'll be back for Chhaya and the cart,' he said.

'Goodbye, Malati,' said Lexy with a sob. 'Thank you for everything.'

Rakesh pushed the boat into the river using one of the oars.

'I wish you a safe journey, my daughter,' whispered Malati. 'My thoughts will be with you always.'

The little boat rocked dangerously as Rakesh rowed them across the river. The smell of burning buildings filled the air and the flames were reflected in the water. In the distance they could hear the hubbub in the town as they glided across the blackness to the bank on the other side. They crossed without being challenged and Rakesh helped Lexy and the children out of the boat.

'Stay right where you are,' he whispered. 'I won't be long.'

Lexy hugged Mattie and Benjamin to her while they waited. It seemed hours before Rakesh returned with Chhaya and the cart. He pulled the boat onto the bank so that it did not drift away, and then they set off immediately to put as much distance as possible between them and the burning town before dawn broke. The squelch of mud sucked at Lexy's shoes and one of them was lost before they had covered more than a few yards. Scarcely faltering in her footsteps, she kicked off the other shoe.

The children sat in the cart in silence; they had not spoken since Benjamin recalled what had happened to his mother and baby sister. When Lexy told them that they must hide their blond hair and blue eyes under the blanket whenever they saw anyone else along the way, they had nodded, wide-eyed and open-mouthed. Their safe and pampered world had disintegrated in one fell swoop. They lacked the language to cope with the enormity of it, and so far there had been no time for Lexy to explain in words they would understand.

By the time the first streaks of yellow dawn lit the horizon they had almost reached the village where Chhaya's aunt and uncle lived. Rakesh had set a good pace and the two women had managed to keep up with him, neither of them wishing to show any sign of weakness to the other. Thistles tore at their clothes and scratched their arms and legs, and stubble had lacerated Lexy's tender feet, but they had marched grimly onwards. Meerut was fifty miles away.

At the outskirts of the village they took shelter in a tumbledown hut. Rakesh sent his wife in search of her relatives to seek whatever help she could from them. Lexy and the children lay down on the earthen floor of the hut to snatch some sleep whilst Rakesh kept watch outside. When Lexy awoke after an hour she felt refreshed. Chhaya had still not returned and Lexy was unable to quell a rising sense of panic. The other woman's hatred had been tangible and Lexy was frightened that she might not come back at all.

'Don't be afraid, flower of my heart,' said Rakesh, reading her thoughts. 'She will not betray you.'

'Can you be sure?' asked Lexy.

'Yes. She is an Indian wife and she will do as I say. Besides, she knows that if she betrays you she also risks her life and mine for having helped you.'

'Perhaps she won't care,' said Lexy gloomily.

Rakesh looked at her thoughtfully. 'Perhaps she won't,' he agreed. 'But if it is her intention to betray any of us she won't do it yet. She will fight you for me first.'

Lexy shivered. 'She does not need to fight. You are taking me to Meerut. You are letting me go, and I am letting you do it because I cannot risk anything happening to Mattie and Benjamin. Your wife will have you without a fight; but only for now, Rakesh. When the troubles are over and we are safe again, I shall come back to you.'

'I will be waiting, flower of my heart. I will wait for you forever.'

Chhaya did not return until the late afternoon. When they saw her coming along the dusty track pushing a sturdy handcart, Lexy could have wept with relief. Chhaya brought milk, tea, chapattis and some cold curry, and they ate greedily.

'I shall thank your uncle personally when we return the cart to him on our way back home,' said Rakesh. Chhaya nodded in silence.

When they finished eating Rakesh transferred the bundle of clothes and the blankets from the old cart.

'We are going on until it gets dark,' he said before Lexy had time to protest. 'We will rest during the night and travel by day.'

'In the heat?' said Lexy.

'Yes, except for the hottest time. We won't attract much attention if we travel by day as long as the children keep their hair covered. If we go by night it will look suspicious. We need to look like an ordinary family going about our business.'

They set off again until it was too dark to see their way and Chhaya's resentment increased when she found that she was to take turns with Rakesh to guard the sleeping memsahib and the children during the night. In the middle of the third day, just as Lexy was lulled into thinking that their safety was assured, she was horrified when two young men sprang from behind a tree and confronted them. They were resting in the shade of some tamarind trees near an evil-smelling pond on the edge of a village. Chhaya had gone in search of food. The children were asleep in the bottom of the handcart and Rakesh pulled a blanket over them. He eyed the strangers warily. They came close, staring at the heavily pregnant woman. With her skin nut-brown from the scorching sun Lexy provoked little more than passing curiosity from the two men. She was obviously not a local woman, but she had been speaking to Rakesh in their own language. Rakesh had forbidden English to be spoken at all during their flight to Meerut.

'What do you want?' asked Rakesh.

'Where are you going?' asked one of the men.

'To the next village. We have kin there. Our home was burnt out.'

The two men whispered together for a moment. 'What's in your cart?'

'We have nothing for you to steal,' said Rakesh. 'We lost everything we owned in the house fire.'

One of the men reached into the cart and grabbed the bundle of clothes. He pulled the bundle apart. 'British clothes,' he said in disgust.

Rakesh shrugged. 'We grabbed what we could like all the other looters. You can have the clothes if you think your women would like to wear them.'

The man dropped the bundle onto the ground and spat. The other man made a sudden grab at the blanket that covered the children. Lexy jumped up to protect them. She turned on the strangers and unleashed a string of invective at them. Rakesh and the two men stared at her in horror, and Lexy had to suppress a nervous giggle at the expressions on their faces. But it was effective: the two men hesitated, and then edged away from the cart. When they were out of earshot, Rakesh turned to Lexy.

'Well, you certainly fooled them,' he said. 'No *pukka* memsahib could possibly know such filthy language. Where did you learn such awful words?'

'Was I really rude?' grinned Lexy. 'I once heard our cook scream at the sweeper and it sounded so deliciously offensive that I couldn't help but remember what he shouted.'

'Rude?' Rakesh was still shocked. 'You were downright obscene and no, before you ask, I have no intention of translating it for you.'

They were still chuckling over it when Chhaya arrived with some chapattis. It was not much for three adults and two hungry children, but it would have to do and it was too hot to want to eat much anyway. Then, as soon as the shadows began to lengthen they set off again. Lexy had torn one of her petticoats into strips to wrap round her cut and bleeding feet. She limped on with her mouth set in a grim line and did not complain.

It took them seven days to reach Meerut. Rakesh had driven them at a hard pace, but he was surprised at the distances they had managed to cover each day. They had travelled without any real danger and without sighting any other refugees, but he was relieved that it was over and Lexy and the children would now be safe from harm. Within sight of the artillery barracks, they sheltered in a *tope* of mango trees to say their goodbyes.

Chhaya stripped Mattie and Benjamin and dressed them in the white party clothes they had been wearing when Rakesh found them. They submitted without protest, used to being cared for by ayahs. Chhaya spoke softly to them, but they remained silent and withdrawn. As yet they had not begun to understand why Indians, people who had only ever shown them their utmost devotion, should have turned on them with such savagery.

'You must also change into your European clothes,' said Rakesh.

'You will have privacy amongst the trees.'

Lexy struggled into the dress her ayah had rolled into the bundle days ago. It could not have been more unsuitable – four flounces of cream silk attached to a tight-fitting bodice. Chhaya pulled and tugged, but she could not lace it properly over Lexy's expanded waistline. Then, to Lexy's astonishment, Chhaya removed her dupatta and draped it over Lexy's shoulders to hide the exposed flesh of her back. Lexy's expression softened as she turned to thank Chhaya, but her gaze met a venomous look of hatred, which was totally out of keeping with the gesture of human kindness Chhaya had made, and Lexy's smile of gratitude froze on her face.

There was no water to wash any of the red dust from Lexy's or the children's faces, and their hair was matted to their heads with dust and perspiration. When they were ready, Rakesh ordered Chhaya into the tope of mango trees out of sight. After she had gone he took Lexy in his arms and kissed her forehead.

'You are safe now, flower of my heart,' he whispered. 'You and our son.'

Lexy was desolate. She clung to him and tears washed a tortuous path through the covering of red dust on her face. 'How can I live without you?' she wept.

Rakesh held her close, imprinting the feel of her in his mind forever; then he took her arms from around his neck.

'Go now,' he said. 'Be happy wherever you are.'

'I will find you again,' sobbed Lexy. 'I can't say goodbye to you. I belong to you now and always.'

They kissed one last and lingering time. 'You must go now,' urged Rakesh. 'Take the children and go where you will be safe from this madness. And remember, flower of my heart, I will always love you.'

Lexy knew that she should leave him, but she could not move. Her legs shook and her heart felt as if it would break. Rakesh pushed her gently forward.

'Take her hands,' he said to the children. 'Walk to the barracks where you will be safe.'

As the blood red sun went down Lexy, Mattie and Benjamin stepped from the shelter of the trees into the open space between them and the barracks. Rakesh watched them go with a dead and empty heart. Chhaya crept forward and peered from behind a tree. She felt a searing moment of triumph. The memsahib had gone. Rakesh was hers alone.

Major Robert Willoughby squinted in the twilight at the woman who emerged from the trees with two small children. She was limping, and each step obviously caused her pain. Even from where he stood he could see that the children were British refugees because their blond hair glinted in the light. He was less certain about the woman. She looked dark enough to be an ayah bringing the children to safety, and yet she wore European clothes. Their progress was slow and heavy, and they walked towards the barracks with apparent reluctance. He thought it odd that they did not hurry. If they had fled the horrors of Delhi or one of the smaller towns he would have expected them to have joy in their steps as they reached sanctuary, in spite of what they may have suffered.

'Something doesn't feel right,' said Major Willoughby to the soldier beside him. 'Prepare to open the gate to let them in, but keep your eyes peeled. It may be a trap.'

Once she started to walk towards the barracks holding Mattie and Benjamin by the hand, Lexy stared grimly ahead, blinded by tears. She dared not turn to look at Rakesh; had she done so she would have run back to him. Rakesh watched her go. The pain of parting was intense, but he had brought them to safety and he would always know that Lexy slept beneath the same moon and was warmed by the same sun as he. She would return to her own country where their son would have a better life, but Rakesh would carry her forever in his heart.

If Chhaya's whining voice nagging him to turn for home had not intruded into his longing, Rakesh would not have left the shelter of the trees, but the sound of her voice, full of reproach and bitterness, roused him from his brooding. He could not let Lexy go without holding her one last time. He stepped from the shadows.

Major Willoughby saw him and frowned. Rakesh took several steps towards the woman and her children, and the major asked himself why an Indian was following her. There could only be one answer – he intended to kill her. He took his pistol from its holster and levelled it. Rakesh began to run towards Lexy, but he did not call out to her so she did not turn round.

'Take one more step, you mutineering little bugger,' muttered Major Willoughby. 'Just one more step, and it will be your last.'

Rakesh called out to Lexy as he took that one last fateful step. The major fired his pistol. Rakesh's cry reached Lexy at the same time as she heard the shot. For a moment she stood in stunned disbelief. The shot whizzed past her ear and she turned to look behind her. Rakesh lay on his back on the ground. A red stain spread over his shirt and dripped into the dust beside him. Major Willoughby had shot him in the chest.

'No!' Chhaya let out a silent scream, stuffing her arm in her mouth for fear of being heard, of giving herself away. 'No!' she screamed again internally, shrinking back into the shadows of the trees.

'No!' screamed Lexy. 'No!' She dropped the children's hands and ran back to Rakesh.

Puzzled and confused, Major Willoughby chased after her. By the time he reached her she was already kneeling in the dust with her head against Rakesh's cheek, her grief too deep for tears. Major Willoughby returned his pistol to its holster.

'He was running after you,' he explained. 'I had to protect you. He would have killed you all.'

Lexy looked up, numb with shock. After a moment her vision cleared and she recognised the major as the man who had trifled with her affections on the voyage out to India all those years ago. She staggered to her feet and launched herself at him, fighting tooth and nail, hysterical with grief and rage.

'We needed no protection from him,' she screamed. 'He saved our lives. He brought us here to safety.'

Major Willoughby battled to catch hold of Lexy's hands, and then held her at arm's length, dodging her thrashing feet. As she calmed down he looked at her more closely. There was something familiar about her, but it took several minutes for him to recognise the dirty, wild-eyed, sunburned hellcat as the beautiful young Miss Nicolson he had hoped to seduce.

'You!' he exclaimed. Then he shrugged. 'Well, I'm sorry, but it is one less devil to worry about. We can't trust any of them any more.' He did not care one way or the other about the death of the native. 'Come, let me take you to where you can rest.'

Lexy took one last aching look at the man she adored, lying in a pool of blood. Already vultures swayed on the topmost branches of the trees. She took hold of the children's hands again, their dirty faces vacant of expression, eyes glazed, dumbstruck from having witnessed yet more bloody violence, and together they followed Major Willoughby into the barracks where survivors of the mutiny in Meerut and fugitives from Delhi were gathered for protection. As darkness fell, the shock of Rakesh's brutal death caused Lexy to go into premature labour, and as stars sprinkled the night sky she gave birth to Rakesh's son.

CAWNPORE

CHAPTER 44

There had been no letter from Lexy for two weeks and Evalina was anxious. Charlotte had not written either, and it was so unusual that Evalina had to quell feelings of panic each time she thought of them. They were both in the habit of writing every week and it was only the fact that Evalina had had no letter from either of them that helped her to stay calm. Something might have happened to the Sandersons or the Cartwrights, but not both. Evalina tried to reassure herself that there must be a problem with the mail, but she remained anxious.

Over the years Evalina had become used to her Indian servants and had learned sufficient of their language to feel comfortable in her dealings with them, but what comforted her most was the very Englishness of life in Cawnpore. There was security to be felt in keeping up appearances, maintaining standards and playing bridge. She had even joined the thriving amateur theatrical society although she lacked both the desire and the ability to venture on stage. Instead, she became a valued member of the costume department, and on more than one occasion had even acted as prompt.

At the balls and parties Evalina and Mungo attended, both in private houses and in the assembly rooms, they formed part of a large circle of people. Some had become close friends, filling the gap left by the absence of family, but they never replaced Lexy and Charlotte in Evalina's heart and she regretted that they were so far away. She had not seen Lexy, Charlotte and the children since just after Benjamin was born. She fretted over poor little Mattie and wondered if Lexy had ever learned to love her. Lexy's letters could be evasive on the subject of her daughter.

As the sun sank lower in the sky, the heat of the day passed. May was particularly hot this year and Evalina had already resigned herself to the hours of daytime inactivity that made the hot seasons seem even longer than they really were. She had never escaped to the hills although Lexy had often badgered her to join them in Simla. Evalina had been too long a spinster to be willing to sacrifice any time with her dear, kind husband for the sake of her own personal comfort.

She made her way to the far end of the garden. It was her favourite spot at this time of day because she could hear the trumpeting of elephants as their laughing mahouts scrubbed them down further along the river. She never tired of this evening entertainment, and there were times when she wondered how she could have been so afraid when she first arrived in India. She clapped her hands and called for a servant to move the table and chairs to the end of the garden and have tea ready for Mungo when he arrived home. Perhaps there would be a letter tomorrow.

The local grapevine was alive with rumour. It had taken four days for news of events in Meerut and Delhi to reach General Wheeler in Cawnpore. Now frantic stories spread like wildfire from the military to the civil lines, the hospitals, the bazaars and into the city. Disbelief, indignation, anger and fear followed in their wake.

The instant he learned of the mutinies Mungo hurried home, anxious to be the one to break the news to Evalina before exaggerated stories reached her. He rode home with a heavy heart, wondering how she would receive the news. He admired the way Evalina had been so determined to be a wife of whom he could be proud. He had watched her grit her teeth and seen the stubborn tilt of her head as she faced snakes, enormous insects, the Indians she feared and the gruelling hot seasons. He had seen her face whatever obstacles this alien land had thrown her way and be determined to cope with them. Yes, he was proud of her and he loved her dearly, but so far she had faced no real danger. That could be about to change. When he heard of the mutinies Mungo immediately recalled Evalina's premonition of disaster when they reached Calcutta. He had given it no thought since then, but in that instant he remembered her terror in every detail. God, give her strength, he prayed. Give us all strength.

He stepped onto the veranda and Evalina called out to him. 'Do come and watch, dearest. It's such fun.'

As he crossed the lawns Evalina could tell from the expression on his face that something was very wrong. Instead of his usual smile of greeting,

Mungo's mouth was set in a grim line and deep furrows knit his brow.

'Whatever is the matter?' she asked. 'Are you ill?'

Mungo shook his head. He took her hand and led her to a chair. A servant poured tea from a silver pot into delicate bone china cups. The lace-edged corners of a starched white cloth covering a wooden table fluttered lightly in the breeze. Evalina watched her husband warily.

'Then what is it? You look so glum.'

'I don't quite know how to tell you,' said Mungo. 'The thing is that there has been some trouble in the north.'

'The north? Do you mean Delhi? There is trouble in Delhi?'

Mungo nodded. 'Meerut first and then Delhi.'

Icy fear clutched Evalina's heart. 'What kind of trouble? Has something happened to Lexy or Charlotte?'

Mungo's eyes as he raised them to meet Evalina's were filled with love and concern. Evalina sat erect and straight-backed in her chair dreading what her husband might say. She knew that he was trying to protect her from something, but he had said too much to stop now. She had to know.

'What is it that you are trying so hard not to tell me, dear?' She squared her shoulders and sipped her tea, determined to remain calm.

Mungo took a deep breath. 'Some of the sepoys have mutinied,' he said. 'There have been some deaths amongst the Europeans.'

'You mean amongst the military?'

Mungo's shoulders slumped. 'Not just the military. The fact is that hooligans from the bazaars have joined the mutineers and there have been massacres of civilians.'

Evalina's heart thudded painfully against her ribs and she felt faint. 'Not women and children, surely?' she gasped.

Mungo nodded sadly. 'Yes, women and children too, but we must not jump to conclusions. There are no specific details and no information that the mutiny has spread any further, so we must pray that Lexy, Charlotte and the little ones are unharmed.'

'That's why there have been no letters,' said Evalina, fighting back tears. 'Oh, Mungo, you don't think they are all dead, do you?'

'There is no reason to think so at the moment. They are not in Meerut or Delhi, and some are bound to have escaped. The mail will have been seriously disrupted, but until we hear differently we have reason to hope.'

Evalina poured more tea. She did not want any more, but she had to do something practical to stop herself from screaming. 'Has the trouble been contained in the north or are we in danger here?'

'I can't answer that, my dear. I am told that General Wheeler is not unduly concerned at the moment. We should follow his lead, but we must keep our wits about us.' Mungo chewed on the end of his pipe for a while before continuing. 'I would like you to leave for Calcutta in the morning whilst there is still time for you to do so, just in case the trouble spreads here. You would be safe in Calcutta.'

Evalina's head jerked up. 'Without you? Never. I have no intention of leaving your side. If my premonition is to be fulfilled, then I would rather be here with you than face it alone in Calcutta. Please don't insist that I go for I will have to disobey you.'

Mungo placed his hand on Evalina's. 'I guessed you would react like this. I won't insist that you leave, but I think it would be prudent to have some bags and provisions packed in case we have to leave in a hurry.'

They said no more. Mungo smoked his pipe in silence. Evalina tried to think of something to say that would lighten their mood, but she could not rid herself of the dreadful certainty she felt that those who were dear to her had been caught up in whatever disaster had befallen Meerut and Delhi, and that her own end was not far away. However, she was determined that she was not going to go to pieces.

'Let us prepare for the worst, Mungo dear, and pray that it doesn't come to that.'

A few days later Jean Tomlinson and Mavis Brandon called on Evalina, rumour and speculation rife between them. The passing on of good news is never done so swiftly nor with as much relish as the imparting of evil tidings. The two visitors vied with one another to tell the most lurid stories.

'And what do you think, Mrs Sibley?' spluttered Mavis Brandon. 'English ladies and young girls have been ravished by their assassins. If any one of those devils laid a finger on me he'd be sorry.' Her corpulent body quivered with indignation.

'We don't know that for certain,' said Evalina. 'My husband says that the sepoys would never defile themselves by doing such things. They consider us unclean, and they would lose their caste if they did as you suggest.'

'Unclean?' exclaimed Jean Tomlinson. 'That is preposterous.'

'We really shouldn't listen to these wild stories,' said Evalina. 'General Wheeler appears to be confident, so we must trust in him and stay calm.'

'Of course he's confident,' said Jean Tomlinson sarcastically. 'His wife is half Indian, so he is bound to think there will be no trouble here. But his European troops are outnumbered twenty to one, so heaven help us if he is wrong. If the sepoys in Cawnpore decide to mutiny, we will all be killed.'

General Wheeler had indeed been unperturbed when he first received news of the mutinies in Meerut and Delhi, but he was a professional and distinguished soldier and did not intend to leave the station unde-fended. On 16 May he sent a dispatch to the Governor-General stating that all was well in Cawnpore, but following the receipt of a telegram from Calcutta four days later, he immediately began to make preparations.

In spite of there being a sturdy magazine more suitable as a position of defence six miles to the north of Cawnpore, General Wheeler chose as the site of his entrenchment four acres of exposed plain close to the native lines and about a mile from the river. He ordered trenches and mud walls to be constructed around his chosen site and placed some of his troops in unfinished red brick barracks outside his trenches. Inside the entrenchment there were two main barrack buildings, one of which had a thatched roof, a water well, privies, two kitchens and godowns for stores. There was an inadequate supply of muskets and ammunitions, and only a few light guns placed in exposed positions. Many of the two hundred European soldiers were unfit to fight, but there were about a hundred European officers together with some native officers and loyal sepoys to defend the entrenchment.

The sight of the hastily built walls, which were only three feet high in places, did little to inspire confidence in those who would expect to find shelter behind them.

'It seems the height of irresponsibility to me,' stormed Jean Tomlinson. 'How does he plan to shelter everyone inside those two buildings? There are thousands of us in Cawnpore, and every one of us will be looking to General Wheeler for protection.'

'I'm sure he knows what he is doing,' soothed Evalina. 'Really, we should be grateful.'

'Well, we will soon find out when it is put to the test. There have already been fires set in the infantry lines, and badmashes have been causing trouble in the bazaars. Did you know that the Wagstaffs and the Martins have left? They are not the only ones either. Several families have taken to the river in the hope of reaching Calcutta before it's too late.'

'Have you thought of going?' asked Evalina.

'What? And leave my home to the mercy of all and sundry? I am not a rat and I refuse to leave a sinking ship. I am not afraid of the locals and I will defend my home until my last breath.'

Concerned about the situation, Mungo, John Brandon and Tom Tomlinson joined a group of civilians and went to see General Wheeler. Mungo was far from being reassured by what he had seen of the entrenchment. He was no military man, but even to him it seemed impossible to defend it without incurring severe losses.

'What did he have to say?' asked Evalina on his return.

'Well, he still seems to believe that there will be no mutiny here, and that even if there is it will be short-lived. He did suggest that we arm ourselves though.' He gave a mirthless laugh.

'What? With guns?' Evalina was incredulous.

'A gun would be more effective than wielding your parasol,' smiled Mungo. 'I will give you my sporting pistol.'

'No, thank you,' said Evalina. 'I have never fired a gun in my life. I'm sure I would be far more likely to hit one of us than one of them anyway.'

Mungo sighed. 'What are we going to do, Evalina my dear?'

She looked at him, saddened to see how much he had aged over the past few days. He looked positively old, with worry etched into every line on his face.

'We will do whatever we have to, my dear, and we will do it side by side. Whatever we have to face we will face it together, and God will strengthen and comfort us.'

On 30 May mutiny broke out forty miles away in Lucknow. The crisis had come. General Wheeler ordered everyone into the entrenchment. He expected it to be a temporary measure and so had only brought in sufficient provisions to last for one month.

Panic erupted. People of every colour and creed, and vehicles of every description poured into the entrenchment. Terrified civilians fled to the protection of the military, desperate to reach safety from they knew not what. Mothers, themselves frightened out of their wits, struggled in vain to pacify screaming children whose terror was heightened by the tangible fear of the adults around them. Husbands and fathers frantically sought accommodation for their families within the two barrack buildings.

'Coo-ee, coo-ee. Over here.' The strident voice of Jean Tomlinson reached Mungo and Evalina above the hullabaloo and they struggled through the crowd to reach her. Jean Tomlinson, Mavis Brandon and their husbands sat in a patch of shade beside the thatched building.

'Why are you out here?' asked Mungo.

'It's no use going inside either of the barracks,' said Tom Tomlinson. 'I've had a look. There's no room to move. People are jammed together, and it is so hot you can hardly breathe.'

Mungo cast his eyes round the entrenchment. Some people were putting up tents, but many others, who had given up hope of finding any room inside, sat on the ground like picnic parties. Europeans who had always sheltered indoors in the heat of the day now sat or walked about beneath the scorching sun. Evalina, Jean Tomlinson and Mavis Brandon sweltered beneath their parasols.

For several days nothing further happened. Jean Tomlinson was all in favour of going back home in the daytime like some of the others were doing, but her husband would not hear of it.

'We are here now and we'll just have to make the best of it,' he said.

'But nothing's happening,' she moaned. 'I swear I will go completely mad before long, and then I won't care at all if I do get shot.'

'Don't be so silly,' said Tom Tomlinson.

Boredom set in, tempers frayed, and Evalina found herself praying for something to happen.

'I wish I had thought to bring some playing cards,' said Mavis Brandon. 'I can't seem to settle to reading my book.'

'Damned Indians,' swore Jean Tomlinson. 'They're doing this quite deliberately. They are trying to humiliate us to break our spirits before they come in and finish us off.'

She looked a fright with her hair stuck to her damp forehead, her top button undone, and her dress crumpled. Water was rationed and there was none to spare for washing. The plump, perspiring wife of a soldier rounded on her.

'Can't yer keep yer trap shut?' she hissed. 'There's children as'll be scared by such talk. You may think you're Mrs High and Bloody Mighty, but you ain't no different to the likes of us now. We're all scared and helpless so shut up, will yer?'

'How dare you speak to me like that?' said a haughty Jean Tomlinson. 'You keep to your own kind, and I'll thank you not to address me again.'

'Oh, hark at her! Yer own kind indeed. We're all one kind in here, missus. Meat fer the butcher's knife, that's wot we are. Said so yerself. But just use a bit o' the brain the good Lord saw fit to bless yer wiv, and stop frightening the little uns.'

Evalina laid a restraining hand on Jean Tomlinson's arm to prevent her from rising to the bait. 'Leave well alone,' she said. 'She's right, after all. We are all afraid and we must try to protect the children, don't you think? At least we only have ourselves to worry about. I can't begin to imagine what the mothers are going through.'

When it finally came, Evalina felt an unaccountable sense of relief. The waiting and wondering were over at last. A cry went up in the entrenchment.

'The city is on fire!'

Pandemonium broke out as people squeezed through the doors of the barrack buildings to see for themselves if it were true. How strange, thought Evalina, that they are not prepared to believe it unless they see it with their own eyes. Why are they leaving the safety of the buildings just to see flames in the distance? An eerie silence fell as they all stood and watched the city ablaze, and as they watched, the reality of their perilous situation penetrated even the most hopeful heart.

CHAPTER 45

The most influential Indian in the district lolled on a pile of cushions feeding on the hatred and resentment he harboured towards the British. His pale face was set in a petulant scowl and his corpulent body quivered with indignation.

'Who do the British think they are?' he raved. 'I'll show them who is master here.'

The focus of Nana Sahib's anger was the pension denied to him by the British. In spite of his protestations of financial hardship Nana Sahib lived in a fine palace, wore magnificent clothes and entertained lavishly. He kept a menagerie and an aviary in his beautiful gardens and was proud to flaunt his possessions in front of his British guests, including General Wheeler, who held him in high esteem.

Nana Sahib was known as the Maharajah of Bithur, but this was a purely courtesy title and was unrecognised in Calcutta. He was the adopted son of the last Peshwa of Bithur who had died six years earlier. When the Peshwa died, the pension he received from the British died with him, and Nana Sahib explored every possible avenue in his attempts to have the pension restored in his own name. He petitioned the Governor-General in Calcutta and he petitioned the Board of Directors in London, but his application was always refused.

Nana Sahib rarely left his palace in Bithur, but in the spring of 1857 he paid a visit to Lucknow. When he left there unexpectedly to return to Cawnpore, his sudden departure caused concern. Sir Henry Lawrence contacted General Wheeler to caution him against placing his trust in the Nana. General Wheeler chose to ignore this advice.

Bitterly resentful towards the British for denying him once again what he saw as his rightful claim to the pension, Nana Sahib hurried from Lucknow with cavalry and infantry amounting to some three hundred men. Once back in Cawnpore they confined their activities for several days to looting and setting fires within the cantonments, which caused panic amongst the residents. Then Nana Sahib sent a message to General Wheeler to inform him that an attack on the entrenchment would begin at ten o'clock in the morning of 6 June. There were some nine hundred souls in the entrenchment, most of them European. Their defences were pitiful, and women and children outnumbered fighting men ten to one.

Mungo watched the rebels mounting siege guns and taking up positions by the windows and on the roofs of buildings outside the entrenchment. The two barracks within the entrenchment were filled with terrified civilians. Those for whom there was no room inside sheltered from the fierce sunshine in tents and beneath women's parasols. They had no protection from enemy fire.

'We've got to get you inside somehow,' Mungo explained to the three ladies. 'It's your only chance. Everyone out here is a sitting duck. Get your things together and we'll try and find some space.'

They pushed their way into the old hospital building where they found refuge squashed together in a corner. It was hot and uncomfortable, but they were out of the sun and protected from the guns. No one managed to get much sleep that night. There was no room to stretch out, and the knowledge that the attack was to begin the next day kept them awake with fear. Some prayed aloud, others sang hymns, and the night passed slowly. In the morning the firing began.

Tom Tomlinson stood up to peer through the window, desperate to see what was happening outside.

'Get down, you silly old fool,' pleaded his wife. 'You'll be killed.'

'Oh, stop fussing,' he replied. 'I can't bear not knowing what's happening out there. The ground is already littered with injured people. Over to the right I can see –'

He never finished the sentence. A shell crashed through the window, knocking it and its frame to smithereens, covering them all with splinters of glass and blowing half of Tom Tomlinson's face away. He fell to the floor with a thud. He was still conscious, but bright red blood spurted from his neck. Jean Tomlinson screamed with horror as her husband's life ebbed away. He died within minutes, and he died with the sound of his wife's screams ringing in his ears. It all happened so quickly that it hardly seemed real. Mavis Brandon put her arm around Jean's shoulders to comfort her, and long after she stopped screaming, silent tears poured unchecked from Jean's eyes.

Mungo spoke softly in Evalina's ear. 'I must give my place to one of the poor ladies outside, my dear,' he said. 'I can't, in all conscience, cower in here in comparative safety when I know that there are women and children without shelter.'

Evalina gripped his hand. 'Be careful, Mungo dearest,' she said.

'You do understand, don't you?'

Evalina nodded and clenched her teeth to prevent herself from begging him to stay with her. He patted her on the head and left quickly. As he stepped from the safety of the old hospital building a musket ball whizzed past his head. He heard the thwack when it reached its target and turned to see a young officer collapse to the ground. Beside him stood his wife with their young son in her arms. She opened her mouth to scream, but no sound came.

Mungo glanced round the entrenchment. Outside it he could see Nana Sahib's men swarming over the countryside. Inside the entrenchment it was a scene of such horror that he was numbed by it. Men, women and children lay where they had fallen, dead or dying, and the firing was intense. Most of the tents were in shreds. People cowered in the trenches, none of which were more than eighteen inches deep, and others clung together beneath the burning sun. Mungo darted forward and grabbed hold of the dead officer's wife.

'Come with me,' he shouted above the noise of the guns. 'You can have my place inside.'

They ducked their heads and ran for the door. Mungo pushed her inside ahead of him and led her to Evalina. Nobody spoke: the sound of the guns filled their ears. They sat, or stood, and waited, and prayed for night to fall. When darkness silenced the guns, Mungo and John Brandon carried Tom Tomlinson outside and laid him in a hastily dug shallow grave with several others who had died that day. Then they drew water from one of the two wells and returned to the barracks with it so that the ladies could quench their thirst. The screaming that had filled the building during the day had stopped and now, except for the groans of the injured and isolated bursts of conversation, it was quiet inside.

Mungo spoke to Helen Brindley whom he had helped bring to safety that morning. 'We have buried your husband in the trench,' he said. 'I am sorry, but I don't think he can have suffered.'

Mrs Brindley rocked her son to and fro on her lap. 'Thank you,' she whispered. She turned to Evalina. 'Your husband is a brave man.'

Evalina smiled. 'I doubt if he felt very brave out there,' she said. 'I am sorry about your husband. How old is your little boy?'

'Jonathan will be two years old on Wednesday,' she replied. 'If we live that long.'

'We must not give up hope yet,' said Evalina. 'I am sure that reinforcements will come.'

Evalina did not know whether a total ignorance of military strategy was a blessing or not. She had no real idea just how perilous their situation really was and several more days would pass with mounting casualties before her mood reached rock bottom.

At night they had little sleep, as frequent outbreaks of musket fire kept them awake. The seemingly endless, dreadful days were spent cowering from shells which knocked chunks from the walls. They battled against the heat, the dust and the flies that swarmed around spilt blood and uncovered wounds, and as the days wore on they began to be plagued by rats.

Mungo took his turn in the trenches in defence of the entrenchment and Evalina lived with the fear that he would not return to her at the end of each day. The heat inside the barracks beneath the scorching sun was intense, and yet they had to limit themselves to sips of water to make it last the whole day. Enemy fire was concentrated on the well, which rendered it suicidal for anyone to approach it before nightfall. Food was scarce because General Wheeler had not expected so long a siege with so many people seeking refuge in the entrenchment.

Many went mad, and this was something that Evalina worried might happen to her. She dreaded the thought of going mad because she was terrified of people who were not in full control of themselves. The terror and horror of it all proved too much for John Brandon and he lost his mind. Mavis Brandon was shocked at what she perceived as his lack of moral backbone. She had already felt ashamed that her husband had cowered inside the old hospital building when other civilians were out in the trenches doing their bit to protect them. Seeing her husband, normally so full of bluster and bravado, show his true colours as a coward had been more of a shock to Mavis Brandon than the mutiny itself; but he was not alone in his madness.

The heat was especially difficult to bear. 'What wouldn't I give for a *punkah-wallah*,' sighed Evalina, flapping a limp handkerchief in a vain attempt to keep cool.

Jean Tomlinson agreed. 'And to think that I used to complain about the awful smell of wet tatties. After this hell-hole, if I survive, I shall never complain about anything ever again.'

When they thought that they had suffered the worst, the worst was still to come. A shell set part of the thatched roof on fire. Blind terror took hold as screaming mothers grabbed their children and stampeded to the door. When they burst through, a hail of rebel gunfire met them. The fire took hold rapidly in the dry, brittle thatch and there was nothing anyone could do to put out the flames. Water was scarce enough for drinking; there was none to spare for fire fighting. Smoke swirled around them, and everywhere there were the frantic screams of those fleeing in panic or caught in the flames. With a cry Helen Brindley suddenly turned back.

'No!' yelled Mungo. 'What are you doing? Come back.'

'Baby has dropped his cuddly. I have to find it.' She hurried into the burning building with her son in her arms.

Mungo chased after her. Before he could reach her he watched in horror as she tripped over her long skirts and fell headlong. A burning spar fell from the roar of the raging fire above. It landed on Helen Brindley's legs and pinned her to the ground.

'Help,' she screamed. 'Help. For pity's sake, someone save my baby.'

Mungo picked his way towards her. Her crinoline had risen to expose her legs and Mungo saw her skin shrivel blackly as her skirts flared. He tried desperately to pull the young mother from under the burning wooden beam, but she knew that she was doomed even though he struggled on and on.

'It's no use,' she said in a calm voice. 'Take Jonathan. Please save my baby. Take him and go. I am not afraid. I shall join my husband, but please help my son to live.'

There was nothing more Mungo could do. He felt his own hair scorch and saw Jonathan's lank hair frizzle. He took the boy from his mother's arms and hurried away. As he went he could hear Helen Brindley chant the words of the Lord's Prayer.

Holding Jonathan's head against his chest Mungo reached the doorway. He peered out and took a deep breath to rid himself of the smell of burning human flesh. Bullets thwacked into the wall beside him. Outside, the rebels concentrated their fire on those who were fleeing the building, and to Mungo it seemed almost welcome after the death by fire that he had just witnessed. The wounded shrieked in agony as they were dragged bodily through the door, their wounds aggravated by the manhandling they received in the frantic attempts to save their lives. Falling masonry and timber fractured limbs; Helen Brindley did not die alone in the fire. And all the medical supplies were lost.

As they emerged from the old hospital building, Jean Tomlinson was shot in the head although the wound was superficial. With no bandages for dressing wounds, Evalina wasted no time in stripping off her petticoats. She lay on the ground surrounded by bodies, living and dead, and tore her petticoats into strips.

The firing stopped when darkness fell, and Evalina was able to get up and attend to Jean Tomlinson's head wound. John Brandon had been shot in the stomach and his wife had had one of her feet blown off. Both had lain unconscious whilst bullets and shells pitted the ground around them. There was no water to bathe any wounds, but Evalina wound strips of her petticoat tightly around Mavis Brandon's shattered leg. There was nothing she could do for John Brandon and she guessed that he had not long to live.

'I'm done for,' he whispered to Evalina. 'Look after my wife for me.'

Evalina looked round for Mungo. He was lying curled up on his side shielding Jonathan's body with his own. Evalina crawled towards them and was flooded with relief to find that Mungo was still alive.

'What has happened to the boy's mother?' she asked.

Mungo shook his head. 'She entrusted her son to our care,' he replied.

Evalina gazed into Jonathan's expressionless blue eyes. This must be why we have been spared, she thought. God has given us this child to care for. She picked up the thin, limp little boy and cradled him in her arms. Whilst Mungo went to fetch water for them Evalina sang a lullaby; it was an incongruous sound amidst all the carnage.

It took Mungo a long time to return with the water. Even at night the rebels had taken to firing at the well, which made fetching water a dangerous undertaking. They were hungry, too. The food supplies were almost used up, and even provisions brought in by those seeking protection were soon exhausted. When a soup made from horseflesh was all there was to eat, they ate it without complaint, but babies starved to death as their mothers had no milk for them. And through it all those few soldiers who remained alive continued to hold their positions in defence of the beleaguered entrenchment.

Then, after three weeks of unimaginable nightmare, Mrs Jacobi, a watchmaker's wife, arrived with a message from Nana Sahib. The survivors of the siege, filthy, starving, and half-dressed in rags and tatters, watched in disbelief as Mrs Jacobi calmly walked into the entrenchment. Mungo left Evalina's side to try and find out what was happening. When he returned he had some amazing news.

'Nana Sahib has offered us safe passage to Allahabad if we surrender.'

'Surrender to the rebels?' Jean Tomlinson was incredulous. 'Surely General Wheeler will not agree?'

Mungo shrugged. 'We are in his hands. I gather that some of his officers want to fight on, but General Wheeler is in despair. His son was decapitated by a shot and the loss has been too much for him to bear. He has given up all hope of any help from Calcutta. My guess is that he will surrender because it's the only chance we have.'

'Well, I wouldn't trust Nana Sahib any further than I could throw him,' snapped Jean Tomlinson. 'Why would he offer us safe passage to Allahabad now when he has just spent three weeks trying to kill us all? It doesn't make any sense.'

But the situation in the entrenchment was untenable. There were no medicines and the wounded suffered unspeakable pain. The food store was virtually empty, and if the monsoons came their paltry defences would be washed away. General Wheeler had little choice but to put his trust in Nana Sahib and he reluctantly set about making terms for their surrender. In return for transport to take the women, the children and the wounded to the river, boats stocked with flour to sustain them on the journey to Allahabad, and the retention of some small arms and some ammunition, General Wheeler agreed to surrender the big guns and the treasury to Nana Sahib.

The guns fell silent. After the terror of the previous three weeks, the atmosphere was one of near jubilation. Those who still had the energy to do so sang and danced. A few children played tentatively, but many had been driven mad by the horrors they had suffered and witnessed.

They ate without worrying about conserving what little food remained. Jean Tomlinson took some water to Mavis Brandon and raised her head so that she could drink. Evalina's firm bandaging had stemmed the flow of blood from Mavis's stump, but it was red and inflamed. It seemed a miracle that she was still alive, but without medical attention she would not last much longer. At Jean's touch Mavis opened her eyes. She slowly focussed her gaze on Jean's face and became vaguely aware that something had changed. She frowned, trying to concentrate. It was quiet. There was no gunfire.

'What has happened?' she croaked through parched lips.

'Shh, don't try to talk,' said Jean. 'It's over. The siege is over. Tomorrow we are leaving here and going by boat to Allahabad. Try to hang on, Mavis dear. If you can just hang on a little longer, you'll have the help you need.'

Mavis's smile was weak. She knew that she could not survive long enough to reach Allahabad, but somehow it did not seem to matter any more. She just wanted the pain to go away.

'Peace,' she whispered. 'All I want is peace.' She drifted back into her twilight world.

Jean Tomlinson sat on the ground beside her and held her hand. What is it that I want, she asked herself. There was no husband or father to tell her what to do. For the first time in her life she was free to make her own choices without reference to anyone else. Home, she thought. I want to go Home. And 'Home' meant the fresh green fields of England, not India which had been her home for most of her long life. No, she would not stay here; she would go Home when it was all over.

That evening they watched three officers leave the entrenchment on elephants. They were going to the Satti Chaura Ghat to inspect the boats provided by Nana Sahib.

'I can hardly believe it,' said Evalina. 'Are we really going to Allahabad?'

'It seems so,' said Mungo. 'You had better pack your things.'

Privately Mungo agreed with Jean Tomlinson's opinion that Nana Sahib was not to be trusted, but there was little point in speculation. They were going to have to do as they were told.

Evalina and Jean Tomlinson collected their few possessions together. Evalina had only a Bible, a little money and a few trinkets, but Jean had brought a casket of jewels and a silver teapot, milk jug and sugar bowl into the entrenchment with her. The silver was set aside and the two women spent the evening and a greater part of the night stitching Jean's valuables into her clothes for safekeeping. Then they did the same for poor Mavis Brandon, who was semiconscious and unaware of the reason for the frequent movement of her skirts, but each flutter of material against her leg made her cry out with pain. When it was done Evalina snatched some sleep with Jonathan in her arms, but Mungo and Jean Tomlinson sat up all night, tense and alert.

'It's the silence,' complained Jean. 'The silence is deafening.'

CHAPTER 46

The survivors of the siege gathered together early in the morning. They were a pitiable sight: half-starved and haggard, wearing ragged oddments of mismatched articles of clothing draped around their bodies. Some wore shoes and stockings, but many were barefoot. Officers and men stood in filthy, tattered uniforms with tarnished buttons, and the wounded lay helpless on the ground. But they were alive. Some two hundred and fifty bodies had been dumped unceremoniously down the well that was situated outside the trenches, and which had been designated its sepulchral purpose when there was nowhere else left to bury the dead. Other bodies lay in the open to be feasted on by vultures; but those who gathered in silence for the first stage of their journey had survived.

The flag was lowered and brought to General Wheeler, and the bedraggled remnants of those who had sought refuge in the entrenchment prepared to leave. There were elephants, palanquins and bullock-carts to transport them to the Satti Chaura Ghat although many would have to walk. Mungo lifted Mavis Brandon onto a cart and Jean Tomlinson climbed up beside her.

'Go on, Evalina,' said Mungo. 'Up you get.'

Evalina shook her head. 'I am not leaving your side. If I get into the cart we could become separated and I couldn't bear that.'

'You can't walk without shoes,' protested Mungo.

'You just watch me,' said Evalina. 'I won't be the only one walking barefoot.'

She peered along the line of survivors clambering onto carts, folding themselves into palanquins or climbing up the hindquarters of elephants, looking for other women preparing to walk the mile to the river. Suddenly she gasped in disbelief.

'Oh look, they are robbing us,' she cried.

They watched in horror as rebels moved down the line, snatching at any valuables they could see. The only jewellery Evalina wore was her wedding ring. Never before had it left her finger, but now she removed it and twisted it into a coil of hair in the bun at the nape of her neck. Jean Tomlinson was too late and was forced to hand her wedding ring to a grinning native, who then snatched her gold cross and chain from around her neck. Mavis Brandon's wedding ring was yanked from her finger, and then the rebels moved on.

'Bloody thieves,' muttered Jean Tomlinson.

Shortly after eight o'clock General Wheeler gave the order to set off. Mungo carried Jonathan Brindley and Evalina trudged along at his side. As the column left the entrenchment swarms of locals rushed in to take what they had left behind.

It took almost an hour to cover the mile from the entrenchment to the Satti Chaura Ghat. When they reached the river, Mungo's heart sank. The forty barges provided by Nana Sahib were not moored beside the bank, and he realised that they would have to wade through the water to reach them. He handed Jonathan to Evalina.

'You take the boy and I'll carry Mrs Brandon,' he said.

'I'm frightened,' whispered Evalina. 'Look at them. They are tormenting us.'

Mungo looked back at the rebels standing on the bank. They jeered and laughed at the difficulties faced by the elderly, the sick and the wounded. Everywhere was chaos as people floundered in the water to reach the boats.

'Don't look any of them in the eye,' advised Mungo. 'Are you ready?' Evalina nodded. 'Right, off we go.'

Mungo and Jean Tomlinson dragged Mavis Brandon out of the cart and shared the burden of carrying her. She was delirious and mercifully unaware of what was happening. Keeping close together they stepped into the water, which cooled Evalina's cut and bleeding feet, and they waded to the boat. Once there, it took a supreme effort to heave Mavis over the side. She fell heavily and screamed in agony. They had nothing to give her for the pain; the best they could do for her was to keep her alive long enough for her to receive medical attention.

Mungo helped Jean Tomlinson into the boat, and then he took Jonathan from Evalina and handed him to Jean. Now it was Evalina's turn to be pushed up and over the side. Finally, utterly exhausted, Mungo clambered up and collapsed onto the deck to recover. He was not a young man, and the effort he had expended in helping the ladies had drained what little strength remained in his starved body.

Every one of the thatched boats was crammed to overflowing, several so heavily overloaded that they sank into the sandbanks and could not be moved. Almost at the end of his physical capability, Mungo lowered himself over the side of their stranded boat and into the water with some of the other men. They pushed and shoved in desperation, but it was useless. The boat was stuck fast in the mud. Further along, equally heroic efforts were being made to free other boats. One did manage to get away, and as it floated free a bugle sounded. On this signal all the native boatmen jumped from the boats and made for the bank. Then a cry –

'Fire! The boats are on fire.'

Evalina leaned over the side and could see that the thatched roofs of some of the boats had been set alight. She cringed at the sound of screams from those who were too wounded to make their escape from the flames. Shocked, confused and frightened, Evalina stood on the deck with Jonathan clutched tightly to her, but before she could make any sense of what had happened some of the rebels opened fire on the boats.

Mungo was still in the water. 'Quickly,' he yelled. 'Over the side.'

Evalina and Jean Tomlinson needed no further persuasion. They joined Mungo in the river, but there was nothing they could do for Mavis Brandon and they were forced to leave her lying unconscious on the deck. Mungo looked round frantically.

'Can you swim?' he asked.

Jean Tomlinson shook her head, but Evalina nodded. She had learned to swim as a child during her summer holidays in Ramsgate.

'Take the boy and make for the opposite bank,' ordered Mungo.

Evalina stared in horror and disbelief at the distance Mungo expected her to swim. Even with the river shrunk to a quarter of its normal size with the hot season, there was still a distance of at least five hundred yards from bank to bank. 'I can't swim that far,' she gasped. 'Even without Jonathan I couldn't reach the other side.'

'You must, my dear,' urged Mungo. 'For my sake, please try.'

The decision was snatched from them as bullets suddenly began to plop into the water around them, fired by rebels Nana Sahib had placed on the opposite bank. Those who had survived the siege were now caught in crossfire. Everywhere people struggled and died.

'Let's wade out as far as we can to give them as small a target as possible,' said Mungo.

They edged their way deeper into the river until they stood with just their heads above the water. Jonathan clung to Evalina in abject, silent terror. The noise of the guns and the screams of the wounded almost deafened them. Then Jean Tomlinson was shot in the neck and disappeared beneath the water. Evalina turned to Mungo.

'It's over, my dear husband,' she said. 'It is a sad way for it all to end, but I can't begin to thank you for my wonderful life with you.'

Mungo reached for Evalina. 'I love you so,' he said. 'But we are together in this awful nightmare, and we will always be together now, in death as in life.'

They stood facing one another with Jonathan squashed between them and gazed into each other's eyes as they waited for death to claim them. They ignored the splash of bullets around them and they closed their ears to the screams. Evalina saw Mungo's eyes widen in surprise, and then they became glazed and unseeing. He slipped silently away until there was just redness in the water where he had been. Evalina was in despair, but she was past tears. She raised her face to the sky.

'Why?' she cried. 'What is it all for?'

Deep in the water she watched helplessly as rebels waded into the river and tore babies and children from their mothers' arms. The poor, starved, terrified or mad little ones were bayoneted to death, and the river ran red with blood.

Evalina's stunned mind began to work again. She decided that she and Jonathan might be safer lying in the bottom of one of the half-burned boats than remain where they were, so she inched her way through a sea of mutilated bodies, but when she reached a boat, what little clothing she still wore was sodden and weighed her down. She could not climb into the boat; instead, she cowered beneath its prow and waited, and prayed, for death.

Nana Sahib was not at the Satti Chaura Ghat. He had remained in Savada House, his headquarters in his camp outside the entrenchment, but he could hear the sound of his guns a mile away. When a messenger arrived with the news that all the enemy were being destroyed, Nana Sahib ordered the killing of women and children to stop.

Evalina sat on the riverbank with the other survivors of the massacre. Numb with shock and grief, she was oblivious to the misery around her, as she had no room in her mind for anyone or anything except Mungo and the colossal emptiness in her heart. She felt as if she was suffocating and she gripped Jonathan, as a dying man will cling to a straw. One of the rebels came to them with a drink of water. She took it, thanking him automatically, good manners being deeply ingrained in her. Then she began to take stock of the others sitting on the sandy bank. There were about one hundred and twenty of them still alive out of some nine hundred souls who had been in the entrenchment, and Evalina was forced to acknowledge that she was not alone in her grief.

There were no men amongst this forlorn group of survivors. All the artillerymen had been killed within the first few days of the siege, and many of the willing civilians who had volunteered to take their places were themselves quickly mown down. Of those who had escaped death during the siege at the barracks all but four then lost their lives during the failed river crossing. These four managed to push one of the boats free, and although most of its occupants were killed as the boat was chased and harried on its course down river, the men survived to reach Allahabad to tell of the siege of General Wheeler's entrenchment in Cawnpore and the massacre at the Satti Chaura Ghat.

After half an hour of sitting in fierce sunshine, the exhausted women and children were led away in groups. Many were injured, many had been driven mad, and most were terrified into a stupefying apathy. They made no protest as they were herded back towards the entrenchment to Savada House where they were imprisoned under Nana Sahib's orders. After three days they were moved again. Now they were incarcerated in the *Bibighar*, a house that had originally been built by a British officer for his Indian mistress.

The Bibighar was a single-storey building set around a courtyard. Its two main rooms measured just ten feet by twenty-one feet, and into them were crammed those who had survived the siege and the massacre, together with a few unfortunate survivors from the mutiny at Fatehgarh which had preceded that at Cawnpore. This last group contained two colonels, a magistrate, and a merchant with his fourteen-year-old son: all males who had inexplicably not been put to death. The captives in the Bibighar numbered just over two hundred, and most of them were children.

Crammed into one of the rooms with countless others, Evalina secured a place for herself and Jonathan in the corner furthest from the door. There was no furniture, so she sat down on the bamboo matting and surveyed her fellow prisoners. Scarecrows all of them, wet and muddy from the river. Swarms of flies worried gunshot wounds and sword cuts. The only possessions left to them were the rags they wore, and Evalina was as bewildered as those others who still had their senses – for the rest, the lack of clothes, shoes, brushes and combs, and all the trappings of civilisation that they had always taken for granted, was of no concern, as they had lost their minds along with everything else. Perhaps it was an advantage, thought Evalina, not to know or care what was happening. She felt in her hair for her wedding ring and was relieved to find that it was still there. Mungo may have gone and Evalina might be alone, but she still had his ring to remind her that the past nine years had been real and not just a dream.

Jonathan Brindley clung to Evalina like a baby monkey. He would not be put down so Evalina sat with him on her lap. His face was expressionless and he had made no sound since he had stopped crying for his mother. Evalina had no idea whether or not he could talk for he made no attempt to communicate with her other than to cling to her for dear life.

They were given dhal and chapattis, and milk was provided for the infants. Then, when night fell, they lay down on the matting or the dirt floor to snatch what sleep they could. There were more children than there were women to care for them. A young girl crouched by herself against the wall close to Evalina. She stared vacantly ahead and made repeated odd jerky movements or just sat rocking back and forth. She appeared to be alone.

'Does anyone know this little girl?' asked Evalina of the other captives in the room.

One or two heads shook a negative reply; no one claimed the child. Evalina struggled to her feet with creaking knees and stepped over recumbent bodies as she went to her. The girl's long dark hair had fallen to her shoulders, her tattered ribbon hanging by a thread. The red hair ribbon and the red sash tied around her filthy, torn white dress looked like angry wounds. There was blood on the side of her face and her bare feet, like Evalina's, had been cut and grazed on the walk to and from the river.

She made no attempt to resist as Evalina took her hand and brought her to the corner she had commandeered.

'What is your name?' asked Evalina.

The girl did not respond so Evalina repeated the question in Hindustani, but there was still no answer.

'Well,' said Evalina. 'You don't have to tell me your name if you don't want to, but I've got to call you something, so I will call you Polly. That was my sister's name. I'm Aunt Evalina.'

With two children to care for now Evalina was prevented from sinking into a well of self-pity. She did everything she could to protect them from falling sick, and every day that they survived raised her hopes that they would be set free. She was glad that she had never escaped to the hills during the hot weather like other memsahibs usually did; without punkahs the heat inside the Bibighar was appalling, but she tolerated it better than those who had never weathered an India summer.

They were nominally cared for by Hussaini Begum, a woman of Nana Sahib's household. They had her to thank for what food they were given and the provision of some fresh clothing. One morning as she washed the tattered remnants of her linen, Evalina realised that it was the first time in her life that she had ever had to perform such a chore for herself.

Before long women and children began to die from cholera and dysentery, and Hussaini Begum decreed that they were to be allowed brief periods on the verandas for some fresh air. Evalina hated going outside where they were an abject spectacle for all those who came to rejoice in their humiliation. If she had only had herself to worry about she would have stayed in the evil-smelling room, but she knew that Jonathan and Polly would benefit from going outside. Jonathan had finally submitted to being put on the floor, but if he was not clutching Evalina's skirt he held fast to the little girl. Neither of the children ever spoke and the only sound Polly made was a strange, low moan that Evalina could only quieten by humming a lullaby.

For fifteen days their imprisonment continued with daily deaths from disease. Then, on 15 July, the five survivors from Fatehgarh, including the boy, were taken outside and shot. Fear spread its icy tentacles through the captives once again, and everyone trembled when Hussaini Begum came into the Bibighar. She had something to say.

'The British are coming.'

*

There was no rush of excitement to greet these words. It could have been a trick, but Evalina's heart lurched with a ripple of hope. The children would be saved. For herself she no longer cared. There was nothing for her now, no purpose to her life. She did not wish to live without Mungo. What would she do without him? Where would she go? All those she loved here in India were gone, as were her brother and sister in England. Better by far to die now than to live alone. She had never been alone in her whole life. But she had managed to keep these two children alive with God's help, and for that she was grateful.

'The British are coming and you are all to be killed.'

It took several minutes for the words to sink in. Then there was a clamour of disbelief, indignation and renewed terror. Evalina put a protective arm around Jonathan and Polly.

'It can't be true,' said one woman. 'Why kill us now? Why did they save us from the massacre at the Satti Chaura Ghat if they planned to kill us all anyway?'

'They will have to kill us now,' replied Evalina. 'They daren't leave any of us alive to tell the tale of what they have done.'

The woman sought out the commander of the sepoy guard. 'Is the Begum telling the truth?' she implored. 'Are we all to be killed?'

The commander shook his head. 'I have received no such orders,' he said. 'Don't be afraid.'

Their relief was short-lived. When Hussaini Begum heard that the sepoys were not going to obey any orders to kill the women and children she was furious. She went to see Nana Sahib. It had to be done. No one must be left alive who could point a finger at any one of them and say 'he was there'.

Hussaini Begum returned with the order and she sent the reluctant sepoys to carry it out. They came into the room and made feeble attempts to grab hold of hysterical women and children, but they failed to drag any of them outside.

Evalina pushed Jonathan and Polly into the corner and stood squarely in front of them, shielding them with her own body. A volley of gunfire burst through the window, but Evalina's corner was safely out of the line of fire. Some of the women and children were hit and fell to the floor. It was only a matter of time now before Evalina and the children in her care would join their loved ones in heaven. Evalina loosed her hair and retrieved her wedding ring. She slid it onto her finger, determined that she would die wearing it. Then, quite suddenly, the firing stopped, and the sepoys refused to fire any more.

But it had to be done. Hussaini Begum sent for her lover, whose mother had been a regimental prostitute. He arrived at sunset full of hatred for the British for the shame he had suffered as a child. He came with two Moslem butchers and two Hindus who were employed by Nana Sahib. They entered the Bibighar armed with tulwars and went from room to room systematically killing seventy-three women and one hundred and twenty-four children: those who had survived the siege and the massacre, and all those who had fled the mutiny at Fatehgarh only to be sucked into the horror of Cawnpore.

Evalina felt oddly detached as she watched the slaughter in front of her, and it was not until she was splattered with a child's blood as his head was severed that she, too, began to scream. One of the Sikhs came for her. She thought that he was going to decapitate her and instinctively raised her arms to protect her throat. Inexplicably he grabbed both her wrists with one hand and dragged her towards the door. This exposed the two children and one of the butchers, his once white apron now saturated with blood, moved towards them. As he sliced into Polly, Evalina screamed again, and Jonathan ran to cling to her legs. The pair of them were dragged out of the house by the Sikh and made to sit against the outer wall. Another woman was already seated, clutching her half-severed arm and rocking back and forth, keening to herself. A short while later, a third woman and three boys were also dragged alive and in various states of mental dissolution to join them.

While the slaughter continued in the house, Evalina watched the three boys as they ran around the well. Jonathan refused to join them and remained tightly clinging to Evalina's legs. There was no joy in the seeming play of the boys, just a need to run, possibly in the belief they were running to their freedom. Evalina wept silent tears, absent-mindedly stroking Jonathan's hair, as she prayed for an end to this madness, but her mind refused to loosen its grip on reality.

After a while the butchers and the Sikhs finished their gruesome task and left. They ignored the three women leaning against the outer wall of the house and the boys who had finally stopped running around the well and lay exhausted in what shade they could find. Evalina shifted to try and find a more comfortable sitting position, but Jonathan gripped tighter to her legs, his eyes squeezed shut as if to force out the visions of horror he had witnessed.

Evalina watched the sun slowly descend in the sky, not sure if she would see it rise again. She did not understand why she had been spared yet again and tried to suppress the glimmer of hope for survival that rose unbidden in her heart.

As dusk fell the insects increased, drawn by the smell of blood and putrefaction emanating from the Bibighar. With death no longer an imminent threat and the glimmer of hope increasing, Evalina once again wrapped her wedding ring in her hair, using the increasing dark and the need to swat away swarming insects as cover. If she was to be allowed to survive this horror she felt sure any gold seen on her person would be ripped from her and she maintained sufficient grip on her sanity to ensure she retained her most precious possession.

The night was strangely silent. Occasional whimpers rose from the sleeping boys and groans from the other women. Insects continued to harass Evalina and rats began their first tentative steps into the house, also drawn by the smell of blood. Evalina drifted in and out of sleep. Her dreams took her back to her earlier life in England and in her wakeful moments she reminisced on her wasted years before Mungo Sibley had rescued her. She had lived more in these few short years in India than all her previous life and she was not sorry to have left her family behind.

As the night slowly ebbed away, Evalina's thoughts were filled with her sister. She relived their childhood, their hopes and faded beauty. She watched with uncritical eyes as the sisters dressed for ball after ball, year after year, never quite relinquishing that hope of a chance of happiness. As she danced one final dance with Mungo, Polly whispered in her ear 'James is coming'.

Evalina awoke with a start. Four sweepers had arrived at the house to carry out the orders they had been given – all the bodies were to be thrown down the dry well near the Bibighar. Although conscious, Evalina was suffering from dehydration and could not understand where she was or what was happening around her. A huge crowd of onlookers from Cawnpore and the surrounding villages gathered to watch the bodies of the memsahibs being stripped of any usable clothing before being tipped down the well.

An uneasiness crept into Evalina that soon became abject terror. She tried to move, but hours of sitting with Jonathan clutching her legs added to the dehydration and ensured her limbs would not respond. Jonathan was ripped from her legs and thrown head first down the well. Evalina tried to scream but could make no sound. She was dragged away from the wall and her clothes were ripped from her body. Fear paralysed her, and she was picked up by two of the sweepers and carried to the well. She felt detached and watched from a high vantage point as she was tossed on top of the other bodies.

'Not like this. Please, God, not like this!' Evalina felt more than said.

But the British were coming.

Brigadier-General Sir Henry Havelock's troops were marching on Cawnpore. It was a small force for the task ahead, and most marched in the stifling heat wearing heavy woollen tunics because not all their summer uniforms had arrived. There were a thousand British infantry, over a hundred Sikhs, some native irregulars and volunteer cavalrymen. Five miles from Cawnpore they engaged with Nana Sahib's force of five thousand men. It was a desperate fight, but the British held the day.

Nana Sahib fled. Hussaini Begum fled. All those who had been in any way involved with the rebellion fled. Nana Sahib's men and thousands of the citizens of Cawnpore fled.

As he marched on Cawnpore Lieutenant James Wickham's fertile imagination portrayed him rescuing his funny old aunt from Nana Sahib's clutches. Men being the primary targets, he suspected Mungo was already dead, but he would not allow himself to think the unthinkable – that Aunt Evalina might also have perished. He was going to save her.

The shocking reality of General Wheeler's ruined entrenchment took his breath away – the shattered buildings and the remnants of the mud walls that had been erected in its defence. There were tattered belongings strewn over the sandy plain; books, papers, scraps of clothing, odd shoes. The desolation brought them up short as they realised something of how terrible the ordeal had been. Lieutenant James Wickham could almost hear the ghosts of the despairing departed reproaching them for arriving too late.

Some of the locals took them to the Bibighar, and here the full horror of what had happened was forced upon them. The rooms swimming with blood and the tangled mass of mutilated bodies piled one on top of another down the well were testament to the massacre of women and children that had taken place only hours before their would-be rescuers reached them. Hardened troops were physically sick at the sight, and they wanted revenge.

When Lieutenant James Wickham reached the well he was loathe to look at the terrible sight. The smell and the horror turned his stomach. He felt he was being watched and looked around and above him nervously. He could see no one, but the feeling would not leave him. He slowly made his way to the edge of the well and looked in. A pair of eyes stared up at him. Evalina breathed his name and smiled at him as she slipped away.

'They were raped first.' The rumour spread. Lieutenant James Wickham knew that this was unlikely, but his grief and anger were such as to make him want to believe it. His fantasies of rescuing his aunt had turned to the nightmare of seeing her die.

Vengeance was the word on everyone's lips, and vengeance they would have. And in exacting their revenge, the British inflicted a punishment as dreadful in the eyes of the Indian as the massacres had been to them. Before they were hanged, captured rebels were made to lick blood from the floor of the Bibighar to break their caste.

KARMA

CHAPTER 47

In the aftermath of her escape to Meerut it was the children who saved Lexy from losing her grip on reality. She was bleak with loss and burdened with guilt, believing that Rakesh's death was her punishment for committing the moral offence of loving where she should not have loved; but she was not alone in her grief for there were women who had been widowed, and there were bereaved mothers and orphaned children. Their shared torments forged understanding and tolerance, and they helped one another to survive.

Mattie and Benjamin were deeply traumatised by the scenes they had witnessed. They would not leave Lexy's side, literally clinging to her and each other. When kind old Mrs Ponsonby tried to take them for a while to allow Lexy to rest, they fought and screamed, and Benjamin bit the old lady's arm so hard that he drew blood. They would not release their hold on Lexy's skirt for days, and at night she cuddled them close, each seeking solace from the comforting touch of one another's bodies. Neither of the children spoke. Benjamin's thumb only left his mouth long enough for him to eat and Mattie chewed her fingernails to the quick.

Lexy named her baby 'Robin'. Born too soon he was a tiny scrap of humanity still covered in the protective hair of the womb. His need for frequent nursing and careful handling helped Lexy in her fight against intense and hopeless despair. His skin was closer in colour to Lexy's own than to Rakesh's, and after startled eyes flew from the black-haired baby to his mother's own foreign appearance, he caused no further comment. Every day Lexy expected someone to denounce her baby as being of mixed blood, but no one did, and she endeavoured to melt into her surroundings so as not to draw attention to him.

Five weeks after Robin was born, Major Willoughby presented himself to Lexy. She sat in a cane chair in the shade of the building and looked every bit as beautiful as he remembered. Her baby was on her lap and the two older children sat one on either side of her. Major Willoughby studied them carefully. He thought it strange that the newborn should be so dark when the others were fair, but then Lexy was also dark. Still, it was odd all the same.

'How are you?' he asked. 'Is there anything I can do for you?'

Lexy turned her face away from him. 'Go away,' she said. 'I have nothing to say to you.'

The Major flicked his leg with his riding crop. He had news for Mrs Sanderson but hesitated to tell her.

'I asked you to leave,' said Lexy.

He raised an eyebrow and cleared his throat. 'I made it my business to try and find out about your husband for you. I hope you don't mind,' he said. 'I am assuming that your husband was Colonel David Sanderson of Sanderson's Rifles? That's what I was told anyway.'

Lexy nodded. She looked up at him warily. 'You used the past tense, Major Willoughby.'

'Yes. I am afraid that I have bad news for you. Your husband died a gallant death fighting the rebels. He was a brave man. I am sorry.'

If Major Willoughby had expected an outburst of grief, he was disappointed. Not so much as a flicker of emotion crossed Lexy's face.

'Thank you for coming to tell me,' she said flatly.

She turned away from him, and Major Willoughby, with a crack of his crop, left her. For a time Lexy sat and stared into space wondering how it was possible to feel nothing for the death of a husband. She did not even feel a sense of relief to be rid of him. They had been married how long – six, seven years? She could not remember. It was as if that part of her life had never really been.

She became aware of Mattie's hot tears dropping onto her hand and laid her cheek against her daughter's head. Poor little Mattie. It had taken Lexy five and a half years to learn to love her daughter. Five and a half wasted years. She kissed Mattie's golden hair, which was so like her father's, and was flooded with guilt. She had blamed Mattie for so much, and she had held her responsible for her inability to love her. Now she loved her dearly and was fiercely protective of her, but it was too late. Mattie had lived without her mother's love for too long and, although she was obedient and keen to please, her heart was like a kernel inside a hard shell: a shell grown to protect herself from further hurt.

When news of the massacres at Cawnpore reached Meerut, Lexy's desolation was complete. She felt no anger or resentment, just an unutterable sadness that reached the very depths of her soul. She was thirty years old and there was no one left in all the world to care about her.

'Your children are your future,' said wise old Mrs Ponsonby when they sat together one evening and Lexy ventured to air her loneliness. 'You still have a life in front of you, Mrs Sanderson, and the children will give you a sense of purpose in that life. And when time lessens the agonies you suffer now, you will find another love. Love is what makes the world go round at your age. At my end of the allotted span, however, it is money that oils the wheels. No one would want to take on an old hag like me, and I daresay I really would find it a dreadful bore to have to learn to accommodate the quirks of another husband, but at least I won't spend my final years in penury, and at my age that is a comforting thought.'

Mrs Ponsonby had taken Lexy and the children under her wing. She was a shapeless woman with freckled skin, blue eyes that had faded until they almost lacked any colour at all, and lips that had disappeared into a thin line over a mouthful of yellow teeth. Her hair was a patchwork of grey and white with streaks of rusty yellow, which she wore in a loose bun from which wisps and strands continually escaped to fall over her shoulders.

She was a great fan of crochet and even now, hot as it was, she sat crocheting endless yards of lace edgings – for what? She had no bed linen or napery of her own left to her now, but the mind-numbing repetitive movements of making crochet lace was Mrs Ponsonby's way of keeping herself rooted in the present. She did not like to think too deeply about what had happened to her husband at the hands of the rebels. It did not matter that she had no need of her crochet lace edgings.

'Will you stay on in India?' asked Lexy.

'No, dear, I shall go Home,' replied Mrs Ponsonby. 'I haven't been back to England for over twenty years, but I do still have some family there who will take me in. India is no place for ladies now. I think we memsahibs should clear out and let the men get on with the task of restoring law and order without having to constantly fret over our safety.'

Lexy remembered how the Colonel had tried to provide for her and Mattie's safety; time that might have been better spent on something more important.

'Perhaps you are right,' Lexy said.

'What will you do?'

Lexy shrugged. 'I don't really know. I have no one in England except for an aunt I scarcely know, but I've no one here either. I'm not sure what to do for the best. My husband wanted me to take the children to his family in Dorset if anything happened to him.'

Mrs Ponsonby nodded. 'Perhaps it would be wise. Some of us are going to Simla for a while as soon as it is safe to travel. Perhaps you would care to join us? We are going to Delhi first because apparently we can go and have a look at Bahadur Shah, the old king, before he goes on trial. I'm curious to see what he looks like.'

Lexy shuddered. 'I couldn't do that,' she said. 'But I would love to go to the hills again. Perhaps I'll be able to come to a decision about the future if I can leave this place with the awful memories it holds for me. But first I need to visit my old home and thank someone who helped me escape the mutiny.'

'Of course, and do leave the children here. It will make the journey so much easier. I would be happy to look after them; it's no trouble. In the meantime, I will write to my old friends in Simla with whom I shall be staying. They live there and I'm sure they would be more than willing to make room for you and the children.'

'Thank you,' said Lexy. 'You are very kind.'

The old walled town was in ruins with buildings burned, and shops and houses plundered. There was little food and many of the local inhabitants had fled to avoid starvation or death at the hands of the British when they retook the town.

Lexy had taken Mrs Ponsonby up on her kind suggestion and had left Mattie and Benjamin in her safe care, but the baby had travelled with her and she held him close now as she searched for the Chatterjees' mansion. She knew that it was just inside the walls and beside the river, so she walked in that direction. She saw a mali working in a garden, trying to restore it to some semblance of its earlier grandeur. She walked through the broken gates towards him.

'Is this where the Chatterjees live?'

The mali nodded and Lexy continued up the path to the front door. The once highly polished wood was splintered and cracked. Chunks of masonry lay where they had fallen, and an aura of decay hung over everything. Had it not been for the gardener Lexy would have turned away, assuming that the place was deserted, but she knocked on the door. It was opened immediately, and she was ushered into a sparsely furnished room off the hallway. Moments later there came the whisper of slippers on marble tiles and Malati Chatterjee stood in the doorway. The two women stared at each other in silence for several minutes before tears of relief, joy and grief overwhelmed them.

Malati ordered tea and led Lexy onto the veranda. They sat down with the heady perfume of jasmine and roses wafting over them.

'So,' said Malati at last. 'This is my grandson?'

Lexy blushed and nodded. Robin was almost six months old and he smiled and gurgled at Malati.

'Rakesh always said that the baby would be a boy. He was born early – even earlier than I had calculated judging by how tiny he was.' Lexy's eyes clouded over as she remembered. 'Do you know what happened to Rakesh?'

Malati looked down at her hands, which were loosely clasped in her lap. 'I know only that he was shot by your people,' she said. A single tear dropped onto the back of her hand.

'It was an error of judgement,' said Lexy. 'I am not trying to excuse the officer responsible, but he had no way of knowing how brave Rakesh had been in smuggling us to safety. The officer was only doing his duty as he saw fit. He saw Rakesh run after me and thought that he was going to kill me. I have relived those moments over and over in my mind. Rakesh insisted that the children and I changed into our own clothes so that we looked like pukka British. Perhaps if we had stayed in Indian clothes the officer would not have been so concerned. I don't know, but I have been able to forgive him his mistake.'

She paused with a faraway look in her eyes. 'Malati, I don't know how I am going to live without Rakesh.'

Malati's eyes glistened with tears. 'Thank you for coming to tell me. Now that I can understand what happened perhaps I may also learn to forgive.'

'Did Chhaya come back to you? Do you know what happened to Rakesh's body?'

'Yes, she came back, but she was incoherent,' said Malati. 'She was gone for weeks and I don't know what she did during that time. I did gather that she left my son's body for the vultures as she had no means of cremating him, or even of burying him. She went into labour a few days after she arrived back here and she gave birth to a daughter. In her mind it was the ultimate failure and she went completely mad. A month after the baby was born Chhaya disappeared and we have not seen her since. I have no idea what has become of her.'

'Did she take her baby with her?' asked Lexy.

Malati shook her head. 'Why would she? What use is a daughter, after all?'

Lexy drank her tea in silence. She thought the Indian attitude towards girls harsh and incomprehensible. She and Malati had been baby girls once, and even though she had not loved Mattie for a long time she had never thought her worth less than a boy would have been.

'Was it very terrible after we left?' she asked.

'Yes, it was. We gathered up our most valuable possessions and some stores of food and took shelter in the tykhana. We were so grateful that Rakesh had found such a wonderful hiding place and we were quite safe there. We stayed hidden for a couple of weeks without leaving it at all, and after that we only did so to replenish our food supplies. It was many weeks before it was safe to live in the house again, and what a mess it was in. If it weren't the badmashes who wrecked our home, then I'm afraid it was your people. They were all desperate for trophies and booty. I'm glad that I have no way of knowing who was responsible. That way I can't harbour grudges.'

'I'm sorry,' said Lexy. 'It makes me feel ashamed.'

'Don't be. People do things in times of war or when they are frightened that they would not otherwise dream of doing. It is done. We did not lose much and none of us was hurt, thanks to the tykhana. Only Rakesh paid the price, and others fared far worse than we did. What are you going to do now, Lexy?'

'The first thing I want to do is to go to my old home near the bazaar. Your sister's jewels and my mother's pearls have probably been stolen, but I have to know for certain. Also, I need to lay some ghosts to rest.'

'And your husband?'

'He was killed in the fighting.'

'I see,' said Malati. 'I am sorry for that. Will you stay in India?'

'I'm not sure. We are going to Simla for a few weeks with a few other bereaved memsahibs. It will give me time to think about what I should do.'

'Rakesh's son would have a better life in your country than in mine,' said Malati.

'What makes you say that?'

'Because neither your people nor mine will welcome him. You know what everyone thinks of half-castes. He falls between two stools, but his skin is fair. There must be a good deal of your father in him. Captain Nicolson had blue eyes and golden hair as I recall.'

'Yes, he did,' smiled Lexy.

'Here in the sun Rakesh's son's skin will turn brown and his eyes will betray him for what he is. Take him to your country, Lexy, where he has the chance of a good life. Rakesh would have wanted that for his son.'

Lexy sighed as she remembered Rakesh voicing exactly those concerns for their child when she first told him that she was to have his baby.

'You are probably right,' she said. 'In any case, I have to think about little Benjamin. He is not my child and his grandparents have a right to decided what becomes of him although it will break Mattie's heart if they are separated.'

After a short silence Malati stood up. 'Would you like me to come with you to your old house or would you prefer to face your ghosts by yourself?'

'Oh, would you really come with me?' said Lexy. 'I would be so grateful. I don't relish the idea of going there alone. Although I have been told that my husband was killed, I have the scary feeling that it is not true and that he is lurking there somewhere, waiting for me to return to him. That sounds awfully childish, doesn't it?'

'Not at all,' said Malati. 'Come, we'll leave your son with my ayah and go there straight away.'

CHAPTER 48

The haveli had been partially destroyed. Debris littered the once beautifully manicured lawns, doors creaked on broken hinges and glass from shattered panes lay inside and outside the windows. Curtains had been yanked from their tracks and piled in the centre of the floor, pictures had been torn from their frames, and the only ornaments left behind lay in broken heaps.

Malati followed Lexy as she wandered from room to room, opening cupboards and drawers. There was no sign of the jewellery casket, and even though she had not expected to find it, she was disappointed nevertheless and upset to have lost her mother's pearls, her only link with the past.

The Colonel's room was the last one Lexy ventured into. It had been ransacked, but lying on one of the beds was the photographic portrait of the Colonel and his first family. The silver frame was missing but the portrait was undamaged, and Lexy picked it up and put it in her bag. She did not want it for herself, but it was something for Mattie to have as a reminder of the father she had loved.

After they had searched each room, Lexy and Malati strolled out onto the veranda at the rear of the haveli. The gardens had been trampled into the ground and a part of the oleander and hibiscus hedge had been torn down to reveal the bibi khana. Lexy stopped abruptly. Her hands flew to her cheeks and she gasped.

'I had forgotten about my husband's bibi,' she whispered. 'She might still be in there.'

The massive explosion in Delhi when the Magazine was blown up shook the foundations of the bibi khana and woke Savita from the drugged stupor induced by her hookah. Fear and shock sent her darting outside in a state of semi-undress. She feared an earthquake, but once outside she could smell smoke, and a dull orange glow told her that a part of the old town was on fire. She ignored the Colonel's command that she was never to enter the main house and ran straight there to seek protection. But the haveli was deserted. Even the servants had gone. Savita's bare feet pattered on the stone floors as she ran from room to room.

'Colonel! Colonel!' she shrieked. Her screams echoed in the empty rooms. She thrust doors open in her search for someone to shield her from danger, but her fear was quickly dampened when she entered Lexy's room and spied the casket on the dressing table. She hastened to open it and found it bulging with jewels. Savita did not hesitate. She grabbed the casket and fled back to the bibi khana where she bolted the doors and shutters. All she could think of was hiding the jewels somewhere no one would think of looking for them.

'Ayah!' she screamed. The ayah came running. 'Help me.'

The two women struggled to move the dais on which the Colonel received his daily pleasure. Beneath the dais was a loose marble tile, which Savita removed. She tipped the contents of the casket into the hole where her other treasures lay concealed, and then she and the ayah heaved the dais back into position. No one would find the jewels and Savita's future was assured. If the Colonel returned she would give the jewels back to him in the knowledge that he would reward her for keeping them safe; but if he did not return, she would sell them for more money than she could ever need for the rest of her life.

She tossed the empty casket into a cupboard and sent the ayah to prepare another hookah. Whilst she waited, Savita lay on the padded dais with her head resting on a red brocade bolster. She put a piece of opium into her mouth and settled down to wait for the Colonel to come to her rescue.

A band of badmashes rampaged through the town and crashed their way into the haveli, looting and destroying as they went. Some of them careered around the gardens, trampling flowers and kicking earth away in their search for buried treasure. When they were done they moved on – except for five of them. Convinced that there should be more in the way of treasure to be found in such a place, five badmashes stayed behind to conduct a more thorough search. Angry at their failure to find any jewels they moved into the rear gardens. They took it in turns to urinate on patches of earth: if the urine disappeared quickly it would indicate that the ground had been recently disturbed, possibly to bury valuables. They found nothing. Tempers flared, and they began uprooting bushes and plants; and in doing this they chanced upon the bibi khana.

They found their way in through a shutter whose hinges had rusted. They forced it open, smashed the window and climbed inside. They found the ayah first. She opened her mouth to scream, but one of the men quickly stabbed her in the neck and she fell to the ground with a sigh. Then the men inched through the bibi khana until they stumbled into the room that was clearly dedicated to the pursuit of sexual pleasure. They stopped in their tracks as they entered, scarcely able to believe their good fortune. Savita, half-stupefied from the opium, lay on the dais wearing nothing more than her jewels and a transparent, gauzy dupatta over flimsy crimson pyjamas. The badmashes stood around the dais and stared open-mouthed at a vision of beauty such as they had never seen before.

Confused and befuddled, Savita opened her eyes. She knew that something was wrong, but she couldn't determine just what it was. She tried to focus on the man who stood at the foot of the dais. He was small, almost black, and filthy, with matted hair and a mouth stained red with betel juice. She glanced at the other four men. They all looked the same to her. She shook her head in an effort to clear her mind and struggled to sit up. Her movements spurred the leader of the gang into action.

'We'll never have another opportunity to sample such a one as this,' he said. 'Tie her down.'

As Savita's hands and feet were bound tightly to the carved poles at each corner of the dais with the same golden cords she had used to tease the Colonel, she became fully aware of her danger. She screamed.

'Sing away, little bird,' cooed the leader of the gang. 'There is no one around to hear your song but us.'

First, they robbed Savita of her jewels – gold rings and bangles given to her by her family, and jewels showered on her by an appreciative Colonel. They argued amongst themselves over who should have what, and all the while Savita screamed. Finally, the leader leant forward and grasped the top of her flimsy covering, ripping the material from her body. Savita squirmed violently, which made them all roar with laughter.

For a long time, confident that no one would discover them in their crime, they did not touch her. They just stood and stared at her voluptuous naked body: the soft alabaster skin without blemish, the perfectly rounded full breasts pointing to the canopy above, and the dark triangle between her spread-eagled legs. They gazed deeply into her private places, feasting their eyes and prolonging the tension for themselves and their captive.

They waited for so long that Savita began to think that they would not rape her after all, but they were fired by whisky they had stolen when rampaging through the bazaars, and they were further intoxicated by Savita's perfume and the smell of smouldering incense in the room. The leader suddenly let his dhoti fall to the ground and pounced.

Savita's screams inflamed them further, and they cheered each other on as one after another they raped her again and again. The stench of their unwashed bodies and fetid breath made her sick, but her ordeal went on and on, lasting most of the night. Then they slit her throat.

The badmashes ransacked the Bibighar, searching through the almirahs and cupboards and taking whatever they could carry. They threw the empty sandalwood casket on the floor and searched high and low for the jewels they knew it must once have contained. When they could not find them, they slashed at all the furnishings, reducing opulent fabrics to shreds in their anger and frustration. Eventually they left the Bibighar, leaving the door wide open, and disappeared into the dark lanes and chaotic streets of the burning town.

The room was full of flies and little of Savita remained. Through the open door the enticing smell of a decomposing body had been released, luring wild animals inside; they had made short work of her remains. No one had entered the Bibighar for months, and Lexy and Malati stood on the threshold and recoiled in horror.

Lexy covered her nose and mouth with a handkerchief. 'Let's go,' she said with a shudder.

'Not without what we came for,' said Malati. 'Look, there's Anjana's jewel casket.'

Malati stepped into the room, moved to the dais and covered what was left of Savita with the remnants of the bed curtains. Lexy edged into the room and looked about her.

'It's empty,' she said. 'Everything has been stolen or destroyed. Let's go, Malati.'

'Wait a moment. Where did you leave the casket?'

'In my room.'

'Hm. That means that this bibi must have found it and brought it here for safekeeping. Put yourself in her place for a minute. Suppose you had found a fortune in precious stones and decided to keep them for yourself or keep them safe until the owner returned, what would you do in those circumstances?'

'I don't know,' said Lexy. 'If she came into the main house and found no one there she must have been very frightened.'

'Not too frightened to think about feathering her nest,' said Malati. 'She brought the casket here, and my guess is that she hid the jewels somewhere. Whoever ransacked this place would have taken the whole casket if the jewels had still been in it. There were too many to be carried loose in their hands. My guess is that the robbers found the casket empty. The big question is – did they find the jewels, or did she have time to hide them somewhere really safe?'

Malati began to examine the floor carefully. She lifted the carpet and inspected the tiles beneath it.

'What are you doing?' asked Lexy.

'We Hindus hide our valuables in the walls. Moslems bury them under the floor. By the look of this place she was a Moslem so she would have buried them.' She put her hands on her hips and surveyed the bed from top to bottom.

'The dais looks heavy and I doubt if the robber moved it, especially with a body lying on it. If I had been in the bibi's position I would have hidden the jewels under the dais if I had had time. Help me move it aside.'

Just as Savita and her ayah had done months earlier, so Lexy and Malati pushed and shoved at the dais. When they moved it to the wall the loose tile was easy to see. With a cry Malati scrabbled at its edges until she was able to lift it out. 'There, I was right.'

Malati was triumphant. Every piece of Anjana's jewellery was there and amongst them was Miriam's pearl necklace. Lexy reached for it with tears in her eyes.

'Oh, Malati, I thought they had gone forever. I can't thank you enough. I could not have done this by myself.'

They returned the jewels to the casket and Lexy fastened the pearls around her neck.

'Let's get out of here,' said Malati.

They hurried back to the Chatterjees' damaged mansion. Over tea Lexy was thoughtful.

'Is something wrong?' asked Malati.

'Not really, but I hope you won't be offended by what I am going to say. The thing is, I want you to have your sister's jewels.'

'They were Anjana's bequest to you,' said Malati.

'I know, and if you have no objection I will keep one necklace as a memento of her love for my father. It is not that I am ungrateful, but the jewels are so beautiful beneath an Indian sun, and yet look so out of place in England. I may return there, but the jewels belong here.'

'You could sell them to give you a fresh start.'

Lexy smiled at Malati. 'That I would never do. I will tell you something that I have never told another soul. I am a very rich woman. My father left me a fortune and my husband has left me well provided for. The truth is that I haven't given my father's fortune a thought. I was embarrassed by it and angry about it because of the circumstances in which he had made us live. I won't bore you with the details. It is only now that I am completely alone that I have even remembered that I am an heiress. Wherever I decide to live, I shall want for nothing and neither will the children. The future for Rakesh's son is secure.'

Malati nodded. 'Very well then, for that reason only I agree to you returning Anjana's jewels to me, but if you do decide to remain in India you have only to let me know and they will become yours again.'

Lexy rose to take her leave. Malati's ayah brought the baby to her.

'Must you go so soon?' asked Malati.

'Yes, I must. I am on my way to Simla with a party of memsahibs. In the hills I hope to come to terms with all that has happened to me over the past nine years. Somehow, I have to learn to live with losing Rakesh, and my aunt and uncle. They perished in the massacres in Cawnpore, and I haven't begun to cope with the horror of that yet.'

Malati sighed. 'There is so much hatred and heartache on both our sides, which will take many years to heal – if it ever heals at all. But life will go on, Lexy dear. We have all suffered and it is not over yet. I will never forget you any more than I ever forgot your father. Meeting you has helped me to deal with my own grief. You mustn't be sad for too long. You still have a life to live, and there's my grandson to care for. Learn to be happy again, Lexy, and put the past behind you.'

In Simla Lexy's wounds began to heal. Mrs Ponsonby's friends, a Mr and Mrs Cameron, were Scots who, like many of their countrymen, deserted their own land to seek fame and fortune in India. The Camerons had not found fame, but Mr Cameron had made a fortune in the tea trade. Now they were living out their retirement in a comfortable house nestled against the hills. Their home was bright with polished brassware and tartan cushions, and it was here, sitting beside a glowing fire in the evenings and eating oatcakes every bit as tasty as those she ate on Toronsay, that Lexy's spirit revived.

One chilly morning she took Mattie and Benjamin to Conrad Gardner's grave. The wooden cross she and Charlotte had placed there had fallen over. Benjamin helped Lexy to dig a fresh hole to plant it more firmly. Then they collected armfuls of wild flowers to put on the grave.

'Who is in there?' asked Mattie.

Lexy found that she could talk about the boy with affection and without pain. 'His name was Conrad,' she said. 'He was a dear little boy. Somewhere in England he has a mother, two brothers and a sister. I'm not sure about his father. He was due to go back to England, but he might have been caught up in the troubles like we were. I don't suppose anyone will come and visit Conrad's grave ever again.'

Benjamin took his thumb from his mouth. 'Is Mama in the ground too?' he asked.

Lexy hugged him to her. 'I don't know. I don't know what has happened to all the people who did not survive. But one day, when this is all over, there will be memorials built to honour and remember them all. And your Mama and Papa and Clara May, and Mattie's daddy will not be forgotten. Nor must we ever forget Rakesh because he saved our lives. What he did was very brave. We will always remember them, and their story will live forever.'

On one of her solitary walks, Lexy paused to gaze at the snow-covered Himalayas and was reminded of the Cuillins on the Isle of Skye. That made her think of Toronsay and in that moment she knew that she had to return there. She felt an intense need to visit her father's grave; until she did so she knew that she would not be able to grieve for him properly. And now that she knew his story, knew the secret his heart had concealed for so long, Lexy felt the need to grieve. But it would not only be the

Reverend Murdo Nicolson, the father she knew, but also Captain Murdo Nicolson, the man she did not know, and for whom she now felt a deep affinity, that she would mourn.

The tale Malati had told her would have seemed hardly possible had Lexy not also loved across the divide of race and culture, but having experienced such love and loss herself, she could at last understand the man her father had become. All her life it seemed that she had hated him and resisted any soft feelings towards him, and now the love she had denied him filled her with self-reproach. Now she understood how he had fled from his pain; why he had sought solace in religion without finding any relief; and how his pain had increased over the years, fuelled as it was by the bitterness of his inability to comprehend Anjana's sacrifice. She recognised the look of haunted grief that had been his constant companion for she saw that same look when she caught sight of her reflection in a mirror, and she understood the hollowness of his religious life.

But Lexy was determined not to repeat her father's other mistake: she would not reject her children like he had rejected her. Old Mrs Ponsonby was right; the children were her future and her love for them would help her through the sea of her own despair. Life for her would not end here in India. She would go Home, that place with the capital 'H' so beloved by all the British here in self-imposed exile. She would go forward carrying Rakesh in her heart until the end of her days, and she would survive. But first she had to return to the Isle of Toronsay and kneel at her father's graveside. Too late she had come to understand him, but she had begun to find peace, and a great surge of love and pity for her father filled Lexy's heart.

THE END

GLOSSARY

Scotland

breeks	trousers
brose	uncooked form of porridge: oatmeal mixed with boiling water or milk
cailleach	crone, hag
canna	cannot
chust	just (Highland); also used in the vernacular in the Islands as an informal device to round off arbitrary phrases (could be translated as a term of endearment)
ciamar a tha thu?	how are you?
Clearances	the forced eviction of inhabitants (of the Highlands and western islands of Scotland), clearing the land of people primarily to allow for the introduction of sheep pastoralism
cromags	hooks
dinna	don't
drap	drop
frae	from
haud yer wheesht	be quiet (hold your tongue)
hougmagandie	fornication
ken	know
kirk	church (Church of Scotland)
Kirk Session	the lowest court of the Presbyterian Church (of Scotland)
machair	grassy plain
mair	more
manse	minister's house
nae	no

oot	out
sae	so
scallags	land labourer, farm servant
skelping	slapping, smacking
spoot	spout
strupach	cup of tea
taibhse	ghost/apparition/wraith, especially seen just after a person's death
wheesht!	quiet!
wifey	old woman

India

ayah	native nurse; ladies' maid
badmash	hooligan
betel	the leaf of an Asian evergreen climbing plant, chewed in the East as a mild stimulant
bibi	Indian wife or mistress
bibighar	women's quarters – often for the Indian wives and mistresses of British Officers
bibi khana	women's house
bobajee	cook
bobajee khana	cook house
char-wallah	tea boy
chowkidar	guard, watchman
dak bungalow	government staging post
derzi	tailor
dholak	barrel-shaped, two-headed hand drum
dhoti	loose loincloth
dupatta	shawl or scarf worn with *salwar kameez*
feringhee	foreigner
gharry	horse-drawn carriage
ghat/s	series of steps/a broad flight of steps leading down to water, particularly a holy river
haveli	courtyard house
John Company	informal name for the East India Company
koi-hai?	is anyone there?
kurta	long shirt worn with pyjama bottoms

maidan	an open space in or near a town, used as a parade ground or for events such as public meetings
mali	gardener
maya	illusion
munshi	teacher
nautch	traditional Indian dance performed by professional dancing girls, often as part of a party or celebration
puja	Hindu prayers
pukka	proper, civilised
punkah	ceiling mounted blade fan used in India before the electric fan
punkah-wallah	one who works a Punkah usually by pulling a cord
River Jumna	also known as Yamuna River
salwar kameez	a Punjabi suit comprising loose fitting trousers and tunic top
sati	Sanskrit for "virtuous woman"; widow who burns herself (through self-immolation) on her husband's funeral pyre
sepoy	private soldier in the infantry
shisha glass	mirrorwork (textiles)
subedar	native officer
syce	groom
tabla	pair of small drums (fundamental to Hindustani music)
tiffin	a snack or light meal
tope	(in South Asia) a grove or plantation of trees, especially mango trees
tulwar	heavy curved Indian sword
tykhana	underground chamber in which to keep cool during the heat of the day
zenana	the women's quarters of an Indian house

Lightning Source UK Ltd.
Milton Keynes UK
UKHW042012050219
336792UK00002B/145/P